A SCION OF HEROES

The World of Captain James Murray

A SCION
OF
HEROES

Stuart J McCulloch

Matador
9 Priory Business Park,
Wistow Road, Kibworth Beauchamp,
Leicestershire. LE8 0RX
Tel: (+44) 116 279 2299
Fax: (+44) 116 279 2277
Email: books@troubador.co.uk
Web: www.troubador.co.uk/matador

ISBN 978 1784621 377

British Library Cataloguing in Publication Data.
A catalogue record for this book is available from the British Library.

Printed and bound in the UK by TJ International, Padstow, Cornwall
Typeset in 11pt CrimsonText by Troubador Publishing Ltd, Leicester, UK

Matador is an imprint of Troubador Publishing Ltd

To Maureen

Contents

List of Plates

Summary Timeline of Captain James Murray RN

c1749	Patrick Murray, father of James Murray, born.
c1756	Eliza Smith née Stewart, mother of James Murray, born.
1775	George Murray, James' grandfather, becomes 6th Lord Elibank.
1778	James Murray born at St. Augustine, Florida
1779-80	American Revolutionary War. British advance into Georgia and South Carolina. Siege of Savannah.
1781	James Murray moves to New Abbey, Scotland.
1783	British colony of Florida handed over to Spain. Remaining settlers, including James' mother Eliza and his three sisters, resettle in the Bahamas.
c1786	James' sisters join him in New Abbey.
1793	Patrick, James' father, purchases seigneury of Argenteuil, Canada.
1796	James joins the Royal Navy at Halifax, Nova Scotia. Becomes a Volunteer 1st Class in HMS Topaz.
1798	Promoted to Midshipman.
1803	Seigneury of Argenteuil handed over to James by his father, Patrick.
1804	Moves to HMS Ruby as a Master's Mate, then HMS Hyena as Midshipman.
1805	Transferred to HMS Centaur. Battle of Dominica. Then on to HMS Northumberland. Battle of San Domingo.
1806	Promoted to Lieutenant and given command of HMS Ballahou.

1807   Takes over the command of HMS Unique.

1808   Joins HMS Neptune. Attack on Martinique.

1809   Promoted to Commander and takes over HMS Recruit. Sells Seigneury of Argenteuil. Attack on Guadeloupe.

1810   Commands HMS Oberon on the North Sea and Russian stations.

1811   James attends party in his honour in New Abbey, Scotland.

1815   James leaves HMS Oberon on half pay and lives at Raehills in Annandale, Scotland, with Admiral Sir William Hope. Takes command of HMS Satellite.

1816   Engaged to Miss Matilda Harris. Attack on Algiers with HMS Satellite.

1818   Leaves HMS Satellite and has extended shore leave. Lives at Castle Leod near Dingwall. Promoted to Post Captain.

1821   Marries Rachel Lyne Tucker. Appointed to command of HMS Valorous on the Newfoundland Station.

1824   Valorous shore party ambushed by Mexican bandits.

1825   Leaves HMS Valorous and moves to Assynt House, Easter Ross.

1827   Establishes home in Ross-shire and builds Craigdarroch House at Contin.

1831   Wife Rachel involved in a scandalous adulterous liaison with Robert R. Mackenzie.

1832   Asked to be a Second in a high profile duel and then involved in an altercation and challenge with two Highland lairds.

1834   Returns to his sister's home in New Abbey. Dies on 29th May.

Preface

Graveyards can be dangerous places. The ghostly occupants of Sweetheart Abbey graveyard are, in the main, a rather benign bunch, but their headstones offer tantalising glimpses of an unfamiliar and engrossing world. The temptation to delve into this exotic domain can be immense, but the penalty may lead to a heavy fine, payable in energy, time and frustration. When the author and his wife bought the former New Abbey manse, situated in the shadow of the majestic Abbey, they knew they were moving into a fine old Georgian property. They were not to know they were also moving into a new world, the world of Captain James Murray RN. Clearly visible from the window of the manse, the house where James lived and died, is the large sandstone monument dedicated to his memory. The size of the headstone hints at the esteem, or possibly the wealth, this person enjoyed in his short life of 56 years, but other than that, there are few clues to tell us anything about the man himself. So began the quest to explore his world; information that James was not going to give up easily. Occasionally the research led into a blind alley, but it would also flow in unexpected, delightful and absorbing directions.

Should a fly on the wall of the drawing room in the manse, circa 1830, chance upon a family gathering, perhaps the conversation in this beautiful Galloway village would be expected to focus on the recent harvest, or conceivably the latest local gossip arising out of the Kirk Session. More likely in this case would be heard first-hand accounts of some of the most tumultuous events in British history. The life, times and connections of Captain James Murray were far from the ordinary.

The period from 1745 until 1834 was a dynamic and eventful one in both Scottish and World history. In the mid-18th century, Scottish politics was dominated by dynastic quarrels between the Jacobites and the Hanoverians and disputes were still settled by sword and shield. The 'United Kingdom of Great Britain and Ireland' was a relatively new state and still remained a shaky amalgamation of nations. By 1835, Britain was firmly established in its own dominion and, despite losing one empire, had gained another and had become the world's greatest economic and military power.

At the beginning of the period kings still clung to their divine right to rule, but less than a hundred years later, many of the world's monarchies had been totally swept away and those that remained were subsumed by elected parliaments. Real progress towards equality amongst men had been made by the abolition of slavery and the tentative democracy of the Reform Acts. The ordinary person, once ensconced in a feudal life of the village dominated by the local gentry, would be experiencing massive changes in agriculture, new industry and, especially in the Highlands of Scotland, a drive towards efficiency and profit which would often take preference over tradition and loyalty.

The spine of this book is the life of James Murray and his immediate family, but the ribs and limbs are the stories of their wider relatives, friends and acquaintances, stories which were wide ranging and often dramatic. Eye witness accounts of some of the most turbulent events in recent British history; a planned assassination of the King, a brutal murder during the American Revolutionary War, life on board a warship of Nelson's invincible navy and one of the largest ever slave rebellions. Their world encompassed the heights of opulence such as that enjoyed by some of the great families of Scotland, but it also experienced the pain of warfare, debt, family breakdown and personal grief.

Society was very stratified during this period and movement

between the social classes was not easy or common. The story of James' life focuses on the tales of some of the movers and shakers of that society; and most of these people came from the aristocracy, the gentry and their aspirants, as they were the only people to have the time and opportunity to move and shake. Furthermore, they were also the people with whom James Murray tended to share his life.

Many biographies focus on an extraordinary life or involvement in extraordinary events. This is not really the case with Captain James Murray. Had the events which defined and documented the planet during his short tenure been captured in a motion picture, he would not have been in line for a premier 'Oscar' nomination. But most principal Oscar winners only reach that lofty position with the help, support and excellence of a host of supporting characters. James would certainly have been in line for a 'best supporting actor' nomination.

Primary sources have been used extensively. It didn't help that the main subjects of this book inconveniently lived in the days before most National Records were kept. Furthermore, the central figures are named Smith and Murray, both familiar and widespread names and it was commonplace to find several similarly named people in the same area at the same time. For example, there were at least three naval officers named James Murray on the Navy List in the same period as the subject of this book. The difficulties were also compounded by the fact that both James and his father Patrick were illegitimate, and thus not formally recorded by the landed family from which they sprang. Fortunately, a few letters and legal papers survive to tell James' story directly and wherever possible the tale has been told through these documents and other contemporary records.

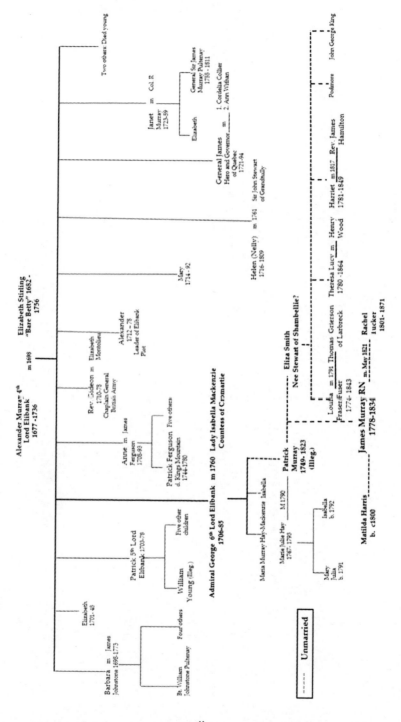

Alexander Murray 4th Lord Elibank 1677-1736 — m 1698 — Elizabeth Stirling "Bare Betty" 1682- 1756

Two others Died young

Janet Murray 1723-59 m Col R

Elizabeth m 1: Cordelia Collier 2: Ann Witham
General Sir James Murray Pulteney 1755-1811

General James Hero and Governor of Quebec 1721-94 m Sir John Stewart of Grandtully

Mary 1714-92

Helen (Nelly) 1716-1809 m 1761

Theresa Lucy m Henry Wood 1780-1864
Harriet m.1817 Rev. James Hamilton 1781-1849

Louisa m 1791 Thomas Grierson of Larbreck 1774-1843
Eliza Smith Nee Stewart of Shambellie?

Podmore   John George King

Rev. Gideon m Elizabeth Montolieu 1710-73 Chaplain General British Army

Alexander 1712 - 8 Leader of Elibank Plot

Anne m James Ferguson 1708-93

Patrick Ferguson Five others d. Kings Mountain 1744-1780

Admiral George 6th Lord Elibank m 1760 Lady Isabella Mackenzie Countess of Cromartie 1706-85

Patrick Murray 1749-1823 (Illeg.)

James Murray RN m May 1821 Rachel Tucker 1778-1834 1801-1871

Matilda Harris b. c1800

Patrick 5th Lord Elibank 1703-78
Five other children

William Young (Illeg.)

Maria Murray Hay=Mackenzie Isabella

Maria Julia Hay 1767-1793 M1790

Mary Julia b. 1791   Isabella b. 1792

Elizabeth 1701-48

Barbara m James Johnstone 1698-1773

Bt. William Johnstone Pulteney   Four others

Unmarried

xvii

Prologue

T he worst part was the silence, that unexpected period of time where contemplation is inescapable. James Murray knew that the dogs of war were about to be unleashed, but whether they would turn on him he knew not.

Only a few brief moments previously the ship had rocked with frenzied activity after the Captain had ordered, "All hands clear the ship for action, ahoy!" and the sinister beat of the drums had echoed his command. Sailors ran in all directions, men snarled and cursed as they took up their station by their guns. Orders were barked out as the bulkheads were expertly knocked away; sand was scattered on the decks to avoid slippage in the blood that was soon expected to be staining the decks. Round shot, designed to penetrate and shatter the enemy's hulls or destroy his sails was brought up and stacked next to the guns and, alongside them, stacked in boxes, was the fearsome anti-personnel grapeshot. Some of James' midshipman colleagues were stationed below, on the berth deck, with orders to shoot any man who attempted to run from his quarters. A lieutenant was shouting instructions on how and when to board, as he furnished the marines and his chosen boarding party with pikes, cutlasses, and pistols. Other marines, fighting and harrying for the best firing points, took up their positions on deck or in the rigging. They were responsible for the small arms fire and concentrated particularly on any officer who made himself too visible on deck.

At last, every man and boy was at his post and the silent gunner crews, slow matches burning by their sides, awaited their orders. James was too excited to feel fear, but he could not avoid the weight of responsibility that was bearing down on his shoulders. James Murray – a scion of heroes? He was an Elibank, albeit an illegitimate son of an illegitimate son, but an Elibank nevertheless. Within living memory many of his relatives had become household names, both famous and infamous for their deeds and exploits. Perhaps now was his turn, but there were no eminent relatives by his side to turn to for advice. He was on his own.

He had seen action before, but nothing like this. Through the limited vision of the gun port the huge bulk of the colossal French ship of the line L'Imperial loomed closer and closer. He could now see many of her 118 guns quite clearly and ruefully reflected that 59 of them were preparing to fire in his direction.

But the moment was broken not by the enemy but by his own guns and the silence reigned no more. James knew that his ship was heavily outgunned, but he was an officer in the Royal Navy. Uneven odds were not uncommon and most certainly had not stood in the way of Admiral Nelson just a few weeks previously at Trafalgar.

HMS Northumberland's guns roared into action as shot after shot crashed into the side of the French ship. Then a new noise was added to the cacophony. It sounded like the tearing of sails high above and was accompanied by a bloodcurdling whistle and shriek, caused by the rush of wind as the enemy's shot entered the British ship. By now the roaring of cannon could be heard from all parts of the ship and, as she shuddered and groaned under the bombardment, it made a most hideous noise. The screams and cries of the wounded rang through all parts of the ship. As men slipped and lurched in the blood and chaos of the gun deck, the wounded were carried to the cockpit as fast as they fell, whilst those who were killed outright were, without ceremony, immediately thrown overboard. The British ship was losing crew rapidly, but still the battle went on. The men cheered with all their might, although many hardly knew why. Some of them pulled off their jackets, others their vests, while some, still more determined, had taken off their shirts, and, with nothing but a handkerchief tied round the waistbands of their trousers, fought ferociously.

A shot neatly removing a hat but leaving the hat's owner unscathed has been a feature of countless battle scenes described in adventure stories and shown in movie films through the ages. Amazingly, in this engagement it really happened. Admiral Alexander Cochrane, directing operations on the deck of the Northumberland, was sharply reminded of the intensity of battle as a cannonball neatly removed his hat. Remarkably, he was uninjured.

The ships continued to engage for almost two hours until James heard a new noise above the pandemonium. A sickening crash heralded the collapse of the ship's main mast as it hurtled down onto the main deck. Now, the once mighty HMS Northumberland had no source of power, and she was drifting helplessly. Finally, she ceased firing, but not in defeat. The French L'Imperial had been forced to run aground and had struck its colours. The battle was over and, unlike many of his colleagues, James was still alive.[1]

He had come through what was his first, and was to become the Royal Navy's last, major large scale fleet engagement under sail. His junior role in the battle had not fully released him from the shadows of his ancestors but he had done well and, he hoped, was now on his way to becoming a worthy scion of his ancestral heroes.

1

Bare Betty

P atrick Murray was not enjoying the best of days. When he regained consciousness a groggy appreciation of his circumstances encouraged him to wish he hadn't bothered. His corps of men, once over 100 strong, had been reduced to just 63 with only 93 cartridges left between them. He was surrounded by hostile American forces and only two of his junior officers were fit for any form of action. A stabbing pain from his arm reminded him why he had passed out in the first instance. The exit wound of the bullet which had passed through his shoulder made it almost impossible for him to get up. The splinter wounds in his posterior made it even worse to stay where he was. He was helped onto a horse by his comrades in arms and, as he led his small corps of men back towards the ship that would hopefully take them to safety, he had a little time for reflection. He didn't particularly fear for his own life. He had great faith in his own ability and that of his men. But he still feared; feared for the reputation of the Royal Americans, his regiment and the centre of his life, feared for the future of the British colony of Georgia but, most of all, he feared for the future of his young son James, who awaited news of him in distant St. Augustine, East Florida.

That fear was not shared by James. The fears of a young child tend not to run to colonialism and mortality and James' main concern would have been based around life with big sister Louisa and baby Theresa. Although blissfully unaware of his heritage, he was an Elibank Murray[2] and the Elibanks tended to fall, or even more often jump, into the nearest available abyss only to be invariably guided down to safety by the nearest available angel. The Murray name has given history more than its fair share of heroes, ranging from Scottish mediaeval leaders, Jacobite Generals and famous tennis players to the eponymous nickname for a popular Asian culinary delight.[3] The Elibank Murrays have been largely forgotten in such illustrious company but they bear comparison with any, especially the remarkable children of 'Bare Betty', Captain James Murray's great grandmother.

The first Elibank title was conferred in 1643, and by the eighteenth century the Elibank family were well established as influential and titled landowners. Alexander Murray, the 4th Lord Elibank, married Elizabeth Stirling around 1698 and Elizabeth, the great grandmother of Captain James Murray, was to produce thirteen children.

Alexander was remembered as a fine man by Patrick, his son and heir. Even allowing for the inevitable praise forthcoming in most eulogies, Patrick clearly had great love and esteem for his father:

> He lived, esteemed and beloved by men of all ranks and parties and his death is universally lamented. No man ever surpassed him in the practice of every social virtue. He was a fond husband, and indulgent parent and an unalterable friend and as he never had an enemy he was never accused or suspected of any vice.[4]

Elizabeth, better known as 'Bare Betty', is remembered as a much more formidable figure. Unfortunately the origin of her nickname is not at all risqué and probably arises from Elizabeth's reaction on being noticed without her customary head-dress. By repute she over-reacted at being seen in such an undressed state and that, of course, ensured she would be reminded of it for the rest of her life by the use of her easily misinterpreted soubriquet.

Bare Betty was not to be underestimated. A tale is told of a suitor who claimed to be deeply in love with her and announced that he was ready to lay down his life for her sake. She replied, "I do not believe you would part with a joint of your little finger for my whole body." The next day the gentleman returned and presented her triumphantly with the joint of one of his little fingers. He was not a little surprised when she gave him an immediate refusal, saying, "The man who has no mercy on his own flesh will certainly not spare mine."[5]

Elizabeth has left her legacy as an imposing, strong-willed woman, but it is her remarkable offspring who were to make their mark on the world stage.

There was troublesome Barbara, who eloped with Sir James Johnstone, the 3rd Baronet of Westerhall, Dumfries-shire. Their third son, Sir William Johnstone Pulteney was, by repute, the richest man in Great Britain when he died in 1805.

And there was brainy Patrick. As a leading member of the 'Scottish Enlightenment' he mingled with many distinguished people, such as his particular friend, David Hume, the internationally renowned philosopher. Patrick was celebrated for his wit and even received accolades from Dr Johnson, who was usually scathing about all things and all people Scottish.[6]

Alexander, his younger hot-headed brother, became infamous in his own lifetime. Today the 1745 rising of Charles Edward Stewart (or Bonnie Prince Charlie as he is sometimes known) is shrouded in romance; peopled by heroic Highlanders with tartans, bagpipes and shattered dreams of glory, but during the lifetime of the children of Bare Betty it was still a very fresh memory. For many people it was far from romantic, representing a potential loss of freedom, the imposition of a dishonoured monarchy, an unwanted religion and a potentially fearful conflict. Following the defeat of the Stewarts at the Battle of Culloden in 1746 Alexander's enthusiasm remained undimmed. After getting into trouble for political misdeeds in London, Alexander wisely decided to make a run for it and in November 1751 he arrived in France. In the relative safety of Paris he was soon deeply embroiled in an outlandish and ambitious plot to bring the Stuart dynasty back onto the British throne. In 1751 a plan emerged in which King George II would be killed or captured and the waiting Charles would emerge from hiding to put his father, James Francis Edward, the son of the deposed James VII of Scotland and James II of England back on the throne of Britain. Initially Alexander Murray argued that he would simply poison the king, but Charles vetoed this and so 'Plan B' was agreed upon. In this, Alexander Murray and MacDonald of Glengarry would lead an attack on St. James's Palace with a body of young exiled Jacobite officers and four hundred Highlanders. They would overpower the guards and seize or kill King George. What could go wrong?

Confidence was high and a medal was even struck to commemorate the event. To their chagrin the plot was flawed in almost every aspect and Alastair Ruadh MacDonald of Glengarry soon carried the tale to the English authorities. Some of the conspirators were captured and Dr Archibald Cameron, a leading Jacobite, was executed for his involvement. Fortunately Alexander stayed in France, kept his head down and escaped the executioner, but the plot, now known as the 'Elibank plot', effectively ended all hopes of a Jacobite return. Alexander remained in exile until April 1771, when the new king, George III, astonishingly pardoned him and allowed him back into Britain. He died, unmarried, in 1777.[7]

The religious one of the family was Gideon, who became Chaplain to the 43rd (later 42nd Black Watch) Highlanders in 1745 and, unlike his brother, would serve on the Government side in the conflicts with the exiled Stuarts. He later moved on to become Chaplain-General of the British Army in 1749.

James, the fifth son, was the soldierly one and was destined to become a famous and influential figure in the military and diplomatic world of his time. The Seven Years' War, fought between Britain and France, saw confrontations in many parts of the world, but the decisive action which finally gave the British control of what is now Canada was the battle for the Plains of Abraham at Quebec. The wounded commander, General Wolfe, upon being told that the French had broken, turned on his side and with his last breath uttered, "Now, God be praised, I will die in peace". Brigadier-General James Murray, took over command and within days Quebec surrendered and the city was turned over to the British. In 1764 the hero James became the first civil governor of the Province of Canada but, as usual for an Elibank, his actions were highly controversial. He was considered too sympathetic to the French-Canadians and was recalled to Britain in 1766. It was not to be the last Elibank Murray contribution to the historical development of modern Canada.

Bare Betty's remarkable family was completed by another son, George, and three further daughters, Helen, Anne and Janet. Helen (Nelly) caused scandal in the family when she married the Hon. John Stewart of Grandtully. John was seventy-five years old, deaf, blind in one eye and up to his ears in debt. Furthermore, Nelly received 5,000 marks as a marriage gift. The luckless John died within three years of the ceremony.[8] The other two girls were also to make their mark, but not for what they did but for the children they produced.

Anne married an Advocate, James Ferguson, and they went on to produce six children, all of whom made their mark in society. The best known was Patrick, their second son. Patrick was to become one of the best known figures of the American Revolutionary War. He was given command of his own elite corps; all armed with his own design 'Ferguson' rifles. His rifle company was successfully employed in several actions and, in the engagement at Brandywine on 11th September 1777, legend tells the tale (and Patrick agreed with the legend), that he had the opportunity to shoot a senior-looking Rebel officer who was riding away from him. His marksmanship would surely have ensured a kill but, as he later wrote:

> It was not pleasant to fire at the back of an inoffending (sic) individual who was acquitting himself very coolly of his duty so I let him alone.[9]

This senior-looking Rebel officer was believed to be none other than General George Washington. Patrick Ferguson was later wounded and lost the use of his arm. He was tougher than he looked and, in spite of his handicaps, his military career continued to flourish, as he learned to fence and shoot with his left hand. Near Charleston, Patrick was bayoneted through his remaining good arm in a 'friendly fire' incident, but seemed undaunted by the experience. For three weeks he rode with the reins in his mouth, whilst propped up in the saddle by his orderlies. He was killed in action in the autumn of 1780, and was much lamented by the British loyalists.[10]

The last girl of the Bare Betty 'brood' was Great Aunt Janet, whose son James, rather like a number of his other Elibank relatives, was to forge a distinguished military career, reaching the rank of Major-General, and then build a second career as the Member of Parliament for Weymouth and Melcombe Regis, becoming a Privy Counsellor and Secretary of War between 1807 and 1809.

These distinguished relatives would provide a rich vein of contacts for any young man of Elibank blood, but they would have been irrelevant to this story had it not been for the indiscretions of George, the final member of Betty's family to be introduced.

In 1740 Commodore George Anson left Portsmouth to begin his famous circumnavigation of the globe; a journey at that time quite epic in scale. Sailing along with Anson was James Murray's grandfather, George Murray, who was commanding the 'Tryal' sloop of war. Britain was, as usual during this period, at war with Spain and the ambitious objectives of the expedition were to attack Spanish possessions by sailing around Cape Horn. With 500 soldiers they would capture a few cities and their treasures, seize the famed treasure galleon, which sailed from Acapulco to Spain, and then instigate and lead a revolt of the Peruvians against Spain. As huge quantities of silver were shipped from Peru to Spain and Spain's Caribbean possessions provided sugar, spices and tobacco, the potential rewards were vast. But so were the dangers. Apart from the massive scale of the objectives, the rounding of Cape Horn in winter had never been done by a European ship before and its winter storms were infamous in magnitude. The story of what happened has become the stuff of legend. By the time Anson returned to Britain four years later, by way of China,[11] Britain was at peace with Spain and at war with France. HMS Centurion was the only ship of his flotilla to make the full journey and after horrific losses, mainly to disease, only 188 men of the original 1,854 survived. Severe overcrowding had led to a devastating attack of typhus, or ship fever, spread by body lice, which thrived in the hot, humid and unsanitary conditions on board ships in tropical lands. To compound their misery, the lack of fresh fruit and vegetables also meant that scurvy was ever present.[12] The objectives to seize Callao, Lima and Panama were not accomplished and the Peruvians were not to rise up against their Spanish masters for another seventy years. Several ships were lost and one of the flotilla, HMS Wager, mutinied, its crew becoming lost or dispersed throughout the Pacific region.

The whole thing could have been deemed a disaster, but that was not how the expectant British public viewed it. Anson and his crew were considered heroes. This was partly due to the massive achievement in simply completing the voyage, but was probably more a result of the huge amount of prize money Anson obtained from captured Spanish ships.

In order to reward and encourage aggression it was customary to pass on all or part of the value of a captured ship and its cargo to the capturing Royal Naval Captain for distribution to his crew. Naval personnel would highly value any captain who had been successful in obtaining prizes, as a crew could make a year's pay for a few hours' fighting. The survivors of Anson's voyage did very well. It was said that one third of all the gold reserves in the Bank of England had come from the Centurion. A number of ships were taken during the voyage and significant prize money was obtained, but the crowning glory of the whole expedition was the capture of the Acapulco galleon. The ship had been spotted near the Philippines and after ninety minutes of intense struggle the Spanish galleon finally surrendered. The galleon was carrying 1,313,843 'pieces of eight'[13] and 35,682 ounces of silver and this was eagerly shipped back to Britain.

The contribution of George Murray to the expedition had been limited because for much of latter part of the journey he was absent in, what seemed to be almost the norm for an Elibank, rather controversial circumstances. At Madeira, Commodore Anson promoted George to Captain and a few months later transferred him to the larger HMS Pearl. In the dreadful South American weather of the winter and early spring the Pearl and an accompanying ship, the Severn, lost sight of the other ships (although it is not clear if they also lost sight of each other as well). The next day the two ships came together and headed north attempting to re-join the squadron. As the weather deteriorated further the officers agreed that unless the winds became favourable they would return around Cape Horn and go back to Britain.[14] A day later they carried out this controversial decision and the crews steeled themselves to face the nightmare of Cape Horn once again. Fortunately on the return journey the southern passage between Tierra Del Fuego and the South American continent enjoyed more benign weather conditions. Nevertheless, when the two ships reached Rio de Janeiro on 6th June 1741, 158 of George's ship's crew had died, 114 were too sick to be on duty and only 30 men were left to work the ship. The two ships finally left Rio in December 1741 and headed for England. When they got home they faced a mixed reception and some gossip of desertion. Both Captains were totally exonerated of any untoward behaviour in the official report and they went on to acquire some very considerable prize money.[15] George Murray's career continued to progress after his ill-fated expedition. Finally, in 1756 he was placed on the list of superannuated Rear-Admirals, but his active naval career was over.

It was probably just as well that George was overseas during the time of the Jacobite rising of 1745. Like his brothers, he almost certainly had Jacobite sympathies and his marriage to Lady Isabel Mackenzie, eldest daughter of the attainted Earl of Cromarty, ensured that Jacobite voices were seldom wanting in his close family. Despite this, in 1778 he became the sixth Lord Elibank and succeeded to the title and the estates. George and Isabel had two legitimate children, Maria and Isabella. George doted upon them for the rest of his life, although not without a tinge of guilt for his illegitimate son Patrick who, on George's death in November 1785, would be excluded from all his inheritance.

2

The suppression of vice and immorality

Perhaps the combination of simple 'joie de vivre' on surviving the Anson expedition and the stress of the accusations against his conduct on that voyage gave George Murray an excuse to allow his ardours to stray from the strictly straight and narrow towards extra marital liaisons. The inevitable result was the birth, circa 1749, of an illegitimate son, Patrick.

Illegitimacy in the pre-Victorian era was not uncommon amongst all sectors of society and Georgian men and women seemed to enjoy a robust attitude towards sex. Nevertheless, for most ordinary people the status of a 'fallen woman' was a horrifying prospect. The legal age of consent was only 12 and parents took great pains to ensure that their girls did not mix with 'fallen women',[16] presumably because such a state was highly contagious. Women who became pregnant outside of marriage were often treated very harshly:

> The principal... reason given for the severity with which females who have fallen from the path of virtue are treated in this country is the necessity of separating them entirely from the virtuous, in order to prevent contamination.[17]

By June 1787, George III had become so worried about the moral health of his subjects that he issued a 'Proclamation on the

Suppression of Vice and Immorality'. It had very little effect, except to provide amusement among aristocratic circles.[18] At a time when most marriages, especially in the upper classes, were organised on the basis of patronage and convenience, it is no surprise that many took comfort in sexual relationships outside of marriage. Within the aristocratic community, especially in military officer circles, it was almost the norm.[19]

Consequently illegitimate offspring were by no means unusual. The attitude towards these children varied considerably, but inevitably they were denied inherited titles or entailed property. Sometimes an illegitimate status acted as a bar to society, especially for females, but the many examples of prominent illegitimate children within influential society circles of the time give a mixed picture. A number of fathers freely accepted their illegitimate children and ensured that they were well taken care of in life, albeit at a lower level than their legitimate children would enjoy. Males, once accepted, would usually take their father's name and would be supported by them, often directed towards a career in administration in the Empire, the Church, or the Military. Illegitimate females, who would usually take the name of their mother, were often supported in obtaining a 'good marriage', so well described in the novels of Jane Austen.

The aristocratic view of illegitimacy was well illustrated by the Elibank family. Towards the end of his life Patrick, the 5th Lord Elibank, was accused by a relative of failing to acknowledge a boy as one of his illegitimate offspring. He angrily refuted this suggestion and as evidence he pointed out that he already had six illegitimate children and went on to name them. In his view, one child more would not have made much difference, so it was outrageous to suggest that he was deliberately withholding an acknowledgement.[20] Despite this, he was deeply hurt by the suggestion:

To find that I have lived seventy four years to so little purpose, that so improbable a tale, so much to my disgrace, should be received by anybody, my reputation in the world must be low indeed.[21]

Patrick did indeed look after his six illegitimate children. The eldest, William Young was supported in what became a glittering career with the East India Company. Patrick, his other son, inherited much of his moveable estate and became the Laird of Simprin in Berwickshire. The other four children, Charlotte, Maria, Ann and Elizabeth, were all left substantial amounts of money on Patrick's death and all went on to have successful marriages.[22] Patrick left the welfare of his illegitimate children in the very capable hands of his brother, General James Murray, who took a keen interest in their welfare, helping the careers of the boys and sending the girls to "the best school in England".[23]

George Murray, now the 6th Lord Elibank following the death of Patrick, his elder brother, had immediately recognised Patrick, his illegitimate namesake, as his son too. Twenty years later he was probably beginning to regret it.

Patrick had grown up under the care of his father, Admiral George and his family retainers. According to George's younger brother Gideon, when George married Isabella Mackenzie, the heir to the estate of Cromartie, at the age of 56, the newly married couple settled down:

George hath retired on a yellow admiral's half pay. He lives at Luffness, drinks hard and grows fat.[24]

The young Patrick was immediately accepted into the family home and grew up with his new stepmother. The marriage produced two legitimate daughters, but the hapless Patrick was destined to miss out on the inheritance of both the Elibank title and the significant financial rewards which would arise from a legitimate inheritance. Patrick didn't seem too downhearted and was proving to be to be quite a handful in the 'Just William' tradition of boy mischief. His step-mother constantly worried about 'little Paty' and despaired of his suitability for any future career. Admiral (as he now was) George Murray had planned an army career for his errant illegitimate son and consequently had purchased an ensign commission for him in the 42nd Foot, the famous Black Watch Regiment. The 42nd were to serve in North America but, in an inauspicious start to his military life, Patrick was left behind in Britain. Admiral George Murray had especially good relations with his now famous and heroic brother, General James Murray, the hero of Quebec, and so he wrote to him asking for help. Perhaps a new start for Patrick, in a different regiment where Uncle James could keep a close eye on him?

> ... you was (sic) so good in your letter to say you would take him off my hands... and put him down for a commission in your own regiment... beggars cannot be choosers... I shall send him out to you by the first Glasgow ship unless you forbid it. The folks here believe him to be yours which proceeds from his being like you and what is worse is a ... resemblance. Nelly (their sister Helen) says that you told her you lay with Sally when Mrs Murray had the small-pox which answers with his birth. This I know to be false and tell it for the joke.[25]

If there was any truth in the rumour, James' wife Cordelia certainly did not suspect it. She wrote to her mother describing her time whilst ill with smallpox:

> Mr Murray hardly ever stirred out of ye room from me ye whole time, so that I had no need for a nurse.[26]

Surprisingly, after such a bad taste joke, General James didn't forbid it[27] and young Patrick Murray made his way to Quebec to meet up with his uncle. Patrick's step-mother graphically summed up the feelings of many mothers, before and since, on the occasion of their little boy leaving home. She wrote to General James:

> I was glad to hear poor Paty arrived safe though the picture you gave us of him upon his first appearance made us laugh very much... I do assure you when he left he was very clean and had his hair trimmed by the best barber in Edinburgh; he had two suits of clothes, one quite new the other very good, a new beg-coat, laced hat, ten shirts, shoes, stockings, comb etc. with a bed, pillow, blankets and a quilt, a trunk to lock things in which I dare say he never did more than his father before him... I think him a very fine boy, I am very glad he has got into such good hands. Nothing vexes me but the Scotch Boy with the Scabed Head (sic), which I fancy was the name he went by in the ship...[28]

Patrick was logged in the records of 1771 as a Lieutenant in the Muster of General James Murray's own regiment, the 1st battalion of the 60th Foot (American Rifles).[29]

Just three years later General James had reason to regret his patronage of the rather wild and carefree Patrick, and he wrote to Patrick's father, George:

> For your sake I hope he turns out better than I expect he will do... He has an insuperable absence and inattention with a proneness to pleasure. These equalities are not likely to loose (sic) force in the hot gay climate of Jamaica.[30]

To General James Murray's astonishment, the 'hot gay climate' of Jamaica did not prove to be the expected undoing of his nephew Patrick. Indeed, James had reason to completely re-evaluate his errant nephew when, just two years later, Patrick was promoted to Captain and went on to a successful military career with the 60th Foot. Patrick's worth would rise even further in the illustrious eyes of his uncle when in 1778 he named his first and only son, the future Captain James Murray, after him.

The 60th Foot began life in 1756 as the 62nd (Royal American) Regiment with a remit to defend the thirteen American colonies from attack. The regiment was different in its structure from its contemporaries and has been described as an early example of a British 'foreign legion'. The officers, all Protestant, were recruited from Europe – not from the American colonies – and consisted primarily of British, Dutch, Swiss and German nationals. The regiment, by 1757 renamed the 60th (Royal American) Regiment, boasted of a more able soldier who was encouraged to use his initiative while keeping his discipline; something not always found in colonial militia.

The new regiment, with James Elibank Murray as its Colonel Commandant, had fought at Louisburg in 1758 and then at Quebec in 1759 in the campaign which finally wrested Canada from France. Although looking like most other British regiments with their red coats and cocked hats or grenadier caps on campaign, their swords were often replaced with hatchets, and their coats and hats were adapted for ease of movement in the woods. Swift guerrilla type movement became the fighting characteristic of the regiment. Although originally the 60th Foot was to be deployed only in North America, the British Parliament had no qualms about the re-defining of geography should it suit them and in 1763 they passed an Act which stated that the West Indian Colonies were now part of North America. This had far reaching implications for the 60th Foot, who almost mutinied at the prospect of serving in the West Indies. Their concern was not based upon any geographical or ideological loyalty to the American mainland, as virtually all the officers and men of the 60th Foot came from Scotland, Ireland or mainland Europe, but was instead based on their own health prospects. Despite their vigorous protests the Act stayed and over the next few years the men of the regiment were to be proved right. Most of the regiment had sailed for Jamaica within two years of the Act and their new barracks were constructed on low-lying swampy ground near Spanish Town. It would have been difficult to find more unsuitable terrain. For the men of the regiment it proved to be a lingering death and over the next twenty-five years, as disease took its heavy toll, the old Royal American Regiment virtually disappeared.[31]

So, 'the hot gay climate' may well have been a reaction to the very short life expectancy which was to be the soldiers' lot in their new station. The soldiers made the best of it, if Lieutenant Colonel Fuser was anything to go by. Quite how the bachelor Lieutenant Colonel Fuser, one of the original Swiss members of the regiment,[32] met Mary Smith, a young widow, can only be a matter for conjecture, but meet they did. The result was that in December 1774 a girl, christened Louisa Fuser, was born.

When a regiment was not involved in combat it was not unusual for the officers and men to develop relationships with local ladies. Inevitably some officers of the 60th succumbed to temptation. Lord Nelson's famous, if inappropriate, quote, "Once past Gibraltar, every man is a bachelor," referred to the senior service but no doubt was equally relevant to the army. To understand the prevailing morality of such liaisons the following incident is illuminating. In May 1778, Lieutenant Nathaniel Fitzpatrick of the Queens Rangers contracted a 'violent venereal disease' and passed it on to his Company Commander (a Captain James Murray, but no relation, it is hoped, to the subject of this narrative) through Mary Duche, their shared mistress. Fitzpatrick was court martialled. The official citation read:

... upon their return to Quarters, it was whisper'd in the regiment and came to the witness's knowledge that during the absence of the regiment he had lain with a woman that liv'd with Captain Murray of the same regiment knowing himself to be poxed, and permitted Captain Murray to lay with her without informing him of it, who was disorder'd and thereby render'd incapable of doing his duty.[33]

Fitzpatrick was acquitted but was criticised for 'improper conduct'. Whilst not suggesting that this was the usual moral stance taken by all the officers of the British Army it is noteworthy that it was known throughout the regiment that Murray lived with his mistress, and this passed without comment. Furthermore, Fitzpatrick was condemned not for what he did but for the fact that, in his actions, he caused the Captain to become unfit for duty.

Colonel Fuser would suffer no moralistic outrage from his regiment on the birth of his illegitimate daughter. He fully acknowledged Louisa as his natural daughter but his relationship to her mother was unclear. Mary is clearly cited as the mother of Louisa in Colonel Fuser's will, made just five years after Louisa's birth, but she is mentioned only as a widow and the mother. She is not left any inheritance, kind words or thanks. This is not entirely surprising in view of what is known about the character of Colonel Fuser. He has been described as "a pretty robust character"[34] and was brought to the attention of Patrick Tonyn, the Governor of East Florida, for being "insufferably rude, even insulting, to Indians and to Florida Rangers".[35] He did have a softer side and in his will Mrs Eberhard, the wife of the Adjutant of the 3rd Battalion of the 60th Foot, was left fifty pounds and his deep gratitude, for her care and attention to both Louisa and himself.[36]

Mary is not heard from again and it is likely that, as was all too tragically common at that time, she did not survive the birth or its aftermath.

3

Help me to be pure
– but not yet

Quote: Saint Augustine

I n 1774, when Louisa Fuser was born, the 60th Foot were still in Jamaica, but trouble was looming in the American colonies. The British government were concerned that the very strong connections of the regiment with America potentially made them an unreliable unit. Indeed, the Colonel-in-Chief of the regiment, Sir Jeffrey Amherst, had already indicated that he did not want to fight his own people in America. To combat this latent ineffectiveness, the first and second Battalions remained in Jamaica and two new Battalions were raised. Early in 1776 the new 3rd and 4th battalions of the 60th Foot arrived in St. Augustine, Florida, under the command of General Prevost. They were to comprise the principal British Regular Army force in Florida throughout the Revolutionary War. The loyalty of some of the regimental officers of the 1st and 2nd Battalions had been questioned but no doubts lingered about Colonel Fuser, Captain Macintosh and the newly promoted Captain Patrick Murray. As part of a regimental 'stiffening process' they were transferred from the 1st Battalion in Jamaica to the newly constituted 4th Battalion in East Florida and in 1776 they arrived at St. Augustine to take up their duties.

Florida had become a British colony in 1763 as an outcome of the Seven Years' War, when Spain ceded Florida to Britain in exchange for Cuba, which the British had captured during the war. The British almost immediately subdivided Florida into two separate colonies. West Florida consisted of the western portion of modern Florida but also included parts of the current states of Louisiana, Mississippi and Alabama, and had its capital at Pensacola. East Florida covered the rest of what is now modern Florida with its capital at St. Augustine. When Patrick Murray first sailed into the harbour of St. Augustine he was not entering a hastily wooden-built frontier town, but a town which had been continuously occupied for over 200 years. It was first settled by the Spanish in 1565 and remained in their possession until the British finally wrested it from them in 1763. The English had tried to take the town many times before. In 1586 Spanish St. Augustine was attacked and burned by Sir Francis Drake, and the surviving Spanish settlers were driven into the wilderness and swamps. They soon bounced back and rebuilt the town only to be subject to another attack 80 years later. This time it was the English privateer, Robert Searle. As a result of this, the Spanish began constructing the Castillo de San Marcos, destined to become so well-known to Captain Patrick Murray and the other officers and men of the 60th Foot. Today, in a very good state of repair, it still stands and is the oldest fort in the USA, a considerable lure for the many curious visitors to this most attractive of cities.

In 1740 St. Augustine was again unsuccessfully attacked by British forces from their colonies in the Carolinas and Georgia. The War of Jenkins' Ear[37] had provided a perfect opportunity for another British assault. It was the largest and most successful and was organised by the Governor of Georgia, General James Oglethorpe. Oglethorpe, with several thousand colonial militia, British regular soldiers and a number of Seminole warriors, laid a furious siege to St. Augustine. Still the fort and town held out and it took a peaceful negotiation between Britain and Spain, in which

Britain swapped Florida for Havana, Cuba, for St. Augustine finally to become a British settlement. By 1776 it had become a very handsome town with a settlement pattern which has remained largely unchanged to this day. The sheltered Matanzas Bay links the Intracoastal Waterway running along much of the shoreline of Georgia and Northern Florida to the Atlantic Ocean and on the western banks of this bay stands the formidable Castillo de San Marcos. Earthworks and wooden fortifications, some still visible today, spread west and south to enclose the town. Less than a mile to the south was an Augustinian monastery which, renamed the St. Francis Barracks, was converted into officers' quarters, around which was constructed a series of extensive and well-planned barrack blocks[38] for the rank and file British soldiers. The barrack blocks are gone but the monastery building and the parade ground, now serving as the car park for the National Guard headquarters, still stand.

Across the road from the barracks stands the oldest house in St. Augustine, called the Gonzales-Alvarez house. This house, built on the ashes of a previous dwelling burned down by English troops in 1702, was purchased by Joseph Peavitt, a former officer of the 60th foot, who had done what thousands of future Americans would dream of doing and retired to St. Augustine. Sadly, he didn't live long enough to enjoy his retirement but his widow Mary, with her new husband John Hudson, opened up the building as a public house for the soldiers across the road. Clearly, the 'hot gay climate' enjoyed so much by Patrick Murray in Jamaica did not entirely disappear when the Regiment moved to St. Augustine, and it takes no great stretch of imagination to see Patrick, billeted just across the road, making frequent use of the gaming table which still holds pride of place in the house. Between the old monastery barracks and the fort stretched the walled town. A contemporary observer conjured up a picturesque vision of the settlement:

Houses are built after the Spanish fashion with flat roofs and
few windows – here and there the English have houses with
more windows... The town was planned for four streets
running North-South but only two are conspicuously built up,
straight indeed but narrow. ... Almost every house has its little
garden, of which splendid lemon and orange trees are not the
least ornaments.[39]

The town even had a theatre which put on several productions
every year. To make sure that this pleasant little town did not erase
all memory of home, its large Scottish contingent set up a St.
Andrew's Society and had an annual march to the parish church,
from which they "returned in due order to Brother Love's Coffee
House to partake of good fare".[40] Although Brother Love's Coffee
House has long gone, the still-active local society meets just as it
did over 200 years ago.

Only a year after the annexation of East Florida, James Grant,
a Scottish army officer, was confirmed as the first Governor and
to attract new settlers he immediately set about issuing land grants
to prominent businessmen. One of the first men to benefit from
this policy was Richard Oswald of Cavens and Auchincruive, a
member of a family close in friendship with the Elibank Murrays.
Richard, a very rich and influential businessman who had made
his fortune through the slave trade, received the huge land grant
of 20,000 acres along the Tomoka and Halifax Rivers, now situated
within the boundaries of Ormond Beach, to the north of
Daytona.[41]

A visitor to this popular tourist area today would still
recognise the massive task facing these pioneers. The low lying
coast is made up of a series of bars and tidal islands which would
effectively block any ship's access to the interior. A short distance
inland lies a natural stretch of water, by no means contiguous,
called today the Intracoastal Waterway. It was not so very different

at the end of the 18th century. A contemporary traveller noted that it was an easy passage from Charleston to Georgia and on to Florida by use of the 'inland passage'.[42] Further south the passage was far from easy. The only navigable inlets linking the coast with the Intracoastal Waterway were at St.Augustine, situated many miles to the north, and the Ponce Inlet, twenty five miles to the south. A broad expanse of sandy beach, so beloved of modern vacationers, blocked any alternative route. Once a ship had entered the Ponce Inlet the troubles were not over. Access to Oswald's plantation was only by the tidal Intracoastal Waterway, a passage notorious for hidden bars and shifting sands. To go overland was even worse, as most of the land was thick virgin forest and swamp, well provisioned with malarial mosquitoes, bugs of all types and a full veneer of alligators.

Richard's representatives[43] were undaunted by the difficulties, no doubt largely because they had access to Oswald's huge reservoir of slaves who would do all the manual labour anyway. In June 1765, several boats filled with a few Englishmen and Scotsmen and approximately fifty African slaves landed at the point which would soon become the 'Oswald Plantation'. The first plantation struggled, but just a few years later a second development in the aptly named Swamp Plantation, six miles to the south, became a roaring success. Soon, over 300 acres of cleared land was studded with several settlements and a sugar mill. The remains of this, the oldest British sugar mill in the United States, which produced large quantities of molasses for the rum trade, can still be seen.[44] Nearby, on the Halifax River, they set up the Adia settlement with 100 acres of corn and rice, an indigo house and extensive slave quarters.[45] It seemed that the new British colony of Florida was up and running.

Richard Oswald was maybe the first but was certainly not the only man to begin to open up the Florida forests. A few miles to the south the massive New Smyrna settlement, which encompassed

101,400 acres (410 km²), was being developed by Andrew Turnbull, another Scot, utilising a 1400 person workforce of mainly Minorcans, recruited by Turnbull from his ships in the Mediterranean Sea. With these and other embryonic developments the plantations were at last beginning to show real promise for the future and St. Augustine was rapidly increasing its trading function.

In 1767, a new man entered the landholding community of East Florida. Lieutenant Colonel Tonyn, through the good offices and patronage of Richard Oswald, was assigned a land claim of 20,000 acres on the east bank of Black Creek, a tributary of the St. John's River,[46] and just a few years later he was appointed the second British Governor of East Florida.

By now the gathering storm in the northern colonies was threatening to engulf the area and it would not be long before open conflict broke out. In the lull before the call to action some of the officers of the 60th Foot became embroiled in the maelstrom of East Florida politics. Patrick Tonyn was a forthright and uncompromising governor who was unlikely to tolerate dissent, especially being geographically very close to the turmoil taking place to the north.[47] In particular he had little regard for the group called the 'Sons of Liberty'. This loose organisation of American patriots was formed to protect the rights of the colonists and to take direct action against what they believed to be the mistreatment of American colonists by the British government. They were best known for the Boston Tea Party in 1773 which led to the British government introducing the Intolerable Acts.[48] This onslaught on illegal activity in the North led to very jumpy administrations throughout British North America, and East Florida was no exception. Even before Patrick Tonyn's arrival a group of men existed in St. Augustine whom he later referred to as a "cabal of dissensionists and agitators". It included planters William Drayton and Dr. Andrew Turnbull and wealthy merchants such as James Penman and Spencer Mann. Allegedly, another name later to join the same group was Lt. Colonel Fuser of the 60th Regiment of Foot.[49] His anger at Governor Tonyn was mainly based around the question of who commanded the local militia but often surfaced in more trivial ways, such as the near-duel situation which arose between them when Fuser accused Tonyn of opening his mail.[50] The closeness and friendship of this so called 'dissensionist' group was further reinforced by the selection of Dr. Andrew Turnbull, James Penman and Spenser Mann as executors of Louis Valentine Fuser's will of 1779.[51]

Captain Patrick Murray was placed in a difficult position, with his immediate superior, Lieutenant-Colonel Fuser, being in direct conflict with Governor Tonyn, a man who was close to and supported by the influential Elibank and Oswald extended family connections. There was to be only one winner and it was Governor Tonyn. By 1778, he had succeeded in quietening down all his antagonists by all means at his disposal, which included disgracing them publicly, removing them from office or simply allowing the war take them elsewhere. Patrick Tonyn then spent the rest of the Revolutionary War successfully maintaining the defences of St. Augustine and was on hand to finally draw the curtain over Britain's short-lived Florida adventure.[52]

The hot, steamy atmosphere of St. Augustine did little to dampen the ardours of young army officers and perhaps some of the ladies too. Enter Eliza Smith, a remarkable woman who, in the little that is known of her, exhibited a lifestyle rarely seen in the strict and narrow society of the late 18th century. Quite how Eliza arrived on the scene is a matter of conjecture but she certainly arrived with a bang rather than a whimper as, in the early part of 1778, James Murray, son of Eliza Smith and Captain Patrick Murray, entered this world.

Like Patrick his father, he entered life as an illegitimate child, but was immediately acknowledged by Patrick and took his father's illustrious name. His mother, Eliza, may have been none other than Mary 'Eliza' Smith, the mother of Louisa Fuser, as throughout her documented life she referred to Louisa as her daughter. However, Eliza never used the name Mary, even in later legal and official documents, and for Mary and Eliza to have been one and the same there would have needed to be a catastrophic breakdown in relations between Eliza and Colonel Fuser at some time between the birth of Louisa and that of James. That she later took some responsibility for Louisa is certain and it is very likely that there was a kinship between the two women, but the mother-daughter terminology was more likely one of convenience and a reflection of filial affection than a biological event.

Louis Valentine Fuser's will left virtually all his estate to his only daughter, Louisa. He also named four of his senior officers, mainly company commanders, as executors. Patrick Murray's name is not one of them but this does not necessarily signify any hostility or distance between the two men, as at the time of the will Patrick was on active service in Georgia. Mary Smith is mentioned, almost grudgingly, as the mother of Louisa[53] and there is no warmth expressed in the choice of words, although it would be a step too far to declare that any hostility could be deduced by the wording of the will. Furthermore, the close military relationship between Lieutenant-Colonel Fuser and Patrick Murray, clearly expressed in Patrick Murray's diary accounts, never seemed to dip below the highly professional.[54]

Eliza, a young lady of independent financial means, was the widow of a Joseph Smith (referred to in references as 'a gentleman').[55] This term was usually used in connection with the younger sons of the gentry or those who held a title. Of the candidates in this prominent field, a leading contender would be one of the vast number of offspring from the family of the Hon. William Smith of New York.

William Smith left England in the early eighteenth century to settle in New York. He soon rose to prominence in the legal profession, ultimately becoming a highly respected Judge of the Supreme Court of New York. He and his French wife, Mary, had 15 children and many of them became equally prominent in their own fields. One of them, Catherine, married the important merchant, John Gordon of Beaufort, South Carolina and the couple were to purchase vast estates in the developing province of Florida. Legal disputes over titles meant that by the time of the Revolution, ownership of the Florida estate had not been finalised and a family presence in Florida would have been necessary. Catherine's elder brother was William, nicknamed 'the Historian', who was to follow in his father's footsteps and become the Chief Justice of New York. He lost that position for his support of the loyalist cause during the Revolutionary Wars but was rewarded by the British government for his loyalty by being appointed the Chief Justice of Quebec, Canada, where he died in 1793, leaving behind at least ten children. Current genealogical studies fail to identify a Joseph Smith who married Eliza and left his fortune to her, but the connection to this Smith family of New York is both plausible and attractive in explaining Eliza's presence in Florida, Georgia, South Carolina and, later in her life, Quebec.

4

Come and take it!

Any romantic vision of a happy Eliza and a smiling Patrick, proudly holding their new baby James as they settled into domestic bliss would have been immediately shattered by news from the North. Hostilities had broken out and all thirteen British colonies were in open revolt against the Crown. Patrick and the 60th regiment were soon to be called into action. Their first task was to defend Florida against hostile incursions from the Northern States. It is rare for any first hand contemporary accounts of the war by a British officer to have survived, but one of the few remaining was compiled by Patrick Murray himself as he played his part in the Georgia and South Carolina campaigns of the Revolutionary War. Inevitably his own role was prominent in the description of the events which follow, but in most cases other evidence supports Murray's account.[56]

Early in 1778 Patrick's, and the regiment's, first campaign followed a confusing period of local but relatively benign skirmishes. Early in the war an attack by the newly constituted East Florida Rangers, of which he was a part, was executed against the rebel held Fort Barrington. Patrick and his immediate superior officer, Lieutenant-Colonel Fuser, made a reconnaissance towards the fort but were spotted by the defending American detachment. The Americans thought that they were the advance guard of a much larger force and, to the delight of Patrick and his men, the American Commander, Captain Wynne, along with 52 Carolina Riflemen and 23 men of the 1st Georgia Regiment, laid down their arms and were promptly marched off as prisoners, escorted by Patrick and 20 of his men. The disarmed Americans were delivered to their own forces and were put under honour not to serve again until they were formally exchanged for British prisoners. The recently captured Americans, not surprisingly, hugely magnified the size of the British attacking force in their stories, and so all the American forces wisely retreated. The next day Murray and his men burnt Fort Barrington and then marched back to St. Augustine, arriving just a few days later. Patrick must have considered that this warfare business was excellent fun. The British had not been shot at, had not fired a shot themselves, and all sides had behaved with impeccable gentlemanly manners throughout. It was not going to last.[57] Just a few days later the American Major Baker, with his Georgian Dragoons, had a skirmish with the Black Creek Indians who were fighting on the British side, and killed two of them. Shortly afterwards Major Prevost, a Company Commander of the 60th Foot, launched a surprise bayonet attack on the same group. Forty of the Georgians jumped into a nearby swamp and were not heard of again. Thirty others escaped and the rest surrendered, but to the horror of the British regular soldiers all but sixteen of the prisoners were then summarily slaughtered by the Black Creek Indians. It was only with great difficulty that the American officers, Major Baker and Captain Fen, were saved from the same fate. The honeymoon period was over.

Patrick then braced himself for an American onslaught, which was inevitable after the actions of the Black Creek Indians and the constant sniping and guerrilla tactics employed by the 'Rangers', a very active Loyalist militia group. These irregular so-called 'Rangers' were a semi–independent militia mainly raised from settlers and loyalists in Georgia and were led by the mercurial Thomas Brown, a recent British settler and now Military Officer.

His impressive successes against the Georgia revolutionaries was a result of his tactical awareness, his alignment with local Indian tribes, but overwhelmingly his own deep personal commitment to the cause. Thomas Brown had only arrived in America in 1774 with every intention of making it his new home. In the Georgia back-country trouble was already brewing and by 1775 he had become known as an opponent of the 'sons of liberty', an independence movement rapidly gaining ground in Georgia. Perhaps one of the reasons they were gaining so much ground was their unashamed policy of intimidation. Thomas was to experience this first hand when nearly 100 Liberty Boys marched to the house where Brown was staying and called upon him to swear an oath to uphold the pro-independence Georgia Provincial Congress. There followed a dramatic doorstep confrontation.

Brown asked to be excused from the oath, saying that he did not want to take up arms against the country that had given him being, but neither did he want to fight against those among whom he intended to spend the rest of his days. Robert Hamilton, the leader of the mob, replied that the oath did not require either of these alternatives but failed to convince Brown. As the mob grew restless Brown was told that he could not remain neutral so he made to go back inside the house. At that point the mob threatened to destroy his property and drag him to Augusta where he would be forced to join the association. Brown returned to the porch, pistols in hand and as the mob advanced he told them that the first person to touch him must be ready to 'abide the consequences'.

A group then rushed towards him and Brown fired his pistols. One misfired but the other hit one of the attackers through the foot. Brown then drew his sword and kept off the attacking mob until one crept up behind him and hit him on the head with a rifle butt, fracturing his skull. Brown was carried off to Augusta in a semi-conscious state. His hair was stripped off with knives and he was scalped in three or four places. He was tied to a tree and burning pieces of wood were thrust under his feet; he was tarred and burned so badly that he lost two toes.

The appallingly injured Thomas Brown was then exhibited in a cart driven through the town of Augusta[58] but, amazingly, he physically recovered from his ordeal.[59] A now absolutely unwavering Thomas Brown was to remain an indomitable thorn in the side of the American Revolutionaries for the rest of the war, even though he was often treated with contempt by regular British officers on his own side, who disdained his non-regular militia status.

It was to pull out this thorn that a large detachment of Georgia militiamen trailed and attacked Brown's Rangers and chased them over the Georgia – Florida border. Brown led the American militiamen right into a prepared defensive position of British regulars, established by Major Mark Prevost on the Alligator Bridge over the Nassau Sound just to the east of present day Callahan. The Battle of Alligator Bridge, fought on June 30th 1778, was the only major engagement in an unsuccessful American campaign to align British East Florida with the 13 breakaway states during the War. Patrick Murray was in the British camp at the time and he takes up the story:

> Presently we heard Whitfield the drummer beating the Grenadiers March and the Rangers (Brown's irregular troops) filing over the bridge.... soon after entering, when the Ranger's drum beat to arms, the Rangers, many of whom had lost their arms in the cabbage swamp, were seen flying into that in front of our camp. Captain Muller of the Grenadiers and his men came running into the camp for their arms, musket balls whistling over our tents while the enemy with sabres and rifles were shouting "down with the Tories".[60]

Official accounts of the battle have suggested that the American troops were deliberately lured into a formal defensive position but

Patrick Murray's account suggests that, if anything, the British troops were caught by surprise by the appearance of the Americans. After a brief but fierce fight the British regulars defending the bridge succeeded in turning back the Georgians.[61] With food stocks declining, the Americans retreated back into Georgia and thus ended their dream of bringing East Florida into the revolutionary camp.

In November 1778, General Prevost, having decided it was time to go on the offensive, launched an invasion of Georgia using the 60th Regiment as the spearhead troops. The assault was part of a much larger strategy, as the Florida force aimed to meet up with General Clinton and Colonel Campbell, who had landed north of the Savannah River in Georgia, and were to march south. The clear aim was the re-conquest of Georgia.

By 24th November 1778 Patrick and his men, commanded by Louisa's father, Colonel Fuser, were landed by boat at Newport, a few miles to the south of Sunbury, and they advanced towards Sunbury and Fort Morris. They encountered little opposition in their progress and on arrival they camped on the slope of rising ground just between Fort Morris and the town. A reconnaissance party advanced towards the fort and found it well defended with cannon and so Patrick and his company were ordered to bypass the fortifications and go straight into the nearby town of Sunbury.

Today the town of Sunbury does not exist and all there is to see are a few archaeological remains and the old Sunbury Cemetery. In 1778 the landscape was very different. Sunbury was founded in 1752 and in 1758 the building of an ambitious town and port was begun. The planned port was laid out with wharves, town lots and three town squares, the main one overlooked by a handsome courthouse. Very soon the embryonic town had grown to rival Savannah as the chief port of Georgia. It was this settlement that Patrick Murray entered on the evening of 24th November. The town was taken with no opposition as the inhabitants, almost to a man, had taken shelter in nearby Fort Morris. Sunbury Courthouse was taken over as the Company HQ, but as it was still in the process of construction, a nearby merchant's house had to be used in lieu. This proved to be a most fortunate change of plan as, with great delight, Captain Murray described how he discovered there a 'puncheon' of rum and informed his superior officer, Colonel Fuser, who then gleefully distributed it. Murray was careful to point out that the soldiers were strictly under orders that there was to be no plundering. Obviously this order did not apply to thirsty British officers.

The next day Captain Patrick Murray was to witness one of the most famous incidents of the American Revolutionary War. A small contingent of Fuser's men, including Patrick, was tasked to take Fort Morris, defended by 200 Americans under Colonel John McIntosh. Colonel Fuser sent a formal surrender demand to the fort, giving the defenders one hour and calling upon Colonel McIntosh to lay down his arms and "remain neuter until the fate of America is determined." Fuser's demand for the surrender of Fort Morris provoked a noteworthy response which has inspired Americans ever since:

> We, sir, are fighting the battles of America, and therefore distain to remain neutral till its fate is determined. As to surrendering the fort, receive this laconic reply:
> COME AND TAKE IT.

In his memoirs Patrick Murray unsurprisingly plays down the reply, simply noting that it was 'spirited'.[62] Colonel McIntosh became an American hero for his courage and defiance at Fort Morris. After the war the Georgia Legislature voted to honour him with a sword, the blade of which was inscribed with his now famous words, "Come and take it!"[63]

Colonel Fuser didn't take up McIntosh's offer and ordered a

retreat so that the extended British forces could regroup further south. They gathered, along with a flotilla of boats, at Cumberland Island off the Georgia-Florida border. The problem now was that the provisions had run out as a result of the constant American harrying of the British supply ships. For three days Patrick and his battalion colleagues existed on a barely subsistence diet of a very small portion of rice and a few oysters found in the inlets of the sea. It didn't help when a gale separated the British ships and Patrick, with a small group of colleagues, was shipwrecked on Little Cumberland Island for three days.

All was not lost. Some rice and a supply of Madeira wine, found in a wreck, all enhanced by some alligator meat, allowed the makeshift battalion cook to offer paella, and plenty of it, on his evening menus for the next couple of days. It goes unrecorded whether Patrick considered this 'paella' an improvement on the horsemeat he was offered on reaching the British HQ and the comparative safety of Jeckyl Island.[64]

By early January 1779 the British were back at Fort Morris, this time with artillery and an indignant (and possibly drunken) Captain McIntosh. Captain Roderick McIntosh, who was serving in Patrick's Company had been recruited from the Scottish Highlands and was inordinately proud of his heritage. By repute, Captain Roderick, having availed himself of rather too much alcoholic hospitality, insisted on summoning the fort to surrender. He strutted out, claymore in hand, and approached the fort, roaring, "Surrender, you miscreants! How dare you presume to resist His Majesty's arms?" The fort commander, who bizarrely knew Roderick personally, forbade anyone from firing and threw open the gate saying, "Walk in, Mr McIntosh, and take possession." "No," said Rory, "I will not trust myself among such vermin; but I order you to surrender." This was the signal for the defending garrison to open fire and Roderick was soon hit by a ball which passed through his face, sideways, under his eyes. He stumbled, and fell backwards, but immediately recovered and retreated backwards, flourishing his sword. Cyrus, his black slave, who had bravely accompanied him on his near solo assault called out to him to run but Roderick's alleged response was still defiant. "You may run, but I am of a race that never runs".

He didn't run, but, with the help of his comrades-in-arms, discretion became the better part of valour and Rory backed safely into his lines. Nevertheless, as a permanent reminder of his folly, he had suffered severe wounds and lost the use of an eye.[65]

Later in the day General Prevost began a bombardment of the fort and the defenders, after suffering a brief but very heavy bombardment, surrendered with 200 prisoners being taken (although Patrick believed the number to be between 300 and 400).[66] A detachment was left to guard the fort; the only choice for the new fort commandant was the now one-eyed Captain Roderick McIntosh, ably assisted by his acting 'aide-de-camp', Cyrus.

On the military front, the British advance was moving swiftly and Savannah was captured with virtually no resistance. The next step was Atlanta, and this town fell by the end of January. Fearing an imminent and massive counter-assault by the American forces, General Prevost decided upon attacking South Carolina in the hope that the Americans would be distracted away from their inland Georgia campaign towards Atlanta. As part of this feint, a force of British troops, including Patrick, landed near Port Royal, south of Charleston, South Carolina.

After missing an easy chance to capture the harbour of Port Royal,[67] the only harbour where a ship of the line could safely dock south of the Chesapeake, the British moved their ships up the Broad River on the west of the Island. They disembarked near the present Laurel Bay and with Patrick commanding the left wing of the advancing British force, they began to move inland, hoping to cut off the Port Royal Ferry from the town of Beaufort. Today, moving up from the south, Port Royal Island presents a relatively flat and physically featureless appearance until a point near Grays Hill where a significant scarp slope suddenly drops from the centre of the island towards the ferry and coastline. On February 3rd 1779 General Moultrie and about 300 Charleston militia had also noticed the slope and chose to use it well, forming up under cover to stem the British advance. Patrick was about to face the fiercest engagement he had so far experienced.

When the two forces collided the situation became the reverse of most Revolutionary War engagements – the Americans were in the open and the British in cover, amid bushes and wild brush at the edge of a nearby swamp. A general but fierce engagement, which lasted about 45 minutes, then began. Finally the Americans, now almost out of ammunition, began a retreat, but the British had retreated a few minutes before this. Consequently the Americans, last to leave the field, claimed the credit for winning the battle, which has now come down in history as an American victory. Patrick's own memoirs furnish rather more detail.

The Americans formed up about 200 yards from the British line and a general engagement ensued. Patrick, commanding his light infantry company on the left wing of the British line, was soon in the thick of things. He was showing the coolness under fire expected by regular British officers when he began to 'dress his men off' to ensure a good straight line prior to the general assault. Some may call this behaviour foolhardy and certainly at this point the Elibank luck deserted him as he was struck in the right buttock by a piece of grape shot. Fierce American fire then drove the British to seek cover behind brush on either side of the road. Major Gardiner, the senior British Officer present, then decided to retreat and sent orders to Patrick Murray on the left wing. Patrick immediately appealed against such a course of action as he claimed that his men were pushing back the Americans. Major Gardiner consequently rescinded his order, but by now the battlefield was a smoke-drenched and confused place with both sides believing that they had beaten their opposition.[68] Seemingly impervious to his buttock wound, Captain Murray rallied his troops and ordered an advance, forcing the enemy to withdraw. A single rifleman (probably a pesky 'Virginian', according to Patrick) stayed behind and with a well-aimed shot hit Murray, the bullet passing through his left arm and exiting between his shoulder blades. The Americans, now out of ammunition, then completely withdrew. Patrick had fainted, probably through loss of blood, but on regaining consciousness he re-joined the rest of his rather confused corps. According to Patrick, a final British charge was made in open order, but the American riflemen did not wait for the bayonet; throwing away their arms, they made off. The small surviving British contingent then retreated towards their boats and a colleague found a horse, enabling the wounded Patrick to regain the ship in relative comfort and safety. The scenes of death and injury all around were very disturbing, as the small British force had suffered badly, with only 63 men of the 160 or so who had begun the action being uninjured. There were heroic acts in plenty, such as that of Corporal West in Patrick's Light Infantry Company who, on receiving a serious wound, had his left arm amputated on the field. The next morning, apparently undaunted and obviously feeling much better, he composed a song about the incident, which regrettably has been lost.

Patrick disputed the American version of events as he argued that the American force had retreated first, leaving the British as masters of the ground. He insists, citing three other officers in his support, that he and his company kept the ground from which the enemy had retreated.[69] It all seems rather a schoolboy argument about who was last to leave the spot in what was, in retrospect, an utterly inconsequential battle, although it did have a minor morale-raising effect on the beleaguered American troops. Whatever the true version of events, Patrick was taken to the newly captured Savannah to begin his recuperation and take up his prestigious new post as an aide-de-camp to the General.

An aide–de–camp on General's Prevost's staff would need to show impeccable behaviour, good decision-making powers and the ability to liaise with enemies as well as friends, and it is to the credit of Patrick that he was chosen for the task.[70] In his memoirs he is quick to demonstrate that he always behaved with great propriety towards the Americans, exemplified by the incident where he burned (with great reluctance, he emphasised) a plantation house belonging to the American Colonel Haywood. Patrick had urged Haywood's sons to come and save the building but they answered him with bullets for his humanity. Nevertheless, according to him, he still ordered all the furniture to be removed on account of the ladies. Perhaps the General recognised that he was the ideal man to liaise with the Americans. Furthermore, Patrick, by his own account, had a prodigious memory. When a secret letter was found by Major Prevost, Patrick was allowed to read but not copy it. The next day Patrick, after he had re-joined Colonel Fuser, copied the letter from memory. Compared with the original, only two words were different.[71]

Defeat from the jaws
of victory

The capture of Savannah was not only strategically significant for the British Southern campaign but was symbolically important too. Savannah, established in 1733 by James Oglethorpe, is the oldest city in Georgia, and even today it largely retains its original town plan. The city was built on the southern bank of the navigable Savannah River and offered a good sheltered harbour under the lee of Hutchinson Island. Oglethorpe, defence always in mind, laid out the city around a series of squares which allegedly would allow local militia units to easily form up using a strong defensive square formation should attack from any direction arise. The original purpose was soon forgotten and around the 22 pleasant squares developed some of the finest housing and architecture to be seen in Colonial and Antebellum America, today attracting millions of visitors who go to enjoy the city's architecture and historic buildings. As one of the great success stories of Colonial America, Britain was anxious to take and then hold the city. The holding part proved to be a bit more challenging than the taking.

The American General Lincoln, tasked with re-taking the important city of Savannah, knew that he would need naval support. He got it from a surprising quarter. The French, although ostensibly at war with Britain and supporting America, had not played a significant part in military operations so far, but this was to change. Vice Admiral Comte d'Estaing agreed to bring his fleet to support a joint American / French attack on the city. General Lincoln left Charleston with around 2,000 men to invade Georgia and by 12th September Admiral d'Estaing had landed a further 3,500 men near Savannah and was able to join up with the recently arrived General Lincoln and his army. The combined force, now sitting poised outside the city, demanded that General Prevost surrender. Prevost refused, of course, and on 23rd September d'Estaing and Lincoln began their bombardment. This continued until well into October, but official reports played down the effects, indicating that little damage had been caused. The besieged defenders didn't all agree. Anthony Stokes, the Savannah Chief Justice, wrote to his wife on 9th November. He reported that much of the city had been destroyed by the cannonades. The women and children, of whom there were many, hid wherever they could find shelter. Mrs Prevost, wife of the General, hid in the cellar of a Captain Knowles' house and recorded how they had suffered a severe and horrifying bombardment. It proved too much and most of the women left the city and sought protection in the nearby Yamacrow Marsh and the adjoining plantation lands of John Gordon on Hutchinson's Island, both out of range of the bombarding cannons.[72]

Whilst not officially recorded, Eliza Smith was almost certainly amongst these huddled and terrified women. Her movements are unclear after giving birth to James Murray in 1778. However, in early 1780 a new addition to the family arrived. Theresa, born in Georgia, is rarely featured with any surname, the only occasion being in Eliza Smith's will of 1806 [73] when she is referred to as Theresa Smith, in the same way that Louisa Fuser was referred to as Louisa Smith. That she fails to carry the Murray name, and is never mentioned by Patrick Murray in any of his correspondence, suggests that Patrick was not the father, although

Eliza's presence in Georgia indicates that she was still attached to the wounded Royal American Officer. The convention for illegitimate children at that time was that if a son was acknowledged by his biological father the boy would bear the name of his father. This was usually, but not exclusively, the case with daughters too, although some would take the name of their mother.

Eliza Smith claimed Theresa as her daughter and James Murray also acknowledged the girl as his sister in the same manner.[74] If Patrick was not the father does this suggest that Eliza was rather too generous with her sexual favours and the father was a third person unknown? In the officer environment of 1780 this is most unlikely, and would certainly be an occasion for a duel, or at the very least the cause of a serious breakdown in a relationship, as James himself would personally discover later in his own life.

Other possibilities do exist. The timing of Theresa's birth was shortly after the siege of Savannah. It was common for families to take in orphans and bring them up as their own and plenty of orphans were in need of care in the period of intense social turbulence that existed in Florida and the Southern States in the late 1770s. Many ill-fated girls were hostages to fortune in those difficult times and had lost their family. Admiral Lord Exmouth, otherwise known as Edward Pellew, the famous frigate captain, was frequently delighted by the wit and gossip contained in letters from his adopted daughter Jane Smith. Jane was said to be the daughter of a seaman killed on duty, but was suspected to be the illegitimate daughter of Pellew himself.[75] The ubiquitous surname of Smith would be the least likely to be fully traced and in the case of Pellew's adopted daughter may have been a fictitious name.

Whilst Eliza and the other women and children cowered in their hiding places around Savannah, the British defenders, with true stiff upper lip, tried to play down the whole desperate situation, indicating that the barrage was of no real consequence. The attacking army, especially the more impetuous French forces, began to get increasingly restless and demanded that the well-defended British positions be assaulted. The British defenders, now reinforced by the arrival of John Maitland, prepared to meet the assault. Maitland, Patrick's fellow officer, had conducted a remarkable forced march through the swamps and marshes from Beaufort on Port Royal Island to Savannah at the head of 800 Highlanders and the gallant survivors of Patrick's battalion from the Port Royal engagement. The first wave of the American / French assault began just after dawn on 9th October and made the ill-advised mistake of assaulting the Spring Hill Redoubt, defended by Colonel Maitland and the same intrepid men who had marched from Port Royal.[76] The French and American attack immediately ran into very heavy British fire and took significant losses. The second wave had some more success but in fierce hand-to-hand fighting, with heroic actions on both sides, the British finally drove the attackers back and inflicted very heavy casualties. After less than a day of fighting, the American and French losses were 1,094 men killed and many more wounded or captured, with British losses reported as only 16 dead and 39 wounded. On 18th October the siege was abandoned, the French fleet departed and General Lincoln retreated back to Charleston with the remnants of his dispirited army.[77]

The siege, so played down by the British, was at a very considerable cost to the city of Savannah. The minutes of the meetings of the Council of Georgia immediately after the siege not only paint a picture of how much the physical fabric of Savannah had been destroyed, but also exemplify how the established social order had broken down, to the terror of many of the population. The unhappy citizens complained of:

the ruinous condition of the chimneys [probably all that was left of many houses], where lives are in constant danger of fire and other accidents; the filth and nastiness of the streets; the indecent practice of burying dead bodies in various places and not confining it to the place appointed for that solemn purpose; the great number of negroes strolling around the town and country, many armed and committing robberies and other enormities to the terror and annoyance of the inhabitants; the want of a house of confinement for negroes; the ruinous condition of the roads and bridges and the want of boats and attendance at ferries; the want of a place for the reception of the poor who pine and die in the utmost distress, destitute and in want of the common necessities of life; and the want of an assembly where grievances could be heard.[78]

By December 1779, Sir Henry Clinton, Commander in chief of the British forces in America, had arrived in Savannah and prepared his forces to continue the assault northwards, this time without the help of the depleted 60th regiment. Clinton, with 14,000 troops and 90 ships under his command, marched north and began a siege of Charleston, South Carolina, on 1st April, 1780. Unable to break out and with no relief expected, the American General Lincoln was compelled to surrender the city and his army of over 5,000 troops on 12th May 1780.[79] It was the largest British victory of the Revolutionary War and only bad news from St. Augustine interrupted the British celebrations. Louis Valentine Fuser, father of Louisa, had suddenly died. Colonel Fuser had returned from active service in Georgia to St. Augustine in early 1779 to take command of the garrison still left in the city. He had been in poor health for some time and it was hoped that his return might hasten a recovery. This was not to be and news of his death met with a mixed reaction. Governor Tonyn was secretly relieved, as he considered that Fuser was part of a 'desperate faction' working against the best interests of British Florida. Not all agreed and despite his often arrogant, rude and uncompromising character he has been described as a "most intelligent and energetic officer."[80]

With Georgia now returned to the crown and Charleston back in British hands, the remnants of the 60th Foot returned to their duties in St. Augustine. Accompanying them were Eliza and Theresa, with Eliza now taking on the additional responsibility of looking after Louisa, the six-year old daughter of the deceased Mary Smith and Colonel Fuser. The burgeoning Smith / Murray family soon had a further addition with the birth of Harriet in early 1781. In a similar manner to Theresa, Harriet was recognised by Eliza later in life as her daughter and by James Murray as his sister. Once again Patrick is silent concerning any responsibility he may have had as a father, a view reinforced by Harriet bearing the surname of Smith. The likely conclusion is that Harriet was also an orphan child, taken under the wing of Eliza in these desperate times.[81]

By 1781, the aide-de-camp duties that the now recovered Patrick Murray owed to General Clinton or to General Prevost had ended with the return of both Generals to Britain. Consequently, Patrick could now return to his regimental responsibilities in St. Augustine and assist Eliza with family responsibilities too. Both West and East Florida had remained loyal to the British crown throughout the American Revolutionary War and as events turned against the mother country, St. Augustine served as a safe haven for thousands of loyalists fleeing from the war in the tenuous 'Thirteen Colonies' to the north. The town also acted as a gaol for a significant number of important 'rebel' prisoners and at one time three of the signatories to the American Declaration of Independence were confined, at the same time, in the town until exchanged for British prisoners held by the American forces.

Although in the main the prisoners were well treated, the residents of the town were discouraged from active dialogue with them, advice frequently ignored by the local population.[82] Some of the soldiers of the 60th Foot were rather less accommodating and one of them was James' father Patrick. It was reported that one of the American prisoners, named William, was abruptly arrested and forced into the Guard House by Captain Murray for a 'supposed trifling libel' against the commandant, Colonel Glazier. He was kept in detention for three days until all charges against him were dropped and he was swiftly discharged. He later bitterly complained of the 'scandalous treatment' he underwent from Captain Murray, in that he unjustly forced him into confinement.[83] Patrick, in his diary, always spoke with respect and consideration for his American opponents, but this event, taking place shortly after his own wounding at Port Royal, showed that his patience and understanding had been stretched to breaking point. He was to receive further bad news.

In 1778, with the war raging in the north, Spain took the opportunity of capitalising on the beleaguered British forces by launching an attack on West Florida. After successfully capturing British positions in Louisiana and Mississippi (then part of the West Florida colony), the Spanish General, Bernardo de Galvez, moved towards Pensacola, the capital city of West Florida. By 1781 General Galvez, with more than 40 ships and 3,500 men, was in a position to launch an assault on the town. Thus began a two-month siege of Pensacola.

The British defenders of the city, almost all regimental colleagues of Patrick Murray, fought bravely but by April 1781 Galvez's total force had increased to 7,800 and they greatly outnumbered the defenders. The final straw came on 8th May, when a Spanish shell struck the powder magazine in the Queen's Redoubt. The magazine exploded with massive force, destroying the fort and killing almost 100 British soldiers. Finally, with this blow, the British forces surrendered after taking over 200 casualties in total from the small garrison of less than 1,400 men.

The Spanish took 1,113 prisoners and British West Florida was lost.

The surviving captured members of the 60th Foot were sent to Havana and later taken on to New York where they were exchanged for Spanish and American soldiers in British captivity. It was a serious blow to British morale and enough for Patrick to seriously consider his family position.

His conclusion was dramatic. In the interests of safety, his son would need to leave North America, and so it was that in late 1781 or early 1782 a three year old James Murray left his mother and 'sisters' and sailed from Florida towards the safety of Patrick's homeland, Scotland. James later told how he was 'brought 'from Florida but does not elaborate. It is quite possible that Patrick himself brought over his young son as he had the available time to do so. He was on the muster for the 4th Battalion of the 60th Foot throughout 1781 and early 1782 but he is described as 'casual' and thus probably not present in person.[84] He was transferred to the 2nd Battalion on the 19th April 1782 but still did not feature on the regimental muster.[85] He appears to have had an extended period of leave, perhaps considered necessary in view of his over-zealous actions in St. Augustine.

The best small village in Scotland

In 2012, New Abbey, a small settlement in Southern Nithsdale and just six miles south of Dumfries, won the national 'Beautiful Scotland' competition and consequently held the title of the 'best small village in Scotland'. The competition success could mainly be put down to the care and attention lavished on the village and its gardens by its fortunate residents but, according to the proverb, 'you cannot make a silk purse out of a sow's ear.'

When James arrived in the village, few would have compared New Abbey to a silk purse, but the foundations and structures which would lead it to receive its prestigious accolade over two hundred years later were already in place and it had left the 'sow's ear' long behind. A beautiful setting, in the lee of Criffel Hill, certainly helped. A visitor wishing to travel along the coastal road towards the distant port of Dalbeattie or the nearer emigration port of Carsethorn would need to pass through New Abbey. The village waiting for James and his sisters was not a bustling metropolis, but did not justify the description of remote. New Abbey in many ways was typical of the small villages to be found throughout Regency Scotland, but in addition it had important historical connections. Visitors today can still gaze upon a village which would be instantly recognisable to James, his sisters and their fellow residents of the late 18th century.

New Abbey, then as now, gave its name to the village and to the surrounding parish. On nearing the village via the new road from Dumfries, a visitor would have realised that they were entering a place of some aspiration. The road, with its views of the rose red Sweetheart Abbey to the left foreground, followed the slope down towards the New Abbey Pow. As it neared the bridge it passed through the ranks of the newly planted avenues of Scots Pine and other native species. This magnificent woodland plantation, representing the burgeoning ambitions of the Stewart of Shambellie family, showed a foresight that still gives pleasure to visitors and locals alike in the 21st century. The bridge over the Pow, at the junction of the Dumfries road and the road from the Snuff Mill at Glenharvie, was constructed in 1715 and a single-span bridge[86] gave access to the winding main street of the village and its mill.

James Murray saw the three-storied whitewashed mill, now under the care of Historic Scotland, when it was still under construction by order of William Stewart of Shambellie. The building itself was almost certainly a modernisation or rebuilding of a much earlier mill built in mediaeval times to serve the Cistercian monks and the surrounding community. This corn mill was a very important part of the New Abbey rural community and the corn harvested around the village was ground here into flour for bread. The mill, carefully restored and in full working order today, is worked by use of an overshot wheel. Water running off the slopes of Criffel is brought to New Abbey and stored in the dammed mill pond above the mill. A mill race and operating sluice bring the water flow to the top of the wheel, where the water fills buckets which are built into the wheel. As the buckets fill, the weight of the water starts to turn the wheel and operate the grinding stones. The water spills out of each bucket on the down side into a spillway which leads back to a lower pond, probably originally a monastic fish pond, and then into the New Abbey Pow.

It is interesting to speculate that James, as a child, was inspired by the success of the new mill and used the memory of its construction and its effectiveness to establish the first ever Canadian water powered timber mill on his estate in Argenteuil, Lower Canada.

The majestic remains of Sweetheart Abbey and the Monastic Mill form the kernel around which the village known to James Murray stands. Sweetheart Abbey, founded in 1273 as a Cistercian Abbey, is an intrinsically beautiful building and its history adds further to its romantic charm. In the thirteenth century the concept of marriage amongst the aristocracy was based firmly around the need to support and enhance security, power, prestige, dynasty and influence. Love and compatibility tended to play a secondary role, if at all, so it is all the more romantic to learn that this Abbey owes its foundation to the love marriage between the parents of King John I of Scotland, namely Dervorguilla, daughter of the powerful Alan, Lord of Galloway, and John Balliol of Barnard Castle. Following John's death the influential Dervorguilla, already, along with her late husband, a founder of Balliol College, Oxford, richly endowed the Abbey and arranged for it to house the heart of her husband. The organ was embalmed and casketed in a 'coffyne of evorie' and laid beside Dervorguilla herself when she joined her deceased husband in 1289.[87]

Five hundred years later Dervorguilla would have had a just cause to be most displeased with the way history had left her legacy. The monks were long gone, victims of the Scottish Reformation, and since 1587 the property, vested in the Crown by the Annexation Act, had acquired a number of owners. Over the years a general decline had led to the Abbey suffering depredation of a severe nature, and by 1779 it was little more than a quarry for high quality building stone, put to good use by the owners, William Newall and William McNish. Many of the present houses along both sides of Main Street, New Abbey village, were built around this time, largely composed of the stone taken from the old Abbey. Ironically, many of these houses are now listed buildings themselves.[88]

The oldest house [89] in the village did not owe its foundation to stolen stones from the Abbey. Situated to the west of the mill, with its gardens sweeping down towards the Pow, it is of at least 17th century origin and its stones may even remember when the Abbey was a hive of activity controlled by the Cistercian community. Nearby, and also of significant age, is Abbey House, just to the south of the Corn Mill. This house, just off the village square but beautifully secluded by mature trees, has a section dating from the 17th century, with most of the rest of the building of the early to mid-18th century. In 1781 this house was used as the main residence for the Stewarts of Shambellie and was very well known to the young James Murray.

A short walk eastwards from the house would lead to the boundary walls of the Abbey. These walls, constructed of massive granite blocks, encircled the Abbey grounds and for much of their length are still visible today. By 1781 the road to Kirkbean ran through the Abbey grounds and the Gatehouse which once guarded the entry to the Abbey precincts, was long gone. However, the Port House at 5 Main Street and the corresponding house across the road at 6 Main Street, still remained, as they do today, although both now widened and heightened. The orientation of the houses, at right angles to the street, gives a clue to their initial function as Port (gate) Houses, a clue strengthened by the remains of the Abbey Walls attached to their gables.

Between Abbey House and the Port was the main section of the village. Many of the houses around the square, especially numbers 5–11, would all have been clearly recognised by James Murray and several had commercial purposes as well as residential functions. Nearby was the King's Arms Inn, later renamed the Wellington Arms. The current village shop is housed on the north side of the square. Its present frontage had not been constructed by 1781 but it is on the site of an earlier important building. The clue to its original function lies in the hugely impressive warehouse still extant and attached to the rear of the property. This four storey and attic structure, built circa 1750, indicates by its size that New Abbey was then a village of significant commercial activity. Across the road stood the old smithy, now indicated by its sliding doors. The plaque above the door informs that it was still a new building in James Murray's time:

by hammer and hand all arts do stand RM 1775.

The narrow main street weaves past the former 'port' houses and beyond it enters an area which was within the former Abbey precincts. Today the road is lined with cottages, and James had arrived in the village at a time when considerable new building was going on in this area. The reason for this was national rather than local. The so called 'agricultural revolution' was changing the traditional labour-intensive system of agriculture which had existed in Lowland Scotland for hundreds of years. Throughout rural Scotland thousands of cottars and small tenant farmers migrated from their farms and small holdings to start fresh lives in the new industrial centres of Glasgow and Edinburgh. Others chose to try their hand overseas, but many simply moved the few miles from their disappearing holdings into the nearby villages. Throughout Scotland, villages as well as towns had to accommodate the migrant rural population and New Abbey was no exception.[90] The single storey cottages on the north of the Main Street, all built with stone from the Abbey, probably owe their origin to this phenomenon, but one of the cottages has a reminder of a much older period. Rosewall, at 14 Main Street, has a painted Cistercian rosette built into the wall. Next to it is a carved plaque, said to have been rescued from the Abbey, representing three figures in a boat. By local tradition these are three women who were used to row pilgrims across the Nith and up the Pow almost to the Abbey itself. Close connections between New Abbey and the Grierson family at Keltonhead, on the far side of the Nith, north of Kirkconnell, indicate that this practice had not entirely ceased by the late 18th century.

On the other side of the main road is Devorgilla Cottage with its coachhouse, now used as a private garage. Whilst this house post-dates the arrival of James Murray it is believed to incorporate earlier fabric, and the coachhouse function of a place to rest and change horses between Dumfries and the emigration port of Carsethorn would almost certainly have been very familiar to James.[91]

Between 1781 and 1784 Britain saw considerable immigration with thousands of returning loyalists coming into the country as a result of the loss of the American colonies. Nevertheless, the arrival of four young children would have been a significant talking point for the 649 people of the parish.[92] Not that the children had anything to fear. A contemporary article describes the 'guid folk' of the parish as:

> a sober, obliging, honest and intelligent set of people , hospitable to strangers, charitable to the poor, just in their dealings and obliging to one another. They affect not elegance nor expense in their dress or diet but are cleanly and comfortable in both, and are truly a set of very worthy and respectable people. Very few incline to the sea, and fewer still to the army. To the credit of the parish it may be added that not a single individual from it has been confined in jail, either on account of debt or the suspicion of any criminal activity for these 20 years past.[93]

It's who you know

James' Elibank antecedents would have ensured that he was known and cared for by the leading families of the area.[94] There were already tenuous Elibank connections to the neighbourhood. In the early 17th century the owner of the Cavens estate at Kirkbean, a few miles south of New Abbey, was William Maxwell. William had married Katherine Weir and a few years after his death she re-married, firstly to a James Murray and finally to Patrick Murray, the 1st Lord Elibank. It was Katherine's third marriage, and his fifth marriage, but for both it was their last. Patrick died in 1649 but the Cavens estate remained in the hands of the Murray family for over a hundred years until it was sold to the Oswald family. By the late 18th century the Elibanks had still retained some land connections in the district. The sasine registers indicate a flurry of activity in the late 18th and early 19th centuries by Alexander, the 7th Lord Elibank, involving the crofts of Powside, Nimbelly and Fellend between Kirkbean and New Abbey and two small estates near Beeswing.[95] A little further away and deeper into Galloway, Isabella and Marie, the legitimate children of George Murray, the 6th Lord Elibank and James Murray's grandfather, Isabella and Maria, held Kilquhanity and Drungans. Most of the remaining local Elibank land was disposed of in 1808, mainly to the land-insatiable Oswald family.[96]

This family, whose path frequently crossed that of the Elibank Murrays, ultimately came to possess huge tracts of land in this part of Scotland. At its maximum extent it was possible to walk from

Trostan, to the north of New Abbey via the coastal plains all the way to Colvend without ever stepping off Oswald land; and a fine walk it would be too. The Oswald family first appeared in the area when they purchased the Cavens estate in the middle of the 18th century. Although the estate played second fiddle to their much larger and more prosperous estate of Auchincruive in Ayrshire, it remained in their hands for a further 200 years. Richard Oswald, a very influential merchant, had amassed a great wealth from his plantations in the United States and the West Indies. Oswald's company owned a slaving fort on Bunce Island at the mouth of the Sierra Leone River and it is estimated that they sent over 12,000 enslaved Africans, mainly from the Temne people, to America, where most were put to work in the rice fields around Charleston. Richard had married Mary Ramsay, the only daughter of a rich plantation owner, and by this marriage he greatly increased his properties in the West Indies and America. His wealth increased further during the Seven Years' War (1754-63) after he obtained a contract to supply the British Army with bread. The Oswalds were not always the most popular local residents and famously Mary, even when deceased, still managed to raise the ire of the poet Robert Burns. Robert was turned out of an inn in Sanquhar to accommodate Mary's burial party on its way from London to Ayrshire and immortalised the moment in a biting poem.[97]

Richard had built the house at Cavens in 1752 and on his death it passed to his nephew, also Richard.[98] This Richard Oswald became well-known for his beautiful wife[99] and for his career as a Scottish Whig Member of Parliament for Ayrshire. His younger brother James was probably even better known. He was one of the leading supporters of the movement that led to the Reform Act in 1832 and one of the first Members of Parliament, elected under the new more democratic procedures of 1832, to represent Glasgow. He is commemorated in Glasgow Cathedral and by a statue in the north-east corner of George Square.

The first Richard's cousin, James Oswald, was a very influential Member of Parliament and was a personal friend and political supporter of General James Murray, and there was frequent and helpful correspondence between the two whilst General James was Governor of Lower Canada.[100] Another relative was Captain John Oswald, who was a member of the Argenteuil Rangers and associated with a place destined to play a significant part in the life of Captain James Murray. John Oswald, later promoted to the rank of Lieutenant-Colonel of the Quebec Militia, was a particularly active Loyalist during the American Revolutionary war and his zeal probably did little to support the diplomatic skills of his kinsman, Richard, in his negotiations with the American Commissioners in 1782. John was the son of Thomas Oswald, who as a Captain in the 60th Foot was a colleague in arms of General James Murray, and would later become acquainted with a young junior officer called Patrick Murray. They lost contact when Patrick went with the regiment to the West Indies, but the Oswald connection would once again be renewed when the regiment moved to Florida and Patrick encountered the multi-tentacled world of Richard Oswald.[101] Through these connections James, and later his sisters, no doubt frequently enjoyed the hospitality and patronage of the Oswalds, even though their base at that time was primarily in the nearby Kirkbean parish. The extensive Oswald New Abbey properties would come later.

The Oswald kin were only one of a number of remarkable families who would have been part of James Murray's early life. Very influential in the New Abbey environs at this time was the Craik family. Although their estate was to the south of New Abbey, William Craik had married into the family of the Stewarts of Shambellie and was also a personal friend of James Maxwell of Kirkconnell. William was a giant in the history of agricultural improvement in Southern Scotland. In 1726 he settled on a small farm called Maxwellfield, belonging to the Arbigland estate, a few miles along the Solway Coast south of New Abbey. Seven years later he cemented his local credentials when he married Elizabeth Stewart, the only legitimate daughter of the influential William Stewart of Shambellie. At the death of his father in 1736 he succeeded to the family estate and twenty years later he and his family moved in to their newly built mansion house at Arbigland. William has entered the history books primarily as an agricultural improver. He drained his land and he experimented with crop rotations, he significantly improved his farm machinery and also took an interest in scientific stock breeding. Although his agricultural innovations were widely admired and recognised, it was his larger than life character that he is best remembered for today:

> ... Mr Craik was a man of great originality, and uncommon powers of mind... Every operation was diligently superintended by himself;... for the greatest part of his farming life, was seldom later in his bed, during the summer season, than from three to four o'clock every morning, – usually breakfasting and dining in the fields, near his labourers, who did the same... The country was, at this period, so far removed from every idea of real civilization, that, to permit one's male guests to go sober to bed, was looked upon as the greatest possible failure in hospitality and good manners... In hard drinking, hard riding, and every other youthful excess, few could equal his notoriety... He understood several languages well, and grammatically, viz. Latin, Greek, Hebrew, French, and Italian; and had made some little progress in Spanish. He was a tolerable architect, – fond of chemistry, – read much on learned subjects, – and usually rendered himself master of whatever he set his mind upon.[102]

By current standards, William Craik was a man who could not be described as an enlightened employer and would certainly not have welcomed trade unions interfering in his employment practices:

> Mr Craik abhorred idleness... he contrived to get some of the wiser tenants to clean... the grain that had been previously thrashed. This, the servants almost unanimously opposed, and threatened to burn the barns of those who persisted in the practice. These threats, however, were not sufficient to intimidate Mr Craik. He fairly gave them the alternative, either of going to Kirkcudbright jail, or yielding obedience to the orders of their employers; and submission immediately ensued.[103]

He was not man to cross and his courage and forthrightness were legendary in the area.

> ... A notorious ruffian accused of murder and other crimes, being brought before Mr Craik (as a Justice of the Peace for the county)... ordered the fellow's hands to be bound, as his conduct was of the most daring and insolent nature... the ruffian, having drawn a long knife, threatened to stab the first man who approached him. Mr Craik, observing that the constables were terrified by this ruffian's threats, jumped from the seat of Justice, and snatching a rope from one of the constables, first wrenched the knife from the fellow, and then forcibly tied his hands behind him, without any assistance whatever.[104]

William Craik, as well as his legitimate children, also had some illegitimate ones. One in particular became very well-known for his American connections. James Craik was brought up in Arbigland and left for America on reaching the age of maturity.

He was educated in the medical line and served for some years in the regiment commanded by George Washington, then a Colonel in the British service, with whom he formed a friendship that continued uninterrupted throughout his life. Soon after the commencement of the American Revolution, General Washington appointed him Physician-General to the United States.

The tenuous Craik connection through marriage to James Murray did not apply to his erstwhile employee, John Paul, despite the exhortations of the local gossips. John Paul, later John Paul Jones, became the first great American naval victor and a national hero, after capturing HMS Drake on 24th April, 1778, the first victory for any American military vessel in British waters. However the New Abbey gossip, no doubt whispered well out of range of any of John Paul's relatives still living in the area, was more concerned with his parentage than his military exploits. His family connections with New Abbey were strong. John Paul Jones' parents, John Paul senior and Jean MacDuff, were married in New Abbey Parish Church on 29th September 1733, just three days after the marriage of William Craik and Elizabeth Stewart in the same church. John Paul Jones' father by this time was working as a gardener on William Craik's estate and John Paul grew up in the New Abbey / Kirkbean area. Following some adverse incidents on home soil he left home and joined the American Navy, much to the chagrin of his family, who were still living locally. Local gossip pronounced:

> We a' ken 'yt his name wus John Paul an yt his faither wus gairdener tae Craik o' Arbiglan, but naething wud ser the dirtery but they declar't he was a left-handit son o' aul Craiks.[105]

There is no evidence to lend this more credence than idle tittle-tattle and it probably originated in the deeply held belief at that time that to achieve greatness, as John Paul Jones certainly did, he must have had some blood of rank. How could a mere gardener produce such a man?

John Paul Jones had an interesting life. He first went to sea when he was just thirteen and at the age of seventeen he went into the slave trade as third mate on the 'King George' of Whitehaven. Two years later in 1766 he transferred as first mate to the brigantine 'Two Friends' of Kingston, Jamaica, but he soon left the slave traffic in disgust, calling it an 'abominable trade'. By the age of twenty-one John Paul had become a Captain, but unfortunately he had a terrible temper. The red mist fell once too often when he punished and ultimately killed the ship's carpenter with excessive lashings from the cat-o'-nine tails. He was accused of unnecessary cruelty and was arrested in Kirkcudbright and charged with murder. Fortunately for him he was acquitted. He then took command of the 'Betsy', and remained in the West Indies in the mercantile business, making himself a small fortune. This only lasted until 1773 when he was forced to leave the area for Virginia after his temper got the better of him once more, when he killed a man in a dispute over wages.

When the fledgling United States Congress formed a 'Continental Navy' Paul Jones offered his services, and he was commissioned as first lieutenant on 7th December 1775. Just three years later Jones carried out a hit-and-run raid on Whitehaven, Cumbria. A shore party of two boats landed in view of the two forts which guarded the harbour. The plan was for each boat to capture one of the forts. Jones' boat did so bloodlessly and spiked the fort's cannon, but when he went to the other fort he discovered that the other boat's crew had all gone to the pub instead. He rounded up the recalcitrants and all his men returned safely, and hopefully sober, to his ship. Four hours later, Jones reached Kirkcudbright Bay to carry out a plan to capture the Earl of Selkirk and exchange him for incarcerated American sailors. The

Americans, despite their foreign uniforms, found that they were able to walk around the area with impunity. John, with his strong local accent, had spread the word that they were a British press gang and this clever tactic ensured that any local men would keep as far away from them as it was possible to be. The raiding party made their way to the family mansion but the Earl was not at home. The Americans looted the mansion and took the family silver, but four years later Jones returned the silver, along with a letter of apology for his impolite actions.

After leaving Kirkcudbright he captured HMS Drake near Carrickfergus, following a sea battle which lasted over an hour. After his daring successes in taking the war to the shores of Britain he was given command of the USS Bonhomme Richard and in 1779 he set sail on another voyage to British waters. On the night of 23rd September 1779 he fought his most famous battle when he engaged HMS Serapis and HMS Countess of Scarborough off Flamborough Head. During this engagement with the 'Serapis', Jones uttered, according to the later recollection of his first lieutenant, the legendary reply to a request from the British captain for him to surrender: [106]

I have not yet begun to fight!

The 'butcher's bill'[107] was horrendous, and over half of the crews of the two ships were either killed or wounded. John Paul Jones was ultimately successful and after transferring his crew to the captured 'Serapis', he sailed to Texel in Holland with over 500 prisoners. It was enough to ensure that he entered and remains still in the American 'Hall of Fame' with the sobriquet of 'founder of the American Navy'.

Another very prominent family of the area was the Maxwell family of Kirkconnell. When the Murray / Smith children played in the area to the rear of Sweetheart Abbey they would take the well-worn route, via the picturesque ford, past Maryfield and Landis with its ancient Abbot's Tower, and on towards the historic estate of Kirkconnell. The first charter to mention the Kirkconnell estate is from 1235, whereby a William of Kirkconnell granted land and certain rights to the Abbey of Whithorn. The Maxwell family, the owners of Kirkconnell for hundreds of years, were great benefactors to the Abbey and Church of New Abbey and prominent members of the New Abbey community. Following the Scottish Reformation they robustly held on to their Catholic faith despite considerable persecution, and Kirkconnell House retained its own chapel where local Catholics could celebrate mass, until a Catholic church was built in the village itself.

James Maxwell, a very colourful character, succeeded to the Kirkconnell estate in 1746. The year before his succession he, with as many local men as he could muster, rode off and joined the army of Charles Edward Stewart. He met up with Prince Charles in Edinburgh, and became a Captain in the Horse Guards and one of the Prince's aides-de-camp. He would have been well acquainted with the Elibank family, especially Alexander, that dedicated servant of the Stewarts. James was present at the battle of Culloden, after which he escaped to France. He is chiefly remembered for writing 'A Narrative of Charles, Prince of Wales' Expedition to Scotland in the Year 1745,' printed by the Maitland Club in 1846, and the fact that he was an eye-witness to the remarkable events of 1745 and 1746 gives great weight to his evidence. Maxwell placed the whole blame for the failure of the rising on John Murray of Broughton (no relation to the Elibank Murrays or to Murray of Broughton and Cally, the founder of the Galloway town of Gatehouse of Fleet). In his opinion, Murray, for selfish ends, persuaded Prince Charles to start the expedition; to secure his own advancement he kept his leader at odds with those who should have been the best counsellors, and in many cases his greed for money brought great hardships on both the Prince's officers and men.

With James Maxwell otherwise occupied when his father died in 1746, the task of keeping the estate together fell to his mother, Janet (although she apparently received much help and assistance from the unlikely, very Protestant, William Craik). There was considerable local unrest among the tenants when, in early 1746, the Duke of Cumberland's army took over the parkland at Kirkconnell and commandeered their 98 horses and 12 Galloway ponies. The tenants argued it was James who was the rebel, not them, and yet they were the ones who would suffer. The Duke of Cumberland was deaf to their protests.[108]

James Maxwell, now pardoned, returned to his estate in 1750 and at once set about enlarging the house and improving the property. For the buildings, bricks made on the estate were used and today the present house has one of the oldest brick constructions in Scotland.

James married Mary Riddell of Swinburne Castle, near Hexham, Northumberland, in 1758, and they had three sons — James, who inherited Kirkconnell, William, who became the friend and physician of Robert Burns, and Thomas, who was a merchant in Liverpool. James Maxwell died in 1762, but his legacy and memory were still strong when the young James Murray was growing up in nearby New Abbey.

William, the second son of James, spent much of his childhood at school in Flanders, but returned to Kirkconnell when he was 15 years of age. In 1784 he enrolled at Edinburgh University to study medicine and three years later he qualified as a doctor. After two half-hearted attempts to start medical practices in London and Dumfries, William set out for Paris. He arrived there on the eve of the revolution, with the city a hotbed of discontent. He chose sides carefully, playing down any aristocratic leanings of his ancient lineage, which was just as well, as his new Parisian friends were to become the leaders of the revolutionary forces that were to purge France of its aristocracy. At his family's pleading, William returned to Scotland late in 1789, but the revolution in France was now well underway and William became an 'underworld' arms dealer for the revolutionary forces. Following the discovery of an illegal order by him to a Birmingham firm for 20,000 daggers, he became a wanted man. William eluded capture and returned to France, where he enlisted in the National Guard and, by repute, commanded the guard that led Louis XVI to his meeting with the guillotine on the morning of 21st January 1793.

On the 1st February of that year France declared war on Great Britain, which led William to change sides and head for home. A now disillusioned William arrived back at Kirkconnell, and in need of funds he took up medicine again. This time he achieved more success and he built up a small but well-regarded practice in Dumfries. Robert Burns held William in high esteem medically and they probably shared many political views. William Maxwell attended Burns during his last and fatal illness, and he prescribed 'sea-bathing in country quarters' and horse riding for the 'flying gout', which he thought was Robert's medical problem. Inadvertently his cure probably hastened Burns' end, and thus William had the regrettable distinction of adding the death of one of the world's finest poets to his existing regicide. Robert and his family clearly did not hold that opinion and Burns' son, born shortly after he died, was named Maxwell in his memory.[109]

8

Keep your heid doon

In the late 18th and early 19th centuries, if you were looking for a bit of peace and quiet in New Abbey, the place not to choose was Shambellie, probably the most raucous place in the village. Resounding to the laughter and screams of countless children, Shambellie was the home of the Stewart family who were to become closely connected to James Murray and his sisters. This family had been in the New Abbey area from at least the early 17th century and came to prominence following the break-up of the Sweetheart Abbey estates during the Scottish Reformation. Originally the Stewarts occupied Shambellie Grange just to the north of the village, but by the early 18th century they had moved into the attractive large house, now called Abbey House, sheltered behind trees, just off the square in the centre of the village. Abbey House, originally three separate buildings, was mainly built on the site of an existing croft called Fuller's Croft and was certainly in existence by 1625.[110] More adjoining land to the south of the croft (now to the rear of the present Abbey Arms) was purchased in 1766 and a major renovation and expansion of Abbey House began. This included a new wing, the north windows of which looked directly onto the new road from Dumfries. It was this view which may have inspired, circa 1775, the planting of the avenue of magnificent native trees which currently adorn the route. Mixed in with Scots Pine is, on the eastern side, an avenue of Limes, planted by Charles Stewart, and on the western side, alternate Limes and Beeches, planted by Charles' son and heir,

William Stewart. In 1855 the Stewart family built the much larger and grander Shambellie House[111] just outside the village boundaries, but James and his sisters would only know the environs of Abbey House and the bewildering number of children who came to occupy it.

Charles Stewart of Shambellie was born in 1716 and, apart from a short time in Dumfries, spent virtually all his life in the village. He and his wife Ann had seven children. One, Dorothea, died very young, but the rest probably survived into adulthood. The eldest son and heir, William Stewart, nicknamed 'the old man', was born in 1750 and lived until 1844. Another larger than life local figure, his great age belied his continual battle with debt and ill-health; not that his father-in-law, James Murray of Cally and Broughton, had any sympathy. His forthright letters often stopped just short of insolence:

> I am sorry to observe from your letter that you still complain of bad health though I am persuaded it is much better than you are disposed to allow it, but if you continue to lay in bed till 10 or 11 o' clock and keep yourself wrapped up in a plaid the little while you are out of doors and take no exercise you may be sure that you can never have a hardy strong constitution or enjoy good health.[112]

William's other defining characteristic, and one which gave him a brief respite from his concerns over his many health issues, was his ability to propagate the species. He is known to have had at least 26 children, but tragically few of them outlived him, and those that did were not without their own problems. Nevertheless, he was inordinately proud of his children, and of his accomplishments in producing them, as evident in his announcement in the local newspaper:

> To Mr Stewart of Shambelly, a son, being Mr Stewart's 25th child.[113]

William's reputation as something of a philanderer has been passed down the generations, and as late as 1940 an old lady in the village recalled her mother saying that she was told that if she encountered 'William the Laird' in the village she was to curtsey politely but:

> keep your heid doon until he's gone.[114]

Despite his many problems, William lived for 94 years in an environment much less conducive to personal health than our own, so it seems that maybe William knew very well what was good for him.

William married three times. His first wife, Ann, was the illegitimate daughter of James Murray of Cally and Broughton.[115] Although these Murrays were not directly related to the Elibank Murrays, the two well-connected Murray dynasties had a lot in common and had a social connection with each other and with the Stewarts of Shambellie.

Murray of Cally's first wife was the long-suffering Lady Catherine,[116] daughter of the Earl of Galloway. Her relationship with the illegitimate Ann Stewart of Shambellie, could have been fraught. In fact it became extremely close[117] and through their social connection James Murray would meet Catherine's brother, Vice-Admiral Keith Stewart. Admiral Stewart was one of a number of acquaintances who influenced and perhaps supported James Murray in his career choice. Just three years separated Admiral Stewart's son, James Alexander, from James Murray and the two became childhood friends[118] and were destined to meet in different circumstances in James' later life.

The second and younger son of Charles Stewart was James,

who went on to a distinguished military career, with the 42nd foot, the famous 'Black Watch', finally retiring as Colonel of the regiment in 1804.

The rest of Charles Stewart's children were girls. The eldest was Marianne, followed by Dorothea (the same name as the child who died when one year old) and finally Elizabeth. The biographer of the Stewart family commented that there was 'nothing much known' about Elizabeth.[119] She was born circa 1756 and was mentioned in 1767 when father Charles made provisions for all his children (apart from William, who was to inherit the estate), leaving £2,500 to be shared amongst them on his death. As he didn't die until 1786 it remains unclear whether any of this money found its way to the recipients, but at least the thought was there.[120] The Shambellie Stewart biographer assumed that Elizabeth had died, although, unlike her peers, no record of her early death was ever recorded.

An alternative scenario exists. Elizabeth Stewart, daughter of Charles Stewart of Shambellie, on marriage became Eliza Smith, the mother of James Murray. The children and dependents of Eliza came to live and grow up in the village of New Abbey and this was no accident. A close family or friend connection to New Abbey was essential. Furthermore, the important connections made by James Murray and the good marriages made by his sisters all indicate that they came from a family of some prestige. Additionally, in a letter discussing James Murray's future prospects, permission was granted for a naval career with the East India Company by James' mother Eliza and Mr Stewart – surely none other than her elder brother, William Stewart of Shambellie,[121] who, on the death of his father, had become the head of the family. On the negative side, there is the complication that Eliza is not mentioned again in the extensive papers left by the Stewarts of Shambellie.[122] A reason for this may be gleaned from an examination of the attitude of the family to Elizabeth's elder sister, Dorothea. Dorothea had become pregnant by a man named as Captain Baker, and they had an illegitimate daughter, named Frances. Even though Baker fully acknowledged that the child was his, Dorothea was ostracised by her family thereafter. She went on to have more children in two legitimate marriages, but throughout her life she was to receive little help and support from her elder brothers, even though for a time she was in dire financial need.[123]

Strong connections existed between the American colonies and the Stewart family. Charles had become involved in the tobacco trade and he, and later his son, had major interests in transatlantic shipping and imports from the colonies. The Glenharvie Snuff Mill, just outside the village of New Abbey, is a reminder of that Atlantic connection. The connection was further strengthened when big sister Marianne's eldest son, Kenneth, became a plantation owner in Jamaica.[124] It is but a small jump to suggest that the headstrong Elizabeth had acted against the family's wishes when she married the American, Joseph Smith, and thus suffered the same fate as Dorothea, leading her to begin a new life on the other side of the Atlantic Ocean.

Some of William Stewart's children were close in age to the Murray / Smiths. William Stewart Junior was exactly the same age as James Murray. Elder sister Louisa was the same age as Catherine Stewart, three years younger than Charles Stewart and one year younger than James Stewart. Harriet Smith was slightly older than Maryann Stewart and just three years older than John Stewart. William Stewart's family had been living temporarily at Boreland, near Gatehouse of Fleet, as William was serving as the factor for the burgeoning estate of his father-in-law, James Murray of Cally. However, ties with New Abbey remained strong. His father lived in the village and William still looked towards Shambellie and New Abbey for many of the family needs and one of them was education.

Enter William Wright: minister, conservationist, early

educator of the Shambellie Stewarts' children and possibly young James Murray and his sisters. For the Reverend William Wright, 'entering' was more easily said than done. When he was appointed to the ministry in the parish of New Abbey he knew that a hostile reception would await him so, when in early May 1769 he and his family made their way to the village to take up the new appointment, they were accompanied by a squad of soldiers.

They needed them. At the March Burn, just south of Martingirth, they were intercepted by an angry mob, mainly composed of well-armed women wielding sturdy sticks and stones. Fortunately a passage into the village and entry to the manse was not accompanied by bloodshed, but it was an inauspicious start.[125]

The issue arousing so much anger was the means by which William Wright was appointed to the ministry in the first place and was not a problem of the parishioners with the Reverend personally. The dispute revolved around the concept of patronage and who should appoint the minister of the parish.

The minister of the parish was a very important appointment, with the local church playing the leading role in many aspects of the everyday life and death of the parishioners. It was considered essential to appoint the right man. Patronage in the selection of a new minister was well established in both custom and law, with the Patron being the King, one of the universities, a town or burgh Council or a large local landowner. During the Scottish Reformation, the 'First Book of Discipline' (1560) and the 'Second Book of Discipline' (1578) both stipulated that Ministers should be chosen by their congregations, but this never became law. Indeed, it was virtually superseded in 1567 by an Act which deemed that 'patronages' were to be preserved. A further Act of 1592, the so-called 'Golden Act', established Presbyterianism as the only legal form of church government in Scotland, but pointed out that Presbyteries were 'bound' to receive and admit any qualified minister who was presented by His Majesty or a 'lay

Patron'. If a congregation refused to accept a suitable nominee, the Patron would be entitled to the stipend, lands, house, etc. which the minister would normally receive. The aristocratic hold on influence and power in Scottish governance ensured that this procedure remained in force, even though the more democratic adherents to the Church of Scotland bitterly opposed it.

A 1690 Act went some way to appeasing the church. It restored Presbyterianism as the only legal form of Church government in Scotland but did not abolish patronage. However, it vested power in the heritors (normally male landowners on the electoral roll) and Elders (exclusively male) of each Parish, and they had the responsibility of proposing a suitable candidate to the whole congregation, to be either approved or disapproved by them.

In 1711 the aristocratic influence once more gained the upper hand with the passing of the 'Church Patronage (Scotland) Act'. This restored patronage to the original patrons, giving them the right to present suitably qualified candidates to Presbyteries in the event of a vacancy. Its clear purpose was to allow the established aristocracy and other Patrons in Scotland to regain control over the parish churches once more. Its effect was to be the restoration of the situation as it was in 1592. The Church of Scotland, through the General Assembly, protested against the Act almost every year. Other more militant ministers, heritors and Elders objected to Patronage on principle, arguing that it compromised the independence of the Church and the right of congregations to call their own ministers. Feelings ran high and many disputed appointments saw popular demonstrations of discontent and, in some cases, violence. This was the background to the protest in New Abbey, with the unfortunate and bewildered William Wright on the receiving end.[126] Despite the widespread protests, the Patronage Act was not finally repealed until 1874, when power once again reverted to the parishioners.

After such a shaky start to his new career, things went from bad to worse. Less than a year after taking up his new post, William and his wife Jean lost their youngest daughter, Cecilia Ann. She was aged just seven years. Her elder brother Robert was the next to go. Robert had gone to the West Indies to make his fortune, but, like so many of his countrymen, he succumbed to disease in those difficult sub-tropical lands. However, he would have had time, in that small and close environment of British adventurers and emigrants, to meet the officers of Patrick Murray's regiment, the 60th Foot, who were stationed in the Caribbean at this time.

Their only remaining son was their eldest, James Wright, and circumstantial evidence suggests a possible connection between the Wright family and the 60th Foot. A James Wright served as the Surgeon's Mate, and later the Surgeon, in Patrick Murray's battalion for many years.[127] His origin is unknown, but he may have been associated with John Wright, a young man believed to be connected to the minister's family.[128]

In May 1771, John Wright wrote a letter from the Liverpool docks to a Dumfries doctor.

> ... I was engaged to go with the Betsey,[129]... for £4.10s per month, a slave, and what other perquisites are common. She is one of the largest and finest ships I see... I only wrote (to) my father (that) I was going to sea but did not mention Guinea as I thought it would give an alarm, nor do I want if possible that they should know but that I'm going to the West Indies. The ship is to go out of dock on Monday and sail in 3 or 4 days after. I have this day ordered my medicines... I don't know anything I will want from my parents. I shall write frequently I have the opportunities on the sea... I expect to hear from my father before I go but (I) shall not write again till I'm going off... [130]

James Wright would have been 17 years of age when the letter was written and was just the age at which a young headstrong boy would leave to make his fortune, as his younger brother Robert did a few years later. On occasions the two names, James and John, were used randomly for the same person. For example, the successor to William Wright as the Minister of New Abbey was James Hamilton, and several letters are extant which refer to him as John.[131] Nevertheless, the forenames James and John, then as now, were perceived as different names and were not usually used as alternatives. Consequently it is unlikely but not impossible that James and John Wright were the same person.

The Betsey was not going to the West Indies. In fact it was going to Guinea – the Slave Coast.[132] The Betsey was a well-known slave ship that was to achieve notoriety just a few years later. The campaign to abolish the slave trade, piloted by William Wilberforce, led to a series of Bills which were debated in the British Parliament. The Bill of 1792 proved to be particularly explosive and Wilberforce used any emotional measures he could devise to gain support for his moral argument against the trade. He recounted one incident where six British captains had fired on an African settlement, killing a number of innocent people, in order to intimidate the local people and thus secure a lower price for the slaves. His opponents, and there were many, argued that this was a tall tale with no basis in fact, and insisted that Wilberforce name and shame the captains concerned. Wilberforce resisted this for a long time, but finally released their names. One of them was the Captain of the Betsey, trading out of Liverpool.[133]

John, a trainee, was to become the Assistant Surgeon on this infamous slave ship. His passage would be part of the famous slave triangle, whereby the Betsey would pick up slaves from West Africa and take them to the Caribbean or the Americas and from there return to England with New World goods such as sugar, cotton and tobacco. John had some moral doubts as to his role in this trade, and despite his bravado, he certainly did not want his family to know what he was doing until he was well underway and it was too late to stop him. Even as early as 1771 many people had serious moral doubts about the slave trade and they may have included the Reverend William Wright and perhaps John / James Wright too. An early association of the ship with the British Army, stationed in the West Indies and Florida, could give a disillusioned young man an opportunity to leave the slave trade industry, perhaps embarking upon a new career in the army by signing on to the 60th Foot, the Royal Americans?

A direct connection between the Betsey and the 60th Foot came to light as a result of an incident a few years later during the turbulent events of the American Revolutionary War.

On 17th December, 1775, the Betsey was captured by American revolutionaries off the coast of New England. Her confiscated secret correspondence revealed that St. Augustine was building up powder and arms for a forthcoming struggle. The 60th Foot were then the regiment charged with the defence of St. Augustine and East Florida and thus were in direct contact with the Betsey.[134] Several ships with the name Betsey were afloat at that time but the final act in the life of this Betsey came in February 1799. The American war was over and the Betsey was back to its usual 'triangle' trade, heading for Liverpool with a valuable cargo of sugar and ivory, when it was captured by the French privateer, Zele. The French put a prize crew onto the ship and headed for Brittany. Just off the coast of Penmarch, Brittany, the Zele was taken by the British frigate, HMS Melpomene. The prize crew in the Betsey made a run for the harbour, but in very heavy weather they failed to make it; the ship was destroyed on the rocks off Penmarch and her slaving days were over.

Yet another James Wright was the 4th Battalion, 60th Foot Quartermaster, and he appeared as an executor for Colonel Fuser[135] (the only beneficiary being James Murray's sister, Louisa

Fuser). Yet another James Wright served briefly as a second lieutenant in the 4th Battalion and this Lieutenant James Wright sold his commission and left the regiment at a similar time as the return of James Murray from St. Augustine.[136]

Conjecture encourages the hypothesis that one of these Wrights may have been James Wright, the son of the Reverend William Wright, and it was he that played a part in ensuring that the four young refugee children from America were able to grow up in the secure and safe haven that was New Abbey.

By 1773 things were looking up for the Wright family in New Abbey and William was becoming more accepted. He became increasingly worried about the apparent building site he could see from the windows of his manse next door to the Abbey, and he feared that the Abbey itself was in great danger of disappearing. William Newall[137] and William McNish, local businessmen who owned the Abbey, had for some years been steadily demolishing the buildings to sell the stones, which they then used for the construction of new houses along the current Main Street. The minister did his own reputation no harm at all when he persuaded the local heritors to take action. Under his leadership a public appeal was launched to prevent the demolition of the main Abbey building and, following payment of the sum of forty-two pounds, an agreement was reached with Newall and McNish which saved the Abbey from any further demolition.[138] When James Murray arrived a few years later he was able to play childhood games amongst the exquisite ruins of Sweetheart Abbey and its impressive remaining boundary wall with its dressed granite boulders. Visitors today still enjoy the very same views.

9

We will die with our
swords in our hands

It seems that James had left Florida just in time. After the surrender of Lord Cornwallis at Yorktown in October 1781 and the inauguration of a new Whig government in London who were well-disposed to a peace settlement, the loss of the American colonies was inevitable. East Florida did not see itself as part of this picture and remained staunchly British. Consequently, when Savannah, Georgia, was evacuated in July 1782 and five months later Charleston, South Carolina, went the same way, the destination for many of the refugees would be to the last remaining British enclave in the south, St. Augustine.

Eliza, with her three remaining dependent girls, now in St. Augustine, were to witness many unwelcome changes over the next few years. Loyalists and their slaves poured into the town in their thousands, often accompanied by the remnants of the provincial regiments returning from Georgia and the Carolinas. The scene became chaotic:

> Large numbers of Indians came and went and many sailors enjoyed a boisterous holiday on shore. The taverns, punch houses, liquor shops and gaming places did a rushing business. Riots and other disturbances frequently occurred.[139]

The situation in East Florida was serious but surely things could only get better? At last the British colony now had enough people to fully develop the low-lying swamp forests and establish the colony on a sound footing. Perhaps they could even get West Florida back from Spain and begin once again to re-capture the British colonies in America?[140] All eyes were now on Paris, where British negotiators were meeting with American representatives to thrash out a peace settlement, but those in Florida felt there was little to worry about. After all, they had one of their own playing a leading role in the talks. Richard Oswald, slaver, Florida plantation magnate and New Abbey landowner was one of the British commissioners who finally brought peace to the continent. The preliminary peace treaty, said to have been formulated in Richard Oswald's Paris hotel room, was finally agreed in November 1782.

To the great shock and horror of the colonists in St. Augustine, the negotiators agreed that Britain would return East Florida back to Spain.[141] There was probably little alternative. Lord George Germain, the new officer in charge, was at his wits' end endeavouring to develop a strategy to defend the colony:

> I have but forty men invalided and no naval force... add to this the small pox is now in every house.[142]

The cession plan finally agreed upon was to disband the militia regiments, evacuate all British citizens and offer all eligible residents new opportunities in Nova Scotia or other British colonies. This news went down like the proverbial lead balloon in the streets of St. Augustine, now crowded with about 10,000 people displaced by the war. A town resident writing to a friend in May 1783 reported his outrage over the cession of East Florida and described the situation:

our troops are ... very mutinous. A few nights ago several were killed; their plan was to burn the barracks, plunder the town, take possession of the fort, arm all the negroes and put every white man to death that opposed them, keeping the country to themselves as they will rather die than be carried to Halifax (Nova Scotia) to be discharged.[143]

Although considered by some to be little more than a rocky outpost, the nearby Bahamas at least would offer the loyalists something they would recognise; a similar climate, landscape and social culture. There was also plenty of room. It was estimated that the population of Cat Island, considered to have the best soil in the Bahamian chain of islands, was only 15 in 1783, and nearby Long Island had not many more, with only 111 people.[144]

There was only one problem. The Bahamas had been captured by Spain in 1782 and incorporated into the Spanish West Indies Empire. Andrew Deveaux, formerly of Beaufort, South Carolina and personally well known to Eliza Smith decided that he would take matters into his own hands. At his own expense he recruited volunteers who would invade New Providence, the most populous of the Bahama Islands, on behalf of the British Government and re-incorporate it, along with the rest of the Islands, into the British Empire. Astonishingly, he was not short of volunteers and at the beginning of April 1783 his force, about 70 men strong, descended upon the Bahama Islands.[145] The main Spanish stronghold on the Island was Fort Montagu and this was the initial objective. In clear view of the defenders, Deveaux landed his small force nearby. In order to convince the Spaniards that they were significantly stronger than they appeared to be he plied his boats back and forth, appearing to land fresh troops each time; the Spanish were unaware that the same troops were being landed over and over again. The Spanish troops seemed to have a particular fear of native Indian troops and so Deveaux dressed a few of his men as natives. A few war whoops later and it was all too much for the Spanish defenders and they surrendered.

Andrew Deveaux was a few days too late. Unbeknown to him, Spain had already agreed to transfer the Bahamas back into British rule and so his almost farcical but brave attempt at re-conquest was quite unnecessary. It did have a useful conclusion in that it raised awareness of the Bahamas as an alternative place of refuge for the loyalist Britons in St. Augustine, but for most it was little better than the alternatives already on offer. It even proved to be of mixed blessings for the champion of the day, Andrew Deveaux himself. An ungrateful British Government concluded that, as he had attacked British territory, he was ineligible to claim compensation for the not inconsiderable costs of the invasion.[146] However, on the plus side, he had become a hero to the people and he would reap the benefits of his new celebrity status later, in Bahamas land acquisitions.[147]

The ordinary residents, especially the single women like Eliza Smith, had plenty to fear at the almost total breakdown of law and order in St. Augustine. An incident involving a young army officer called Ensign Manning demonstrates just how much law and order had dissipated. Manning and a group of his soldiers called at a tavern near to the fort which was run by a Minorcan named Lorenzo Capo and his wife, Maria. Guilty of no other crime than allowing the Ensign and his men to drink too much, the Capos were both taken to the fort. There Maria was locked in the guard room and repeatedly raped. Her husband was then forcibly returned to the tavern to serve more alcohol to the extremely intoxicated soldiers. Ensign Manning was charged with rape and in his almost deranged state blew his own brains out. Angry soldiers from the regiment blamed the Capos for the incident and took their own retribution by rioting and totally destroying the Capos' tavern. No further actions were taken.[148]

The soldiers' general anger was mirrored by the ordinary

citizens. The British Association of American Loyalists made their feelings absolutely clear in a plea to the British authorities.

> that we… all of that description of men who have taken an active part in the American war, and whose fortunes have been sacrificed, are bereft of our slaves, abandoned by our sovereign, deserted by our country, are reduced to the dreadful alternatives of returning to our homes to receive insult worse than death to men of spirit or remain in constant dread of assassination, go to the inhospitable regions of Nova Scotia or the Bahama Islands where without slaves poverty and wretchedness stares us in the face or last of all, deny our religion and renounce our country and become Spanish subjects.
>
> … rather than accept any of the alternatives in our choice we will die with our swords in our hands, for we are almost driven to despair. Let us therefore beseech your Excellency to take care of your fellow subjects, who have so greatly suffered in their country's cause.[149]

They didn't die with their swords in their hands; at least not on this occasion. The evacuation began in late 1783, reaching its peak when fifteen vessels made thirty four trips to Kingston, Halifax and Nassau laden with refugees and their property.[150] One of these miserable refugees, fleeing from their past and living with the uncertainties of their future, was Eliza Smith. Most of the refugees were described as "Clerks, Apprentices, Discharged soldiers, Paupers and Vagabonds,"[151] but some of the more prominent citizens, mainly military officers and those of a mercantile, landholding or professional background, were named in a list of the fifty two arrivals in Nassau from East Florida by June 1784. On that list was Eliza, accompanied by her dependents, comprising three white children, almost certainly Louisa, Theresa and Harriet, and two black slaves, the long serving family servant Fortune

Smith and Rosetta Smith, possibly her daughter. Once more demonstrating her strength and independence of spirit, she was one of only five women on the list and shared her exile with some illustrious company. Passengers on ships to Nassau included luminaries and former military colleagues of Patrick, such as Colonel Deveaux and Colonel Brown, the erstwhile feared and hated leader of the Florida Rangers. Most of the named refugees were single men and they had fewer dependents travelling with them than Eliza.[152] In common with her fellow travellers Eliza initially received six months' support for her family and later was promised a grant of 100 acres to establish a plantation.[153]

It was almost over in Florida. On 12th July 1784, Vizente Manuel de Zespedes, the new first governor of Spanish East Florida, took over responsibility and the British flag was lowered for the last time over St. Augustine, to be replaced by one of Spain. In a dignified but muted ceremony Governor Tonyn handed over the symbols of power accompanied by a fifteen gun salute and three volleys of musketry.[154] A new era in Floridian history was just beginning and Patrick Tonyn quietly left to board HMS Cyrus and sail away from St. Augustine for ever.[155]

Or at least that was the plan, but it didn't quite work out like that. The Cyrus had been quietly rotting away in the harbour for a few months whilst the Governor sorted out final arrangements. As she left harbour and the anchor was being weighed, the wind caught the massive flaying anchor and drove it straight through the rotten timbers of the ship's hull. The Cyrus immediately began taking in large quantities of water and soon became quite incapable of sailing. Governor Tonyn, tail firmly between legs, was forced to return to St. Augustine and ask the new governor if he could stay on for a while. On 19th November, over two months later, two transports finally arrived from Nassau and in an ignominious final farewell, Patrick Tonyn left Florida forever.

Those like Eliza, who had left Florida for the Bahamas were

soon to find life difficult. By April 1785 over 6,000 loyalists and their dependents had arrived at Nassau, soon swamping the original inhabitants and causing serious food shortages.[156] At that time Nassau had only one main street, lined with wooden buildings, and it was soon reported that all the buildings were filled with refugees and many others were living in tents,[157] leading an official report to comment that the refugees "sit where they can."[158]

The aim was to distribute the loyalists through more of the islands of the Bahama chain[159] but the new settlers had serious concerns over the fertility of the soil and its ability to support a considerable influx of new people. They soon began to understand why there had been so little agricultural activity prior to their arrival.[160] The ground would not support crops of sugar, rice or tobacco, the mainstay of American mainland plantation agriculture, but it was discovered that good yields could be obtained from cotton, a crop soon to become pre-eminent in the Americas. Early reports in the islands' only newspaper, the Bahamas Gazette, were highly optimistic, but gradually the cotton plantations ran into increasing problems.

Within a very short period of time the number of new settlers from the former British colonies outnumbered the original inhabitants throughout the island archipelago.[161] The Bahamas were overseen by a governor, appointed by the British parliament, and a local elected assembly, a system which had worked well for very many years. However, it failed to recognise the new demographic, the new culture and the new political outlook now becoming dominant in the colony. Tensions soon arose between Governor Maxwell, clinging to the status quo, and the new settlers, who were looking for more equitable land allocations (as they saw it) and representation on the assembly for the loyalist incomers.[162] Violence was not unknown and major clashes occurred over land allocations.

Many of the earlier incomers, including Colonel Thomas

Brown, had taken up land in Abaco[163] and this was one of the places in the Bahamas where there were serious disturbances. The new settlers, many from New York and some from the South, failed to agree on virtually anything and soon began to fall out amongst themselves. Their disagreements rose to such a height that it was reported that they were very close to taking up arms against each other.[164] Furthermore, Colonel Brown and some of his fellow officers from the former King's Rangers soon discovered that their land in Abaco had poor fertility and so began to transfer their holdings to Caicos. Eliza would have watched the actions of the influential Colonel Brown carefully because by 1802 she held plantation lands in Abaco, but also had a plantation in the Caicos.

Ultimately the unpopular Governor Maxwell was recalled and in April 1785 he was replaced by James Edward Powell. Governor Powell died in office just one year later, but had done little to satisfy the loyalists and had failed to significantly change political representation in the Island Assembly. Great hopes were placed in the new Governor, the Earl of Dunmore, who was also an American exile and shared a common experience with the displaced loyalists. Unfortunately, Dunmore had no more success than his predecessors and perhaps was even more unpopular. He had strong views about the status of free negroes, a view not always popular amongst the slave culture of most of the loyalist incomers.[165] He also followed self-interest in an unashamed fashion, and in his manner and approach he had the rare ability to upset almost everybody.[166] Eliza had arrived in Nassau and despite her plantations in other parts of the Bahamas she always referred to herself as living in New Providence. A prominent tavern / meeting house in Nassau, very popular with the more illustrious Loyalist immigrants was referred to as Mrs Elizabeth Smith's Tavern,[167] and conjecture suggests that she may have been the owner, as the 'mine host' and 'buxom barmaid' roles do not sit comfortably on Eliza's shoulders. That she was a business woman of some ability is not in doubt and furthermore she seemed to socialise in prestigious company, so it seems that any role of this nature would be in the capacity of owner rather than active worker.

In mid-september 1785, a hurricane hit Abaco and the nearby islands, uprooting trees, devastating crops and destroying the cotton harvest.[168] In late October the next year another hurricane finished off what had not been accomplished by the previous one.[169] Along with the constant agricultural struggle and the insidious political unrest, the natural disasters may have been the straw which 'broke the camel's back'. Louisa, Theresa and Harriet were to set sail for Scotland and join younger 'brother' James, now firmly settled in the village of New Abbey near Dumfries.

In New Abbey, Shambellie House was a bit quieter than usual. Charles Stewart, now a widower, still lived in the house, but eldest son and heir, William, had gone to live in Boreland, near Gatehouse of Fleet, where he was the factor on the estate of his powerful father in law, James Murray of Cally and Broughton.

James Murray, son of Eliza and Patrick by now was well settled in the village. He may have occupied the relatively empty Shambellie House, but it is also possible that he was living in the church manse with the Reverend William Wright. Having children in the Wright household would not be a novel experience.

William Wright had a formidable intellect. He had been employed in the public school at Annan, Dumfriesshire, where he enjoyed considerable success and developed a strong reputation for scholarship. Doctor James Bell, a renowned medical practitioner and diarist, was educated by the Reverend Wright and resided with him and his family. When William moved to New Abbey, James Bell moved with him to continue his education, ultimately going on to a highly successful career at Glasgow University.[170] The fond memoirs left by Doctor Bell illustrate that William Wright was accustomed to having children living in his home and his wife, after the noise and bustle of bringing up four children of her own, was faced with the all too quiet prospect of a home without any of them. James Murray, in his later correspondence, demonstrated that he was a fluent and articulate writer and clearly had received a very sound education. The village facilities for children were only adequate. There was one parochial school with an average of 50 pupils, and two smaller seasonal schools. Indeed the school proudly boasted that it had gained a slate roof as early as 1755. In a time when social class divisions were so strong it was unlikely that the school was considered adequate for a young boy of James' lineage, particularly so as the schoolmaster, Robert Farries, was a most eccentric figure. For reasons best known to himself, he declared that he would only wear clothes that he could take from scarecrows, and from 1792 to 1806 he indeed wore nothing else.[171] An alternative education was preferred by the ambitious Shambellie Stewarts and they looked to William Wright to provide it. He very successfully tutored William's sons, James, William and Charles[172] (who with their problems at school would prove a sore trial for any pedagogue),[173] and in all likelihood he provided a similar service to James Murray and perhaps his sisters.

In 1786, Charles Stewart of Shambellie died and his son William, although remaining at Boreland, took over leadership of the family. The funeral may have been the catalyst which encouraged Eliza and her three charges to come over to Scotland from New Providence and there was certainly plenty of space in the empty Shambellie House for them all. The girls would never return to the Bahamas.

10

Go to sea, young man

Despite his illustrious and privileged relatives, James Murray's illegitimate status meant that he would have to make his own way in the world, although there was no shortage of people willing to help him. Like many younger sons of the gentry, a career in administration in the colonies was thought to be a possible vocational option; and who better to help him pursue this than his cousin William Young? William would have been very sympathetic to the potential difficulties facing young James Murray. He too was an illegitimate child, the oldest illegitimate child (of at least six) fathered by Patrick Murray, the 5th Lord Elibank and friend of Dr. Samuel Johnson. When only sixteen years old, William had taken employment as a writer with the East India Company, a huge enterprise responsible for the administration and development of British India. He soon rose to become a factor for the company and thereafter his progress was rapid. By 1779 he was the third most senior official in the company and had responsibility for hundreds of employees and millions of pounds. Despite this lofty position he was not so busy that he couldn't take an interest in the welfare of his relatives.

He had been asked to find James Murray a junior position with the company, but he was gloomy about any future prospects, as he explained to his uncle, General James Murray.

> ... in regard to my cousin Murray... I have thought of a surer
> way of promoting his affairs than sending him to India... the

Civil service is cut down to nothing now and the charter expires in 1790 when the ministry will take the company into their own hands;[174] it is an event I hold certain, and when it happens the servants of the East India Company... will have no other alternative than to end their days in that country in penury and misery or come home and follow some other pursuit.[175]

William was not entirely pessimistic and he put forward an alternative suggestion.

I therefore think it best to send him to sea in an East India ship. He must make one voyage as a midshipman; he may then become a mate before his return. He must then sail as 3rd or 4th mate, then as a 2nd. I think that at the end of four voyages I shall be able to give him a ship... He is sure of becoming a captain of an Indiaman if I choose it, whenever it can be safe to trust him with such a command, and they all make large fortunes, sometimes £20,000, £30,000 or £40,000 by a single voyage.[176]

There seemed to be little to stand in his way.

The boy likes the proposal and his mother and Mr Stewart both approve it. He shall be an East India Captain and... it will be his own fault if he does not become a man of fortune.[177]

The call of the sea was strong but James did not take up the splendid offer from his cousin William. Instead he sailed to Canada.

By early 1789, when James was just eleven years old, changes were afoot on the other side of the Atlantic Ocean. His father, Patrick, was to take a major change of direction in his life and James was going to be part of it.[178]

With the signing of the Treaty of Paris back in 1783, the

American Revolutionary War had finally come to an end. Patrick Murray, just a year or so after James Murray had left North America for Scotland, was back serving his regiment in their new base at Hampstead, Montréal. As a reward for his stalwart if interrupted war service and his duties as aide-de-camp to the General, Patrick was transferred to the Second Battalion, the 60th Foot, and was almost immediately promoted to Major. After the upheaval of wartime, life was to take a quieter turn for a few years, mainly revolving around routine garrison duties and patrols, in an effort to ensure that the newly independent United States didn't try to expand their borders into Canada once again. The relatively quiet garrison life was not to last and Patrick's appointment as the commandant of Fort Detroit in 1788 was just the beginning of the new chapter.

In 1760, Fort Ponchartrain du Detroit came under the authority of the British Crown following the capture of Montréal. At this time, Fort Detroit covered an area of approximately 200 by 100 yards, with an estimated 300 buildings existing within the palisades and giving a village population of around 500 inhabitants. From this humble beginning was to grow the present city of Detroit with, still at its core, the old historic area occupied by the fort. The main task of the new Commandant was to liaise with the native peoples and the established French settlers, whilst at the same time encouraging new settlers to come into the area from Britain, especially Scotland. It was a job Patrick was eminently suited to. His long experience as an army officer had given him strong man management skills, and his memoirs about his active service days supported the view that he was a man who could empathise with local inhabitants and behave in a civilised manner towards them. In Florida and Georgia the local Indian tribes had frequently supported the 60th Foot in combat, and Patrick understood their ways and customs.

It was not always thus, and he had some pre-existing issues to tackle. Earlier commandants had collected taxes to support the garrison as well as requiring each local family to supply wood to the fort. As tax revenues increased substantially, some saw this as a pocket-lining venture. In addition, some earlier commandants had found it difficult to trust the Native Americans, developing a business relationship with the tribes but failing to establish any trust or mutual sympathy. Significant problems had surfaced too when General Amherst, fearing a possible uprising, had ordered a limit on the ammunition sold to Native Americans and French settlers. This led to a belief that the British had an ulterior motive for their actions and were trying to take away a primary means by which the tribes and the earlier French settlers could support their families. Many tribes left the area, and those who remained often had negative feelings toward the garrison and some of the settlers. Many of the French settlers left too, often moving from the village to outlying farming areas.[179]

By the time that Patrick had become the Commandant of Fort Detroit British attention was turning to land acquisition. Several huge land districts, to be supervised by a Land Board, were created by the Canadian Council and Major Patrick Murray headed the Land Board for the nearby District of Hesse (this was the area which included all land west of Lake Erie's Long Point to Fort Detroit and then northwards to an undefined border).[180] The Land Board had the task of overseeing land matters, settling disputes regarding land and boundaries and facilitating settlement. Their chief activity soon became a desire to establish a legal status in the occupation of the extensive native lands and as a result negotiations with local native tribes tended to dominate proceedings. The actions of these Local Land Boards have since become very controversial but give an insight into how the vast lands of Canada and the United States were initially acquired. The four local tribes, the Ottawas, Chippewas, Potawatomis and the Hurons, were brought into a series of negotiations, primarily instigated by Board member Alexander McKee. By May 1790 an agreement was reached by which the crown would legally occupy 1.35 million acres of land, comprising most of the southern peninsula of Ontario. The four Indian tribes would relinquish their titles to this land and in return they would be given 1,680 blankets, combs, hats, rum and other assorted minor items. It has since been calculated that the Indian tribes received 0.214 pence per acre for this transaction, and this was only the first purchase of many,[181] until the Land Boards were abolished in 1794 and the land granting process was centralised through the Executive Council of the Canadian Government. It is not recorded how Patrick viewed this massive purchase, but as Chairman of the Board he would certainly have been influential in the negotiations. They proved to be his last and he stood down as Commandant of Fort Detroit in 1790. His successor at Detroit was Major John Smith, who also replaced him on the Land Board. A Mr Claus held the command at Fort Detroit for a brief time after Smith left in 1792 and, no doubt, this did a lot to encourage the potential immigrants in the younger age groups to settle in the area.[182]

Patrick's service on the Hesse Land Board convinced him that it was time to move his career in a different direction, and he didn't waste any time. He decided that domestic bliss was to be the lifestyle of choice in preference to the ordered existence of Garrison life. He had already decided to end his army career and his son James was now living with him. He sold his commission and then, for the first time and at the age of 49, he got married.

His 23 year old wife was Marie Julie Hay, the daughter of John (Jehu) Hay, a former officer of the 60th Foot. John was American by birth, born between 1730 and 1740 in the British colony of Pennsylvania of Scottish parents. Like an early mirror of Patrick Murray's life, he fought as an officer in the 60th Foot (in the Seven Years' War) and then served at Fort Detroit, being later appointed as town mayor. Throughout the American Revolutionary War he was a loyalist and in 1778 he was active in the Wabash area. The local American Commander believed that he, along with one other person, was responsible for encouraging Indian raids on frontier settlements in Kentucky and the Ohio valley. He was captured and for a time it looked like he would be executed as a murderer, but fortunately he was spared Death Row. He was freed in 1781 in an exchange of prisoners and sailed for England later in the year, perhaps on the same ship that was taking young James Murray to Scotland. In London he received the appointment of Lieutenant Governor of Detroit. In 1783, with Detroit remaining in the British Empire after the peace settlement, he re-joined his family, but by now the rigour of past life was having its say and his health was poor. He died just two years later, on 2nd August 1785,[183] just five years before his loving daughter Marie Julie married his fellow officer and former colleague, Patrick Murray.

Marie Julie had little time to make her mark in Detroit society. She gave young James Murray two half-sisters; Mary Julia Murray was born in 1791 and Isabella Murray was born the following year, but, alas, she was not to have the pleasure of watching them make their way through life. Tragically, illness struck her down and she died just one year later and was buried in the Chapel of St. Amable, aged just 26 years.[184]

Shortly after his wife's death on 8th May 1793, Patrick completed the purchase of the seigneury of Argenteuil, near Montréal and with it gained almost 54,000 acres of land.[185]

The Seigneurial system was a form of land distribution and organisation established in French Canada in 1627. It was inspired by the feudal system and involved the personal dependency of the tenants on the Seigneur. Initially the land was granted as fiefs (called Seigneuries) to the most influential colonists who, in turn, granted tenancies and bought and sold the land. The Seigneuries varied considerably in size and shape but tended to be approximately five by fifteen km in size, and were often shaped into long rectangular strips along a water source, thus gaining access to the river or lake which would be the principal communication route. To gain a seigneury was a mixed blessing and not all Seigneurs made their enterprises financially viable.[186] Income was derived from their tenants and prosperity was based on the success of attracting and keeping industrious tenants on the new land. The Seigneurs also faced a number of obligations, such as the protection of their settlers and establishing and maintaining communications with the outside world.

The first inhabitants of the Argenteuil area were tribes of Algonquians who were already living along the north side of the St. Lawrence River. The French authorities established the Fief and Seigneury of Argenteuil in 1680, the place taking its name from a castle in Argenteuil-sur-Armançon in Burgundy. Argenteuil was situated 80 km west of Ville-Marie (Montréal) and comprised a large block of land and several islands. An early description of the Seigneury gives a flavour of its topography and appearance.

Perhaps through all the upper part of the district of Montréal, no tract of equal extent will be found of greater fertility, or possessing more capabilities of being converted, within a few years, into a valuable property. The land is luxuriantly rich in nearly every part, while the different species of soils are so well varied as to afford undeniable situations for raising abundant crops of every kind. The lower part bordering on the Ottawa is tolerably well cleared of wood; there are large patches of fine meadows and pastures; in the back parts the woods run to a great extent, and yield timber of the different kinds of first-rate size and goodness, which hitherto have been very little thinned by the labours of the woodman. [187]

The description was written with potential settlers in mind but, despite the rave review, settlement was slow and by 1740 only five

French families were established along the edge of the Ottawa River. Profit was hard to come by and over the next few years the Seigneury changed owners several times before becoming the property of Pierre Louis Panet in 1781. Twelve years later he, in turn, sold it to Major Patrick Murray for the sum total of 1,931 livres and five shillings.[188] Patrick Murray, as a result of illegitimacy, had no claim on the Elibank estates and titles, which after the death of his father would revert to his cousin as the nearest legitimate male relation. But at least Patrick had moved on and up in the world. He was now a proud and substantial landowner in one of Britain's most important colonies and his son James, with two new half-sisters, was the son of a laird. But James had little time to enjoy his new life. The time to make his way in the world and begin his future career could be put off no longer.

The Royal Navy in the late eighteenth century was not always the most popular of careers for a young man. It was renowned for its ruthless impressment of recruits, its cramped living conditions, its poor food and its harsh discipline, but for the seventeen year-old James, inspired by his grandfather Admiral George, this was all of no consequence.

Britain had been at war with France off and on since 1689 but the wars of the late 18th century were fought over deeper principles than the mainly colonial tussles earlier in the century. The forces of the country were mobilised to an extent never seen before and the Royal Navy was the spearhead of the British war effort. Britain had first declared war on revolutionary France in 1793 and began in alliance with Austria, Prussia Spain and Naples. One by one the allies left the struggle and by 1796 Britain was effectively isolated in a war against France, Spain and Holland. The country needed every volunteer it could get and James determined to be one of this number.

It was not quite as simple as that. It was not easy to gain a commission in the senior service; it required effective patronage and significant funding. Fortunately James had a number of patrons who could assist him to further his embryonic career choice to become a naval officer.

Patronage was an essential ingredient of 18th-century society and nowhere more so than in the Royal Navy. It allowed the best officers, those who held the prime commands and won the key battles, to pick their followers. As professional men they chose juniors who would reflect credit on them, and perhaps help to secure military victories, prize money and profit. Similarly, ambitious young officers sought the patronage of the best Captains. Sometimes the officer had humble origins but in most cases the patronage system relied upon and used the extensive network of the British ruling classes.

It wasn't cheap.[189] James, like other young officers, would need significant funding to finance the costs involved, such as the initial purchase of his commission, his uniform expenses and the myriad other demands made upon a young gentleman hoping to enter a prestigious, exclusive but expensive career as a naval officer.

There was an illustrious set of potential patrons to whom James could have looked for support. Admiral James Gambier, a former Lord of the Admiralty, was the son of Lord Gambier, the former Lieutenant–Governor of the Bahamas. Admiral James had kept his connections with the Bahamas. His mother, Lady Gambier, had received a large grant of 4,000 acres of land on Cat Island in 1789,[190] and she, of course, was a close neighbour and friend of James' mother Eliza, who held her substantial plantation lands nearby.

Unfortunately most of the rest of James' potential patrons had died just before he began his naval career. His grandfather, Admiral George Murray, 6th Lord Elibank, had died the previous year. The Shambellie Stewarts had introduced him to the Earls of Galloway. Admiral Keith Stewart of Glasserton was the son of Alexander Stewart, 6th Earl of Galloway, and was father to James' friend, James Alexander Stewart-Mackenzie, who was later to become Lord Seaforth. Admiral Keith would also have been in a position to give James the start he desired but sadly, he also died in 1795. In fact, the deceased nature of his patrons was of little importance to the commencement of his naval career (although of great importance to the deceased) as the ongoing influence of such illustrious patrons, deceased or not, would have been considerable.

It could almost guarantee a good start for James, so the main issues now remaining for him were which ship and which station to choose to begin his career. His decision was influenced by another distinguished, but once again deceased, connection. Admiral John Campbell, the son of the minister of the village of Kirkbean, close to New Abbey, was something of a local hero and his family were well known to James. Campbell had also entered the Royal Navy at an early age and in 1740, along with George Murray, James' grandfather, he had sailed around the world as part of Commodore Anson's expedition. He later became known as a navigational expert and was, from 1782 to his death in 1790, the Governor and Commander-in-Chief of Newfoundland, which happened to be the nearest British naval station HQ to the young James Murray.

11

A career begins: The Topaze

S o it was that after spending Christmas 1796 with his father in Argenteuil near Montréal, James Murray headed east to Halifax, Nova Scotia, to be entered on the muster of HMS Topaze as 'volunteer, first class'.[191] It seems incongruous that James, with no knowledge of seafaring, should have the rank of 'first class' but this title was enshrined in the contemporary system for officer training. To the credit of the service, the Royal Navy insisted that its officers would undergo practical hands-on experience, and ideally this would include the lower deck as well as the officers' quarter deck. The regulations demanded that to be classed as Midshipman or Master's Mate the candidate should have served not less than three years at sea and 'be qualified in all respects'. In 1794 a new class called 'volunteers first class' was created which would be composed of:

> young gentlemen intended for sea service; to be styled volunteers and allowed wages at the rate of six pounds per annum.[192]

These youngsters were often placed in the care of the gunner and lived in the gunroom. From there they would train in all aspects of life at sea. James could not have had a much better ship to begin his naval training.

The Royal Navy was forced to admit that the French ships were usually very well built and often superior in many ways to similar

British ones, but to balance this, the British usually claimed superiority in tactics and leadership. HMS Topaze, hopefully exhibiting the best of both worlds, was itself a captured French 32 gun frigate, originally built in 1791 and thus still relatively new. Captain Stephen George Church, an experienced officer, had taken over the ship the previous year and had overseen the commissioning of her into the Royal Navy. Frigates such as Topaze were smaller than a ship-of-the-line, but were formidable opponents for the large numbers of sloops, brigs, gunboats, privateers and merchantmen sailing the seven seas. They had a very long range and were often used as scouts for the fleet, but were also quite capable of carrying out raiding and cutting-out missions and conveying messages and dignitaries. For most officers and men a frigate was the posting of choice as frigates often saw action, which meant a greater chance of glory, promotion, and prize money.

Even though the American Revolutionary War was now over, James was not beginning his career in some safe backwater. The Americas, even excluding the former colonies of mainland America, were commercially pre-eminent among British colonies at that time and the trade in slaves, sugar, coffee, wood, and tropical goods was central to the British economy. Lord Dundas had emphasised this point when he commented as early as 1796 that far more harm would result to our commerce and credit from a French invasion of Jamaica than an invasion of Great Britain or Ireland. The French probably shared that view and by 1796 French forces and their allies were becoming very active in the West Indies, making frequent moves against the British colonies and their shipping trade. It was a concern to military leaders. Even Lord Nelson seemed a bit worried:

> ... The West Indies... is more likely for them (the French) to
> hurt us in than this country. We have but few troops to defend
> our islands and recent conquests.[193]

Fortunately the Royal Navy gained the upper hand and by 1810 all the French, Dutch and Spanish colonies of the West Indies were under British control. The young officer James Murray was to play a full part in this eventual triumph, but at that moment in time he was blissfully unaware of such machinations which were to take place in those far off islands. He was heading for the cold waters of Newfoundland to join his first ship.

Had he joined the Topaze a few months earlier he would have been a bit richer, after partaking in a small share of the prize money for the capture of the Elizabeth, a 36 gun French frigate. On the morning of 28th August 1796, the Topaze, part of a larger British squadron, was becalmed near to Cape Henry off the American coast. Suddenly the cry went up from the watch of 'strange sails to starboard' and soon the 'strange sails' were recognised as three French frigates. The ship cleared for action amid great excitement and bustle, but a lack of wind made an immediate chase impossible, so it soon all became rather anticlimactic. However, after an agonising wait, probably just as bad for the French as for the British, the Topaze was the first to catch the breeze and set off in pursuit. About five and half hours later Topaze came within firing range of the French ship Elizabeth, with a crew of 297 men. There was not much of a fight. The French vessel fired a single broadside towards the Topaze, which singed the whiskers of a few of the crew but caused no casualties. Elizabeth, clearly seeing that she was outnumbered, had no stomach for a further fight so she lowered her colours and surrendered. HMS Assistance and HMS Bermuda then took possession of the prize and accompanied her to Halifax while Topaze, along with the rest of the squadron unsuccessfully pursued the other two French frigates before she returned to Halifax to pick up her prize money and, of course, her new 'volunteer first class'.

James was to stay on Topaze for almost eight years. He needed to serve at least three years before he was eligible for midshipman and during that time he would hope to learn his basic trade as a seaman. He was unlikely to forget the first weeks of his new career. Conquering sea-sickness can take time for any man[194] but James didn't expect to have to find his sea legs in some of the worst weather that an Atlantic storm can offer. On 1st January 1797 the Topaze sailed south out of Halifax harbour heading for Bermuda and immediately ran into strong gales. As they rounded the Sambro lighthouse the weather showed no signs of abating. The next day the winds got even stronger and on 3rd January the gaffs of the main and mizzen topmasts were blown away.

Over the next few days the ship's carpenter worked overtime in appalling conditions, now made even worse by heavy snowfalls. Remarkably, he managed to repair the masts, enough for the ship to give chase to a strange sail that had been spotted. Not surprisingly they failed to catch it, which was probably just as well, as even worse weather was soon to arrive. The master wrote in his diary that 'on Tuesday there were strong gales and very heavy seas'. The Topaze had been sailing with a squadron of ships but by midday she had lost sight of them all. At 2.30pm the foresail blew away from the yard and half an hour later the mizzen topsail and the fore and main staysails were all gone. This was soon followed by the loss of all the ship's yards and booms. The sea had staved in many of the cabin deadlights and the hammock boards had been washed overboard, as was virtually everything else that was not fully pinned to the deck. By 4pm the ship was under bare masts and was in serious danger of broaching,[195] a terrifying prospect even for experienced sailors. Thankfully the ship survived the night, and it managed to limp into a sheltered harbour on the island of Grand Turk. James had had a steep learning curve. When he joined the ship just two weeks previously he barely knew the difference between the futtock shrouds and the bowline boomkins, but by now he not only knew what they were, he had probably watched them being swept overboard.

The ship anchored in Bermuda on 30th January 1797 and the small squadron restocked and recuperated before taking up their blockade duties. The squadron, now consisting of the Topaze, the Thetis, the Andromeda[196] and the Lynx, had the task of being part of the Royal Naval blockade of the seas around the French and Spanish possessions in the West Indies. It had a simple yet ambitious objective; to strangle all foreign trade between their colonies and the outside world. Over the next few months life aboard the Topaze was rarely dull. Between late January and July the Topaze, patrolling the waters off the eastern coast of the United States, took part in 46 chases of 'strange sails' and of these 30 were boarded, although only one prize was taken.[197] A boarding could be a gentlemanly affair with the captains exchanging greetings and perhaps victuals but there was little evidence of this with the Topaze. Once a chase had begun, the Topaze would fire across the bows of the ship if it did not immediately heave to for boarding, and even an exchange of fire was not unusual. Between 9th May and 28th June the Topaze, sitting off Cape Canaveral in Florida, boarded 16 ships, almost all of them American and none of them involved in any activity which could cause concern to Britain.[198] It must have been galling in the extreme for the American ships, often in sight of their own coasts, to be continually stopped and searched by ships of the Royal Navy. As they were also in danger of losing seamen by impressment, it was not surprising that Britain and the Royal Navy became even more unpopular in the United States, the only wonder being that war between the nations was not declared until 1812.

By early July the Topaze was heading back to Halifax, Nova Scotia, for an extended shore period and James was able to look back with some satisfaction on his first six months afloat. He had experienced and survived serious storms, had taken part in numerous minor enemy actions and had rapidly learned the tricks of his trade in the West Indies environment. But the last leg of his first cruise was still to hold a sting in its meteorological tail.

On Friday 30th June the ship ran into terrible weather once again, and very strong gales combined with particularly heavy seas made the storm on the outward journey seem like a breath of fresh air. At 7am, as the struggling daylight reached a dark grey colour, the main and mizzen top rails disappeared overboard. It was not long before the bowsprit and the foremast itself were carried away too, shortly to be followed by the mizzen mast. The Topaze now had only the mainmast left and at 4pm this went the same way as the others. The ship was now little more than a floating hulk and was in very serious danger of sinking. Even the Master, who turned understatement into an art form, was prompted to note that 'the ship was labouring very much'.[199] The next day brought only a brief respite as the furious weather continued. The Topaze frantically tried to reach the other ships in the convoy by firing her guns, using blue lights and false fires, but no ship answered. Finally, the Clairvoyante answered the distress call, but she was in no better state herself and was unable to assist. On Sunday 2nd July it took heroic efforts by the crew to enable a jury mast to be rigged[200] and to the huge relief of James and all the ship's sailors the Topaze limped into Halifax harbour on Wednesday 5th July 1797. A very welcome and deserved extended shore leave was given to almost all the crew, and the Topaze did not go back into active service for almost two months.

The Topaze continued its blockade duties for another year until it was finally ordered back to the Spithead anchorage off Portsmouth Harbour.

It had not been an uneventful year. James was now a full midshipman. Furthermore, on 22nd April 1798 the Topaze, along with HM Ships Resolution, Asia, Assistance and Hind combined to capture the French privateers, the Soutier de la Patrie and the Amicable Johanna and were able to bring them safely back to Halifax, Nova Scotia. Although James had not made his fortune when he arrived back in Portsmouth, at least he was a bit richer, gaining a prize money share of £2. 15 shillings and 8 pence for his part in the capture of the privateers[201] and after a nine year absence, could now visit his old friends in New Abbey with considerable pride.

During his time with the Topaze, for misdemeanours unknown, James was dis-rated to Able Seaman and took his place with all the other seamen below decks.[202] No doubt this was an experience which, although not welcomed at the time, would serve him well in the future by helping him to understand the difficulties and frustrations the men below decks could experience as part of a 'Man-O-War'. Fortunately for him, his 'Able' rating only lasted eight days and on the 9th February 1798 he was promoted to midshipman, thus taking his first step on the ladder to becoming a commissioned officer in the largest and most successful navy in the world.

Midshipmen could be as young as 12 or 13 but James, at 21, would not have been out of place. About 25 per cent of the midshipmen came from the younger sons of the aristocracy and landed classes, with most of the rest being from professional families. Sons or grandsons of naval officers, such as James himself, made up about a quarter of all naval officers.

He would now live in the midshipman's berth, still grossly overcrowded, but a distinct improvement on the life he experienced below deck as an Able Seaman or even when he was a Volunteer – First Class. He was still very much a learner and would be expected to take part and assist in all the pursuits and skills expected of a naval officer. Some Captains laid down a regular curriculum timetable for their 'mids'. A typical curriculum, practised aboard HMS Amazon in 1802, was:

Monday: training at casting the lead (establishing the depth of water the ship was sailing in) and practising on the mizzen topsail yard (the upper sails).

    Tuesday: exercise with small arms

    Wednesday: knots and splices and general seamanship.

    Thursday: once again on the upper sails

    Friday: exercise at the great guns.

    Saturday: Attending with the Boatswain

In addition to a fixed programme like the one above, they would spend a considerable amount of time with the Master, and perhaps the Captain, working on navigation, mathematics etc. From time to time, especially as they became more senior, they would be given more exciting tasks, such as acting as an aide to the Captain, taking part in cutting-out operations against land forces and even assisting a Lieutenant in operating a division of guns.[203]

Midshipman Murray was to spend another six years on the Topaze, and they were not without incident. The Topaze, like many other ships of the Royal Navy, was making an absolute nuisance of itself against foreign cargo ships crossing the world's oceans. As France was attempting to do exactly the same to the many British merchant ships engaged in similar trade, in April 1799 the Topaze, along with HMS Eurydice and HMS Castor, took up duties as a convoy escort.[204] The first convoy was from Spithead, across the Atlantic Ocean to Newfoundland and Quebec in Canada and by 21st June they were moored in Quebec harbour. The trip back to Spithead was equally uneventful and the Topaze then had a period of local duties, much closer to home. A short cruise to Ireland and extended leave in Bantry Bay in early 1800 was followed by another short cruise to Gibraltar. In February 1801 the Topaze took up convoy escort again, this time accompanied by the Britannia and Heureux. The huge convoy of 86 sails would take a lot of looking after and this cruise to the West Indies was not without incident. By 27th February, just twelve days after leaving Spithead, the convoy was down to 82 British sails, but that was partially balanced by the addition of three prizes, all safely reaching Carlisle Bay in Barbados by the end of March. The convoy continued on around other islands in the West Indies and their escort ships buzzed around them in search of prey.

So did the enemy ships. On 10th May the Topaze, accompanied by the Juno and Syren, was cruising off Havana when a Spanish ship of the line decided to introduce herself. Topaze, clearly choosing to ignore the fact that the Spanish ship had a broadside four times that of herself, cleared for action and at 5.30pm was in position to open fire. She gallantly managed to fire several broadsides into the huge Spanish ship, but unfortunately the Spaniards managed to do the same. The Topaze's bowsprit was carried away in the attack and she was forced to break off action.[205] However, the impetuous behaviour of the Topaze had unsettled the Spanish giant, and she bore away with all speed, hotly pursued by the Juno and Syren. Night brought an end to the action and by the following day the British had lost sight of the ship. Despite this, James Murray learned a lesson central to the success of the Royal Navy in her pursuit of victory against the forces of Napoleon; British ships, whatever size, would aggressively engage the enemy and 'do their duty.'

After a brief shore leave, the Topaze, this time in the company of Melampus and Juno, was once again involved in action when she captured an armed brig bound for Havana from Vera Cruz. The Topaze's log records that it was a Spanish Brig, but it turned out to be the Volant, a French privateer,[206] which was a private ship carrying a 'Letter of Marque'. This government license authorized the ship to attack and capture enemy vessels and bring them in for prize money. It was essentially licenced piracy, but was considered an honourable calling by all those involved in both the British and the French navies. In the same squadron, the Heureux, a fellow convoy ship, was involved in an epic confrontation. The Heureux was particularly fast and was described as, the most complete flush deck ship I have ever seen, copper fastened, highly finished and of large dimensions.[207]

In a 16 hour chase, with the Topaze being unable to keep up, the Heureux captured the 16 gun French sloop, Egypte, from Guadeloupe. By repute the Egypte was one of the fastest vessels in the French West Indies, but it was no match for the Heureux, which ironically was herself a captured French ship.

A further period of shore leave in Port Royal, Jamaica was followed by a journey back to the UK and a period in home waters, ensuring that Napoleon Bonaparte did not invade England. Topaze continued her prize capturing exploits and gained a new Captain, Willoughby Lake.[208] It was time for James Murray to move on, but it had been an eventful eight years, both on the high seas and on land.

From the House of Shame
to the House of God

Whilst James was playing his part against Britain's enemies on the high seas, back in New Abbey, Scotland, James Murray's sisters were growing up. Louisa, his illegitimate half-sister, was four years older than James and was probably around twelve years of age when she arrived in New Abbey. Her surname, Fuser, was unfamiliar to the New Abbey folk and was soon adapted to become Fraser. Her connections through the Manse at New Abbey led her to meet the Reverend William Grierson, minister of Glencairn, and his son, Thomas Grierson, who was soon to become the Reverend Grierson, minister of the neighbouring parish of Kirkbean. These Griersons, although closely related, should not be confused with the Griersons of Larbreck in Northern Dumfriesshire and Keltonhead on the opposite side of the River Nith from New Abbey. Young Thomas Grierson of Larbreck, a frequent visitor to the village, had become a close acquaintance of Louisa and as the years passed this friendship grew into a more intimate relationship. In 1792, in her village of New Abbey and at the ripe old age of 17, she became Mrs Louisa Grierson of Larbreck.

In fact her husband, Thomas, was well known to the Murrays. He was the son of Colonel James Grierson of Larbreck who had played a prominent part in the British administration of Georgia during the American Revolutionary War years. Towards the close of the War, James Grierson was the victim of an infamous assassination, hotly debated for many years. Colonel James seemed to have divided his time between his family estate at Larbreck and his colonial home in Atlanta, Georgia. He had made his name as an Indian trader and merchant in Georgia and had become a respected Justice of the Peace and Colonel of the local militia.[209] When the American Revolutionary War broke out, Colonel James sided with the Loyalists and was to pay dearly for his choice. He was a leading figure in Georgia throughout the war years and was well known to Patrick Murray and the other officers of the 60th regiment. He was also well known to Thomas Brown and as Brown's uncompromising reputation grew he became perhaps too closely associated. Colonel James was assassinated in June 1781, two days after he had surrendered to the American forces besieging Augusta. A contemporary account described the tragic event:

> Colonel Grierson, who had rendered himself peculiarly obnoxious to the enemy by his spirited and unwearied exertions in the cause of his country, was under the custody of the main guard.[210] ... His spirit and unshaken loyalty in every change of fortune marked him out as a proper victim to sacrifice to their savage resentment. One of General Pickens' men, named James Alexander, entered the room where he was confined with his three children, and shot him through the body. He was afterwards stripped, and his clothes divided among the soldiers, who, having exercised upon his dead body all the rage of the most horrid brutality, threw it into a ditch.

> Thus fell the brave, unfortunate Colonel Grierson... by the hand of a bloody, sanctioned, and protected villain, in shameful violation of a solemn capitulation.[211]

The death of Colonel Grierson had a huge impact at the time. British reprisals were soon forthcoming and the hanging of Colonel Hayne of the South Carolinian Militia was partially blamed on the Grierson murder. Even the American leadership was horrified by the assassination. American General Greene called it an 'insult to the arms of the United States and an outrage upon the rights of humanity.' He even offered a reward of one hundred guineas for the arrest of the guilty party but no arrest was forthcoming.[212]

The full story is perhaps rather more complicated. The family, like many others, may have had split loyalties.[213] Many of the rank and file Georgians believed that the killing was justified, claiming that James Alexander shot Grierson for:

> his villainous conduct in the country. Grierson had exposed his prisoners, amongst whom was the father of Captain James Alexander, to the fire of their relatives and friends, for the purpose of screening his men from the besiegers.[214]

Whatever may have been the causal factors for the slaughter, it was a horrendous experience for the children of Colonel Grierson, who were to witness the murder of their father. Thomas and his younger brother William were taken to safety and put on a boat for Scotland, William taking up residence at Larbreck and Thomas at Keltonhead, just across the River Nith from New Abbey. As the Griersons returned to the New Abbey area at the same time as James Murray, it is interesting to speculate that they may all have arrived together and, by virtue of a common background, a close bond developed between the Griersons and the extended Murray-Smith family.

Thomas was to die in 1798, tragically young at only 28 years of age, and 24 year old Louisa inherited the Larbreck estate, which she later ran with the assistance of the Reverend James Hamilton, her sister Harriet's husband.

1. Captain James Murray: This miniature shows James Murray as a Royal Navy Commander and was painted between 1809 and 1816 by Samuel John Stump, (reproduced by kind permission of Bonham's Ltd, London).

2. The Stewart family: Evidence suggests that Eliza Smith, the
    mother of James Murray, was the youngest daughter of
    Charles Stewart of Shambellie and his wife, Ann Hay. Eliza's
    older brother was William Stewart, who inherited the
    Shambellie estate in New Abbey, Scotland.

2a. Ann Hay

2b. Charles Stewart

2c. William Stewart

(All reproduced with
thanks to Lou
Greenshields,
descendant of the
Shambellie Stewarts.)

3. James Murray's Birthplace: This building in St. Augustine, Florida, is the home of the National Guard. In 1778 it served as the St. Francis barracks and officers' quarters for the Royal American Rifles (60th foot).

4. St Augustine: This delightful city in Northern Florida still has many buildings remaining from the British colonial period and has kept its original street layout.

5. Patrick Murray, James Murray's father, took part in the British advance from Florida into Georgia and South Carolina:

5a. Fort Morris. The 60th foot attempted to take the fort on November 25, 1778. When Colonel John McIntosh, the fort commander, was asked for its surrender he famously replied, "Come and take it!" (author).

5b. The Battle of Port Royal, near present day Beaufort. Captain Patrick Murray was leading his men up this slope towards the American lines when he was twice wounded (author).

6. Panorama of New Abbey: Developing around the 13th century Sweetheart Abbey and in the shadow of Criffel Hill, New Abbey was the childhood home of James Murray and his three sisters (author).

7. Old New Abbey, 19th Century: A much changed scene today, this picture shows the old church and the Schoolhouse nestling in the shadow of Sweetheart Abbey. The former manse, once home to James and Harriet is probably the house on the right (public domain).

8. James Murray: Hero of the Battle of Quebec and the first British governor of Lower Canada. James was the uncle of Patrick Murray, James' father (author). This bronze bust, by Michel Binette, is situated in Des Braves Park, Québec.

Theresa was the second sister, born in war-torn Georgia in 1780.[215] As she grew up in New Abbey the many connections through the acquaintances of the Elibank Murrays brought her into contact with some of the leading businessmen of the area, including Henry Wood. Henry conducted his business mainly in the rapidly growing city of Glasgow and was making his name as a sugar importer. He felt that his growing fortune would be better served by expanding into the source of the trade itself and so he, along with other members of his family, left the shores of Scotland and moved to Hoff Van Aurich, Demerara (now part of Guyana) in South America. They were accompanied by Theresa, now Henry's new wife. [216]

The mainstay of the Demeraran economy was sugar, grown on huge plantations which were worked by slave labour. The population of the colony in 1823 was estimated at 2,500 whites, 2,500 freed blacks, and 77,000 slaves. It is on record that in 1822 Henry possessed 26 slaves ranging in age from babies to a 60 year old.[217] A study of James Murray's world of the late 18th and early 19th century shows many parallels to life today, but the ubiquitous impact of slavery and the trade associated with it is a sharp reminder of the many significant differences. The rise of the Oswald family, at the very heart of the trade, has already been described. Their activities led to immense wealth coming back to the areas of New Abbey and Kirkbean as the family acquired land and developed public services, but attitudes to the trade were gradually changing. When James Murray began his naval career, a secondary task of the British fleet was to protect and safeguard the transatlantic trade in people. By the end of his career he was active in eliminating the same trade. In fact it was not until 6th April 2010 that slavery was specifically made illegal in the UK,[218] but in reality the Slave Trade Act of 1807 had abolished the slave trade throughout the British Empire. By this time the economy of both Great Britain and the United States had benefited, and would continue to benefit enormously from the profits of this barbarous trade.

Joseph Smith, likely kin to Eliza Smith's husband, was a mariner hailing from British New York. He was a crew member of the brig Royal Charlotte, one of several ships owned by Samuel and William Vernon of Newport, Rhode Island.[219] The Royal Charlotte would carry just about anything if it could be traded, and indeed it did transport cotton and a wide variety of tropical and sub-tropical goods. However, its primary trade was in human beings and Joseph was an active crew member on the ship, under the captaincy of William Taylor, in the early 1760s. The Royal Charlotte successfully utilised the 'triangle trade'. Profit was made by, firstly, purchasing slaves in Africa with rum or other tropical and sub-tropical goods from the colonies; then secondly, selling those slaves in the West Indies or the mainland of Central America. The triangle was completed by using the money obtained, minus overheads and profit, to purchase molasses and rum from the colonies or processed goods from Britain itself, and thus continue the triangular cycle of trade.

The Royal Charlotte, on reaching the African Coast, would contact agents, such as Richard Brew in Ghana, who would sell the outward cargo for them and would organise and acquire the slaves for the return journey. One of the main slave routes operated between Anomabu, Ghana, and Williamsburg, Virginia. A local businessman, Richard Adams, was the chief customer and he operated a busy slave market. In 1763 he proudly reported one transaction amongst very many when he sold 15 slaves for the grand total of £702 17s 6d, with the best price paid being £58 10s for an adult male.[220]

Another lucrative market was St. Croix in the Virgin Islands, where Cornelius Durant operated the market. In 1768 he undertook the sale of 95 slaves from the Royal Charlotte. He sold 93 of them for the accumulated sum of £4710 3s. 0d, with two small girls and a small boy sold for £112 4s 0d. Two slaves were unsold; one man and one girl, about whom it was written that she would "go in the brig". The Bill of Sale does not record the reason for the girl to go in the brig, or indeed the fate of the unsold male slave.[221]

The slaves themselves were not entirely browbeaten and submissive, as the Royal Charlotte crew were to discover to their cost in 1763. The Newport Mercury of Rhode Island described such an incident:

NEWPORT, 6 JUNE

The Brig Royal Charlotte arrived here last Thursday... by whom we have affecting intelligence of the tragical Death of Capt. George Frost, and Mr William Grant, his Mate... which was perpetrated by the Slaves on board his Sloop, as she lay at Anchor in the River Gaboone, in the Month of November last (1762). Capt Frost having occasion either for some Wood or Water, sent two Men and a Negro on Shore for that purpose, himself the Mate, and a Negro who belonged to the vessel, remaining on board; and in the men's absence he disastrously permitted the slaves, to the Number of about 60, to come upon deck, who immediately seized him, with the Negro Man, and threw them both overboard. Mr Grant, at this time lay sick in the Cabin unable to rise. Capt. Frost swam up to the Vessel, in order to get on board again; upon which the Slaves threw a Lance at him, which penetrated his Body, where it remained, and with which he attempted to gain the Shore, but after swimming about half the way, he sunk, and was seen no more. The Negro, who was thrown over with him, had the good fortune to get safe ashore—The slaves having now the command of the Vessel, they brought the Small Arms, with several Barrels of Powder, upon Deck... the Slaves on board began firing with their Small Arms, but through Ignorance soon set the Powder on Fire, and in the Explosion about 30 of them were destroyed. The Sloop was retaken three days afterwards.on entering the Cabin, the corps(sic) of Mr Grant was immediately discovered, with his throat cut in a very shocking manner, which was supposed to have been done as soon as Capt. Frost and the Negro were thrown over.[222]

Even more serious slave uprisings occurred on land, and during Theresa's residency in Demerara she was to witness one of the most significant events in slaving history. The Demerara rebellion of 1823 was a major uprising which involved more than 10,000 slaves. Its after-effects were to vibrate all across Britain and in 1833, its legacy was to play no small part in the passing of the act which finally abolished slavery throughout the British Empire.

There was a general belief that if slaves were influenced by religious teachings they would become more docile and obedient, and so in 1808 the London Missionary Society erected a chapel on the 'Le Ressouvenir' plantation. In 1817 John Smith took up the position as pastor and he, like his predecessor, received a hostile reception from John Murray the new Governor (no connection with the Elibank Murrays), and from many of the colonists who believed he was a spy for the abolitionist movement in London. Similar situations existed on many of the other plantations too, so the Governor declared all meetings after dark illegal and made religious observation for the slaves generally difficult.[223] Pastor Smith later reported to the London Missionary Society that:

> ever since I have been in the colony, the slaves have been most grievously oppressed. A most immoderate quantity of work has, very generally, been exacted of them, not excepting women far advanced in pregnancy. When sick, they have been commonly neglected, ill-treated, or half starved. Their punishments have been frequent and severe.[224]

110

Furthermore he complained that the Governor had told him that:

> planters will not allow their negroes to be taught to read, on pain of banishment from the colony.[225]

This ran counter to the opinion of the established clergy who believed that it was essential for all followers to be able to read the Christian Bible for themselves. Furthermore, religious instruction for slaves had been endorsed by the British Parliament. As a result, the plantation owners were unenthusiastically obliged to permit slaves to attend church. Reports from the colony to the, often absentee, owners were frequently incorrect and the quality of the local managers left a lot to be desired:

> ... the injudicious managers under whom too many of the slaves are placed; half educated men of little discretion, or command over their own caprices; good planters perhaps – but quite unfit to have the charge of bodies of men, although they might take very proper care of cattle.[226]

Things finally reached a head on Monday 18th August 1823 when slaves on 'Success' plantation began a revolt against their harsh conditions and maltreatment. Those on 'Le Ressouvenir', where Smith's chapel was situated, immediately joined them. The unrest quickly spread to over fifty estates located between Georgetown and Mahaica. Accounts from witnesses indicate that the rebels exercised restraint with only a very small number of white men killed, although some slaves took revenge on their masters or overseers by putting them in the stocks. Slaves went from plantation to plantation in large groups and entered the estates, ransacked the houses, seized weapons and ammunition and locked up their former masters, promising to release them in three days.

The Governor immediately declared martial law. The 21st

Fusiliers and the 1st West Indian Regiment were dispatched to combat the rebels who were armed mainly with cutlasses and bayonets on poles and a small number of rifles captured from plantations. By the late afternoon of 20th August the situation had been brought under control. Most of the slaves had been rounded up and some were shot whilst attempting to flee.

On 25th August, Governor Murray constituted a general court-martial to try the rebels. A variety of sentences were handed out, including solitary confinement, lashing and death. Those who were considered ringleaders were executed by a firing squad; then their heads were cut off and nailed to posts

Pastor John Smith was also court-martialled, found guilty and was given the death sentence. He was sent to prison, where he died of consumption in the early hours of 6th February 1824. News of his death was published in British newspapers and provoked enormous outrage:

> The 1823 revolt had a special significance. It attracted attention in Britain inside and outside Parliament to the terrible evil of slavery and the need to abolish it. This played a part, along with other humanitarian, political and economic factors, in causing the British parliament ten years later in 1833 to take the momentous decision to abolish slavery in British Guiana and elsewhere in the British Empire with effect from 1 August 1834... The slaves were finally freed on 1 August 1838.[227]

The Wood plantation had emerged without serious harm from the revolt but only months after the event, Henry Wood died, leaving his whole estate to Theresa. She stayed for a few more years in Demerara and then sold most of her slaves and moved back to the UK, where she bought several properties in Bath. She now had a significant fortune, much of it originating from the exploitation of slaves in the sugar plantations, although she and her husband are not on record as ill-treating their charges in any way.

After Henry's death Theresa kept one personal slave and, when freedom finally arrived for the slaves, Theresa Wood received compensation of £27 18s 9d for her loss.[228]

Harriet Smith, the third and youngest of the sisters, was born in Florida in 1781 and moved to the Bahamas with her mother Eliza. Harriet seems to have been a quiet, studious girl[229] and little is known of her early life. She lived with her family in Scotland, but James went to Canada and then joined the Royal Navy, her two sisters got married and, in 1806, William Stewart, heir to Shambellie, returned to New Abbey from Boreland, Gatehouse with his huge brood of children and wanted his house back. The 25-year-old Harriet, facing homelessness, would look for support from the close family friend, the Reverend William Wright. The Reverend Wright, the outrage at his initial appointment now forgotten, had served New Abbey very well:

> parishioners fought hard to prevent him coming in and would have fought as hard to prevent his going out.[230]

Not only had the long serving Rev. Wright rebuilt the new Manse in 1802, but he had organised the campaign and funding which led to the saving and preservation of the fine building next door, the nationally important Sweetheart Abbey. His energy undiminished, in 1816 he organised and led the campaign, and badgered others for financial contributions, to build the imposing Waterloo Monument which today still dominates the skyline behind the village of New Abbey.

William Wright was now living on his own and beginning to feel his age. It is only speculative that Harriet then went to live in the new and expanded Manse,[231] taking on companion and surrogate daughter duties. There was no doubt though about the next chapter in the story, as in 1817 Harriet Smith married the Reverend James Hamilton. Harriet would have met James Hamilton at least as early as 1813 when he took on the difficult task of following the ailing Reverend William Wright into the New Abbey ministry. The newly married couple lived together with the Reverend William Wright in the Manse of New Abbey, William remaining in the house until his death there in 1819. It was not all sadness in the Manse, as just before William Wright died, a marriage took place in the house. The remarkable 59 year old William Stewart of Shambellie married again, this time to 18-year-old Bethia Donaldson, and was to go on to have at least ten more children.

The Hamilton family were prominent in Dumfriesshire and could look back on a proud covenanting background. James Hamilton's elder brother, Archibald, used to relate with pride how he had served alongside Robert Burns in the Dumfriesshire Yeomanry and had ridden side by side with him on many occasions. James Hamilton himself had the honour of being one of the squad who fired a salute over the poet's grave at his formal burial cemetery in St. Michael's churchyard, Dumfries, in July 1796.[232] Archibald was the maternal grandfather of Archibald Hamilton Charteris, who was to succeed James Hamilton as parish minister in 1859 and would later move on to become Professor of Biblical Criticism at the University of Edinburgh. Archibald was to make his name as a leading voice for Church reform and is also credited as being the father of the Women's Guild.

13

The angel of salvation

Storm clouds were gathering over Patrick Murray's head back in Canada as he tackled the harsh realities of land ownership and pioneering development in a new colony. He had already borrowed money to purchase the seigneury but the venture continued to drain his finances. Events came to a head in 1802 when decisions made in the Court of the King's Bench, Quebec, in 1800 and 1801 meant that Patrick now had to pay back over £2,200, with £1,275 still owing to Louis Panet, from whom Patrick had bought the estate. A surprising angel of salvation stepped in to bail him out. Eliza Smith had moved from the Bahamas and was now residing in Quebec.

Eliza had not been idle in the intervening years. In an era when women rarely owned property, with business and money management considered very much the man's realm, she bucked the trend. Eliza had a difficult balancing act to perform. She was developing her business enterprises in the Bahamas, but also had the responsibilities of her children in Scotland. As the children got older and more settled into their life in New Abbey she was able to devote more of her time to her agricultural interests. Most of the plantations in the Bahamas were small and the owners occupied houses which, even with the largest stretch of imagination, could not be described as grand.[233] Eliza's reward came on the 17th August 1789 when she was awarded 540 acres of land in Cat Island[234] and just four months later a further 100 acres of land on Long Island, plantations well above the average in size and value. In the period between April 1788 and December 1789 a total of 605 land grants were given in the Bahamas, most to the former American loyalists.[235] Five people were given over 20,000 acres of land between them,[236] and of the rest Eliza was one of the larger recipients. Of all the Bahama land awards, only 41 were larger than that awarded to Eliza, and only seven people had larger grants on Cat Island itself. Of the seven landowners, one was Lady Gambier, the wife of the former Governor and recipient of the largest grant of all.[237] Of the others, most were prominent men heavily involved in Loyalist politics, including James Hepburn, the main opponent and antagonist of Governors Maxwell and Powell and Chairman of the Board of American Loyalists,[238] and Andrew Deveaux, hero of the assault on the Bahamas a few years earlier. Eliza, with her property on New Providence, Cat Island and Long Island (later replaced with land on Abaco and Caicos), was now a prominent member of the Bahamian society; all the more remarkable in that she was a woman and the mother of at least one illegitimate child.[239]

The loyalist dreams of a new and rich plantation life in the sunny Bahamas had been shattered by 1800. At some stage the 'chenille' caterpillar had entered the island crops and soon began to spread with great rapidity. The weather also refused to cooperate with the loyalist dream. In 1797 the cotton crop largely failed due to a combination of the chenille bug, very heavy rains and a hurricane. In 1800 the crop failed once more. [240] It was reported that most planters had abandoned their cotton crops to the bug and reverted to more subsistence corn, peas and some grain.[241] This does not paint the even blacker picture which faced the Bahama loyalists. It was reported that there was a strong spirit of emigration and Thomas Brown estimated that 7,300 loyalists had already emigrated, their surprising destination being the southern states of the USA, especially Georgia.[242] Only a few years earlier some of their number had attacked American sailors (often bringing in much needed supplies) on sight in the streets of New Providence.

Long Island was almost deserted[243] and all but four families had left the Caicos due to the French / Hispanic War nearby. Even in Abaco it can be gauged that plantation life was over when a survey revealed that there were only 15 slaves left on the island, and they provided the essential manpower for the plantation agricultural system.[244]

Eliza, her plantations virtually abandoned, was considering joining the exodus from the Bahamas when word reached her concerninég the difficulties facing Patrick Murray in Canada. It was not a giant step for her to take in deciding to relocate to Montréal to see what she could do. She quickly began to get her house in order before the move. Firstly, she examined the position of her two family slaves, Fortune and Rosetta. There had been a number of slave revolts in the West Indies, notably in Haiti, but slave conspiracy was rare on the Bahamas. Nevertheless, concern was rising and three slaves had been hanged for sedition in Nassau in September 1797.[245] Governor Dunmore had encouraged manumission[246] amongst the slaving community[247] and of the 439 manumissions awarded between 1782 and 1800, 139 of them came from the Governor via a Government Certificate. Lord Dunmore also granted freedom to eight of his own slaves during this period.[248] In this climate of rewarding good service, Eliza did not forget her two slaves, who had accompanied her slaves when she first arrived in New Providence in 1784. She granted freedom to Fortune Smith in 1800, noting her faithful service to the family. Shortly afterwards Rosette Smith was also granted her freedom.[249]

Rosette's freedom may be connected with an incident which took place in 1800. An indentured baker named John Minns from Reading, England, absconded from his apprenticeship and ran away to sea, only to be shipwrecked off Nassau. By repute, he was rescued by a slave girl called Rosetta whom he subsequently married. If the Rosetta of this story is none other than Rosette Smith[250] it may have been this incident which encouraged Eliza to grant Rosette's freedom in the same year and consequently allow her to marry. Rosetta and John went on to raise a family and one of her grandchildren, Alan, became the first non-white mayor of Thetford, Norfolk. Another grandchild was the first non-white Anglican priest in the Bahamas. Two other grandchildren also did well for themselves, both becoming doctors.[251]

Eliza kept ownership of her three plantations and, in later correspondence, she alluded to her slaves, so it was unlikely that her plantations were totally abandoned on her relocation but were left under the care of a manager. Eliza once more stepped into the unknown and moved north to the British colony of Quebec to enter the complex and potentially cataclysmic financial domain of Patrick Murray. At least she was now reasonably wealthy, but most of her wealth was tied up in land and slaves and their values were decreasing almost daily. Nevertheless, she was considered creditworthy enough, and shortly after arrival she took a deep breath, signed on the dotted line and took over Patrick's £1,200 debt. [252]

Despite Eliza's guiding hand,[253] financial issues continued to plague Patrick, and in 1803 he relinquished overall control of Argenteuil in favour of his son, James, for the sum of £7,000.[254] James Murray, still just a Master's Mate on HMS Topaze, did not have the necessary capital to purchase such an estate outright but still he paid £2,700 up-front, mainly by borrowing £1,500 from Sir John Johnson. Patrick had initially borrowed money from a number of sources, including Nicolas Montour, a writer from Pointe du Lac in the district of Trois Rivieres. Sir John Johnson had bought up these debts from Nicolas Montour and consequently had a significant interest in the fate of Argenteuil.[255] Patrick, James and Eliza had been unable to clear their earlier arrears and in order to proceed with the transfer of the seigneury they subrogated to Johnson all the rights and privileges towards Argenteuil if the debt was not paid back within two years. [256]

Sir John Johnson was a very wealthy landowner. In 1774, on his father's death, he inherited a baronetcy and 200,000 acres of land at Johnson Hall (Johnstown), in the Mohawk valley. Already a successful Army Officer, he accepted the commission of Major-General of the district militia and went on to serve with distinction as a soldier and an Indian Department official. When Upper Canada was created in 1791, it was generally expected that Sir John would be named its first lieutenant-governor, but he was not. He was bitterly disappointed but managed to bounce back. In 1796 he was appointed to the Legislative Council of Lower Canada and he continued his duties as Head of the Indian Department. Sir John put a great deal of effort into the acquisition of property. He renovated the Château de Longueuil on Rue Saint-Paul in Montréal and became engrossed in a pursuit of even more real estate.[257] He had taken on the additional role of Seigneur in 1795 when he purchased the seigneury of Monnoir with its 84,000 acres and was gazing around hungrily for even more when he entered into financial arrangements with Eliza Smith, James and Patrick Murray. This was not the end of the borrowing. A further huge sum of £8,000 was borrowed from William DeLorimier, an Indian Department Official, taken with an interest of 6% repayment annually.[258] In order to raise the necessary money Eliza, guarantor of James, directed John Armstrong, her friend and attorney in Nassau, Bahamas to:

> sell and dispose of all her plantations and Negroes on the Caicos, and her lands, Tenements and property of every discription(sic) in Cat Island in New Providence aforesaid, to and for the best and highest price.[259]

James, now the proud but indebted owner of Argenteuil, was able to get on with the business of running his estate. Or at least he could have done if he had been present, but his Royal Navy career still took precedence. James, now mainly an absentee landlord, passed a power of attorney to his father (dangerously) and mother (sensibly), giving them full power and lawful authority to conduct and manage his affairs when he was absent from the province on naval duty.[260] Amazingly, this arrangement seemed to work very well for a while and mother, father and son, 'Team-Murray', brought about a rapid development of the area.

Not surprisingly, the Murrays were keen to encourage settlement from any quarter. Some of the earliest settlers were Americans from Massachusetts. For example, Peter Benedict, Benjamin Wales and Elon (Captain) Lee had arrived in 1799 and at least two of them had served in the American Revolutionary Army. It is ironic that these men had no sooner seen the success of their military campaign and the achievement of independence for the United States, than they left their new country and once again went to live under the British flag. Despite his military service, Captain Lee had deep reservations about American independence and his house later became known as a safe rendezvous for Americans who desired to escape military service during the 1812 war against Britain. Benjamin Wales had also been in the American Army and he was a paper maker by trade. His skills were soon to become very useful in the area.[261]

The American settlers were soon outnumbered by a significant influx of immigrants from Scotland. A feature of the Scottish settlers was the distinct separation of the Highlanders, who settled on the banks of the Ottawa River and around St. Andrews, from the Lowlanders, who tended to settle around Lachute. An early commentator sang the praises of the new Scottish settlers:

> The early settlers in that part of the county, had very little knowledge of farming, their chief dependence for a living being

in the manufacture and sale of potash... About that time, a few Scotch emigrants came to the place, and finding that farms could be bought cheap from these men... secured their own, and wrote for their friends to come. In a short time a small colony of thrifty, industrious farmers was established, who brought not only knowledge of the best system of agriculture known and practised in the Lothians, but who also brought the best and most improved agricultural implements, and also the best tradesmen. Being careful and frugal, as well as of the most industrious habits, a marked change was soon visible in the appearance of the country, and in a short time the desert rejoiced and blossomed as the rose.[262]

One of the first Scottish settlers was John Fraser from Inverness-shire. He had a lonely existence until more settlers came into the area, partly as a result of an advertising campaign by Patrick Murray. John McMartin of Glenlyon, Perthshire, was one of the new settlers. He had decided to emigrate to the New World and headed for Montréal. Once he arrived, he learned that his newly purchased estate was an unbroken wilderness and that his nearest neighbour would be thirty miles away. At this time he met Patrick Murray, who was in Montréal endeavouring to obtain new Scottish settlers. He persuaded Mr McMartin to sell his land and, along with his brothers, take up a new residence in Argenteuil. Accordingly, in 1801 the McMartins purchased two lots on the south side of the River Rouge. A small log house and clearing were here on his arrival, but in a few years John had built another house, which, apparently, is still standing. Dr. Henderson came from Doune near Stirling. He was a very able man, and at the age of 16 he entered the University of St. Andrews. He studied Divinity and by the turn of the 19th century he had his own ministry in Carlisle, England. From there he looked for a new challenge and left for Montréal. Leaving his wife and three small children in Montréal, he came to Argenteuil and preached to the people as a visiting minister, the parish not yet having its own full time minister. The devout congregation were pleased with him and offered him the first Presbyterian ministry in the Seigneury. He was happy to accept and remained the parish minister for the next fifty-nine years.

Some Scottish settlers came to Argenteuil via America. For example, Duncan Macgregor came from Perthshire and settled in the American colonies. On the outbreak of the Revolutionary War he felt too loyal to fight against King George so he removed to Canada and lived near Quebec until 1802. He then finally moved to Argenteuil and his descendants were to live in the same area for very many years.

It was not only the Scottish settlers who helped the Seigneury to grow. There was a surprising number of black settlers, an astonishing aspect in view of the fact that at the time both Britain and America still had legalised slavery. However, the anti-slavery movement in Britain had many adherents and was rapidly gaining support under the indefatigable leadership of William Wilberforce. Whether James and his father Patrick were motivated by these ideals or were simply after monetary gain is unknown, but the legacy of so many free pioneer black settlers in the Seigneury of Argenteuil is present today:

> Outside Montréal, several blacks secured Seigneurial lands in this period, by grant from a Seigneur or by purchase from the previous occupant. The Seigneury of Argenteuil, on the Ottawa river is particularly striking in this regard.[263]

In May 1793 Pierre-Louis Panet granted to the 'negre' Ben a life lease of a plot within his Seigneurial domain. This was the day before Panet sold the Seigneury to Patrick and he would have known Ben and encouraged the lease. In return for his lease Ben was to act as gatekeeper and was to maintain the road running by the property. He also had to pay the Seigneur two bushels of grain or corn per year.

Other early black settlers included a man called Hyacinthe and a Mr Gad Way who had recently arrived from the United States. James Murray granted Way a lot in 9 Prince Edward Street, in St Andrews. This property was 90 feet wide by two arpents (approx. 116 metres) deep. For this lease Way was to pay James one Spanish dollar or five shillings each year. Joseph Freeman from Boston, and bearing a name which hints at his status, bought Lot 10 in November 1804. The lot next to it was leased to Edward Thomson, "an affricain late from Albany (New York)". In both cases the price of the lease was not in money but in labour. Freeman was to clear four or five acres of land and prepare it for seeding and cultivation by the following May and Thomson was to cut down eight acres of wood. In a busy period for leasing later in November, Patrick Murray, acting for absent son James, granted another lot to Benjamin Rorberson (alias Robertson) for an annual payment of one Spanish dollar and three bushels of grain or corn.

A descendant of another black settler, James Robinson, has left a full description of the terms of occupancy facing newcomers to Argenteuil in the early 19th century. By the spring of 1804 James Robinson and his wife Mary were established in the Argenteuil Seigneury where a son, named Jean Baptiste, was born on 28th April. James Murray granted Robinson his land on 21st November 1804. It measured three by thirty acres and had no buildings on it. To keep his land, Robinson had to obey all the seigneurial rules, which were:

· Taking his grain only to the seigneurial mill or facing a heavy fine.
· Living on the land at least one year and one day from date of signing the lease.

- Paying the taxes to the Seigneur, which were one Spanish dollar or five shillings and one bushel of wheat, on November 11th of each year.
- The Seigneur reserved the right of the retreat lignager. This meant that if a tenant wanted to sell his land, the Seigneur had the preference over anyone else to buy it.
- Having his land measured and the boundaries clearly marked by the Land Surveyor.
- Construction material like wood (oak and pine), stones, limestone and sand belonged to the Seigneur. He could use them to build a church, mill, or presbytery, or for his personal needs, without paying for them.
- Respecting the neighbour's decouvert, building good fences and making all the roads that the Seigneur should think proper for public utility. (The decouvert is the rate at which someone clears the trees off his land. It is not allowed to let the trees on your land slow down the growth of your neighbour's crops. You must clear your land at the same pace.).
- Cultivating the land in such a way that the taxes could be easily paid from its products.
- Doing public work as required (like every other tenant of the Seigneury).
- The Seigneur retained the right to take any parts of the tenant's land to build any kind of mill or deviate the river if necessary or desirable. Experts would be appointed to evaluate the damages that were done to his land and he would be compensated for them.

If the Robinson family broke any of these rules, the land could be repossessed by James and would become part of his personal demesne again.[264]

Officially slavery ended in Quebec in 1834, but in practice the numerous free men of African origin in the area demonstrated that it had disappeared very much before that. Some proud residents have long argued that slavery was never part of the Quebec mentality, and although this has little basis in historical evidence, the numerous leases granted to black settlers in Argenteuil gives an indication of the progressive way Quebec and Canada were moving in this very important social issue.

It would be nice to think that the progressive views regarding black settlement were also to be seen with regards to native settlers. Regrettably that does not seem to be the case. Patrick, in his days with the 60th Foot in Georgia and South Carolina, had fought with and led many Native Americans and generally the two groups had worked well together. However, there is no record of any Native American Indian settlers moving to the Seigneury of Argenteuil. Perhaps they did not want to settle under a conditional regime they considered irrelevant to them. Patrick's actions as the chairman of the Land Board of Hesse indicated that he was far from committed to Indian settlement in the area. In a later letter to his Aunt, Lady Cromartie, Patrick seemed rather proud of his Indian Land purchase and suggested that an answer to her financial woes could be to emulate himself in his dealings in Canada. He wrote:

> I conceive… to be entitled to a grant of land not less than 5,000 acres for obtaining for the Government by purchase, for the trifling sum of £1,200 in Indian Goods from the store, a country around Lake Erie and Lake Saint Clair of 3,000 square miles. This if effected may be of service to my daughters.[265]

The first village to develop in Argenteuil was, not surprisingly in view of the strong Scottish links, called St. Andrews. The village, situated on the banks of the North River near its confluence with the Ottawa, enjoyed a pleasant location.[266] The river was navigable for much of the year and as river communication was the most effective method of transport in the early 19th century, it was able to develop a trading function. Its chief claim to fame was that the very first Canadian paper mill was established in the village, and this business, utilising the natural wood resources of the region, ultimately became one of the leading industries of Canada itself. The paper mill was started in 1803 by two New Englanders, Walter Ware and Benjamin Wales, with the intention of manufacturing writing, printing and wrapping papers. They obtained a 30 year lease from James Murray for the necessary water power and use of other utilities. The owner of the land was Mr James Brown, a Lowland Scot who had moved to St. Andrews from nearby Montréal. To aid the mill, a dam was built across the river and a canal was dug to provide water power. As a large quantity of timber would be required for the erection of the paper mill itself, a saw mill was built at the head of the canal. As a result the paper mill had sufficient water power to drive the machinery required.[267] For many years the mills and their accompanying industries provided the leading employment for many of the local men and inspired others in Canada to develop similar enterprises. Patrick Murray apparently took an active interest in the development of the area and an early account relates that:

> so little did the first settlers know of the geography of the country, or understand the way of economising space, that for a long time they conveyed grain up the Ottawa River, thence by boat to the North River, and up to the village and mill. Major Murray, the Seigneur, happening at this time to visit the settlement and learning this custom, pointed out to them the amount of toil they were needlessly expending; and then, showing a map of the Seigneury, convinced them that, in a direct course, a road through the woods to the mill would be much more direct.[268]

As a result a new road was opened and Seigneur Murray got all the credit. That was the brief upside. The downside came with the reality of Seigneury ownership, which proved to be less financially attractive than it had first seemed.

A glance at some of the aforementioned lease arrangements show that the annual rent would produce only a modest sum of money. Profit-making in Argenteuil would only be forthcoming over a very long time period, and this was something that James Murray didn't have. As a result, the Murrays were constantly in financial difficulty, and by 1806 Eliza, tired of the stress and strain of running the seigneury in the absence of James, determined to return to New Providence, Bahamas. She began to sort out her affairs and they proved to be challenging. These affairs, complicated enough, were compounded by a number of debts, most accruing from Patrick Murray, who still owed large sums, including £1,200 to Sir John Johnson.

Firstly Eliza drew up her will. Her estates in the Bahamas had still not been sold and so these she left to her children, although whether natural or adopted is not known:

> Share and share alike between the said John G. King, Podmore Smith, Theresa Lucy Smith, Harriet Smith & Louisa Grierson...
> all children of her, the said Eliza Smith her residuary heirs forever.[269]

Notable by his absence from this list of children is James Murray. In fact, he was singled out in the will to receive the modest sum of 25 pounds. This may appear to be an insulting sum to her eldest son, but more likely represents the fact that Eliza had already put very significant funds into James' business deals in order to expedite his purchase of the Seigneury of Argenteuil.

In further transactions on the same day, Eliza, holding a mortgage based upon the estate and Seigneury of Argenteuil, passed on the powers of attorney to her attorney, James Reid, for the debts still accruing.[270] She also entered into an agreement with Sir John Johnson in which she took over the responsibility of Patrick Murray's outstanding debt to Sir John for £1,200.[271] This is the last mention of James Murray's mother in Canada and, as she promised, she left the colony shortly afterwards and returned to New Providence.

Eliza Smith was a complex character. She married at a young age and her husband was taken away all too soon, but at least she inherited a substantial fortune, making her a desirable catch, especially for Patrick Murray. He was a dashing officer, well respected by his contemporaries and colleagues and capable of turning an impressionable young lady's head but Patrick, denied the Elibank inheritance as a result of his illegitimacy, showed little foresight and acumen in his business dealings. Eliza proved to be remarkably loyal to him, moving with him from Florida to Georgia, back to Florida and, after a period of several years, to Canada. Her physical relationship with Patrick did not survive long but she was there to support him and their son many years later. Without her financial assistance the Murrays would not have been able to purchase and keep hold of the Seigneury of Argenteuil as long as they did. She was able to move back to the Bahamas still a wealthy woman, and in a day when women took on very little commercial responsibilities this suggests that she was a strong and capable character. However, her puzzling personal life suggests otherwise. After becoming a widow she may have had at least four further partners and at least six children, yet she never re-married. It seems that this strong woman would not easily lose her individuality and her wealth through a marriage settlement. Her status in life and the respect she seemed to enjoy indicate that these children were not all illegitimate and, apart from James, may have been adopted. In the rigid and conservative environment she moved in, the correct social mores, so well depicted in the novels of Jane Austen, suggest that she would have been the subject of, at best, malicious gossip and, at worst, exclusion from 'polite' society.[272] There is no evidence that this was Eliza's lot in life. Nevertheless her relationship with her family was fraught. Her three daughters were with her when she left Florida for the Bahamas but within a few years they were in New Abbey, Scotland, almost certainly living distant from their mother for long periods of time. Eliza did not forget them completely and they were left equal shares of her property in her will, as was Podmore Smith and George King, children that she had acquired in the Bahamas. What is not open to doubt is the mutual love and respect between her and her eldest son, James. James expressed his esteem for his mother in his later letters to his wife Rachel, and Eliza clearly gave enormous support to James, especially in his business and land dealings.

Alas, the support was not enough and as debt continued to mount up, the land hungry Sir John Johnson began the process of acquiring the Seigneury. As early as March 1807 the seigneury was seized by the sheriff by virtue of a writ of execution at the suit of Sir John Johnson against the lands and tenements of Patrick Murray, James Murray and Elizabeth Smith, and a notice of sale of the Seigneury was placed in the local newspaper.[273] It was not a complete sale as Patrick, acting for James, was involved in at least two further sales and land concessions in the Seigneury after this date.[274] However, by March 1810 Sir John is clearly designated as owner of the Seigneury[275] and although the exact date of transfer is uncertain,[276] James' career as a Canadian estate owner was over.

14

Hero: San Domingo and Dominica

J ames, despite his foray into land ownership, had made it clear by passing on powers of attorney to his mother and father that his first priority was to further his naval career, and to do that he now needed to broaden his experience. He had been lucky in gaining his initial experience on board an active frigate, the ship most likely to gain prizes and increase personal wealth. The ships of the line were larger and more powerful than the frigates but were also too expensive and sometimes too unwieldy to do chase duties after smaller ships. Consequently, they were mainly occupied in blockade duties with the aim of keeping hostile navies in port so that they could not do mischief to British shipping. Overall this blockage policy was very successful and consequently major naval engagements involving the mighty ships of the line were rare. Regrettably, this led to service on the ships becoming very tedious and could frustrate a young and ambitious junior officer, keen to demonstrate his mettle in action. The small brigs and sloops, excellent ships in themselves, were too small to challenge most 'Men-O'-War' and had to content themselves with carrying and coordinating duties. But all the ships required different skill sets which, to be a successful officer, needed honing to a high degree. So James had to look for new experiences.

He found them in a couple of temporary transfers, firstly to the Ruby, a 64 gun ship of the line. He served for only a month, all on shore duties,[277] before he moved on to the Hyena, a small 28 gun frigate which had once been a civilian transport and was soon to become an RN store ship. This convenience posting took him over the Atlantic back to the Leeward Islands station in the Caribbean and, as the fateful year of 1805 dawned, he joined the Centaur, a 74 gun ship of the line. He was only on the Centaur until April of that year but it was four months that James was not going to forget.

On the 22nd February 1805, the island of Dominica was attacked by a combined French naval and land force of some strength, consisting of 10 ships of the line and almost 5,000 troops. The French force, flying the British flag, sailed from Martinique and arrived off the town of Roseau in South-West Dominica. Keenly watching on shore was Brigadier-General George Prevost, the son of Augustine Prevost, commander of the 60th foot during the American Georgia campaign twenty years previously. George Prevost, who as a junior officer had fought alongside Patrick Murray in the later stages of that campaign, was now The British Commander-in-Chief of the Forces in Dominica. He had experience on his side, but still managed to completely fall for the French ruse with the British flag, and sent the Captain of Fort Young to conduct the supposed British Admiral and his fleet to a safe anchorage. He was rowed right alongside the Majesteuse, the huge French flagship of 120 guns, before he realised his mistake. Immediately afterwards the French fleet lowered the British colours, hoisted the French ones and disembarked its invasion boats, now packed with French troops. They pushed off for the shore and at once began an attack on the fort and town of Roseau. With the Majesteuse and the other seventy-fours and frigates pouring broadside after broadside into Fort Young, the enemy assaulted time and again, but each time they were repulsed. The enemy broadsides had done little damage to either the fort or the town but the luckless inhabitants of Roseau had not bargained for the friendly fire from their own fort. The cannon fire from the British positions in Fort Young led to flames drifting with the wind onto the town, and the whole place was burned to the ground. The remaining British troops then decided to retreat to a safer haven, the garrison at Fort Shirley, by Prince Rupert's Bay in the north west of the island. The French pursued and four days later there was a stand-off at the fort. George Prevost was offered terms for surrender but he refused. The General then made preparations for a long siege by ordering cattle to be driven into the fort and obtaining stores of water from the river and the bay.[278] Over the next few days the French forces, keen to take the fort before the Royal Navy could retaliate, embarked on a vigorous siege of the defenders.

As news slowly filtered through of the invasion, the Royal Navy began to respond. HMS Centaur was one of the first to arrive on the scene and midshipman James Murray was keen to impress. In his own words:

> I, of all the officers under Sir James[279] Hood volunteered to carry... succour to Sir G. Prevost when blockaded by (the French) squadron at Prince Rupert's, Dominica (and) succeeded beyond his expectation. He chose, before all his staff, to term me 'the gallant son of a dear father, who he was pleased to call his friend'.[280]

It seems that the siege was lifted by the young midshipman. Sir George Prevost in his official letter commented:

> On the 27th the enemy's cruisers hovered about the Head; however, the Centaur's tender, Vigilante, came in and was saved by our guns. I landed Mr Henderson, her commander, and crew, to assist in the defence we were prepared to make.[281]

It is not clear whether the Mr Henderson referred to in the above letter was the commander of the tender or was accompanying the Commander and his crew, but it seems likely that this is the incident described by James Murray. Whether or not James was the commander of the tender he would have been present in making this dangerous dash for the shore through the heart of a very strong French squadron.

This action helped to dishearten the French invaders, who saw that the fort was still secure and the Royal Navy was likely to arrive in numbers at any time. A day later the French fleet embarked its soldiers and withdrew from Dominica. They were never to return and the British colony was finally safe. The French had lost over 300 of its men and several officers of rank in their forlorn assault. British losses were described as trifling.

This was the Centaur's last campaign in the West Indies and she made preparations to return to the European theatre. James, now a senior midshipman and valued as an officer with promise, was needed for other things, so he remained in the West Indies and the Centaur sailed without him.

Maybe it was just as well. The Elibank luck was once again to help one of its sons. The Centaur, on its way across the Atlantic in a very heavy sea, ran straight into hurricane force winds. The real worry of a strong wind when combined with a high sea is that the vessel will broach. If the bow of the ship is not kept pointed into the waves, they can push the bow aside, thus turning the boat side-on. Since a sailing ship cannot steer unless the sails are providing forward motion, all control will disappear and effectively the ship will be lost and will often capsize.

The horrific Atlantic storm, with its gigantic waves and driving rain, soon destroyed the Centaur's masts and sails and threw them overboard. It carried away her rudder and smashed all her boats into firewood-sized pieces. Any escape would now be out of the question should the ship capsize. Fortunately it didn't, but it began to leak very badly, partly as a result of damage caused when the Centaur had run aground a few weeks earlier. The crew vigorously laboured at her pumps and for sixteen hours it was touch and go whether the amount of water coming in to the colander-like ship would overwhelm the heroic efforts of the men at the pumps, and sink the ship. Things momentarily got even worse on the second day of the storm when a colossal wave brought the vast first-rate ship, the St. George, to within centimetres of crashing into the Centaur. Fortuitously, after that the winds gradually lessened, the seas became a little calmer, and the crew were able to get a sail under and around the hull of the ill-starred ship. This did just enough to reduce the leaks. The danger wasn't completely over yet as the Centaur was now much weakened by her battering and so the crew were forced to throw most of the heavy guns and all the disposable stores overboard. She still had no masts or steerage but fortunately HMS Eagle, a 74 gun third-rate ship, was on hand and was able to tow her into Halifax on the Newfoundland station. During the repairs at Halifax, it was discovered that it was not only the storm that almost caused the loss of the ship and all her hands. It was reported that:

> 14 feet of false keel was found off from the fore-foot aft, which occasioned the leak.[282]

Sailors at that time were notoriously superstitious and the Centaur now was not considered the luckiest of vessels. This was not altogether surprising, because amazingly a very similar incident had occurred to the last ship called HMS Centaur. As this was only 23 years previously, it was still in the living memory of some of her crew.

None of the current Centaur crew had first-hand experience of the earlier disaster because virtually no-one survived. The

Central Atlantic Hurricane (as it became known) of September 1782 was one of the worst disasters ever to befall the Royal Navy, when it descended upon the fleet of Admiral Thomas Graves sailing across the North Atlantic, and led to the death of over 3,500 seamen.

This early Centaur was a 74-gun ship of the line, originally belonging to the French Navy, but captured by the British at the Battle of Lagos in 1759. It had a useful if undistinguished career in the Royal Navy until its capabilities were tested against the overwhelming forces of nature in the 1782 hurricane. As the ships neared the Newfoundland Banks, the winds reached over 150 miles per hour, accompanied by 50 foot waves, and the Centaur was thrown upon her beam ends. The ferocious winds and driving rain took away her masts and her rudder and inevitably she eventually foundered, despite the most strenuous efforts of the crew over several days. The Captain, John Nicholson Inglefield, along with eleven of his crew, managed to reach one of the ship's boats, which remarkably had not been battered to pieces, and using sailors' ingenuity they managed to devise a makeshift sail. It was largely ineffective so it was astonishing that sixteen days later the open boat arrived at the Azores, having sailed almost across the Atlantic without a compass or a quadrant. The twelve men subsisted on a few bottles of French cordials, some wet bread, a small amount of ship's biscuit and rainwater wrung out into a bailing cup. All but one of the 12 survived[283] but over 500 of their shipmates were less lucky, perishing in the Centaur when she finally sank beneath the waves.[284]

James Murray's Centaur had more luck and fully recovered from her ordeal. She went on to an illustrious later career and was involved in several desperate sea battles and storms, surviving them all. She was finally broken up in 1819, her Jonah tag well forgotten.

Whilst the hurricane raged in the Mid-Atlantic, James was

getting to know his new shipmates on HMS Northumberland, a 74-gun third-rate ship of the line.

A lot had happened since James had sailed off on the Topaze back in 1796. Britain had come perilously close to being invaded in 1797, but a series of spectacular Royal Navy victories had secured its border. The mercurial Admiral Lord Nelson had become a national hero in his naval encounters with the French fleet, but when in 1802 Britain reached peace terms with France at the Peace of Amiens, it seemed that the wars were finally over. The Royal Navy then began a massive demobilisation and many of James' fellow young officers were left without ships to serve on. Fortunately, James was not of that number and his career service remained unbroken. It was just as well because the peace lasted barely a year and by April 1803 war had broken out once more and most of the British fleet was vigilantly patrolling home waters, ensuring that the invasion force of Napoleon Bonaparte would never land on the shores of Britain.

The morale and confidence of the Royal Navy had never been higher following the string of victories against the fleets of the European powers and the British naval policy was now twofold, concentrating upon blocking merchant ships who were attempting to enter the ports of France and Spain, whilst at the same time blockading these ports to keep their huge war fleets away from the open sea. It was a very successful policy until finally Admiral Villeneuve, under pressure from Napoleon, broke out of the port of Cadiz and was brought to battle by an outnumbered Admiral Nelson and his twenty seven ships of the line. The ensuing Battle of Trafalgar was an emphatic and outstanding victory for Nelson, marred only by his own death on board HMS Victory. The outcome was a severe blow to the fleets of Spain and France, but perhaps led to a slight overconfidence by the British government in believing that the naval forces of France were unable to threaten Britain again. The guard was lowered and there was an ill-advised relaxation of the blockade. The breakout from Brest of a significant French squadron, led by the 118-gun Impérial, soon emphasised the inadvisability of that relaxation but Vice Admiral Duckworth and his fleet were on hand and immediately set off in pursuit.[285]

Admiral John Duckworth had been present at some of the great naval battles in the wars against France and Napoleon. He had served as captain of HMS Orion, a 74-gun ship of the line, and led the ship during Admiral Lord Howe's stunning victory at the 'Glorious First of June' of 1794. By 1798, and now a Commodore, he commanded the squadron that supported the capture of Minorca in November, and as a result gained promotion to Rear Admiral. Appointed Commander-in-Chief at Barbados and Leeward Islands in early 1800, he almost immediately captured a large Spanish convoy, gaining a small personal fortune as his share of the prize money. In early 1801 he seized the islands of St. Bartholomew, St. Martin, St. Thomas, St. John, and St. Croix from the French colonial occupiers and gained himself a knighthood in the Order of Bath for his troubles. By 1804 he was a Vice Admiral. His next tour should have been to join Admiral Nelson's fleet, but his presence at the Battle of Trafalgar was not to occur, through no fault of his own. As a result of a major shipyard issue his ship refit was not completed in time and was not ready for action. He finally put to sea in HMS Superb, leading a force of seven ships of the line, but having missed the Battle of Trafalgar, he was then ordered to oversee the blockade of Cadiz.

When he received intelligence of the French squadron which had broken out of Brest and was now operating against British convoys, he abandoned the Cadiz blockade and rushed off in search. By 5th February 1806, and after what had seemed to be a wild goose chase, Duckworth, by now off San Domingo in the West Indies, finally spotted the French squadron. His squadron was a bit stronger too, having been joined by two ships of the line under Rear Admiral Alexander Cochrane.[286] One of the ships was HMS Northumberland, a relatively new 74-gun ship. Amongst its crew was midshipman James Murray; having left the Centaur he was now with new shipmates on the powerful Northumberland, and was eagerly awaiting his orders.

Lookouts, usually midshipmen, were sent aloft at daybreak to scan the horizon and continued to perform the same function throughout the day.[287] On the morning of 6th February 1806, the lookout on the foretop mast of HMS Magicienne excitedly informed his Captain that five French ships of the line and two frigates were anchored in a line at the entrance to San Domingo harbour. Signals were hastily sent to Admiral Duckworth on the Superb and he, not losing a moment, ordered the squadron to bear down and engage the enemy.

The French admiral, Leissègues, alerted to the British approach, rushed to re-board his flagship Impérial and immediately got the French squadron under way. Duckworth, now close to the French ships, divided his force into two divisions, one to windward, which consisted of his flagship Superb (74 guns), Northumberland, Spencer (74 guns), and Agamemnon (64 guns), and the other one to leeward, led by Rear Admiral Thomas Louis, which included Canopus (80 guns), Donegal (74 guns), and Atlas. On board the Northumberland there was frantic activity. The order to clear for action had already been given and the crews took up their stations by their guns.

It was a frantic and dangerous time for James as he prepared to face his sternest test yet in his short naval career. It is not recorded just what his duties were, but he may have been in charge of some of the gun crews, and competition between the young officers on who could achieve the fastest rate of fire[288] was intense. He may have had a role on deck, acting as an aide to the Captain, with the added spice of needing to dodge enemy grapeshot to deliver orders to the relevant personnel. He may even have been aloft, tasked to ensure that the men reacted quickly and efficiently to orders from their officers below.

As the British ships closed on the French squadron, the leeward group began to fall behind. Superb was the first ship to open fire, on the leading French ship, the Alexandre, and this was closely followed by James' Northumberland engaging the much larger French flagship, the Impérial. Northumberland was aided by HMS Spencer, but a series of dramatic manoeuvres allowed the Imperial to focus its fire on the Northumberland and the Superb. The Northumberland returned fire, broadside after broadside. The Northumberland Captain's Log graphically recorded the heat of action:

> At 1010 the enemy hoisted French colours and the ships began to engage. By 1115 two French ships had struck their colours. The Northumberland, in close action with the French three decker (the Impérial), was much cut up. At 1123 another French ship struck and at 1146 the Northumberland ceased firing, being totally disabled in masts and rigging. At midday the main mast, being shot through in several places, fell forward onto the booms. It broke all the boats to pieces and carried away three or four mid-beams. The other masts were much wounded and the rigging and all the sails were cut to pieces. All hands were employed in clearing the wreck and repairing the rig.[289]

The Northumberland was not alone in attacking the Impérial and soon a melee of other ships were engaged in this intense battle. Several ships focused on the French three-decker and succeeded in toppling its main and mizzen masts. The French ship, now crippled, steered for shore, but the British Canopus continued to press the attack. Approximately ten minutes later, the Impérial ran aground, and was soon followed onto the reef by its companion, the Diomède. The battle was effectively over.

The fierce two-hour battle was a complete victory for the Royal Navy, but not without cost. The British suffered the loss of 74 men and the wounding of 264 and on James' ship, the heavily damaged and dismasted Northumberland, 21 men were killed and 74 men wounded, the highest casualties of any British ship in the battle. For the French, the battle had been a complete disaster and resulted in the loss of all five ships of the line, with over 1,500 casualties.

The Battle of San Domingo, now virtually forgotten in the aftermath of the exploits at Trafalgar, helped to remove the remaining threats to British shipping in the Atlantic and the significance of the victory was understood and widely celebrated at home.[290] It proved to be a celebration day for James too, and for his excellent service he achieved promotion. His lieutenant examination states that:

> He possessed diligence, sobriety and obedience in command. He could splice, knot, reef, sail, keep a reckoning of a ship's way by plain sailing and Mercator, observe by the sun and stars, find the variation of the compass and is qualified to do his duty as an able seaman and midshipman.[291]

He could now put his hard-acquired skills to the test in his new capacity as a Royal Navy lieutenant and as a commander of his very own ship, HMS Ballahoo. He had served his time as a rating below decks and on the quarterdeck as an under-officer. He had been involved in many individual and fleet actions and, having come through all the hoops and ladders put in his way, he had emerged with flying colours. Providing that the politicians didn't spoil things by making peace he was all set for a long and distinguished naval career.

15

You'll laugh when it's all over

James would have reflected that in his first command he was walking in 'a dead man's shoes', as the previous captain, Lieutenant H.N. Bowen, had been killed in 1806, but that was just the way it worked in the navy. His ship, HMS Ballahoo launched in 1804, was the first of a new class of Royal Navy schooner and was built in the renowned shipyards of Bermuda. These schooners were originally intended as despatch boats, chosen for their speed and windward ability, but were used for a myriad of other naval tasks. Ballahoo was a small but very fast vessel that carried a crew of 20 and packed a hefty punch, with its four 12-pounder carronades. It was flattering to James that in his first command he had been entrusted with a ship that needed expert handling to get the speed required. On the other hand, the Ballahoo class was quickly acquiring an untoward reputation. They were to attain a high rate of loss, primarily to wrecking or foundering, but also to enemy action. As despatch boats they served a useful purpose, but it was reported that they were also "sent to 'take, burn, and destroy' the vessels of war and merchantmen of the enemy", and in this they were notably unsuccessful.[292] The same source noted that:

> Their very appearance as 'men of war' raised a laugh at the expense of the projector. Many officers refused to take the command of them... Moreover, when sent forth to cruise against the enemies of England... these 'king's schooners' were found to

sail wretchedly, and proved so cranky and unseaworthy, that almost every one of them that escaped capture went to the bottom with the unfortunate men on board.[293]

Ballahoo was based around the Leeward Islands and was tasked to patrol the surrounding seas, enabling James to continue his service in the Caribbean, an area about which he was now developing considerable expertise. The Ballahoo went some way towards dispelling the poor reputation that her class of ship had acquired. She enjoyed considerable success in keeping the waters around the Leeward Islands free from pirates and Frenchmen, whilst at the same time gaining James and his crew a fair amount of welcome prize money. In February 1807, the sloop Port d'Espagne and the brig Express captured two foreign brigs and, luckily, Ballahoo, sailing in the vicinity but not part of the fight, acquired a share of the prize money. On 4th August 1807 Ballahoo, accompanied by the schooner Laura, of 10 guns, was this time in the midst of the engagement. Patrolling off Tobago the two ships encountered the Rhone, a French privateer. They gave chase and after a running fight of several hours, and several broadsides, they captured her. The Rhone had severe casualties, with two dead and five wounded out of her crew of 26, but the British had no casualties.

Only two weeks later Ballahoo's boats destroyed a small privateer in the Bay of San Juan and, showing that things come in threes, the Ballahoo, in early September, assisted HMS Port d'Espagne in capturing another small privateer, the Rosario, in the same bay; not too bad a record for a class of ship enjoying such poor standing. James was able to move on from the Ballahoo almost immediately after the capture of the Rosario with his good reputation still intact.

He was then employed in supervising the fitting-out of a recently captured French vessel now entering the service of the Royal Navy. This ship, the Unique, of 12 guns, had a chequered past. Captains in naval engagements would often avoid the use of full broadsides if possible as the main aim was to capture a ship and thus gain prize money so consequently, the ships often swapped sides. This led to busy careers for the sign writers who were kept permanently occupied by the need to replace English signs with French ones, only to change them over again a few months later. The Unique illustrates this point well. The Unique was originally HMS Netley, which was captured by the French in 1806. It was then used as a 21-gun privateer called the Duquesne. In early 1807 HMS Blonde captured Duquesne, and this, renamed HMS Unique, became the ship James Murray eventually commanded, taking over in November 1807. It was to be captured by the French once more, but after James Murray's period of command.

James made an inauspicious start with his new ship and his new crew. He joined it at anchor in Barbados and after a couple of days gathering stores the Unique prepared to set off in convoy for Antigua. A Captain of a Man-of-War faces a myriad of problems to solve and challenges to meet and almost immediately James faced his first one on his new ship. As they prepared to sail away his crew ran into difficulties in weighing the anchor.[294]

Anchors are immensely heavy in order to be effective in their task of anchoring the ship by digging into the sea bed. The anchor is hauled up from the sea bed by its cable and this cable, extremely thick, heavy and wet, is tied to a smaller but very strong rope which is looped around a circular drum on deck, the capstan. Capstan bars, about three metres long were inserted into the Capstan and the crew would put their weight against the bars and walk round, sometimes to music or a chant. This would wind in the rope and lift the anchor cable. When the anchor had cleared the water the final process was to haul it up and secure it to the side of the ship, and it was this procedure that caused the problem. Captain Murray just did not have enough able bodied men to complete the action. Plenty of panicking, shouting and swearing did little to help the process and even when help, in the form of more men, arrived from a nearby ship it was not enough. A swinging anchor, if it fell on another ship, could go right through the deck and cause huge damage and James certainly didn't want to lose a whole ship. Reluctantly, with a very red face, he made the decision to let the anchor fall, and there it still sits on the sea-bottom of Bridgetown Harbour. It was certainly the right decision, but the whole episode would have led to elements of derision from the other commanders and would not have helped James' reputation with his new shipmates.

At least he was underway. His task was to patrol the Caribbean Islands, taking a route which, for a modern cruise ship, would sound delightful, but was less luxurious and infinitely more dangerous for a Royal Navy brig at war with two of the leading European powers, France and Spain. From Barbados the route was northerly via St. Lucia, past the French controlled Martinique and Guadeloupe and on towards Antigua and the Virgin Islands.[295]

His success would depend very much on his decisions and the skill of his crew to carry them out. The Unique had a crew of 68 men plus four boys and seven marines. Most of these came from the British Isles (26 from England, 20 from Scotland, 16 from Ireland and four from Wales), but four of the crew came from the West Indies and also present were an American and a Canadian. Completing the multinational complement were two men from Europe (one from Sweden and one from Venice). Apart from the ship's boys, the youngest crew member was 17-year-old James Hogg from Ireland and the oldest was, amazingly, 74-year-old James MacDonald from Scotland. However, the vast majority of the crew were between 20 and 39 years of age.[296]

In the close confines of a 'Man O' War', far more terrifying than enemy action was the threat of disease. Large numbers of men accommodated in cramped and damp conditions, often with poor nutrition and polluted water, provided a fertile breeding ground for disease, and its spread could be rapid. In 1810, at the height of the Napoleonic Wars, 50 per cent of deaths in the Royal Navy were a result of disease compared to eight per cent from enemy action.[297]

In early February 1808 the dread of disease became a reality on board the Unique. As an outbreak of fever swept through the ship frantic efforts were made to isolate the victims and limit any further spread of the disease. The tactic had limited success and the outbreak was controlled, but this didn't help Able Seaman Hanlow. On the 6th February, James Hanlow, after three days of despair, finally succumbed to the fever and died. Following the long-standing naval tradition, he was sown into a sailcloth weighted with a cannonball and, with Lieutenant James Murray conducting a full burial ceremony, the hapless Able Seaman Hanlow silently slid over the side into the blue Caribbean waters.[298]

Health and disease were always a concern to those serving in the West Indies. The Atlantic slave trade had introduced an influx of diseases, especially malaria and yellow fever, from Africa to the Caribbean. Both malaria and yellow fever were spread by mosquitoes and these were plentiful in the many low lying swampy islands of the West Indies. Exposure to these diseases could be almost assured and very many succumbed. To this horror add typhoid and typhus, so common in the overcrowded living conditions endured by soldiers and sailors at that time. In short, the outlook was not very optimistic and service in the West Indies could often be a death sentence. In 1796 it has been suggested that 41 per cent of European soldiers serving in this arena died within a year of their arrival. From 1793 to 1802 an estimated 1,500 officers and 43,500 other ranks died from fevers whilst stationed in the Caribbean, far more than were killed in action.[299]

Just over a week after Able Hanlow's untimely death the ship was to suffer another loss, this time to enemy action. On Sunday 6th March the lookout reported a sighting of two launches. Unique gave chase and they proved to be two Spanish ships heading for Porto Santo. The two launches landed on the shore and James sent one of the ship's boats after them, under the command of his first Lieutenant, Robert Hutchison. It was a trap. On nearing the beach the British boat came under direct heavy fire from the Spaniards on shore. Almost immediately three men were wounded, one of them mortally, and he died in two hours. The men of Unique did not give up the fight lightly and there was fierce hand-to-hand combat, which led to the reported loss of a cutlass and two muskets. James later testified that he had used eight full cartons containing boxes of ball cartridge; a testimony to the fierceness of the encounter.[300]

The combined fleets and armies of the antagonists provided a substantial challenge to Great Britain during this period but an additional challenge was to be heaped onto the broad shoulders of the Royal Navy. In 1807 the slave trade was abolished, not only for the British overseas colonies but also for the United States. To police the world's oceans whilst conducting a full scale war was too much, even for the mighty Royal Navy, but there were some successes. In 1808 the first British anti-slavery patrol, made up of the frigate Solebay and the sloop Derwent, was stationed on the West African coast. Despite this it was inevitable that some of the determined slave ships would still manage to get though their cordon. In March 1808 one of the escapees was caught by HMS Melville and the slaves were moved onto the Royal Navy ship. Unfortunately conditions aboard the Melville were little better than most slave ships. When the Melville encountered HMS Unique it prompted James to write in his log:

> The schooner, being short of provisions and water was unfit to keep company.[301]

HMS Melville was a captured French brig, the Naiad, but by 1808 she had deteriorated and was in very poor condition. The 89 slaves rescued by the Melville were transferred onto the Unique and the Melville was left under the care of James' former ship, HMS Ballahoo. Shortly after the slave incident HMS Melville returned to British waters and was, not surprisingly, sold out of the Royal Navy. At least her last cargo was not destined to suffer the same fate.

Almost as soon as the Unique gathered way it was hit by foul weather and it seemed that lady luck had deserted the ship, just as it had deserted the slaves so many times before. The slaves, morale at rock bottom, had their spirits raised by rescue, dashed by the condition of the Melville, hopes raised once more by their move on board the Unique, but they now feared that all was in vain, this time by drowning or at best shipwreck. The strong current and heavy swell certainly made life difficult for the Unique, but it skilfully rode the storm. All was going as well as could be expected until James, nearing land, sent a boat onshore. Alas, the heavy swell meant that it never reached its destination. She overturned and threw the desperate crew into the waters of the bay. In the midst of a forlorn and hopeless rescue attempt by the Ballahoo, the Melville and two captured Spanish vessels, John Mullins, ordinary seaman, was drowned and thus had the ill-fated distinction of becoming the third member of James' crew to lose his life since the beginning of the cruise.[302]

With sadness the small convoy set off for Port of Spain in Trinidad. They arrived on 2nd April and the slaves were transferred to the port authorities. The Unique now took time to resupply and give her crew some rest and recreation, but it all proved a bit too much for seamen Henderson and McNeill. They enjoyed their time ashore rather more than the officers had intended and on the 16th April, just the day before the ship weighed anchor to resume her cruise, the two ran off and deserted. Just over a month later, as the ship docked in a small port on the northern coast of South America, William Hodge and James Green also, to use the naval expression, 'ran'. Five days later another three men, Bryden Smith, Alasdair Kelly and James Aldston, deserted too.[303] This had now become a major headache for James as he had lost seven men out of a total crew of only 50. It took a long time to train a seaman and to replace them, particularly during active service, was very difficult. He could not afford to lose any more men.

In reality, desertion was not an uncommon phenomenon in the Royal Navy at that time, even though the 'Articles of War', the rules under which the Navy operated, clearly stated that:

> every person in or belonging to the fleet, who shall desert or entice others so to do, shall suffer death, or such other punishment as the circumstances of the offense shall deserve, and a court martial shall judge fit.[304]

It has been estimated that during the period of the French and Napoleonic Wars desertion rates actually fell slightly, but prior to the war they had been running at almost 25 per cent. Admiral Nelson in 1803 noted that, since 1793, more than 42,000 sailors had deserted. The much maligned impressment method of recruiting was often blamed, on the assumption that many men were on board ship unwillingly. In fact, desertion rates varied little between volunteers and pressed men. At the beginning of a cruise they would be high, and then fall significantly after a few months. After a year of service the desertion rate was almost zero. It didn't help the prospective deserter that his navy pay often ran months or years in arrears and desertion would mean the loss of a large amount of pay and possibly prize money too.

Even though it may have had little impact on the desertion rate, the impressment method of recruitment to the Royal Navy was a controversial topic. The central issue was that the American

Revolutionary Wars and then the Napoleonic Wars required a huge influx of manpower to service a burgeoning fleet. Estimates suggest that the Royal Navy had around 12,850 men in 1775. By the end of the American Revolutionary Wars this had risen by over five times to 67,700 men. At the time of the Battle of Trafalgar in 1805 the Royal Navy had almost doubled again to 120,000 sailors, of which half were pressed men.[305] To put this total in perspective, the total population of Great Britain in 1801 was 10.5 million. The population today is over 60 million, so that if the UK was to have a modern navy of equivalent manpower to that of the Napoleonic era it would require over 600,000 men.

To obtain such a huge level of manpower often required drastic measures, and there was little more drastic in popular imagination than the press-gang. The impressment system meant that, by law, a press-gang could only take men between the ages of 18 and 55 who also had experience of seafaring and / or river craft. When appropriate, a warship would form temporary press-gangs from members of their crew under the command of an officer. Those recruited were usually merchant sailors or British sailors working on foreign boats. On land the Impressment Service was tasked with recruiting men from all over Britain. Most naval officers did not want a ship full of recalcitrant landsmen and so, in reality, impressment tended to focus on those who had maritime experience. Unhappily this was not always the case and even if it was, any rumours of a press-gang in the vicinity would cause panic and unrest amongst the young men of the locality. Because of the difficulties of long-distance communication, men taken by the press-gang effectively disappeared and a family might not know their man had been pressed until he returned, sometimes years later. Even for families aware of what had happened there was no system of finding out how long a man might serve, on board what ship, and where. Furthermore, the loss of the main income in a family could often cause severe hardship and consequently many families were left destitute.[306]

The Impressment Service covered every port in Great Britain. On British soil it was rarely sailors who made up the impress team so the senior officer involved would often hire some of the local hard men to form his press-gang. The gang was then sent out in search of suitable recruits and was paid according to the number of men it pressed into service. They often supplemented their income by a bit of corruption and many men would happily pay out a discreet bribe to the press-gang rather than be taken away.

Both the press-gang and their potential victims had to resort to subtle methods to achieve their ends. Avoidance of the approaching gang was a practised art form and so flamboyant action by the searching gang, as so often depicted in fiction, such as charging around the bars and pubs of a town with flaming torches in hand, were unlikely to pick up many men:[307]

> We had intimation of a lot of seamen hid in a small public house, and after a scrimmage secured some very prime hands; such a scene; a wake was got up, women howling over a coffin where a corpse was said to be, but our lieutenant would not believe them and sure enough out popped a seaman, who laughed himself when all was over.[308]

The gang didn't always get it their own way and running battles were frequently fought between the press-gang and locals, often trying to retrieve a man who had been captured by the gang:

> One evening... a sailor was seized by the press gang and whilst they were dragging him along he slipped his arms out of his jacket and ran away hotly pursued by the gang

Some local workmen saw the rumpus and rushed off in support of the captured sailor. Soon a sizeable mob had formed. They managed to liberate the sailor but, still very dissatisfied, they continued to pursue the gang. The huge mob soon surrounded the house where the press-gang were sheltering and, despite the 'riot act' being read out to them, they went on to completely wreck the building in the hope of turning the tables on the press-gang members.[309]

Although 50% of Nelson's Navy was made up of pressed sailors it is perhaps ignored that this means that 50% of the crews were not, and hence were volunteers. There was no difficulty in recruiting officers, as the service was regarded as a means of social advancement. Many officers could rise to a higher level in social circles and, in addition, had the possibility of making their fortune from prize-money awarded for the ships they may have captured. On board, the higher-ranking officers ate well most of the time and had their own servants and often their own cooks.

In fact the sailors often didn't do too badly either. Conditions aboard were certainly very cramped, private life didn't exist and punishments could be arbitrary and excessive. Not very tempting to a potential recruit, but it had to be compared to the conditions that he could reasonably expect should he stay on land. Poverty was still widespread, food was often in short supply and punishment for wrongdoers was every bit as brutal as on the high seas.

Maybe the sea was not so bad after all. A volunteer was relatively secure, surrounded by colleagues and friends, ate regularly and usually got paid. He could even gain a bounty, and many men caught by the press gang decided to change their status to volunteer in order to get their bounty and advance pay rather than stay as pressed men and get nothing.[310] Volunteers made up the backbone of the navy. 'Better one volunteer than three pressed men,' was an expression used widely at the time and an expression which has persisted into more recent times; probably last used in reference to the more modern equivalent of impressment – that of conscription.

The shortage of crew and the need for stores led James to head towards St. Lucia and then on to Carlisle Bay, Barbados, which they reached on 30th April 1808. Bridgetown in Barbados housed the largest garrison of all the British overseas colonies and had extensive supplies of all the very necessary stores. It also held the garrison hospital and James made good use of that for his men. The Unique remained in Barbados until 12th May and during that time John Davy, Robert Hallo, James Stewart and William Lean all attended the hospital, although the reasons for the visits are not known. There were no reports of any additional crew members joining the ship, so it was with a much depleted crew that the Unique set off for a cruise westwards along the northern coast of South America. She headed first for Trinidad and Tobago and then moved onwards past Barcelona towards Curaçao and Panama. The objective was to impose a blockade on Spanish ports and cause as much annoyance as possible to the Spanish colonies of that area.

James didn't have a lot of luck. On 1st June the cry of 'sail ahoy' was received from the lookout and James immediately made sail in chase of a suspected enemy launch. The small ship proved to be too fast for him so the Unique fired her bow chasers in an effort to intimidate the launch or hopefully damage her enough to slow her down. James had no success and his prize escaped his clutches. By early July the Unique had sadly completed an uninterrupted and peaceful sail right past Curaçao in Venezuela and was working along the coast nearing Panama. James was now in dire need of wood and fresh water, but all that was available was to be found in nearby hostile Spanish territory. Nearing desperation by 4th July, he sent a boat towards the shore under a flag of truce. The flag didn't help and the boat was refused permission to land. The ship itself then came under fire from a command post at the nearby village[311] and so a much put out James Murray returned fire and reluctantly headed back out to the open sea. The Captain's log simply states that:

> Being much in want of wood and water sent the boat onshore with a flag of truce to obtain a landing; it being refused commenced firing upon the village. After discharging three broadsides weighed and swept out to sea.[312]

Fortunately, a few days later relief arrived in the shape of HMS Amaranthe, an 18-gun brig sloop, and James was able to partially re-stock. A full re-stocking of wood and water was not possible until 16th July, but the hardships of the crew were mitigated somewhat when they received 30 gallons of rum from the Amaranthe, as they had run out of the 42 gallons of rum they had taken on board just five weeks earlier. On 10th July James sent his cutter in chase of another suspected enemy launch, but once again the launch escaped. It was to be the last time the ship would engage with the vessels of Spain and a few days later, on 18th July, James received an order from Captain Beaver Wells in HMS Castor to cease hostilities. The war against Spain was over; [313] now just France remained.

16

Martinique and Guadeloupe

The conflict against Bonaparte and the extensive French possessions in the West Indies certainly weren't over but at least Britain could now concentrate upon the campaign without worrying about Spain too. The first island to come under scrutiny was the Island of Martinique, home of Napoleon's wife and consort, the celebrated Josephine. HMS Unique, in the company of Amaranthe and a number of other brigs and sloops, began to make their way eastwards in order to gather off Barbados and initiate a tightening of the blockade against the French possessions and prepare for the invasion of Martinique itself.

The journey eastwards was not without its drama. On 12th September James received a signal from HMS Éclair informing him of a French sail in his vicinity and the next day he spotted it. For once, James was successful in his chase and he took the French launch, with all its crew. He sailed triumphantly into St. Georges Bay, Grenada, the next day with his prize and packed all his French prisoners off to the prison ship anchored in the bay.[314] The Unique and Lieutenant James Murray had done well, but time was to tell against the ship. Just one year later the Unique was to finish her days as a fire ship against the French vessels moored in the harbour of Guadeloupe. With the hold now packed with gunpowder, the ship sailed majestically into the middle of the French ships. Once in their midst, the Captain set long fuses and a just few minutes later the Unique met its end as it exploded with dramatic effect.

That Captain was not James Murray. When James had served on HMS Northumberland during the battle of San Domingo, the squadron had been under the command of Rear-Admiral Alexander Cochrane. When Admiral Cochrane was appointed as the commander of the expedition to capture the Island of Martinique he needed good, reliable officers to serve in his flagship, HMS Neptune. He looked no further than Lieutenant James Murray.

On 13th November 1808 James left his command of HMS Unique and took on the weighty responsibilities of a Lieutenant on board the 98-gun flagship, HMS Neptune.

The Neptune had an interesting background. She was launched in 1797 and almost immediately became caught up in the events of the mutiny at the Nore. On 12th May 1797 the sailors at the Nore, an anchorage in the Thames Estuary, perhaps inspired by the example of events the previous month at Spithead,[315] mutinied. It began when the crew of HMS Sandwich seized control of their ship from their officers, an action almost immediately repeated on several other ships. Not wishing to get involved in any mutiny, some of the moored vessels sailed away, but the mutineers, attempting to use force to hold the mutiny together, fired upon them. The situation rapidly escalated out of control. The leaders, in no mood for conciliation, presented eight demands to Admiral Buckner, all concerned with pardons, increased pay and modification of the Articles of War. They might have extracted some sympathy from independent observers of a navy which had refused any change in pay and conditions for almost 100 years until the recent mutiny at Spithead. However, when the mutineers expanded their demands to include the King dissolving Parliament and making immediate peace with France they lost a great deal of their potential support. The Admiralty, now feeling that some of the leaders had more of a political agenda than just a desire to improve pay and living conditions for the sailors of the Royal Navy, offered nothing except a pardon in return for an immediate return to duty. The mutineers then raised the stakes by attempting to blockade the port of London and they tried to prevent merchant vessels from entering the port. The mutinous leaders even advertised their plans to sail their ships to France, but this just served to alienate both the regular English sailors and the general public even more.

The blockade soon collapsed. While lying at Gravesend further up the Thames, Neptune and the 64-gun ships HMS Agincourt and HMS Lancaster, together with a fleet of gunboats, were ordered to intercept and attack the mutinous ships. When the leaders of the mutiny hoisted the signal for the ships to sail to France, most of the other ships refused to follow, very aware of the Neptune and the other 'Men O' War' lying in wait for them. Fortunately, the Neptune was not called upon to use its formidable broadside against its own people. No naval engagement took place and thereafter the mutiny quickly collapsed. It was swiftly followed by the hanging of 30 of the mutinous leaders, and other lesser leaders and conspirators suffered flogging, imprisonment or transportation to Australia. However, the vast majority of men involved in the mutiny were not punished at all.[316]

Just a few years later, the Neptune had plenty of opportunity to display her broadsides when she was sternly put to the test in the Battle of Trafalgar. She was the third ship from the lead in the line of battle and her Captain, fervent as ever, had been promised a position second behind Lord Nelson aboard HMS Victory. Captain Fremantle was not satisfied with that and enthusiastically tried to slip past Victory and lead the line into battle. They only achieved a rebuke from Nelson:

> Neptune, take in your studding-sails and drop astern. I shall break the line myself.

Neptune did, and close astern of HMS Victory, she went into action with her band playing. They were not all completely insane, as everyone, except the officers and the band, was lying down on the deck to protect themselves from enemy fire. As Neptune passed the French flagship, Bucentaure, her gun crews now alert and standing by, she discharged a double-shotted broadside from her larboard (port) guns. Captain Fremantle then swung hard to starboard and fired two more triple-shotted broadsides from nearly 50 guns, at a range of less than 100 yards, into the beleaguered French ship.

Captain Fremantle then steered towards the huge Spanish four-decker, Santísima Trinidad. Opening fire with his larboard guns, the two exchanged heavy fire for the next hour. Santísima Trinidad, heavily battered by Neptune's guns, as well as those from the 74-gun ships Leviathan and Conqueror, ultimately became completely dismasted and covered in debris. After what seemed to be an interminable period of time the Spanish giant finally struck her colours, having sustained heavy casualties, with 205 dead and 103 wounded. The Neptune did not get off easily with 10 seamen killed and 34 wounded. She also suffered considerable damage to her masts, most of her rigging was cut away and she had sustained nine shot holes to her hull. Immediately after the battle the weather worsened into a storm but when the calm came she had the honour of towing the battered Victory, carrying Lord Nelson's body, to Gibraltar.[317]

A complete refit later, the now spick and span Neptune sailed for the Caribbean and joined the West Indies squadron. By January 1809 the British, with an invasion force of 44 ships and 10,000 troops, were all in position just off the coast of the French colony of Martinique and the Neptune flagship, with Lieutenant James Murray on board, was waiting to lead the attack.

It began on 30th January when British troops were successfully landed on both the southern and northern coasts of the island with little French resistance. James was busy organising landing details but had time to meet his father's old colleague, Major-General Sir

George Prevost, who had taken control of the north of the island. The British invasion force, now pushing inland away from their bridgehead, soon met some severe resistance, but by 9th February the entire island was in British hands except for Fort Desaix, which was guarding the capital, Fort de France. The sensible option now was a siege of the fort, and for nine days the British soldiers and sailors brought ashore large quantities of supplies and equipment and constructed gun batteries and trenches in readiness for a lengthy siege. The bombardment began on 19th February and lasted for four long days. French casualties in the overcrowded fort were very grave and on 24th February the French Admiral commanding the fort was left with no real choice and he surrendered unconditionally.

The last remaining source of resistance on the island had fallen and Martinique became a British colony, remaining under British command until the restoration of the French monarchy in 1814, when it was returned to French control.[318] The capture of Martinique was a significant blow to French power in the area as it eliminated an important naval base and virtually the only safe harbour left open to French shipping. Lieutenant James Murray came through the experience unscathed, but not all his colleagues were so lucky. The British experienced 97 men killed, 365 wounded and 18 men missing. The French total losses were uncertain but the garrison, in that short but terrible bombardment, suffered at least 900 casualties.[319]

James had proven to be a sound officer in combat and his reward was soon forthcoming; he was promoted to Commander James Murray and after a period of leave he would take command of a new ship, the 18-gun Cruizer class brig-sloop, HMS Recruit.

The Recruit was a new ship, only being commissioned in August 1806, but it was soon enmeshed in controversy. In June 1807 Recruit, in one of its first cruises, cast off for the West Indies station under the stewardship of Commander Warwick Lake.

Lake had the difficult task of moulding the new crew, including many landsmen, into a disciplined fighting force. To achieve this, a captain, virtually omnipotent in his own ship, had to attain a disciplinary balance and the margin between a taught, disciplined, yet happy crew and a commander who over-relied on harsh corrective measures was often very small. Commander Lake was to have a sharp lesson early in the cruise on what not to do, but probably not as sharp as the lesson received by the ill-fated recipient, Robert Jeffrey.

As the ship reached the first scattered islands of the West Indies a young press-ganged sailor named Robert Jeffrey was discovered to have stolen some of a midshipman's beer. Commander Lake, no doubt thinking that a hard line would send a clear message to the rest of the crew, ordered him to be marooned on the island of Sombrero, thus effectively condemning him to death. Sombrero was a small uninhabited island to the north of Anguilla, measuring only 1.67 kilometres in length and 0.38 kilometres in width, with a land area of only 94 acres. Its nearest habitation was Dog Island, which was 38 kilometres (24 miles) away. Months later, a furious Sir Alexander Cochrane discovered what had happened and immediately ordered Lake to attempt to retrieve Jeffery. The Recruit set out for Sombrero but Jeffery was not to be found. Miraculously, he had managed to attract the attention of a rare passing American ship and was taken to New England. He was found in Massachusetts three years later, working as a blacksmith. He eventually returned to Britain and received compensation for his nightmare experience. Commander Lake was court martialled and dismissed from the Royal Navy.[320]

Prior to taking command, James was given a period of leave, spending most of it trying to get his Quebec affairs in some sort of order but, much to his annoyance this leave coincided with an action which would make HMS Recruit famous. The French colonies had suffered severely as a result of the Royal Navy blockade and they had sent urgent messages to France looking for assistance and re-supply. France responded, and in March 1809 three 74-gun ships and two frigates under the overall command of Commodore Troude arrived at Iles des Saintes, just south of Guadeloupe. There he learned the shocking news that Martinique was now in British hands, British ships were swarming around outside of the harbour and he was now effectively blockaded in the port. His only recourse was to surrender or fight his way out. While Troude made up his mind what to do, the jolly boat from the Recruit was sent inshore to observe the French movements. When it returned, the breathless boat commander informed his Captain that the French ships were on the move.[321]

On 14th April the French ships broke out of Les Saintes and a running fight with the British blockaders began. The French squadron was attempting to use the cover of darkness to escape and the scene soon became chaotic, with broadsides unleashed and blue lights and rockets continually illuminating the night sky. The running battle was to last three days. The speedy Recruit, leading the chasing British squadron, was able to follow the French ships and was soon at the receiving end of fire from all of the French squadron's stern guns. Nevertheless, the plucky little Recruit managed to annoy the much larger French ships and succeeded in delaying d'Hautpoult, one of the French 74-gun vessels, long enough so that the main British squadron, including Murray's old ship the Neptune, was able to attack and overwhelm her.[322] The remainder of the French squadron managed to escape, with the two surviving ships of the line sailing directly for France, eventually reaching Cherbourg in May.

It was all anticlimactic for the crew of the Recruit once their heroic action was over and the new commander, James Murray, had come aboard. An uneventful cruise amongst the northern islands of the West Indies and the eastern seaboard of the USA was enlivened slightly when James Hall, one of the ship's boys, who was probably larking around in the ship's upper reaches, managed to fall overboard. He was rescued by the jolly boat and all was well, but this was to be just a lull before another man-made storm threatened to descend upon the ship. In December, the Recruit joined the huge assemblage of British ships and military personnel at Fort Royal, Martinique, which had been gathered to conduct an amphibious operation against the French forces on Guadeloupe.

The attack on Guadeloupe began on 28th January 1810 and only after a fierce battle, lasting until 3rd February, did the heavily outnumbered and outgunned French finally surrender. The Recruit, playing an important yet rather mundane supporting role in this engagement, was involved in delivering signals and messages and moving personnel and stores, and was able to escape any direct action. Not all were so lucky. British casualties in the operation numbered 52 killed and 250 wounded, but French losses were heavier, being in the region of 500–600 dead and wounded with over 3,500 soldiers captured.

The British policy of blockading the French West Indies had been vigorously pursued by Commander James Murray and his fellow officers and with the fall of Guadeloupe, the last remaining French territory in the Caribbean, the entire region (except the independent state of Haiti) was now in the hands of either the British or their new allies, the Spanish. With the absence of French privateers and warships there was a boom in trade but little need for a strong Royal Navy presence. James Murray had spent most of his military career in Caribbean waters, but by May 1810 those days were over. With an inevitable sense of trepidation he returned to the colder and less familiar home waters and a new ship. He had been appointed as the Commander of the 16-gun brig-sloop, the Oberon, and was now about to play his part in a new theatre of war, the North Sea and the Baltic.

17

It wasn't us Sir

HMS Oberon and the North Sea.

HMS Oberon, commissioned in September 1805, had spent its service in the home waters to the south and east of the United Kingdom. She had seen action; her most celebrated victory being the capture of a French 14-gun lugger, the Rafita, together with 38 prisoners, in 1807. Admittedly at the time the Rafita only had two guns operating but that was not the fault of the Oberon, who was only too happy to claim the victory and prize money.

The Oberon was to play its part in defeating the Continental system imposed by Napoleonic France against the United Kingdom. By the end of 1806, Napoleon Bonaparte had either conquered or entered into an alliance with every major power on the European continent, but did not have the resources, especially the sea power, to defeat Great Britain. His new strategy, with the introduction of the Continental system, aimed to destroy Britain's ability to trade. He believed that if he could isolate Britain economically, by use of a continental trade embargo, Britain would soon collapse. Consequently, he ordered all European nations, including Russia, to stop trading with Britain.

The policy met with some success, but to achieve ultimate victory the French and their allies needed to gain control of the seas. The Oberon and her fellow ships on the North Sea station were there to ensure that this did not happen.[323]

Commander Murray took command of the Oberon at a time when Britain was still embroiled in the Anglo-Russian War, which began in 1807 when Russia ended its war with France. In reality it wasn't much of a war and hostilities were limited primarily to minor naval actions in the Baltic and Barents Seas. Czar Alexander restricted Russia's involvement in the war against Britain to the bare minimum by closing off trade and Britain, understanding his position, limited its military response accordingly. Some naval actions did take place in the far north and there were several forays by the Royal Navy into the Barents Sea in 1810 and 1811, with the busy Leith station, commanded by Vice Admiral Sir William Johnstone Hope, coordinating the attacks. Meanwhile, relations between Russia and France had been growing progressively worse and in June 1812 Napoleon Bonaparte ordered his disastrous invasion of Russia. This encouraged Britain and Russia to sign the Peace Treaty of Orebro on 18th July 1812 and hostilities between the two countries ceased.[324]

Some British sailors almost started the whole thing up again, and it was the crew of the Oberon that got the blame. Commander James Murray responded firmly to the accusations against his men in a letter to the Admiralty:

> In reply to your letter of the 1st November last, which I only received this day, transmitting the copy of an extract of a note from his Excellency Count De Romanoff relative to depredations stated to have been committed by 15 seamen who had been sent onshore from an English ship of war in the district of Kola in the province of Archangel I beg leave to state that there was no communication between HM Sloop (Oberon) under my command and the shore from the period of our leaving Long Hope until our arrival at Archangel during the outward passage and none from our leaving that place until our arrival at Leith.
>
> Jas Murray[325]

The years of the Anglo-Russian War overlapped the so-called Gunboat War against Denmark-Norway. As a result of the British destruction of much of the Danish-Norwegian fleet during Admiral Lord Nelson's assault on Copenhagen, the Dano-Norwegian government decided to build gunboats in large numbers to compensate for the loss. They produced more than 200 gunboats, ranging from the larger gunboat with a crew of 76 men and an 18- or 24-pounder cannon in the bow and another in the stern, to the smaller barge type boat that had only 24 men and was armed with a single 24-pounder. At first these boats were able to capture cargo ships from convoys and occasionally defeat British naval brigs, though they were never strong enough to overcome the larger frigates and ships of the line. Despite this, by 1807 the British had wrested overall control of Danish waters and the Oberon's task was to make sure that it stayed that way.

And the Oberon did very well. In October 1812, in conjunction with HMS Clio and HMS Chanticleer, the Oberon captured a Danish vessel, the Jorge Henrick. The following day Clio and Oberon snapped up a Danish privateer, the Wegvusende. Making sure that the crews had a good Christmas with even more prize money to look forward to, the Oberon and Clio captured yet another Danish privateer, the Stafeten on 24th December.[326]

Prize money was central to the Royal Navy's policy of encouraging aggressive action in engagements against enemy ships. Any enemy ship legitimately and legally captured, whether it was a Man O' War, a privateer or a merchantman, could be taken to a harbour and the ship and contents sold, the crew receiving shares in its value. In addition, the Crown added 'head money' of five pounds per enemy sailor who was aboard a captured warship. The prize money was not shared out equally but was based mainly on 'eighths'. One eighth went to the Commander in Chief who signed the ship's written orders. Two eighths of the prize money went to the ship's Captain and a further eighth was divided among the Lieutenants, Master, and Captain of Marines, if present. One eighth was divided among the Wardroom Warrant Officers and another eighth among the Junior Warrant and Petty Officers, their Mates and Midshipmen. This only left a quarter of the total, which was split amongst the rest of the crew, share size depending on seniority and rank.[327]

Nevertheless, it meant that a good prize could be worth a year's normal pay for the crew. Aggressive captains, even if they were sometimes rather strict with discipline, were often popular amongst the men as the likelihood of prize money was perceived to be greater. Similarly, service in the often independent commands enjoyed by frigates and sloops of war, where prize money was more likely, was more popular than in a large ship of the line where engagements would be much less frequent.

1812 had been a good year for the war and for the Oberon and she returned to Sheerness for Christmas and the New Year in good spirits. For some individuals the spirits were perhaps rather too good. In response to a later court martial, Commander Murray wrote the following letter in support of certain of his crew members:

Oberon, Sheerness Harbour, 12 Jan. 1813

James McCurdy, Gunner.
I consider him a most valuable man, being uncommonly steady and attentive to every part of his duty while on board, he has always had charge of a watch while in this ship and I have always had reason to be highly satisfied with his conduct on-board, though in 2 or 3 instances his conduct while on leave has not my entire approbation. I beg it to be understood that it was only when on leave I have thought him faulty and have never known an instance of inebriety whilst on the boat. He has been a gunner for 10 years.

William Southwaite, Carpenter
I consider him a very well-meaning steady man always diligent
and attentive to his duty and have never known an instance of
his inebriety. He has been a carpenter nearly 3 years.

John Maclean, Boatswain
I have always found him active to his duty and particularly
careful of the stores committed to his charge and have never
known an instance of inebriety. He has been a boatswain for 2
years

J. Murray, Commander.[328]

Behind the scenes this catalogue of events was not far short of
disaster for Commander James Murray. As a result of the
misbehaviour on shore he was now facing the prospect of losing
three of his most valuable warrant officers. The boatswain, gunner
and carpenter held very important positions in a sailing ship. They
were warranted to a particular ship, in this case the Oberon, and
they were experienced, highly trained men with significant
responsibility. It would be very difficult to replace them quickly
but that is what James had to do, with mixed results. Certainly by
December of 1813 he was looking once again for a new boatswain,
having to replace the man who replaced John Maclean in early
1813:

21 December 1813
Mr Thomas Wardle, boatswain of HMS Oberon having been
dismissed of HM service by the sentence of a court martial held
upon him on the 20th (December). I have to beg you will request
their lordships to appoint another boatswain to the said sloop.

J. Murray Commander[329]

Despite his crewing difficulties James Murray and the Oberon set off once again for a cruise across the North Sea to Scandinavia and Russia. The ship moved up the east coast of England and by February was sitting off Scarborough. James Murray, who had been away from the ship, probably on court martial duty, returned to his charge but almost immediately ran into horrendous weather which was to stay with the ship until the end of April. Strong gales and very heavy swells continued to batter the ship and simple operations became severe challenges; a sharp reminder, if any was needed, about the perils involved in working on-board a ship on the open sea. It was too much of a challenge for poor George Brandon as, sadly, in very heavy gales, he fell overboard and was drowned. Following the Naval tradition a simple service was conducted by James Murray on Sunday 7th March and George Brandon, sewn in sailcloth weighed down by a couple of cannonballs, was consigned to the ocean. This 'burial' was then followed by a 'sale at the mast', when the possessions of the deceased were disposed of to the highest bidders. George's possessions raised just £2 13s 6d.[330]

He was not the last of James' crew to be lost as, just a month later, Andrew Carmichael died on board. The crew losses didn't seem to affect the fighting qualities of the ship as the Oberon was to continue where it left off in 1812 and was to have a most successful time. It fought through the snows and gales off the English coast and headed for the no more hospitable seas off Denmark. On the 25th March a strange sail was sighted through the low swirling clouds and the Oberon set off in pursuit. They failed to catch the ship, but their luck changed just a week later when a Danish ship was caught and boarded. On the 13th April another chase took place and once again the Oberon caught up with the Danish vessel and captured her without any bloodshed. Just six days later another Danish ship, bound for Greenland, was chased and boarded. The weather had been consistently dreadful and it was a very damp, battered but rather happy Oberon, content that its mission had been accomplished, which eventually returned to British waters. With sighs of relief all round, the Oberon and its three accompanying prizes anchored in Scapa Sound in Orkney on May 23rd for a well-deserved rest and refit.[331]

For much of the rest of the year the Oberon was on convoy duty to Northern Russia, following a route that was to become infamous for its hardships during the Russian convoys of World War Two. Fortunately the Oberon sailed without major incident and by the end of November the ship was back on the Leith Roads.

It was effectively the end of the war for the Oberon and the end of the command for James Murray. In January 1814 Denmark / Norway was forced to seek peace and the Treaty of Kiel ended the brief war with Britain. Four months later Napoleonic France also finally admitted defeat and surrendered. For almost the first time in twenty-five years Europe was at peace. Huge celebrations accompanied the British victory and the ending of Napoleon Bonaparte's tyranny, but within the ranks of the Royal Navy celebration was distinctly muted. Not to welcome peace would have been churlish in the extreme, but the reality was that for many sailors this would mean significantly fewer chances of career advancement at best, and redundancy at worst. Britannia was going to continue to rule the waves, but it was going to do it with far fewer ships and far fewer men.

The Oberon was no exception to this and in mid-1814 it was paid off from regular service into the ordinary (the naval reserve). Even Napoleon's dramatic return from exile and his resumption of power in France during the 'Hundred Days' between March and his final defeat at Waterloo on 18th June 1815 failed to bring the Oberon out of retirement. From 1814 Commander James Murray, now without a ship, was placed on the half pay list and was wondering what to do with his time and where his next command would come from.

18

Too much hope

A t least the break in command gave James the time and opportunity to catch up with his dispersed families in Quebec, Canada, and New Abbey, Scotland.

Visits to Canada carried an element of danger at that time because once more Britain was at war with the United States and British Canada was very much on the frontline. James' father, Patrick, had continued to live, rather more modestly, near to the Seigneury of Argenteuil but, now in his sixties, he naturally thought that his military life was behind him. The War of 1812 caused him to think again.

The War of 1812, largely forgotten in Britain but of great significance to Canada, was a 32-month military conflict between the United States and the British Empire. The causes of this almost war were multiple and complex but many of the settlers in Canada thought that the principal reason was an attempt by the United States to annex British Canada. Whilst the theatres of war raged from the south of the United States to the Atlantic Ocean, it was certainly the case that a determined effort was made by the United States leadership to bring Canada under their control. The British were potentially most vulnerable along the stretch of the St. Lawrence River where it formed the frontier between Upper Canada and the United States. Over the winter of 1812 and 1813 the Americans launched a series of raids from the American side of the river. The man tasked to stop them was none other than Patrick's old comrade-in-arms, General George Prevost. On 21st

October 1811, Prevost took over as governor-in-chief of British North America and commander of the British forces, and immediately set about organising the Canadian defences. At the Battle of Ogdensburg in February 1813, the Americans were defeated and this victory removed all American regular troops from the Upper St. Lawrence frontier for the immediate future. It didn't last long. Later in 1813 the American Army made two determined thrusts against Montréal. The city was not seriously threatened as both attacks proved to be ill thought-out, poorly executed and ultimately unsuccessful. [332]

This was just as well, as 63 year old Patrick Murray had been dragged out of retirement to counter the perceived American threat to Montréal. In 1812 he was given a Colonel's commission in the 5th battalion of the Lower Canadian Militia and, in Montréal he raised a corps of lawyers, known jocularly as 'the Devil's Own', referring more to views on their profession than to their fighting prowess.[333] Fortunately, they were not called upon to deal with the Americans and they did not fire a shot in anger.

With neither side ultimately gaining any real advantage, peace was declared. Canada was safe once more and it seemed that Patrick's militia would no longer be needed. Shortly after the war ended, the 5th battalion was abolished but was reorganised under the heading of the 'Canadian Chasseurs'. James Murray was furious at what he saw as a deliberate slight to his father:

I will therefore only observe that his (General George Prevost) conduct to my Father has not at all astonished me, because the Coward is always unjust and ungrateful when he can be so with impunity;... did he not... deprive my aged father of the command of that regiment he rose and formed, to give it to who? Why to De Courcy the younger Brother of that Michael De Courcy whose promotion the gallant and the Zealous Sir James Hood thought it his duty to stop for having failed to attempt the execution of those orders which I carried into effect, on three separate occasions.[334]

James' last visit to New Abbey was for the New Year celebrations of 1810-1811, and then he was treated as a popular returning hero. The local newspaper recorded the event with some pride:

> New Abbey Jan 1
> As a public testimony of high esteem and affectionate regard for Capt. James Murray of his majesty's ship the Oberon, there was held a numerous meeting of the inhabitants of this village, both old and young, among whom he had resided in his youth and who was universally beloved. After repeatedly toasting his health and success with loud and cheerful huzzahs a ball was opened by a great number of neatly dressed, healthy and happy young people, excellent dancers – the cheerful glass went round, and the evening was spent in temperance, harmony and social mirth. The company having partaken in a comfortable repast of bread and cheese washed down with a wangle of nut brown mulled ale, parted at a late hour highly pleased and happy.[335]

Of his New Abbey family, Louisa was now married and living nearby at Keltonhead, Theresa was in Demerara and Harriet had remained in the village. In 1813 a new minister, the Reverend James Hamilton, had taken up his post and was living in the New Abbey Manse alongside the old and frail Rev. William Wright, and in all likelihood, James' 'sister', the thirty-two year old Harriet Smith. The Reverend James Hamilton was later to become a strong and faithful friend to James at a time when he most needed strong and faithful friends, so it was to prove a most fruitful arrangement when, just four years later, Harriet and the Rev. Hamilton got married.

It was not uncommon for officers on half pay and waiting for their next cruise to stay at the home of a senior officer. Admiral Sir William Hope Johnstone, the Leith Station commander and family friend, had his palatial home at Raehills, just south of Moffat in Dumfriesshire, and this was to be James' next destination.[336]

Admiral Hope was a distant relative of James and had also been his immediate boss when he was the captain of the Oberon. James had put a fair amount of prize money in the Admiral's direction through his command of the Leith station and the two men had become friends as well as colleagues. James was to stay at Raehills for six months and much of that time he used purposefully to seek patrons who would support his applications to the Admiralty for his next command.

Admiral Hope had entered the navy at the age of ten and served with distinction on a number of ships. Controversy engulfed the young officer in 1786, when he was stationed aboard the frigate HMS Pegasus, commanded by Prince William, the Duke of Clarence (the future King William IV). Hope and Prince William did not see eye to eye and ultimately had a major disagreement which, by repute, led to the Duke of Clarence sporting a black eye for a few days. Not too surprisingly, William Hope was soon transferred away from the Pegasus and was moved on to the frigate HMS Boreas, at that time commanded by Captain Horatio Nelson. Hope later served in many stations including the West Indies, the coast of Guinea, the North Sea and Newfoundland where, in HMS Portland, he worked under the command of Vice-Admiral Campbell from Kirkbean, Dumfries. He achieved his Post-Captain rank whilst serving on the famous HMS Bellerophon, and in 1794 he took part in Lord Howe's famous engagement of the French in the Battle of the 'Glorious First of June', in 1794. He was later temporarily invalided out of the navy and, in 1800, began a second career in politics, gaining the seat of Dumfries Burghs in the House of Commons. In 1804 he was elected to the seat of Dumfriesshire and he stayed in this post until his retirement from public life in 1830. When his health improved he pursued his naval career once again, this time in tandem with his largely inactive political life. He became a Lord of the Admiralty, Knight Commander of the Order of Bath and was promoted to Rear Admiral and later Vice Admiral of the Red. In 1813 Admiral Hope served as commander-in-chief at Leith where he was James Murray's commanding officer. He was largely inactive in later life and was no doubt able to spend plenty of time swapping naval tales with James Murray during his brief sojourn at Raehills. As a postscript, in 1830 Admiral Hope became a privy councillor and was appointed by none other than King William IV, who seemingly had forgotten their earlier tiff.[337]

The good Admiral was a heavy hitter at the Admiralty, and James Murray would have been very grateful for his support in his quest for a new command. Very many sea officers, most having at least as good a social connection as James, were now chasing the few commands available, so James was elated when he learned that he was to receive another command. On 10th September 1815, with the deep satisfaction of appreciating that he was a well-considered officer in Admiralty circles, Commander James Murray took up his position on-board HMS Satellite as her new Captain.[338]

19

The trident vibrates

HMS Satellite, with a crew of 100 men, was a fairly new (commissioned in 1812) 18-gun brig-sloop[339] and James wondered whether, with peace having descended upon the world almost for the first time in his life, he would ever have to use his 18 guns in anger. He had no need to ponder too much, as the British government still had a few scores to settle and a few wrongs to be righted. Such was the situation in North Africa when the Satellite left Britain for the Mediterranean Sea.

With France now out of the way, considerable political pressure was building up to end the practice of enslaving Christians, a practice employed for hundreds of years by the Barbary States. These North African states, mainly the city-ports of Tunis, Tripoli and Algiers, operated under the flag of the Ottoman Empire in Constantinople, but in practice were virtually independent slave trading states. It has been suggested that between one and 1.25 million European Christians were enslaved by the Muslims of North Africa between 1530 and 1780. The northern reaches of Europe were not exempt from these outrages and through most of the 17th century the English lost at least 400 sailors a year to the slavers.[340] Even the fledgling United States became involved when, in 1784, Morocco became the first Barbary power to seize an American vessel after independence. The United States later managed to secure peace treaties with the Barbary States but these obliged the new country to pay tribute for protection from attack. Payments in ransom and tribute to the

Barbary States were not cheap and amounted to 20 per cent of the United States Government annual expenditures in 1800.[341]

By 1816, the Royal Navy had wrested full control of the seas in the Mediterranean region, but to the fury of interested onlookers, especially those who had suffered at the hands of piracy, Britain seemed unwilling to respond to the situation. William Shaler, the American Consul in Algiers, reported that:

> Britain with a single vibration of her Trident might annihilate the pretensions of these barbarians, force them to abandon their abominable practices and seek their living in honest industry; and its failure to do so could only be to encourage the insolence of the Algerines towards other nations.[342]

The Royal Navy had not twitched its trident and the Barbary States continued to defy Europe by its slavery practices. In fact, during the recent wars Britain had deliberately turned a blind eye to the Barbary pirates and their antics, as it needed the support of the Barbary States for a source of supplies to Gibraltar and the Mediterranean Fleet. Now the wars were over there was no such need for compromise and Britain was ready to act. The first step taken was to increase the British naval presence in the area and HMS Satellite, commanded by Commander James Murray, was just one of the ships to make up that extended presence.

The campaign escalated when Admiral Pellew, Lord Exmouth, was tasked with visiting the main Barbary ports of Tunis, Tripoli and Algiers with a small but powerful squadron of warships. The Satellite was not part of this squadron but was sent to the Mediterranean to provide any additional support which may have been needed. The Satellite left Britain in late February and made its way southwards to arrive in Gibraltar on 7th March. She stayed there a few days and then continued the cruise, via Minorca, to anchor at Malta. For a few days, the Satellite was based in the central location of Valetta Harbour and able to link up with the British squadron, whether it be at Algiers, Tunis or Tripoli.[343] Lord Exmouth was then anchored in the Bay of Algiers and on 1st April he entered into negotiations with the Dey of Algiers. This man was not an enemy to be ignored. It was estimated that Algiers could call upon 600–1000 large cannon to defend its port, circa 40,000 armed men and a navy which consisted of four frigates, five corvettes and 30–40 gun and mortar boats. It had successfully withstood bombardment and siege on countless occasions and, despite the awesome reputation of the Royal Navy, they must have been confident that they could withstand anything that Pellew was able to throw at them.

On this occasion their confidence was not put to the test because the Dey, for once, seemed conciliatory, but carefully and resolutely he refused to totally commit to the British demands. In the belief that progress had been made, Lord Exmouth set off for Tunis and then Tripoli, where he was joined by the Satellite and Commander James Murray. On 23rd April Lord Exmouth raised his signal for the Captain of the Satellite to come aboard and the two met in conference.[344] It is likely that at this meeting James Murray was informed of the progress made so far and briefed on the next stage of the campaign.

Both the Deys of Tunis and Tripoli had agreed, without any overt intimidation, to cease the practice of taking Christian slaves and they soon released all those that they held. Lord Exmouth, having made this breakthrough, decided to return to Algiers in an attempt to reach a similar conclusion with the Dey of Algiers. James Murray, now fully in the picture, returned with the Satellite to the central base at Valletta and Lord Exmouth moved on to attempt further negotiations with the Dey of Algiers. This time things did not go so well.

The Dey, less cooperative, played for time once more and the discussions ended in a furious disagreement. Finally Lord

Exmouth, patience at an end, threatened war if an agreement could not be reached.[345] In the interim he informed the Dey that he was going to take the British Consul, Hugh McDonnell, on board his ship for safety. The Dey refused to give a safe conduct and as Exmouth and McDonnell's party made their way back to the harbour there were extraordinary scenes. The diplomatic party were jostled and pushed by an angry mob and in the confusion they became separated so that Exmouth returned to his ship and McDonnell returned to the British Consulate to await further developments.[346]

He didn't have long to wait. The Dey, in a fit of temper, ordered all British subjects to be arrested,[347] but after tempers had quietened down Lord Exmouth made another and more successful visit to the Dey. Finally, on 20th May, Exmouth and his fleet returned home, as had the Satellite, which by now was in Falmouth. All the participants were well satisfied with the outcome, feeling that a great service to mankind in general and Christians in particular had been accomplished as a result of the signing of a treaty with the Dey. It would end the slavery of Christians once and for all.

They were soon to realise the emptiness of the Dey's promise. Only a few days after the signing of the treaty, Algerian troops massacred around 200 Corsican, Sicilian and Sardinian fishermen who were under British protection. The British public were outraged and Lord Exmouth and Commander James Murray hardly had time to hang up their coats before they were making ready to set off once again. By the end of July 1816 the Satellite was back in Malta and Lord Exmouth's squadron, this time comprising the 100-gun Queen Charlotte, five other ships of the line, ten frigates, four sloops, four bomb vessels and two transports, were well on the way towards Algiers.

With conflict now inevitable, an audacious plan was devised to rescue the McDonnell family, who were still at liberty but confined to the consulate in Algiers. Captain Dashwood, from the sloop Prometheus, was sent ahead to Algiers to attempt the extrication of the family. He arrived in Algiers on 31st July, but met with an unwilling McDonnell, who was concerned about the impact on other British personnel should he and his family leave. By 6th August the situation had deteriorated further and it was clear that that evacuation of McDonnell, his wife, teenage daughter and their baby was the only option. The two women were disguised as ship boys and the baby was drugged with an opiate to keep it quiet. The girls, now midshipmen to all intents and purposes, got on board the Prometheus safely but the rest of the party, including the baby, were arrested (the baby was subsequently returned to its mother), probably because the drugged baby had not been drugged enough and had started to cry. The consul and his entourage spent that night in chains in the Algiers gaol, accompanied by eighteen unlucky members of the Prometheus' crew.[348]

James Murray's main contribution to the campaign came on 13th August when the Satellite arrived in haste at Gibraltar and a breathless Murray requested an immediate audience with Lord Exmouth. Exactly what was discussed at that meeting is unclear but it was regarded as significant, and led to Exmouth making haste towards Algiers and the subsequent bombardment. One account suggests that Murray brought intelligence concerning the failed rescue bid and the subsequent imprisonment of McDonnell and some of the Prometheus' crew.[349] Other accounts suggest that he brought a complete plan of the fortification of Algiers.[350] Unfortunately, the ship's logs give no indication that the Satellite was anywhere near Algiers at the time in question. In early August she was off the coast of Barcelona and was anchored there until 8th August. On 11th August she was near Malaga and heading for Gibraltar, where she arrived on 13th August. Algiers is about 400 kilometres from Barcelona and it would have been difficult, but not impossible, for the ship to have gone to Algiers during this period.[351] A good wind and some fine sailing might just have done it, but whatever the Satellite reported it was enough for the Commander in Chief to issue his orders to all his captains and his newly joined Dutch allies almost immediately. Within just a few hours of their meeting the squadron had weighed anchor and set out for Algiers.

Exmouth's squadron met very strong headwinds and could only make slow progress towards Algiers, but the Satellite took a different route and headed for Cape Malabata off the bay of Tangier. Lying in the waters of Cape Malabata was a so-called 'Turkish' squadron, but they may have been the ships associated with Algiers. Consequently, if this is the case, some of the Algerian naval ships were unable to confront Lord Exmouth in the forthcoming Algiers action. Indeed, this may have been the task assigned to the Satellite in its reconnaissance of Tangier. James Murray indicated his willingness for a fight when he cleared for action against a brig flying the Turkish colours and belonging to the emperor of Morocco, but conflict was avoided when it became clear that this ship was not going to interfere with Exmouth's action further east in Algiers Bay. By Monday 19th July the Satellite was back in Gibraltar and was then ordered to make its way back to Britain, much to Commander Murray's disappointment as he was fully aware of his Commander-in-Chief's planned fireworks at Algiers to the east.

The Commander-in-Chief might have welcomed some more support. The Dey had refused his final ultimatum and the inevitable confrontation began just seven days later. Lord Exmouth brought his ships into the bay to an area where the Algerian shore batteries could not fully play and he began a massive bombardment of the city. It was later estimated that over 500 defenders of the city died in just these opening broadsides.[352] The small Algerian naval force that was present tried in desperation to board some of the British ships but suffered horrendous losses in their attempts, with over thirty-three of their boats being sunk. The Royal Navy did not escape scot-free. A number of the ships, including HMS Impregnable, had anchored out of position, both reducing their effectiveness and exposing them to fierce Algerian fire. By 2am, with firing beginning to slacken, a terrible thunderstorm began and the British ships withdrew out of range. Casualties on the British side were high and HMS Impregnable was hit 233 times, losing 111 seamen, 11 officers and 17 boys, with 742 men wounded.[353]

The only wonder was that the commander, Lord Exmouth, was not one of the fatal casualties:

> When I met his lordship on the poop, his voice was quite hoarse, and he had two slight wounds, one in the cheek, the other in the leg; and it was astonishing to see the coat of his lordship, how it was all cut up by musket-ball, and grape; it was, indeed, as if a person had taken a pair of scissors, and cut it all to pieces.[354]

Overall, casualties in the squadron amounted to 16 per cent of the total force, a high butcher's bill. Sadly, the butchers were even busier in the city of Algiers, where casualties were estimated to be between 3,000 and 6,000 people killed. It was too much for the Dey. Lord Exmouth sent his demand for surrender the next morning:

> Sir, for your atrocities at Bona on defenceless Christians, and your unbecoming disregard of the demands I made yesterday in the name of the Prince Regent of England, the fleet under my orders has given you a signal chastisement.
>
> As England does not war for the destruction of cities, I am unwilling to visit your personal cruelties upon the unoffending inhabitants of the country, and I therefore offer you the same

terms of peace which I conveyed to you yesterday in my Sovereign's name. Without the acceptance of these terms, you can have no peace with England.[355]

Exmouth further warned that if his terms were not accepted he would continue the action. The Dey reluctantly accepted, but his answer may have been rather different had he been informed that the whole thing was a huge bluff by Lord Exmouth. The fleet had already fired off virtually all of its ammunition.

A treaty was signed on 24th September, 1816, which led to more than 1,200 Christian slaves, the British Consul and the crew members of the Prometheus being freed, together with a commitment by the Dey to completely abolish slavery in the future. Furthermore, there was to be restoration of 382,500 dollars to the British consul plus repayment of any outstanding hostage and tribute monies. In total, over 3,000 slaves were later freed and it should have been the end to Christian slavery. Alas it wasn't, but all the participants could take pride in knowing that significant steps had been taken to stop the ghastly trade in human beings, so endemic in North Africa at that time. On a more prosaic note, many of the Royal Naval personnel who had participated in the campaign gained promotion. One of them was Commander, now to become Captain, James Murray.

20

A nest of idle vagabonds

J ames Murray's command of the Satellite came to an end in
September 1818 and once more he faced the prospect of a long
period onshore on half pay.[356] As he waited and hoped for a
new appointment he began to look around for a more permanent
home base and his immediate focus was on his family and relatives.
Lady Maria Murray Hay-Mackenzie of Cromartie, the legitimate
daughter of grandfather George Murray, 6th Lord Elibank, was an
important family link, as the Cromartie family had strong
connections to the Elibank Murrays. Maria's mother was Isabella
Mackenzie, who had inherited the vast Cromarty estates in 1796
and administered the estates until her own death in 1801. Maria
with her new husband, Edward Hay, later Hay-Mackenzie, of
Newhall, brother of George Hay, 7th Marquis of Tweeddale, then
inherited all the estate. The estates had recently carried the title of
'Earl of Cromarty', but the colourful background of the Cromartie
Mackenzies, especially when mixed with Elibank Murrays, was
bound to lead to trouble.

The first Murray-Mackenzie link came in 1701 when John
Mackenzie, the 2nd Earl of Cromartie, married Mary Murray, the
daughter of the 3rd Lord Elibank. Their son George, born in 1703,
became the 3rd Earl of Cromartie. Although popular and well
respected, his behaviour during the rising of 1745 was to tear his
family apart and lead to the loss of the Earldom. It had been
expected that George would raise a regiment on behalf of the
Hanoverians but, to the surprise of all, he declared for the Jacobite

cause and raised a regiment of almost 500 men. He served with the army of Charles Edward Stewart until April 1746 when he was taken prisoner in Sutherland after the fiasco of Littleferry in Sutherland, when most of his men were either killed or taken prisoner, including George himself. For his involvement he found himself before the House of Peers in Westminster Hall, London, to answer a charge of treason; the same place and the same charge brought against William Wallace over 400 years previously. Unlike Wallace, Cromartie pleaded guilty, but the penalty to be paid was only slightly less harsh. He was sentenced to beheading.

It is a fortunate man who can count upon the support and strength of a good wife and the emollient and resolute Isabella Gordon, the Countess of Cromartie and Maria Mackenzie's grandmother, was certainly that. She was heavily pregnant and had her large family of young children in tow, but she incessantly begged for her husband's pardon. She waited personally on every member of the Cabinet, and then presented a separate petition to each of them, pleading for mercy. Her master stroke was when she went to Kensington Palace, dressed in deep mourning, and managed to obtain an introduction to the Princess of Wales and King George II himself. According to eye witness accounts, surrounded by her ten young children, she waited in the entrance of the Chapel through which the King had to pass. As he drew near she gave way to grief and completely broke down. She fell on her knees and seized him by the coat tails. Between loud sobs she presented her petition to him and then immediately fainted. King George helped her to her feet and received her petition for clemency. That did the trick. On 9th of August the Earl of Cromartie was granted a conditional pardon, and he was at once set free.[357]

It would be nice to report that they all lived happily ever after, but sadly that was not to be the case. A condition of release was that George, who already had all his estates confiscated and his title forfeited, did not ever go north of the River Trent. He lived in a small property in Soho Square, London, for a number of years but was reduced to extreme poverty.

A great clan chief, who could raise hundreds of devoted clansmen in arms, had fallen dramatically from grace. However, a letter still exists which shows the remarkable continuity of loyalty the Earl could still command. The tenants of his estates in Coigach, a remote and mountainous area of the Western Highlands of Scotland, were considered amongst the poorest people of Scotland and probably had little for which to thank their Laird. Nevertheless, thank him they did:

To Roderic MacKenzie of Akilibuy and George MacKenzie of Coigach

Gentlemen:-

Your letter of 22nd August was delivered to me only the day before yesterday by Alexander MacKenzie of Bishopgate. It gives me great pleasure to prove that my friends in Coigach have not forgotin me, and that ye think of the present condition of me and my family which could not be represented to you in a worse situation than what by experience we find it to be. Any aid or assistance from my friends will be a seasonable relief to us and it will be a double pleasure to have it from my farmers of Coigach, because it will be a testimony of their friendship and regard for me which cannot be more than that which I still retain for them. What they think fit to give, may be sent to Medeat, who will remit it to me, and at the same time you may write me a letter with the names of those who do contribute officing(sic) their several names with their place of abode, that I may know them to whom I am obliged, and I hope to live to be so obliged – believe me to be very sincere[358]

He went on to receive significant funds from his tenants which helped to relieve his near destitute condition, until he died on 28th September 1766. He had not gone north of the River Trent again, thus keeping within the terms of his pardon.[359] It was ironic that, within a hundred years, the tenants of Coigach would be cleared from the land by a future Mackenzie Laird, to make room for sheep.

George Mackenzie's son John had followed his father into the Jacobite fold and was also convicted of high treason and sentenced to death. Fortunately for him he received a full pardon and the family estates were eventually restored to him, but not the title 'Earl of Cromartie'. He built the fine Tarbat House, a house which became the home of the Hay-Mackenzies and was to become well known to James Murray, but is today a sad ruin.

Just two more generations brought the family line to Maria Murray Hay-Mackenzie. Maria was the legitimate eldest daughter of Admiral George Murray, the 6th Lord Elibank and, of course, James' grandfather through the illegitimate line of his father, Patrick Murray. Maria's mother was Lady Isabella Mackenzie, who had inherited the Cromartie estates in 1796 from her cousin Kenneth Mackenzie of Cromartie. Maria had married Edward Hay of Newhall in East Lothian and from then on they both took the name of Hay-Mackenzie. Together they ran the vast estates of Cromartie until Edward died in December 1814 and Maria took on sole responsibility for their management. Maria and Patrick Murray had kept in touch with each other as brother and sister and Maria and James had formed a strong bond, even though both Patrick and James were illegitimate. Thus it was to Ross-shire and the hard pressed debt ridden Cromartie Estates that James turned when his tenure as Captain of the Satellite ended.

He took up a temporary residence at 'the moorings' by Castle Leod, Strathpeffer, near Dingwall and kept himself busy in assisting Maria with the running of her estate. Maria had inherited

Castle Leod, once the historic and principal seat of the Mackenzie Earls of Cromartie, but by 1818 it was sadly neglected. The Countess of Sutherland described the property in 1824 as:

> a very old chateau of the Hay-Mackenzies in Strathpeffer called Castle Leod. Quite a ruin, the roofing alone has cost £500. It was completely deserted except by crows and requires entire restoration.[360]

The Hay-Mackenzies planned to restore the castle to make it fit for human occupation again and Maria suggested that it was to be made habitable for one of her Murray relatives, almost certainly James. Sadly, the funding necessary for such a huge project was not available, as Maria lived constantly under the threat of debt and the need to balance the books. Restoration did finally take place at Castle Leod, but not until 1861, far too late for James Murray.[361]

After the hardships of life on a Royal Navy ship, even a semi-ruined chateau would have seemed luxurious to James. Maria Hay-Mackenzie and her children had a different perception of luxury and the family constantly lived in surroundings which their income could not sustain. Their main seat in Cromarty was Tarbat House, but they spent much more of their time commuting between their southern estate mansion house at Newhall, East Lothian, and very expensive accommodation on the newly built and rapidly developing Princes Street in Edinburgh.[362]

James frequently wrote to Maria from his base in Castle Leod and, although showing the respect and deference due to a lady of Maria's standing, he was not shy in giving his opinion on how the estate should be run. In a delightful letter of 1819, James illustrates just how his life has changed from being a Naval Officer in a life or death struggle against European dictatorship to the more practical concerns of estate management and woodland depredation in Highland Scotland:

Castle Leod Nov 26 1819

My dearest Madam, I would have written yesterday but I was seized with a pain in my right side in consequence I suppose of having got my feet very wet with snow water. I think it easier today and with care I trust it will like all my other complaints not last long. I have not been able on account of the snow, to go to the moors, of course old John could not go either, but as soon as the... (weather eases)... I will find you some grouse. In the mean time I send a small case of Woodcocks... I could only go out in the forenoon or I would have sent more, although I am confident Georgina only asked me to send some as she believed I could not shoot them, therefore let her pay for the carriage... I am sorry to say that the Polecat has destroyed the four pheasant Hens I sent from London, therefore send/find four or six more as soon as possible as we must persevere without we losing either Temper or patience, it is consoling to know that they will succeed for of those used in the garden only one out of nine of the last clutch died a natural death. The others that died were by accidents – I found that the greatest depredations were committing on the Timber of Ballmulach, and by those who from Proffered respects to you, aught not to have kept a servant one moment after detection (as they put all Blame on the servants)... I mean our Fodderty friends, I am told the Major will be quite angry when he knows it, as he was anxious for the Preservation of the Wood, time will show how he treats those who have sinned?

James was less than impressed by some of the employees who had been brought in to work the estate:

Tomorrow Corbett comes, as Laing (Lady Maria Hay-Mackenzies Factor) has again hired him notwithstanding his ingratitude to you, independent of which I am confident he is a very unfit man for this charge. He is a simpleton, a coward and moves like an Elephant whereas the Preservation of those woods require an active and a resolute man, it is true I am here and will keep a Bright Eye on him, but it is not because I feel that I will not be relieved from either my anxiety or fatigue by Corbett and Laing placed in charge of the wood that I feel annoyed, it is because I firmly believe your interests will not be advanced... on this point I differ from Laing, and it is the only one; however as he has only hired him from month to month it is of less consequence as we can get another if he does not answer – I think Laing a most worthy good man and one who really wishes to act up to your (*Lady Maria Hay-Mackenzie*) interest, and I am sure thinks Corbett the best he can get at present, although I think otherwise... [363]

Your devoted servant

J Murray

By 1819 the area of Strathpeffer, which then stood on land divided between four farms (all part of the Cromartie estate) had become well known for the quality of its waters. The belief in the curative property of water is of ancient origin and by the 18th century 'taking the waters' had become a very popular activity for the European upper classes. The town of Bath in England was one of the most prestigious towns in Europe at the time and its emulation in the Highlands of Scotland was something to dream about for hard-pressed estate owners.

When sulphur springs were discovered in the vicinity of Strathpeffer in the 1770s, the talk quickly moved on to the possibility of the establishment of a spa. The springs were fenced off to prevent their pollution by cattle but little further development took place until the early 1800s, when Dr. Morrison from Aberdeenshire declared that his arthritis had been cured by the waters. Word soon began to spread about the miracle cures on offer:

> It is found to be highly beneficial in all cases of ill health which result from a relaxed state of the system, especially in the great variety of disorders occasioned by nervous debility; in gouty, rheumatic, scrofulous, and cutaneous complaints; in affections of the kidneys and bladder, the water being highly diuretic; in cases of dyspepsia, and for constitutions which have suffered by long residence in tropical climates.[364]

When the railway arrived in 1862 much of the construction of the village, to a 'grand European design', got underway. The Spa Pavilion was soon built to provide entertainment and the large number of visitors were housed in a number of grand Victorian hotels, most of which still grace the town.[365] But in early 1819 the Strathpeffer as is known today was still at the early conceptual stage. Maria was just considering fencing off the spa area and building a grand pump-room, 40 feet long and 20 feet broad, over the lower well. For the cash-strapped Cromartie estate this would be a major investment. James Murray was not impressed by the concept at all and advised strongly against it:

> The Moorings under Castle Leod, 27th June 1819
> ... and I will now my dearest madam proceed as the parson says – to give you the ideas that have forced themselves into my mind since I have been here in relation to the fencing (of) the houses at the pump so soon and the more I see and reflect what will be ultimately for your comfort and son's happiness the more decidedly I am of opinion by giving feus for ninety nine years you will for the annual additional income of £150 or £100 create a petty republic of Bachus; drunkards, thieves and

vagabonds of both sexes in the centre of the finest part of your property... [366]

No doubt calling upon his experiences when he lived at Raehills in Annandale, he recollected his impressions of what is now considered to be one of the most attractive towns in Southern Scotland, and drew parallels with the proposed development at Strathpeffer:

> ... the town of Moffat has been created within these 40 years and the morality of its inhabitants is proverbial as a nest of idle vagabonds, it is the pest of the county.[367]

Maria did not heed James' warning and in late 1819 the newly built pump room was opened to visitors and the development of Strathpeffer, Highland Spa Town, had begun.

It wasn't always wise to cross Captain James Murray. Whilst not always agreeing with the financially beleaguered Maria, he was a tower of strength in more ways than one. His addendum to the Strathpeffer letter illustrates all the 'get off my land' mentality to be expected from a Highland Laird of the early 19th century:

> I was forced to get up to separate the dogs from fighting when Behold I saw a drunken fellow amusing himself with making all the dogs worry one another, and to make the thing better he swore he would give me a d(amned) good hiding if I did not go about my business or attempted to prevent him. I, of course, was forced to give the gentlemen a dressing he will not forget in a hurry and in doing this I have hurt my thumb.[368]

21

The perfect girl?

Although the 'country squire' role sat easily on James' shoulders he did not lose sight of other priorities. In November 1818 he was in London, meeting with Robert Dundas (Lord Melville), the First Lord of the Admiralty, to petition him for a new sea command:

> I am happy to say that I have seen my Lord Melville and he has desired me to remain in London as he will see what he can do for me... I have also seen Mackay, his Lordship's secretary who has also appraised me that all was going on well and I confess had I not seen so many officers already passed over my head I would have no reason to fault the sincerity of their professions.[369]

A new command was not the only thing on James' mind. During his stay at Raehills he had occasion to travel south in search of his next command and clearly his focus has slipped. He had found the perfect woman. James informed Maria:

> ... Tom told me that you had said to him that I was married? which I am sorry to say is not the case, although I have been engaged to a young woman whom I feel satisfied if you knew you would like much, for the last eighteen months... my intended is humble in her wishes, frugal in manner of living, having been educated in the strictest economy; and pleasing in

her manners, she is excellent at her needle, can make a capital pudding and is not only a good musician, she plays well on the piano... and guitar but speaks Italian and French as well as English. She is in addition the very best tempered good hearted unaffected girl you could know, and she thinks me a perfect nonesuch, which is as it aught to be you know... [370]

Later marriages were not uncommon amongst sea officers and it seems that the forty-year-old James was at last considering settling down. This remarkable young lady was not given a name but was described as the second daughter of Colonel Harris, who commanded the Royal Artillery at Plymouth.

John Harris, later to become General John Harris, was born on 10th May 1765 in Maidstone, Kent. He married Margaret Marshall in Perth, Scotland on 13th Sep 1788 and had a number of children. The birth date of his second daughter, Matilda, is unconfirmed but is no earlier than 1800. In a contemporary portrait,[371] James is revealed as a handsome man who, very dashing in his naval dress uniform, would turn the head of many a young lady. The very young (maximum 18 years old) Matilda seemed an unlikely match for the 40 year old James but the military background and the Scottish connection worked in her favour,[372] although it is unlikely that Matilda's father saw things in quite the same light.

James had reason to believe that perhaps the extended shore leave on half pay was not so bad after all. His contentment was not to last. In a surprise letter from Canada towards the end of the year he received the shocking news that his father Patrick was destitute. He wrote to Maria Hay Mackenzie to inform her of her brother's sad situation:

Castle Leod 3rd December 1819.
Never did I sit down to address you under feelings of such severe affliction as I labour under by the weight of letters from Canada,

192

> I have a letter from Mary (Patrick's daughter and James Murray's
> half-sister) depicting my poor father to be as deplorable as the
> human mind can conceive, depending for subsistence on the
> charity of those who knew him in his better days.[373]

Patrick had fallen on hard times in the years after his final
retirement as Colonel in the Quebec militia. An examination of
Patrick's life inevitably suggests that James should not have been
too surprised by the turn of events. Patrick was constantly in debt
and had it not been for the support of his female companions he
would have been in even worse straits. Now, however, his wife
was dead and Eliza Smith had returned to New Providence in the
Bahamas. Isabella, his youngest daughter, had recently married
George Gordon, a Scottish immigrant merchant from Lachine,
Argenteuil, and had departed her father's home. This left the 28-
year-old Mary Julia, his eldest daughter, and she was still devotedly
looking after Patrick, but in hard straits herself. James, in debt
himself, needed to convince his aunt to request her factor to
relieve him of the necessity of immediate payment of these debts
for a limited period of time:

> ... the instance I saw the letters I sent off the only money I had in
> my agent's hands and which was intended to meet any demand
> Laing might make against me for the different little accounts he
> may have paid for me here, which places me under the Painful
> necessity of requesting you to write to Laing (Maria's factor) not
> to call on me for payment until Spring, as I will not be able until
> then to get money without borrowing it... nothing less than the
> urgent claims of a starving Parent could have found me to convert
> to another use the monies I had prepared to pay a just debt... [374]

James tended to the dramatic in his letters but there is no doubt
about his depth of anguish:

.... .my head aches as if it would burst, whither from the want of sleep or the most horrible of all, a parent starving while I am enjoying a comparative affluence, I cannot tell, for should anything happen to the packet which carries out my letter for Lord knows how they are to get through the severity of a Canadian winter. It strikes me that the Almighty has asked this on purpose to try what I am made of ; of course I am not to shrink from my duty... although I should also display a degree of fortitude which nothing but a conscious rectitude can inspire. I trust that there is no respite of personal suffering that the lot of man is subject to, that I could not (indulge) with as much resolution as my neighbour; I have undergone privations and hardships nearly to the extent of human suffering of which ample testimonies lie on the admiralty shelves, covered with dust, but ... you , and all my friends, will do me the justice to acknowledge that... of what has been my lot to experience, surely then I cannot be deemed Puerile, in lamenting the untoward fate of an honourable minded Parent, whose misfortune it was... the question is not at present whither my father has been imprudent or not, He and his family are in actual distress and it becomes my bounded duty to relieve them to the utmost of my power. I have done so; and all I want is the authority of your name to prevent Laing, from making any demands on me until May.[375]

With the help of James and his family Patrick Murray survived the severe Canadian winter and when he wrote to Maria in 1820 he seemed none the worse for the experience. Patrick was perhaps the last person to dish out financial advice as he had faced all too many financial difficulties of his own. However, in his eyes he had not been without success in his Canadian enterprises and he was not slow to point this out:

I conceive himself (Patrick) to be entitled to a grant of land not
less than 500 acres for obtaining for Government by purchase,
for the trifling sum of £1,200 in Indian goods from the store, a
county on Lake Erie and Lake Saint Clair of 3,000 square miles,
this if effected may be of service to my daughters.[376]

This may refer to his less than commendable land purchase from
the indigenous Indian tribes when he was chairman of the Hesse
Land Board or may be an entitlement for his service as Colonel of
the militia in the war of 1812. The deal was nevertheless held up
as 'an instructive model for the partial extrication of families from
their intergenerational financial problems',[377] but was not a path
copied by the Hay-Mackenzies. The last letter extant from Patrick
was written to Maria Mackenzie in July 1822, just one year before
his death. His financial position had improved, although he was
growing rather infirm. His second daughter, Mrs Isabella Gordon,
was now living with him and he was pleased to inform his sister
that his eldest daughter Mary had married a Mr Mechter:

… a gentleman of Brussels long resident in this country, he has
employments in this town which bring him in four or five
hundred pounds per annum, besides being a major of militia, he
is a man of talent and bears a most excellent character, his good
conduct to his first wife who was older than him, and had the
misfortune to be for some years unable to leave the house
through infirmity, and Mary's not inferior merit induce me to
conclude she is happily married.[378]

Patrick was entitled to land for his wartime services, but he did
not live long enough receive his reward. He died on 14th July 1823
at the very respectable age of 74 years. His life had been full and
although not always successful or indeed praiseworthy, it was
rarely boring. As a young man he was certainly a handful for his

father and his uncle, but later demonstrated his worth as a soldier and officer in the American wars and wrote with obvious pride about his son James and his naval career. His dealings with money were problematic and he seemed to lurch from one crisis to another. He relied, perhaps over-relied, on others, especially the long suffering mother of James, Eliza Smith, but his instincts proved sound and he was befriended with great loyalty. His two daughters in Canada, Marie Julie Murray and Isabella Murray, were rewarded for his service just one year after his death:

> The humble petition of... girls and (only) heirs of the late Patrick Murray, Esquire, in his lifetime, Lieutenant Colonel of Militia, resident in the city of Montréal. Expose your Lordship humbly, that the said Patrick Murray was Lieutenant Colonel, commander of the Fifth Battalion of Select Embodied Militia in this Province during the last war with the United States of America. That the said Patrick Murray, their father, died almost suddenly before his present request to Your Lordship to obtain land that His Majesty, in his goodness, has kindly granted to those that have served during the last war.
>
> In the hope that your lordship will extend the favor(sic) of His Majesty to them, they plead that the land had been granted their Father, they are granted... [379]

Their petition was granted and, although they were inaccurate in their statement that they were the only heirs of Patrick Murray,[380] they gratefully received a substantial grant of land in Abercromby, a few miles to the north of Montréal.

22

Valorous

The novel experience of peace throughout post-Napoleonic Europe meant that new naval appointments were few and far between. An inevitable peacetime contraction in the enormous size of the Royal Navy had taken place and large numbers of sailors had to find new occupations on land, a terrifying prospect for many who had spent the bulk of their lives afloat. Happily, James was not to be one of these unfortunates; he had been given a new command.

HMS Valorous, a 26-gun frigate, was still quite new, having been built and launched from Pembroke Dockyard on the south side of Milford Haven in 1816 and then immediately modified at Plymouth Dockyard by the addition of quarterdecks and forecastle. Although small by modern frigate standards, it was still a formidable ship, with a crew of 135 and 18 very powerful 32-pounder carronades on the upper deck and six 18-pounder carronades on the quarterdeck. Along with a couple of nine pounder Bow Chasers on the forecastle to complete its armament, it was a match for all but the largest frigates. When James took over on 14th February 1821[381] it was the largest ship he had so far commanded.

His new command and, of course, Matilda, his betrothed back in Plymouth, were not the only thing on Captain Murray's mind. Shore leave and petitioning for a new command had meant that James had spent some considerable time at the Admiralty offices in London. During the visits he had become well acquainted with the Cornish family of Benjamin Tucker, a very well-known name in naval circles in the early years of the 19th century.

Benjamin, for much of his early career, was secretary to Sir John Jervis (later to become Earl St. Vincent), one of the most famous names in British Naval history. Earl St. Vincent is best remembered today for his grumpy demeanour and uncompromising character. St. Vincent had many attributes, but strength as a team player was not one of them. His favourite expression, 'the die is cast,' gives a clue to his style of discussion. He imposed a strict and equal disciplinary code on both officers and men and his punishments were often immediate and harsh. For a relatively minor offence St. Vincent once ordered that a young midshipman, little more than a boy, should have his head shaved, a notice hung around his neck describing his crime and that he should clean the heads (toilets) until further notice. For a more serious offence, St. Vincent once ordained that two men, tried and convicted for mutiny on a Saturday, were to be executed on the Sunday. He could be less unforgiving when circumstances dictated, especially if the perpetrator was a young Horatio Nelson. During the battle of Cape St. Vincent, Nelson and his crew left the line of battle without orders and attacked and captured two enemy vessels. Nelson boarded and captured the first and then, crossing her deck, he captured a second which had collided in the general melee of the battle. When Admiral Jervis was queried about this breaking of orders he replied:

> It certainly was so, and if you ever commit such a breach of your orders, I will forgive you also.[382]

In addition to his successful naval career as hero of the battle of Cape St. Vincent, he commanded both the Mediterranean and the Channel fleets and he was also prominent against what he termed "the enormous evils and corruptions in the dockyards."

Working for Earl St. Vincent would have tried the patience of any man, but Benjamin Tucker seemed to cope admirably with the strains and was ultimately well rewarded for his loyal service. In January 1804, and again in February 1806, Benjamin Tucker, through the influence of his illustrious mentor, received the appointment of the Second Secretary to the Admiralty, a civil position of enormous influence in naval circles (the First Secretary was by tradition a political appointment). When political opinion swayed against the Whiggish Earl St. Vincent, Benjamin lost his job, but was then appointed to the position of Surveyor-General to the Duchy of Cornwall, a position he held until his death in 1829. This position was not without authority, particularly in the Tucker homeland of Cornwall, and allowed Benjamin to maintain both his interest and his influence in naval circles. Together with his brother Joseph, (who, as 'Surveyor to the Navy', was a member of the Navy Board and held overall responsibility for the design of British warships) he continued the St. Vincent crusade against dockyard corruption and bad practice, making some friends and many enemies along the way.[383]

Benjamin Tucker also made a great deal of money and was able to buy Trematon Castle, by now a picturesque ruin. Some called him a vandal in that he was not slow to demolish some of the original bailey walls when they blocked his view or where he considered them not suitable for purpose, but it is in his favour that he also arrested any further decay of the castle. He built a nine-bedroomed house in the bailey, two lodges and a great length of drive that zig-zagged up the hill. He landscaped the grounds, laid out gardens, created a huge walled garden and built an orangery, glass-houses, stables and other outbuildings. He filled his house with all sorts of valuable furnishings and established his own museum of natural and ethnological exhibits, including a 2,500-year-old Egyptian mummy and its two coffins.[384] Such a wealthy man with so many contacts would be a most useful ally for any aspiring naval officer. Would it not be absolutely perfect if he had an eligible young daughter as well?

When, on 30th May 1821, Captain James Murray married the 20-year-old Rachel Lyne Tucker, eldest daughter of Benjamin Tucker,[385] he was welcomed into her family with a very flattering speech from her doting father and her three ambitious and very able brothers.[386] His future seemed rosy indeed, despite the loss of the breath-taking attractions of Matilda Harris. The reasons for the breakup of this engagement are not reported, but perhaps the huge age difference did not help.

Still, Rachel was a 'catch' that Captain James Murray would not have been too despondent about, although it would not have escaped his notice that the age difference was similar to that between him and Matilda. A large age gap was not uncommon in relationships involving naval officers, so there was nothing to worry about – was there?

As well as planning his wedding, James was additionally responsible for preparing his new command for sea, as he was due to sail in July. He was also in Plymouth and, following the break-up of his engagement to Matilda, was probably dodging the unwelcome attentions of Matilda's father. John Harris was a very fiery character and Captain James Murray was certainly not on his Christmas card list.[387]

Initially James commenced an intense period of recruiting. In a muster, listed in June 1821, it was recorded that 11 men had 'run', the terminology used for desertion. In a complement of only 125 men this was quite a high percentage, particularly as most of the men were Able Seamen,[388] and they urgently needed replacement. As it turned out that was not too much of a problem because with the contraction of the Royal Navy following the defeat of Bonaparte there was a plethora of skilled men, especially in the traditional seafaring towns, who were looking for a new ship. James had been bombarded with volunteers and on 16th February alone he was able to add 16 new volunteers to his crew.[389]

Another volunteer, although not featuring on the ship's muster, was Rachel Murray née Tucker. With so little time together James was unwilling to give up his new wife so quickly and solved his dilemma by combining career and newly married life. When the Valorous weighed anchor and sailed out of Plymouth harbour towards Newfoundland on Sunday 8th July, Captain James Murray took Rachel with him.[390]

Women were permitted on board Royal Navy ships, when they were in port, at the Captain's discretion. In theory, the women aboard were only supposed to be the sailors' wives and were signed on board by the seaman who were responsible for their conduct. In practice, wives were very much in the minority and the majority of the women who came on board were more inclined towards carnal relations than marital affection. As a result, the scenes below deck, where there was no privacy, were not for the easily shocked and offended. At sea, Admiralty regulations did not allow the carrying of women but, as with many regulations, this was often ignored. At the Battle of Cape St. Vincent at least 23 women and 20 children were aboard Royal Navy ships.[391] Some wives, such as the Gunner's wife (who often looked after the children on board), were even encouraged. It was not common but certainly not unknown for Captains' wives to travel with their husbands, although the practice was more widespread in peacetime. Captain James was happy to unofficially add to the statistic.

Rachel Tucker was still a very young woman and had been doted upon by her father and her three brothers. Despite having many naval connections in the family, it would have been quite an eye opener for her to live in the crowded, damp and very masculine conditions aboard a Royal Navy frigate. To this can be added the very real discomforts of sea-borne life in the Newfoundland station, especially in the winter months. The conditions off the eastern seaboard of northern Canada were amongst the most challenging in the world and it required expert seamanship and a great depth of experience to successfully patrol the wild seas. The Valorous arrived at St. John's, Newfoundland, on the 14th August and after a couple of weeks it began its tour of duty around the coasts of Nova Scotia, Labrador and Newfoundland.

The Newfoundland Station owed its origin to fish. John Cabot had first drawn the area to the attention of Europeans in 1497 when it was remarked that it was just necessary to let down a basket and the fish would swim into it. It soon became a summer mecca for the fishing fleets of many nations, but by 1610 it had become established as an English colony. Thereafter it became an area of British settlement and the Royal Navy established a base to protect both the fishing fleets and the local inhabitants. This protection didn't always run to the indigenous local inhabitants. The British settlers had better relations with the Inuit people than the local Indian tribes as the white men and the Indians had developed a mutual distrust and tended to kill each other on sight. Inevitably, lurid stories had circulated about the local Indians .

The indigenous peoples were said to be extremely dextrous in the use of bows and arrows. They could take four arrows, with three between fingers of the left hand, with which they would hold the bow whilst the fourth would notch the string. The arrows were discharged as quickly as they could draw the bow and with, it was said, great certainty in their aim. They were particularly feared for their practice of scalping. Their technique was to skin the whole face at least as far as the upper lip. Joseph Banks had in his possession a scalp taken from Sam Frye, a fisherman who was shot by the Indians as he tried to swim away from them. The Indians kept the scalp a year but the features were so well preserved that when the same Indians were being pursued by British settlers they dropped the scalp. It was immediately recognised as the unfortunate Sam Frye.

Rachel and James had little to worry about though, as by the time they reached the area the shameful extermination of the native peoples had been going on for many years. By that time the Newfoundland Indians were almost extinct and only a handful remained. [392]

By 1821 the civil authorities had begun to take over responsibility for this northern station outpost from the military and the Governor of the Province was now considered an important position. Nevertheless, the Royal Navy was still the main vehicle to impose authority and law. The naval squadron sent annually to Newfoundland usually consisted of at least two rated warships and an armed sloop, with the Commodore on the Newfoundland station often commanding a 50-gun flagship. The fishing boats typically began to arrive in early May and the naval squadron usually arrived a little later, in July or August, and returned to England, often via Lisbon, by the end of October. Because of the great dangers inherent in the severe winter weather the ships, both military and civil, rarely stayed in Newfoundland for more than ten weeks each year.[393] So it was with the Valorous. Between August and 26th September the Valorous patrolled the remote coastlands of Labrador and Newfoundland with only one substantial break in Halifax harbour taken in mid-September. A couple of minor brushes with potential smugglers was all the action the Valorous could boast of before it set sail, in early November, for Europe. Rather than Lisbon, the usual port of call, the Valorous spent Christmas and New Year in Cadiz, Spain, and by late January she was back in Plymouth.[394] A similar cruise took place later in the year and in May 1822 the Valorous swept out of the Hamoaze to cross the Atlantic once more, but this time it was without Rachel. She had not enjoyed an easy first cruise. Gales had accompanied the ship over much of its journey, especially on the homeward passage. Even well into August, the ship had come close to numerous icebergs and at some stage a collision must have occurred as the Master's log reported that the ship was taking in a considerable quantity of water.[395] The dangers were emphasised just the next year when on 23rd June HMS Drake, with mail from England, was completely wrecked on the south coast of Newfoundland.

23

I was not sober one hour

Rachel's first Royal Navy cruise had revealed that the ship was not a particularly happy one and for the crew, punishments seemed all too frequent. [396] The commander of a Royal Navy ship was virtually omnipotent at sea. This was even more the case with the captains of the smaller ships, the frigates and sloops, who were often sent on individual carrying or reconnaissance missions and had no recourse to a Flag Captain or Admiral for their orders. In their isolated positions they would be able to enjoy the benefits but also suffer the disadvantages of sole command, and they would be judged according to the results of their decisions. Any obvious or perceived misdemeanour on their part would lead to court martial, an automatic event if a ship was lost or severely damaged.

At the back of every officer's mind must have been the fate of Admiral Byng, who was blamed for the loss of Minorca in 1756. He was court-martialled for his actions and was found guilty of failing to 'do his utmost' to prevent Minorca falling to the French. His sentence was to be shot by a firing squad, an action which was carried out on 14th March 1757. Harsh treatment indeed, but it probably did wonders in concentrating the mind of every Royal Navy Captain on doing their duty. They would ensure that all their crew did the same and measures would be taken to enforce such a path.

The perception of punishment in the Napoleonic-era Navy involved a code that was often considered to be unduly brutal, with the men suffering frequent beatings, usually involving the infamous 'cat o' nine tails'. Although there was an element of truth in this accusation, it should be studied in the context of a brutal normality where, in civilian life, the death penalty could and would be prescribed for very minor offences and transportation for life was seen to be the softer option. Instant obedience to orders on board a ship of war was a necessity in times of emergency, and such obedience was sometimes enforced by the use of severe punishment. On 30th April 1808 James Murray and his crew in the Unique observed a 'flogging round the fleet' in Barbados. It was not recorded what the offence was for the doomed wrongdoer, but his sentence was 300 lashes. He was to be rowed from ship to ship so that each ship's company could witness the punishment. At 6.30 in the evening it was the turn of the Unique. On coming aboard, the sentenced seaman was seen to be in a pitiful state, having his back covered in lacerations and suffering from a severe loss of blood. His sentence was still carried out, but after 36 lashes from the Boatswain's Mate the Unique's surgeon intervened and deemed that he should receive no more at the present time. He was taken on board HMS Nelly, his home ship, and, after a brief respite, his punishment was resumed when he was deemed medically able to suffer the consequences.

This was the customary procedure and sentences could take months or years to complete, depending on how much damage a man could sustain at any one time. Following a bout of flogging, the hapless sailor's lacerated back was frequently rinsed with brine or seawater, which served as a crude antiseptic. Although the purpose was to control infection, it caused the sailor additional pain and gave rise to the expression, 'rubbing salt into the wound.' Normally 250-500 lashes would lead to the death of the wrong-doer as infection would usually spread as a result of the wounds received.

Punishment was not always quite so dramatic. Until it was banned in 1809, 'starting' was used as a quick punishment for a man not thought to be pulling his weight or moving fast enough to comply with an order. To 'start' a man, a seaman would be hit across his back with a cane or short length of rope, usually administered by the Boatswain's Mate. This practice was often deeply resented by the men as its use was arbitrary and very dependent on the captain. By 1809 only the most sadistic of officers were still allowing the practice to take place on their ships but a more formalised punishment by use of flogging was still very common.

In 1806 new regulations had been introduced which stated that a captain was not to order punishment 'without sufficient cause, nor with greater severity than the offence shall really deserve'. The maximum number of lashes that could be awarded to any individual was fixed at twelve and any more was supposed to be dealt with by a court martial. This rule was routinely broken, quite openly, with Captains writing in their journals the number of lashes awarded. James Murray was no exception, as illustrated in his actions towards Seaman MacNamara, one of his new crew members when he took over command of HMS Satellite in 1816. On 25th March 1816, just before James took command, James MacNamara,[397] not for the first time, had received 24 lashes for drunkenness, in the company of Richard Thomas, who received nine lashes for insolence and neglect of duty. The following day MacNamara received another 48 lashes, a very severe number. The log does not indicate the reason for the second punishment, but its severity may have something to do with MacNamara's position on the ship.[398] He is referred to as Mr MacNamara and this prefix was normally only used for senior NCOs, officers and the 'young gentlemen' on board a ship. It is difficult to avoid the conclusion that HMS Satellite had a morale and discipline problem at that time. For example, a month later, three punishments of 24 lashes were awarded for riotous conduct and fighting and just two weeks after that, on 16th May, Saul Campbell and William Young received 24 lashes each for a variety of offences including drunkenness, neglect of duty, theft, absence without leave and insolence. On 17th May two further punishments were awarded and a further four more took place on 24th May. Part of the problem was the extended period of time the ship had been laid up in Valetta harbour as it was much easier to maintain discipline whilst at sea than compete with the constant attractions of a nearby seaport. Despite this, the heavy amount of flogging on such a small ship would inevitably have had a deleterious impact on crew morale.

The crew breathed a sigh of relief when James Murray took up his position as Commander but James, whilst not a 'flogging captain', was no pushover and laid out his position early in his command when he sentenced Seaman Hearne to 48 lashes for mutinous behaviour, being drunk and neglecting his duty. Hearne was not alone at the flogging ceremony as, inevitably, he was accompanied by Mr MacNamara, back up to his old tricks again and receiving 36 lashes for repeated drunkenness.

The pattern of punishments in James Murray's last command illustrate the difficulties of discipline whilst in harbour. James, by now a very experienced officer with many years of command, had an all-volunteer crew when he left Plymouth in HMS Valorous on 4th July 1821 for the Newfoundland station. The honeymoon period ended on 26th July when the first punishments were awarded. By now the Valorous was in St. John's Harbour, Newfoundland, after a speedy but otherwise unremarkable passage across the Atlantic Ocean. Whilst in port, William Heedon enjoyed the delights of St. John's rather too much and was rewarded with the heavy sentence of 36 lashes for drunkenness. This quietened the ship down until 16th October when two seamen were punished following a court martial, although it is possible that these men did not belong to the Valorous. No further punishments were recorded until the ship, by now on its way home, reached Cadiz in Spain on 17th January 1822. Once again, shore leave brought out the worst in some of the men, with George Samford receiving 30 lashes and James McWilliams and David Fraser 24 lashes each for drunkenness and neglect of duty. The ship quietened down once more and there were no further misdemeanours requiring correction until the ship reached the home port of Plymouth. James McWilliams again, maybe not drunk this time but clearly disaffected, got 24 lashes for being absent without leave, as did William Hall. Finally, Robert Pally received 12 lashes for 'intolerance'.[399]

All formal punishments followed a certain ceremonial path. The crew were summoned on deck to 'witness punishment' and the drama was enhanced by a drum roll. With heads uncovered to show respect for the law, the ship's company was read the Article of War that the offender had contravened. The wrongdoer, or any supporting officer, was then asked if they had anything to say in mitigation of punishment. This was followed by the removal of all their upper clothing and their hands were secured to the rigging or the grating. At the order "Boatswain's mate, do your duty", a seaman wielded the 'cat' (a short rope to which was attached nine waxed cords of equal length, each with a small knot in the end) on the bare back of the offender. A regular dramatic routine then followed which would include pauses, the untangling of the tails of the 'cat', a drink of water etc. After a dozen lashes, a fresh Boatswain's Mate continued the punishment. After each stroke the cords were drawn through the Boatswain's Mate's fingers to remove the clotting blood. Left-handed Boatswain's Mates were especially valued by the more sadistic Captains because they would cross the cuts and so mangle the flesh even more. [400]

The experience of James Murray and his crew on the Unique supports the observation that as a punishment flogging was often ineffective, with the same men, such as the hapless James MacNamara, being flogged for the same offence time and again.

Some captains were known as 'flogging captains' for the ease
and frequency with which they resorted to corporal punishment.
Equally, a difficult and recalcitrant crew could make it impossible
for a captain to work his ship in a professional and efficient
manner. It was a difficult line to draw but the punishment log for
HMS Ruby tends to suggest that there was a serious underlying
problem. From April 1804 Captain Ferris' log detailed a
horrendous number of punishments. On Friday 13th April he
punished John Joly with 24 lashes for drunkenness and soiling his
hammock, George Durham with 33 lashes for drunkenness and
urinating between decks, James Chappel with 12 lashes for
filthiness and William Thomson with 12 lashes for showing
contempt to a junior officer. Just a few days later another four
more men were punished. Matters quietened down for a month
or so until 30th May, when five more punishments were carried
out, including to Thomas Donaldson who was awarded a serious
42 lashes. Just a week later, another five punishments took place.
Things reached a peak on 14th June when eight punishments were
carried out for a variety of offences, including insolence and
disobedience. Between 14th June and 23rd July another 14
punishments were awarded with one, William Clare, receiving 48
lashes.[401] In the navy at that time it was generally expected that
offences would increase when the crew had the time and money
to partake in the delights of shore leave, but when this continued
whilst at sea it suggested a more deep-seated problem.

A harsh or sadistic captain could make his crew's life a misery.
Despite this, there was a surprising acceptance of flogging as a
punishment by the sailors. In the mutinies at the Nore and
Spithead, where the complaints of the ordinary sailors were heard
and recorded, flogging was not mentioned, and whilst the ships
were under control of the mutineers at the Nore they also ordered
floggings to be carried out. However, this was not the universal
view and some individual accounts of life below deck rail against

the injustice of flogging.[402] On occasions, many of the rank and file sailors enthusiastically participated in physical punishment themselves in a particularly effective form of deterrent against crime. Aboard the Topaze on Thursday 6th April 1797, John Game and Richard Derrick were sentenced to 'run the gauntlet' for theft, as a few years later were Seamen Owen, Nulty and Denness, on the same ship.[403] Theft was a particularly heinous crime in the overcrowded world below decks and the convicted seamen could expect little sympathy from their shipmates. The crew lined up in two rows, chanting and shrieking, and the luckless Game, Derrick, Owen, Nulty and Denness were forced to run between the rows as they were continually struck by small rope whips and any other weapons the vengeful crew could lay their hands on, short of sharpened blades.

Flogging was finally abolished in the Royal Navy in 1881, but running the gauntlet continued in an unofficial capacity for many years longer.

The punishment records of James Murray's ships show that many of the disciplinary issues occurred during and immediately after shore leave, especially if the sailor had received his pay or prize money:

> I think I was not sober one hour when I was awake while the (prize) money lasted.[404]

The drinking culture had a firm hold on the seafarers of the period. It owes its origin, at least in part, to the difficulties in obtaining fresh water. Water, even in casks, would not keep indefinitely and the longer-lasting wine or beer was partially substituted, to stretch out the ration. This became formalised with the regular ration of a gallon of beer per day per man. Rum was introduced in the 18th century as the colonies in the West Indies were opened up for trade increasing the availability of molasses. Soon a half pint per day rum ration was being issued twice a day, with the rum mixed with water to form 'grog'; a drink beloved by generations of sailors.

Not surprisingly, drunkenness was a big problem throughout the navy, contributing to a large percentage of the floggings ordered. The effects of drink were sometimes very severe. In 1808 the entire Royal Marine garrison on the recently captured island of Marie Galante was reputedly incapacitated by excessive consumption of rum. The men in question had to be replaced by captured French slaves who worked on the promise that they would not be returned to their former owners. They stuck to their defensive tasks admirably.[405]

Captain Murray was very aware of the potential problems arising from grog. In an analysis of the punishments awarded on board James Murray's ships, just over 30 per cent of floggings were a result of drunkenness,[406] but these figures only tell part of the story. Drunkenness was tolerated on board to an extent, but was swiftly dealt with if there was any suggestion of it causing a dereliction of duty. Modern evidence shows that even small amounts of strong alcohol will have an effect on behaviour and response speed but in the early 19th century this was not understood. It was only necessary not to have any visible effects from alcohol over-consumption to escape censure. It remains a matter of conjecture just how much alcohol affected the efficiency of the sailors as they performed often very dangerous tasks at sea.

The flogging statistics for drunkenness do not tell the entire story. The vast majority of cases were as a result of shore leave and there were relatively few cases once the ship was at sea. In James Murray's ships the exception was HMS Ruby, where an exceptional amount of flogging for drunkenness and the harmful effects of such drunkenness (urinating in hammocks etc.) slewed the statistics. In a tough life, the alcohol intake would help to relieve some of the real hardships often borne by the hardy seamen and any attempt to cut the rum ration would be strongly resisted by a ship's crew. When, in September 1808, the Unique restocked in Trinidad there was no rum available. This could have been a cause for mutiny, but James Murray defused the situation by a careful substitution, and the ship took on eight barrels of brandy instead. No complaints were registered.

The food seemed less of an issue, but for many seamen it was equally important. In an analysis of the Master's and Captain's Logs written on board James Murray's ships, only the weather gets more prominence than drink and food:[407]

> Englishmen and more especially seamen, love their bellies above anything else... to make any abatement on the quantity or agreeableness of the victuals... will sooner render them disgusted with the king's service than any other hardship put upon them.[408]

The food was of variable quality but, despite its popular reputation, usually good and for many the quality and quantity of food was significantly better than they could expect on shore. In fact, meal times were often considered to be the highlight of the day. Food was often salted or dried and then stored in casks. Despite their poor reputation the despoliation rates for the casks were, in most cases, less than one per cent.[409]

Scurvy had been largely overcome by the end of the 18th century, thanks mainly to an acceptance of the experimental proof demonstrated by James Lind from an examination of the ships' logs of Commodore Anson and George Murray's circumnavigation of the world in 1740.

The ships biscuit, or bread, "a sort of bread... good for a whole year after it is baked,"[410] has become notorious and, in truth, was often very old and invaded by voracious weevils. It was baked by dedicated supply yards situated in the main port bases, the one at Portsmouth being called, with grim coincidence, 'the weevil victualing yard.' The officers had the same food as the men, but usually it was supplemented by food and wine bought at their own expense. The officers and, on good days, the men, were also supplied with fresh food from the chickens, pigs and sometimes cows housed aboard the ship. In addition fishing was common and fresh fish often appeared on the menu.

24

The last cruise

Life at sea could also be very tedious, particularly in the confined quarters of a naval frigate, and when in May 1822 the Valorous sailed for her second Newfoundland cruise, Rachel decided to stay with her father and brothers, sharing her life between the office in London and the comfortable surroundings of the family home at Trematon Castle in Saltash, Cornwall.

The Valorous arrived back in St. John's on 18th June 1822 and then completed a similar uneventful patrol to that of the previous year. The main excitement for Captain James Murray on this cruise was his passenger list. Patrick Murray, writing to his sister in July, informed her of the news:

> I had a letter two days ago from James, he is on the Newfoundland station and tells me that his Admiral Sir Charles Hamilton proposes this autumn to hoist his flag on board Valorous and return with Lady Hamilton in that ship to England.[411]

Sir Charles Hamilton had established his headquarters on board the Valorous and his dealings emphasised the difficulty of life in Newfoundland at that time. Sir Charles had taken up office in 1818 at a most inopportune time. In the previous year a devastating fire had destroyed much of St. John's and reconstruction work had proved to be too expensive since the cod industry had collapsed and poverty was widespread. In addition, the role of combined Admiral / Governor had served Newfoundland very well in its earlier years but was now seen to be outdated. Sir Charles took it upon himself to fight a rear-guard action to defend the role. He was only the second Governor to live in the colony on a full time basis and was the first to be accompanied by his family. Nevertheless, he was unpopular, mainly because of his intense conservatism and reluctance to change. He appreciated the importance of fishing and supported measures to help the industry, but he completely dismissed any agricultural development, simply stating that the soil was too poor. He was involved in helping the many people in poverty at that time, particularly after receiving a petition from the people of St. John's with over three pages of names detailing the misery and distress of the poor. However, most of the money at his disposal was spent in getting rid of them, mainly by deporting them to Britain or the other North American colonies.[412]

His dispute with the Newfoundland Chief Justice, Francis Forbes, reached an almost farcical level. Chief Justice Forbes had frequently overturned Hamilton's pronouncements as not having the force of law. In response, Hamilton refused Forbes permission to return to England on leave. Forbes then countered by threatening to resign immediately, and his stomach condition, not previously a problem, mysteriously and immediately got much more serious. Forbes got the leave he desired when medical reasons finally necessitated his removal from the island.[413]

Sir Charles kept up a continual stream of correspondence whilst on board the Valorous. He seemed particularly concerned with law and order, and he wrote to Lord Bathurst:

Due to the rising number of capital crimes in the province, I urge the necessity of the Chief Justice returning after his four

month leave, as none but the Supreme Court can convict such
cases.

There is the lingering suspicion that it was the speedy return of
Forbes, rather than a rising crime rate, which was uppermost in
Hamilton's mind at that moment. However, there was some
serious crime and Hamilton described at length the situation with
three dangerous convicts who were imprisoned in HMS Ranger,
which was to follow the Valorous into Portsmouth harbour. Of
the three convicted men two were later sentenced to life
transportation and one to death, but Thomas Sturgess, the one
condemned to death, was later to receive a conditional pardon.[414]

It was probably with some relief that on 1st November 1822,
Captain James Murray could decant Sir Charles and his entourage
onto home territory, leave colonial politics behind and reflect on
his next cruise, back to the familiar West Indies and the relatively
uncomplicated life at sea.

The Valorous arrived in Barbados on Monday 3rd February
1823 and embarked upon a marathon cruise to South America and
the southern Caribbean. They arrived back in Barbados in
September and after re-victualing they embarked upon the second
part of the itinerary, arriving in Vera Cruz, Mexico, in early
February 1824.

Tours of duty of this sort, without critical deadlines and
without the possibility of being blown out of the water by a French
Man-O'-War were of immense popularity to adventurers,
botanists, anthropologists and others eager to expand their
knowledge of the many marvels still to be found in the relatively
untraveled world that most people could then experience. Names
who have availed themselves of such opportunities include such
luminaries as Sir Joseph Banks and Charles Darwin. Another such
person was Mr Crawford, an American gentleman. At that time,
Mexico was a highly unsettled region of the world, particularly in

the aftermath of their War of Independence, and roaming gangs of bandits were by no means uncommon. Why Mr Crawford and an accompanying party from the Valorous set off on a tour of the interior of Mexico is now unknown, but the potential delights of spotting rare fauna and flora would, to them, far exceed any possibility of an attack from bandits.

They got it badly wrong. Inland from Santa Cruz, just after the road climbs from the Hacienda of Santa Gertrude, there is a wild and rugged spot. Here the unlucky Valorous party was ambushed by the celebrated Mexican bandit Gomez. Gomez has been described in not very flattering terms:

> The enormities committed by this monster in human shape are scarcely to be paralleled in the histories of the most barbarous savages. He robbed equally friends and foes... on whom he committed every refinement of cruelty, mutilating them in a manner too shocking to describe.[415]

The short but brutal confrontation that then followed left all the Valorous party bound, gagged and relieved of their possessions. Mr Crawford presumably had resisted and was brutally murdered for his attempt to thwart the robbery. The official account stated that Crawford was travelling with Captain Murray, and so it can be assumed that James Murray was one of the 'lucky' travellers who escaped with being only robbed and bound.

A much shaken Captain Murray lived to weigh anchor and sail his Valorous via Havana, Cuba, back across the Atlantic Ocean to Plymouth, where on 23rd July he ended what turned out to be the final act of his distinguished naval career.

James remained on half pay, but the much smaller navy had no further need of his services. Although he did not have the opportunity to command any ships of the line, he had shown his mettle as a sailor, effectively handling his ships in some of the most difficult seas in the world. In combat he had played his part in most of the major engagements of the French Revolutionary and Napoleonic Wars in the West Indies and the North Sea and had always shown the courage and coolness expected of a Royal Navy officer. He had demonstrated that he had the personal skills and the diplomacy of decision when it was needed and, although he ran a taut ship, he was never accused of being a flogging captain. Indeed, a published paper on the 'benefits of flannel', identified him as a caring and considerate officer:

> The advantages of flannel as a preventative from disease in warm as well as in cold climates is now well understood... Captain Murray, late of HMS Valorous, told me that he was so strongly from former experience... of the protection afforded by the constant use of flannel next the skin that, when on his arrival England in December 1833 after two years' service amid the icebergs on the coast of Labrador and the ship was ordered to sail immediately for the Indies, he ordered the purser to draw two flannel shirts and pairs of drawers for each man and instituted a regular daily inspection to see that they were worn. These precautions were by the happiest results... with a crew of 150 men, he visited every island in the West Indies and many of the ports in the Gulf of Mexico and... returned to England without the loss of a single man or having any sick on board on his arrival.

That the superior health enjoyed by the crew of the Valorous was attributable chiefly to the means employed by their humane and intelligent commander is shown by the analogy with the Recruit, for although constant communication was kept up between the latter and the other ships in which the sickness prevailed and all were exposed to the same external causes of disease, no case of sickness occurred on-board the Recruit. Facts like these are truly instructive by proving how far man possesses the power to protect himself from injury when he has received necessary instruction and chooses to adapt his conduct to his situation.[416]

His personal qualities were such that he was able to attract officers to serve on his ships, such as Sir John James Hope-Johnstone, the son of Admiral Hope, and Lieutenant Thomas Ball, who had loyally followed him on several ship contracts. He was inordinately proud of his service in the Royal Navy and, had the war continued and had he survived, he would have almost certainly emulated his grandfather George and displayed his own banner as Admiral James Murray.[417]

25

The day will come

T he recently married James and Rachel had so far spent very little time together as man and wife, so the prospect of a prolonged shore period on half pay was met with some enthusiasm. The couple moved to the Highlands of Scotland and rented Assynt House, a property on the estate of Hugh Munro of Novar, magnificently situated in the hills above Evanton in Easter Ross and not too far from Tarbat House, the home of Aunt Maria Mackenzie of Cromartie.

Whilst at Assynt House, James and Rachel were able to search for a more permanent residence in the area. They focussed on an attractive site in Contin near Dingwall, close to the shore of Loch Achilty and took out a 99-year lease from the landowner, Sir George Mackenzie of Coul. There they began to build their new house and, additionally, James ensured that he would join the prestigious county land-holding class by taking on a separate 31-year lease from Sir George Mackenzie on 600 acres of adjoining land. There, like so many other land owners in the area, he established a sheep farm.[418] In a prominent descriptive text of the time, the ensuing property was wholesomely praised:

> The principal recent improvement in this parish is at Craigdarroch, where Captain James Murray of the Royal Navy has erected a beautiful residence within a short walk of Loch Achilty. The house is a substantial and comfortable building, and stands in a romantic situation, commanding a view of the lake and surrounding scenery.

The garden and grounds have been laid out with great taste, and a track of barren moor has been, by persevering industry and judicious outlay, converted into productive soil.[419]

Captain James and Rachel entered their beautiful new home in December 1827. The house had two large public rooms, four bedrooms, two dressing rooms, a large kitchen, scullery and full servants' quarters. Unusually for the time, the house also enjoyed the luxury of piped water. Adjoining the main house was a two-stall stable block and a coach house.[420] Whilst not being a house of the first rank, it was comfortable, modern and quite acceptable to entertain some of the more prominent families of the county. Life looked good. In Captain Murray's own words, Rachel and he then 'lived together as married persons and enjoyed uninterrupted domestic confidences and felicity'.[421]

The Murrays soon achieved their objective of being socially accepted by the 'first families' of the area. Apart from his aunt and the Cromartie family, James had become very friendly with another Mackenzie family in the area and this one was right at the very top of the social hierarchy. Lord Mackenzie of Seaforth was the titular chief of Clan Mackenzie. The Mackenzies were considered one of the most powerful clans in the Scottish Highlands and at their greatest strength their territories and influence had stretched from the Outer Hebrides right across Scotland to the Black Isle. Even as late as 1715, Seaforth had raised an army of 3,000 men in support of the Jacobite Cause.

James Alexander Stewart-Mackenzie of Brahan was the present incumbent chief, although he would have been better known to James as the son of Vice Admiral Keith Stewart, the son of the Earl of Galloway and brother to Catherine Stewart of Shambellie, from his childhood village of New Abbey in the Stewartry of Kirkcudbright.

James Alexander Stewart-Mackenzie only had a connection to

the ancient line of the Seaforths through marriage, but this marriage threw him directly into the middle of the infamous prophecy of Coinneach Odhar, the Brahan Seer. By the early 19th century Coinneach Odhar had become a legendary figure of Scottish Highland history, and Highlanders even then would recall a significant number of prophesies which were attached to him, including the coming of the Caledonian Canal through Inverness:

One day ships will sail round the back of Tomnahurich Hill.[422]

The coming of the road network:

The day will come when the hills of Ross will be strewed with ribbons.

The Highland Clearances:

The day will come, and it is not far off, when farm-steadings will be so few and far between, that the crow of the cock shall not be heard from the one steading to the other.[423]

The Battle of Culloden:

Oh! Drumossie, thy bleak moor shall, ere many generations have passed away, be stained with the best blood of the Highlands. Glad am I that I will not see the day.[424]

And the coming of piped water, electricity and gas:

The day will come when fire and water shall run in streams, through all the streets and lanes of Inverness.

It is difficult to verify the historical accuracy of these prophesies as they were part of an essentially oral culture and thus were passed down by word of mouth from one generation to another. It is even difficult to verify the existence of the man called the Brahan Seer. He seems to have been an amalgamation of several people, one being a fairly harmless historical individual from the Seaforth Brahan estates and another being a legendary earlier character who was executed as a witch. It is even likely that many of the prophesies attributed to Coinneach Odhar have been an amalgam of predictions from a variety of other sources; for example some similar predictions were made by the mediaeval Thomas the Rhymer, from the Scottish Borders.

Whatever the origin, the 'Curse of the Mackenzies', the most famous of the Seer's prophesies and the one which is associated with James Murray's friend, James Alexander Stewart-Mackenzie, is so precise as to invite wonder. Particularly so, as a number of prominent people, such as Sir Humphrey Davy (who may have confused him with Thomas the Rhymer), Walter Scott (who certainly didn't) and Mr Morrit of Rokeby (MP for Northampton), all verified that they had heard the prediction before it came to pass. A prominent local laird, Duncan Davidson of Tulloch Castle, Dingwall, wrote in 1878 that he had heard the 'curse' over 70 years earlier and well before many of the revelations had come to pass. As a personal friend of Seaforth, he insisted that the Mackenzie family were very familiar with the 'curse' too.

The 'Curse of the Mackenzies' arose as a result of the Brahan Seer, a worker on the Brahan Estates and already well known to have prophesying skills, being asked by Lady Seaforth how her husband, away in France on business, was faring. The reluctant answer from the Seer was that he was faring all too well, and was having liaisons with the many beautiful ladies of the French court. Lady Mackenzie, a lady of indifferent temperament, was furious in her anger and ordered the immediate execution of the Seer. By tradition, he was burnt in a spiked tar barrel at Chanonry Point, near Fortrose and a stone slab by the lighthouse is said to mark the spot where he died. Coinneach Odhar had the presence of mind before he died to utter what became the infamous prophecy, which would foretell the end of the Seaforth Mackenzies:

> The line of Seaforth will come to an end in sorrow. I see the last head of his house both deaf and dumb. He will be the father of four fair sons, all of whom he will follow to the tomb. He will live careworn, and die mourning, knowing that the honours of his line are to be extinguished forever; that no future chief of the Mackenzies shall bear rule at Brahan or in Kintail.

> His inheritor will be a white-coifed (hooded) lass, who will kill her sister. As a sign that these things are coming to pass, there shall be four great lairds in the days of this last Seaforth, the deaf and dumb chief. One shall be buck-toothed, another hare-lipped, another half-witted, and the fourth a stammerer. Chiefs like these shall be the neighbours of the last of the Seaforths; and when he sees them, he may know that his sons are doomed to death, that his lands shall pass away to the stranger, and that his race shall come to an end.[425]

Francis Humberston Mackenzie (1754-1815) was the Chief of Clan Mackenzie and, like all his forebears, he was traditionally known as Seaforth. As a boy he suffered from scarlet fever, which resulted in the loss of his hearing and almost all his speech. Ominously, the predicted four lairds living in Francis' environs, i.e. one buck-toothed, another hare-lipped, another half-witted, and the fourth a stammerer, have all been historically identified and verified. Francis' legitimate children were William Frederick Mackenzie, George Leveson Boucherat Mackenzie, William Frederick Mackenzie (same name as the pre-deceased younger brother) and Francis John Mackenzie. Alas, as predicted, all died before Francis. This left the Hon. Mary Elizabeth Frederica Mackenzie as heiress to her father's estates. She had first married Admiral Sir Samuel Hood and was thus known as Lady Hood. She had been in the Far East with her husband and when he passed away she returned to Brahan wearing the traditional Indian white coif of mourning (thus becoming the 'hooded lass from the East'). In 1823 Lady Hood, accompanied by her sister, Lady Caroline Mackenzie, was in control of a pony carriage returning to their ancestral seat of Brahan Castle. For reasons unknown, the ponies bolted and the carriage overturned. Lady Caroline Mackenzie was thrown out and later tragically died of her injuries. A short distance west of the site of Brahan Castle, close to the Dingwall–Ullapool road (A835), is a monument to Lady Caroline Mackenzie. The Latin inscription on the monument translates as:

> At this point, according to the prophecy, Caroline Mackenzie,
> daughter of Francis, Lord Seaforth, was snatched from life: her
> sister who shared the same hazard was the last surviving hope
> of restoration of his house. 1823.

Coinneach Odhar predicted that, 'the lands will pass away to a stranger' and the stranger was none other than James Murray's old friend, James Alexander Stewart Mackenzie.[426]

James Alexander, on taking over the estates in 1815 by virtue of his wife, was a colourful character in his own right. The Mackenzie family had owned the Seaforth estate, which included the island of Lewis in the Outer Hebrides, since 1610, but by 1815 the estate had fallen into severe financial difficulties. A Lewis historian suggested that contemporary opinion was not flattering towards the latest head of the Seaforth estate:

> Mrs Stewart Mackenzie was a most outstanding person and
> probably the ablest of the Mackenzies, but had a husband whose

imaginative ideas for increasing his rapidly diminishing income were not matched by his power of accomplishment. [427]

James Alexander Stewart Mackenzie was destined to play a major part in James Murray's life, especially after he entered public service as the Member of Parliament for Ross-shire in 1831 and for Ross and Cromarty in 1833. His personal incompetence did not stop him becoming a Privy Councillor, Governor and Commander-in-Chief of Ceylon (1837-41), and Lord High Commissioner of the Ionian Islands (1841-43). He even tried to issue his own banknotes for use in his estates. It is likely that Stewart Mackenzie issued less than a thousand of these notes, and their short life suggests that the note-issuing scheme was not a success.

They live in the midst of filth and smoke

Another Mackenzie family, The Mackenzies of Coul, also became close friends to the Murray family. The baronetcy of Coul was created in 1673 and by 1822 the incumbent was George Steuart Mackenzie, 7th of Coul. The Coul family were distantly related to Captain Murray through Sir John Mackenzie, 3rd of Coul, who in 1703 had married Helen, daughter of Patrick, 3rd Lord Elibank and the aunt of Admiral George Elibank, James' grandfather.

Sir George Steuart Mackenzie's chief claim to fame was his interest in science, especially geology. He first became known to the scientific world in 1800, when he proved that the constituent of diamond was carbon, demonstrated by a series of experiments in which he was said to have made free use of his mother's jewels. It is not recorded how the proud mother reacted to her rather over-inquisitive son.

George's inquisitiveness later paid off when he became a fellow of the Royal Societies of both London and Edinburgh. In 1810 George undertook a journey to Iceland, and later the Faroe Islands, to study their geology. On his return he presented an account of his observations before the Edinburgh Royal Society. A book entitled 'Travels in Iceland' was published and George contributed the sections concerning the voyage and the travels, the mineralogy, rural economy, and the commerce of the island. This was the first of a large number of learned publications to come from the pen of George Mackenzie of Coul. In addition to science he turned his pen to the subject of agriculture, but with this topic he entered rather more contentious ground.

The central core of the issue was the subject of agricultural improvement. In an era when almost all of the land was in the hands of a few landowners and the vast majority of the common people were engaged in small scale agriculture, often of a subsistence nature, any change in agricultural practice would inevitably have a severe impact upon the resident populace. By the early 19th century Galloway landlords had become aware of the extra profit that could be made from cattle breeding for export to the expanding markets of England. Arable land, often land previously used for subsistence, was laid down to grass and enclosed by dykes. Some of the small scale farmers, accustomed to the use of common grazing and open fields, were soon forced out of agriculture. The practice was not helped by some landlords increasing rents and serving eviction notices:

> That same year many of the proprietors enclosed their grounds to stock them with black cattle, and by that means turned out a vast number of tenants at the term of Whitsunday, whereby numbers of them became destitute.[428]

As young James Murray grew up in nearby New Abbey he became familiar with the debates raging over land practices, and would have seen first-hand the impact of rapid change in land management and tenancy procedures in the estates of notable agricultural improvers such as old William Craik from Arbigland.[429] James would have also heard the tales of protest at such 'improvements'. A group of small tenant farmers and cottars, nicknamed the 'Levellers', took direct action to stop these hated 'improvements'. They broke down (leveled) some of the hated dykes which enclosed the land and hindered common grazing, and their actions caused panic amongst the established landed class. In the summer of 1724 the local landlords called for state intervention and troops of dragoons were brought in. The 'rising' was soon crushed and the ringleaders were imprisoned or sent overseas. Murray of Cavens, a descendant of the Elibank Murrays, was one of the landowners to be targeted, although no large scale disturbances reached the Kirkbean area.[430]

One very significant result of these 'improvements' was the migration of large numbers of people off the land to new towns and villages or to the overseas colonies. James Murray lived close to the village of Carsethorn where thousands of emigrants took their last look at their native homeland before sailing to North America, the West Indies or Australasia. It would have been a common sight in New Abbey to see virtually destitute people making their way through the village towards nearby Carsethorn carrying their few possessions with them as they hurried to catch the emigrant ships such as the Lovely Nelly, which in 1775 took 82 emigrants to Prince Edward Island.[431]

By the early 19th century the Highlands of Scotland were experiencing a different and more virulent form of agricultural improvement and Captain Murray's closest associates were amongst those who were at the forefront of the movement.

The years following the Jacobite Rebellion saw a sharp rise in the population, which put pressure on the use of the limited available agricultural land.[432] Highland landowners (chiefs) had evolved a different relationship with their tenants to elsewhere in Scotland. In return for a minimum rent, the chiefs had a ready-made source of labour and a fighting militia to support them. Land ownership was different too because a large number of small tenantry with very tenuous legal rights occupied large areas of land owned by just a few landlords. The rationalisation of the land into small farms, as had happened in southern Scotland and much of

England, had not taken place here. The failure of the Jacobite risings of 1715 and 1745 and the extreme measures taken by the Government to destroy clan power afterwards would ultimately force the clan chiefs to look at their land in a new way. The clan concept of a heritable trusteeship of a group of loosely related kinsmen ultimately gave way to a legal title to the once collective land and the end of the traditional agricultural methods. The forces of capitalism spelled the doom of the old clan kinship system.[433]

The Highland lairds had seen the success of enclosure and new methods of farming in the Lowlands and they now began to introduce similar measures which had, at their core, the concept of monetary profit. Indeed, by the end of the 18th century the strategic management of almost all Highland estates was dominated by maximising opportunities in the marketplace and thus increasing the estate income. The proprietors of some of the massive and ancient Highland estates saw that a way to realise a greater income from their lands was to get rid of their tenants, who were often living on subsistence terms and paying only minimum rent. Thus began the age of the Clearances.

Not all landlords behaved in the same way. There were some who tried to improve agriculture without disturbing or losing their tenantry. Others tried to industrialise and diversify their estates. Some attempted to subsidise their properties from their own incomes. Some lairds ignored change completely and closed their eyes to the opportunities and others blundered on until they fell into the widening pit of bankruptcy. Most, eventually, adopted some policy of population reduction.[434]

New factors or managers were introduced to oversee the changes and many of the traditional tenants in chief, the tacksmen, began to lose their position in local society. New schemes to move the populace to coastal areas for fishing or kelp enterprises, or resettlement abroad in North America or Australasia, often went side by side with voluntary migration. Sometimes the opportunity of migration was eagerly grasped by the poverty stricken former clansmen as a way to improve their quality of life,[435] but, sadly, in other cases, the re-settlement or emigration came after the people had been forcefully evicted from their homes and had seen their roof-timbers burned down. Inevitably the greatest loss was faced by those people at the bottom of the social scale, the people without tenure of the land. They included the squatters, the under tenants and the 'scallags' who were the most numerous and the most vulnerable members of Highland society.

James' new adopted homeland, Easter Ross, was of mixed topography. To the west the land was hilly, boggy, isolated and difficult to farm, but to the east there was a great deal of arable land on the flatter, more fertile, soils. The Highland areas of Easter Ross were soon under threat from extensive sheep farms and the arable areas faced similar problems to those already described in lowland Scotland, namely population reduction caused by the parcelling out of the land to make small consolidated farms. James, his friends and new acquaintances were faced with stark choices, and in most cases chose the 'improvement' road. Sir George Mackenzie of Coul was a particularly outspoken supporter and in 1813 he wrote a book justifying the clearances with the clear message:

> The necessity for reducing the population in order to introduce valuable improvements, and the advantages of committing the cultivation of the soil to the hands of a few... [436]

George was also a firm supporter of sheep farming:

> We have heard but a few feeble voices exclaim against the necessity of removing the former possessors to make way for shepherds.[437]

He had little sympathy for the ancient tenantry, those people who would suffer dispossession:

> They [the landless Highlanders] live in the midst of filth and smoke. That is their choice. They will yet find themselves happier and more comfortable in the capacity of servants to substantial tenants than in their present situation.[438]

James Murray himself had established a sheep farm in his newly acquired 600 acres of land at Contin. However, unlike many others, in doing so he did not dispossess any indigenous tenants.

Another local man at the centre of agricultural change in Easter Ross was Hugh Munro of Novar, James Murray's acquaintance and contemporary. He was the son and heir of Sir Hector Munro and administered the large Novar estates in Easter Ross and Southern Sutherland. General Sir Hector once held the position of Commander-in-Chief of India before retiring to his estates in Ross-shire, and in 1782 is credited with building the Fyrish Monument near Evanton, Easter Ross. Land clearance for sheep and consolidation of arable farms was already taking place on his land on a significant scale, and considerable local unemployment was the result. As a job creation scheme he organised the building of the Fyrish monument, its appearance to represent the Gate of Negapatam, a port in Madras, India, which he captured for the British in 1781. Local legend tells that after the villagers had transported large boulders to the top of the hill where the monument was to be situated, Sir Hector Munro rolled all of the stones down the hill again so that he could then pay the villagers double the amount for them having to complete the task twice. Obviously, Sir Hector enjoyed the support and admiration of many local tenants, but it should not disguise the fact that he was nevertheless an 'improving' landlord and had brought in the new farming methods and the extensive sheep farms in the first place, thus creating the unemployment.

In view of the admiration shown to Sir Hector, it is ironic that the largest rising against the incursion of sheep, which was to take place a few years later, was centred on the glens north and west of Fyrish, on the Novar estates. The so-called '1792 Insurrection' began at Kildermorie in late 1791. To make way for a new sheep farm the old tenants were pushed up to higher ground and the loss of the better grazing land for their cattle threatened ruin for them. Bad feeling then arose between the old tenants and the new sheep-farmers. When local cattle were corralled by some of the immigrant sheep farmers a small skirmish broke out, resulting in a perceived symbolic victory for the original tenants. In July the following year a wedding took place in nearby Strathrusdale. A good time was had by all and the home-brewed ale flowed easily, perhaps too easily. Buoyed up by the heady brew, a number of the guests devised a plan to collect all the sheep in the counties of Ross and Sutherland and drive them across the Beauly River, there to wander at pleasure outside their county boundary.

On Tuesday 31st July about 200 people assembled at Strath Oykel and proceeded to Lairg. They then began to drive all the sheep they could find towards the Beauly River. By the following Saturday they had reached Boath near Kildermorie, with a flock of several thousand sheep. By now alarm was spreading throughout the land-owning class and soon the Sheriff of Ross became involved. He, accompanied by Sir Hector Munro of Novar and three companies of the 42nd Highlanders (Black Watch) from Fort George, marched on Boath. When they encountered the group, the drovers immediately fled, but some of the less fleet-footed protesters were caught and subsequently taken to gaol.

The incident was reported in the press throughout Scotland and reports varied in support, from a fear of popular insurgence (the French Revolution had entered a new and more radical phase

9a. James Murray joined the Royal Navy in Halifax, Nova Scotia. In the Halifax Royal Canadian Naval Dockyard few buildings remain from this period, but Admiralty House, now a museum, would have been a familiar building to Captain Murray (author).

9b. The infamous press gang, commemorated in this Halifax Pub Sign, would have been a familiar and feared presence in the dockyard inns (author).

10. The Battle of San Domingo: This famous 1808 painting, by Nicholas Pocock, shows the French 'Imperial' in the right centre foreground of the painting. To its right and beyond is the partly dismasted 'Northumberland', the ship of James Murray (reproduced courtesy of the National Maritime Museum, Greenwich).

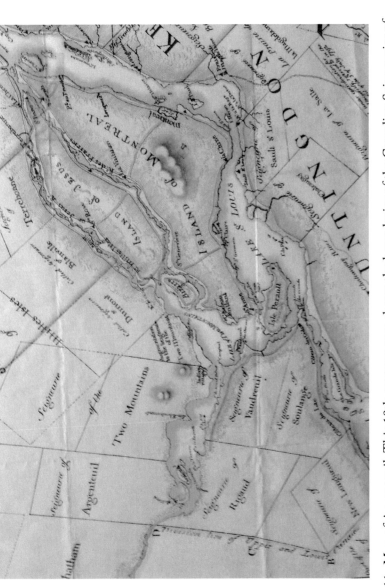

11. Map of Argenteuil: This 18th century map shows the boundaries of the Canadian Seigneuries of the Montreal area. Argenteuil is clearly seen in the centre left of the map (author).

12. St Andrews: This town, was established by the Murray family. This painting, attributed to Salomon, shows the old village in October 1844. (reproduced courtesy of Musée régional d'Argenteuil, Saint-André-d'Argenteuil, Québec).

13. Craigdarroch: This house was built for Captain James Murray in 1827 and this photograph shows the house circa 1908. In recent years the house has served as a Country House Hotel and is now a private residence (reproduced courtesy of Mr Mark Garrison).

14a. Robert Ramsey Mackenzie: He had a scandalous affair with Rachel Murray and was forced to leave Scotland for Australia. He later became the Governor of Queensland (public domain, John Oxley Library, State Library of Queensland).

14b. Colonel Rose Ross was a colourful character who tended to resolve his problems by challenging his opponent to a duel. James Murray was one such protagonist (reproduced courtesy of the Head Teacher of Tain Royal Academy).

15a. Tarbat House: This fine house was the seat of the Cromartie Mackenzies. The house today is a sad ruin (public domain).

15b. Coul House, Contin: Built as the home of Mackenzie of Coul. The scene of secret assignations between Robert Ramsay Mackenzie and Rachel Murray but now a Country House Hotel (author).

16. The Old Manse in New Abbey, Scotland: Outwardly little has
    changed in appearance from the house where James Murray
    spent his last days in the company of his sister Harriet (author).

with the arrest of the King) to outright encouragement for the drovers. For example, one account incorrectly claimed that:

> Accounts of a serious nature have been received from Ross-shire. The people there, exasperated at their being turned out of their farms by the present prevalent custom of the landlords letting out their grounds for extensive sheep walks, and rendered desperate by poverty, had assembled in great numbers and proceeded to several unjustifiable acts of violence, particularly in destroying the sheep, no less than 3,000 of them belonging to one gentleman having been drowned. Some woods are also said to have been burnt.[439]

Two days later the same paper reported that all the gunpowder in Tain and Dingwall had been captured by the rioters. In fact, no people and no sheep at all were harmed during this incident and furthermore no property was damaged. The same paper took a more sympathetic stance later:

> Every gentleman has doubtless a right to make the most of his property, but surely in the exercise of that right much is due to humanity—we may add, to justice. The lower class of people in this country, particularly in the northern parts, have hitherto been remarkable for the regularity of their deportment, and a respectful submission to the laws of their country. Some measures, therefore, more than commonly oppressive, have, we apprehend, given rise to this outrage; and we trust it will excite the immediate attention of the Legislature. While we are commiserating and giving assistance to the distressed inhabitants of Poland, let it not be said that we suffer oppression to stalk uncontrolled at home.[440]

The drovers that were captured soon faced legal justice but the first eight put on trial were acquitted by a jury. Six others were convicted but three of them shortly afterwards escaped from their prison, the Tollbooth of Inverness. It appeared that few, if any, active steps were taken to bring them back to prison and the common view was that the feeling in the country as to the unrighteousness of the sentence passed by the judge was so strong that the prison door was opened so that the prisoners could escape. Of the other three convicted men, one who had failed to appear at all was outlawed and the remaining two were released.

This incident was the first and last effort of the old Highland society attempting to hold back the sheep farms introduced by the 'improvers'. Sir George Mackenzie, of course, had more to say on the matter:

> The firmness with which it was met completely quelled the spirit of rebellion amongst the people in general.

The year 1792 became remembered, not for the Ross-shire insurrection, but as 'Bliadhna nan Caorach' (the year of the sheep), as the Highlands saw the first large scale introduction of the Cheviot sheep. Its large size, its hardiness and tolerance of Highland conditions and its production of great quantities of high-quality wool and meat meant that volume sheep-farming could become even more profitable and thus even more attractive. Large-scale clearances soon took place throughout the Highlands, including areas under the direct control of James Murray's friends and colleagues. In 1820 Hugh Munro of Novar cleared his estates at Culrain along the Kyle of Sutherland, an event which led to considerable civil unrest that was only crushed when the Sheriff and the Military arrived. The estates of Seaforth were largely spared widespread evictions until later in the 19th century, but in the late 1790s Francis Humberston Mackenzie, the father of Lady Hood, issued a summons of removal to over 358 families from the Island of Lewis and advertised the whole of the Uig district for sale as a single sheep farm. For all his limitations, his successor and friend of James Murray, J A. Stewart-Mackenzie of Seaforth, had clear reservations about clearance. In 1800 the advisor to the Earl of Seaforth had calculated that the entire population of Lewis could be reduced to 120 shepherds and their families and those who could make a living from kelp and fishing. The implications of this would have meant that the remaining 10,000 inhabitants of the island would have to leave. Fortunately, Seaforth did not act on that advice, although in the years to come many Lewis families moved to Canada, some to Argenteuil, perhaps as a result of the influence of Seaforth's friend, James Murray.

Despite perpetual and chronic debt worries, the estates of Cromartie had only ordered limited and piecemeal evictions. This policy was to change dramatically later in the 19th century when the infamous Strathconon clearances were ordered. For many tenants this was the second clearance they had faced and the influx of squatters displaced by the earlier clearances, as well as the accumulating effects of population growth, led to some farms which initially had been leased to only two tenants then possessing up to 15 families. From 1840 to 1848 Strathconon was almost entirely cleared of its tenantry to make room for sheep, deer and extensive forest plantations. It is estimated that from four to five hundred people were thus driven from Strathconon; but this was in the future and was not to occur on James Murray's aunt Maria Hay-Mackenzie's watch.

Maria had been under some pressure to re-evaluate her estates, and even James Murray felt the need for reform and change:

The grazings of Knockfarrel, Balmillach and Foresters croft will be set at Whitsunday at their real values, at least double their present rent. I told the Major that they were to be valued, as the present rent is far beneath their actual worth.[441]

Maria resisted the advice of James and others in the overwhelming tide of 'improvement', and was appreciated for her stance. A letter of 21st April 1820, written by the Minister at Bonar Bridge shortly after the disturbances, describes how he was outraged by the actions taken against his parishioners:

> I am happy that you signify your approbation of my conduct... The removal of so large a population in such circumstances... is as impolitic as it is inhuman. All who know your character, Madam, are convinced that no consideration would induce you to commit such an outrage on humanity – 600 souls to be turned adrift without a cot to shelter them.[442]

Much has been written on the overall impact of the Highland Clearances but each individual action was a personal tragedy for the family involved. Lady Maria Mackenzie was all too aware of that fact, as a result of the many appeal letters she received. Some of the recipients had followed her family for generations, and the feared Highland Regiments, serving with such distinction throughout the empire, had been composed of such men:

> Having now become an old feeble poor man and being summonsed a few days ago for £3 18s, being my arrears of rent here for the last two years I have come to the (...) of stating my situation and handing this personally to your ladyship, in the firm hope and belief that you will be graciously pleased to order your Law Agent at Dingwall and incur no more expenses, as I have had neither horse, cow or sheep since I was removed from Achacall but was always till the last two years regular in my small Rent. I was only 15 or 16 years old when I first began to pay rent to your family and my predecessors have been upwards of 100 years doing the same. Three years after my first becoming your tenant, Colonel George prevailed with me to go to the army and

accompanied him to Gibraltar where I was wounded about 40 years ago, which induced him to send me home and how soon he returned to Britain he would procure me a pension, but his premature death to my (most?) misfortune prevented that.

My humble request is now to beg the indulgence that I may not be saddled with new expenses and in the hope that your Ladyship should see proper to comply to my request. I faithfully promise that the greatest part of my arrears will be paid off at Michaelmas next, as my children, who are now able to do for themselves, promise to aid me in discharging this debt should every other power fail me, and I have the honour to remain,

Your Ladyship's Most obedient servant
John MacLeod X

(Signed with his mark)[443]

The bewildered Mary Forbes exemplified a heart wrenching case, not untypical of the plight facing many of the poor people in the area:

The reason of my troubling you at this time is that if you would have the goodness to inform a poor widow such as I am what will be done with me, your ladyship I am sure recollects that you promised to alow (sic) me in the house or gave me meiloraation (sic) if you would think it proper I would wish to be alowed (sic) in my present houses as I have no cattle to trouble you or any person you will have the goodness as to let me know what will be done by me as I have none to help me but to trust in the Almighty, I am afraid to be turned out of doors every day.

I am your most obd. Servant
Mary Forbes Widow.[444]

At least this case was followed up, although with only limited success. Mr Laing, Maria's factor, wrote to Maria that he had a letter from the trustees (perpetrators of the proposed clearance in the name of road improvement) saying that they knew nothing about such a matter. He was furious and insisted that Maria write again and he emphasised that he would take legal action against the perpetrators once he knew exactly who they were. There are no further records of this distressing case.

By the mid-century many parts of the Highlands had been almost emptied of their indigenous population:

> In but too many instances the Highlands have been drained, not of their superfluity of population, but of the whole mass of inhabitants, dispossessed by an unrelenting avarice which will be one day found to be short-sighted as it is unjust and selfish.[445]

27

Has he told everything?

On Thursday 24th August 1831 Sir Francis Mackenzie of Gairloch, a friend and near neighbour of James Murray, sent a message asking James to meet him at his home. An inquisitive but not overly concerned Captain Murray then travelled the couple of miles to Conan House, Sir George's beautiful mansion home on the banks of the River Conon. At that moment Captain Murray's world collapsed.

Sir Francis Mackenzie, fifth Baronet of Gairloch had a sorry tale to tell. Rumours concerning Captain Murray's wife, Rachel, and Robert Ramsay, the son of George Mackenzie of Coul, had been circulating for some time and it was apparent that everyone but Captain James knew the story. Prior to this meeting Sir George Mackenzie, on speaking earlier to Sir Francis, had approached his son, Robert Ramsay, with the rumours. His son spilled the beans, telling all and supporting his tale by showing his father a series of letters from Rachel Murray to himself, presumably in his defence and with the clear implication that she had done the chasing.

George Steuart Mackenzie, the great 'improver' laird was born in June 1780 and was thus of a similar age to Captain James. Robert Ramsay was his fourth son. As near neighbours and distant relatives, the families of Coul and Murray soon became close friends and visited each other frequently. The nineteen year old Robert frequently accompanied his father on visits to the Murrays, and, before long, he and the 29-year-old Rachel became firm friends. The 'official line' would suggest that Robert was responsible for the development of the friendship into something more:

> ... being possessed of various opportunities afforded by a previous acquaintance and habit of intimacy with the family of the pursuer (Captain James Murray)... (Robert) sought and frequented the society of the pursuer's said wife (Rachel) and paid her many and assiduous attentions, so as finally to overcome her affections for the pursuer and her regard for her nuptial obligations, whereby... she was led and betrayed into an illegal and adulterous intercourse with the said Robert Ramsay Mackenzie.[446]

Robert, not surprisingly, took a different view, suggesting that Rachel was the instigator, and he used her rather indiscreet letters to him as evidence.

On hearing the news at Conan House, James Murray refused to believe the stories about his wife and reacted angrily, with considerable indignation. On speaking to Sir George, also at the house, and being informed about the letters from Rachel to Robert, he was forced to face the truth, and he did not take it well. Captain James broke down and was most fortunate in that his friend and doctor, James Wishart, was with him and able to give him the medical care he needed.

The story gradually unfolded and was embellished with obvious relish by those who were called upon to give evidence. The 'below stairs' gossip-factory had gone into full production.

James Ferguson, Coul's Butler, had often seen them together and once, he especially remembered, he saw them together in the passage where Mrs. Murray's bedroom was situated after the rest of the family had gone to bed. They were conversing in whispers. His view was that there was an:

... improper intimacy between them. Indeed this was the general
view of the servants in the house and throughout the county.[447]

Duncan Campbell, Mackenzie of Coul's footman, admitted that he
often carried letters between the two and was asked to show
secrecy and discretion. He noted that they almost always sat
together at table. Ann MacDonald, a housemaid at Coul, talked of
a visit by Rachel to Coul in the summer of 1831. Robert's room
was a few steps from Rachel's. She testified that before breakfast
Robert had looked out of his door to see if the coast was clear and
then Rachel came out of his room and ran into her own. Ann
testified that she suspected that 'something improper was going
on'. Isabella Morris, the laundry maid, supported this story adding
that Rachel appeared to be 'in confusion'. Margaret Mackenzie,
also a housemaid at Coul, told a similar story, using circumstantial
evidence to indulge in malicious gossip. Margaret used to
accompany Mrs. Mackenzie to her room before going to bed. One
night she saw Robert come out of his room and walk along the
passage towards Rachel's room. She had often seen the two
together after the rest of the family had gone to bed. One particular
night she saw Rachel go to the stairs leading to Robert's room
(eight steps), cough and then return to her own room. Off the
stairs where they had been seen speaking there was a dressing
room which contained an unoccupied bed. Margaret stated that
she had often seen the bedding crushed down, as though persons
had been lying in it.

The earliest evidence of impropriety came from Lady
Mackenzie's maid, Helen Henderson. In early 1831 she had
accompanied Lady Mackenzie to Tulloch Castle in Dingwall, the
home of the Davidson family. James and Rachel were in one room
and Robert was in an adjacent room. Immediately before dinner
Rachel had left her room and set off in the direction of Robert's room:

She was in a state of undress; did not have her gown on, her stays were unfastened and her bosom was uncovered. Robert came out of his room and met her. They began whispering together. Rachel then saw me and immediately got very flustered. She called out loudly "oh, Robert, I've lost my comb". Robert offered to help her look for it but she then cried out that she had found it and rushed back into her room.[448]

Where was Rachel's husband, James, whilst all this evidence was unfolding? Clearly he was not observant enough concerning the whereabouts of his errant young wife, as there were also indiscretions nearer home. Elizabeth Kemp, a resident of Contin and near-neighbour of the Murrays at Craigdarroch, said that she frequently saw Rachel and Robert out walking arm in arm. One day in particular she was out collecting wood when she saw Rachel on the road walking up and down. She then saw Robert on the side of the loch (Loch Achilty) coming towards her. Rachel and Robert met and Robert put his arms around Rachel and fondly kissed her. They then went into the woodland and sat down. Robert repeatedly kissed Rachel and she offered no resistance, but finally, obviously concerned about being seen, she stood up, smoothed her gown and left the wood. Elizabeth, apparently needing to collect wood in the very spot where the two had sat down, testified that she had investigated the vegetation and had seen that the heather was broken and pressed down.[449]

The really damning testimony concerned events that allegedly took place in late February / early March 1831. Rachel, Robert and a young lady by the name of Joanna Matheson left Coul by carriage early in the morning to go to Inverness to visit relatives and do some shopping etc. They had booked a breakfast at the Royal Hotel, Dingwall, to be taken en-route. They left Coul about 7am and reached the Royal Hotel at Dingwall about 8am, whereupon they went upstairs into a parlour and were served breakfast.

Shortly after breakfast Joanna left and it was arranged that Robert and Rachel would pick her up later when they were ready to move on to Inverness. Alexander MacDonald, a waiter, then stated that he received a message from Joanna telling him that she had left a book in the breakfast room and he set off to get it for her. Joanna did not remember asking for a book but she accepted that this could have been the case. As Alexander began to enter the breakfast room he saw Rachel in an armchair stretched out on her back, her clothes lifted up and her legs separated. A gentleman was standing between her legs. Alexander obviously spent some time studying the scene as he was able to describe the characteristics of the soles of her shoes. He had seen enough to believe that he had caught them 'in flagrante delicto'. Alexander then entered the room looking for the lost book and, not surprisingly, the guilty pair were very startled, but nothing was said. Shortly afterwards they left the hotel, picked up Joanna in Dingwall and set off for Inverness. There Joanna left to meet with her sister and Robert and Rachel checked into Wilson's Hotel. They then later left to visit the Dowager Lady Mackenzie of Gairloch and met up again with Joanna the next day. Joanna had become suspicious of the relationship between the two by this time, as she was of the opinion that Rachel had not done any shopping, which was a main reason for the trip in the first place. She said that there was:

> ... something in their behaviour towards each other that made
> me feel anxious without being able to say what it was.[450]

These testimonies were heard during the later divorce hearing but on that fateful evening of Thursday 24th August, Captain James knew none of this. He was first informed in the drawing room of Conan House and he was made fully aware of the outline of the sorry tale by the sympathetic utterances of Francis Mackenzie. Despite all, he still refused to believe the story unless it was corroborated by Rachel herself. Consequently, Doctor Wishart, who had been present throughout the disclosures, left Conan House and made his way to Craigdarroch. It was about midnight when he arrived. He rapped on the door and Rachel and her brother Benjamin, who was visiting, opened up in some alarm. On seeing the doctor Rachel was immediately alarmed and feared that James had taken ill or some accident had befallen him. Wishart told her that was not the case, but did not immediately elaborate. He was reluctant to tell Rachel exactly what had been said at Conan House earlier in the evening, but as Rachel insisted, he outlined the series of events. Rachel looked hard into James Wishart's face and exclaimed, "has Robert told everything?"

On receiving an affirmative answer, she left the room and Doctor Wishart, accompanied by Benjamin Tucker, made his way back to Conan House. Early the next morning Doctor Wishart and Mr Tucker returned to Craigdarroch and found Rachel clearly lacking sleep and in a very agitated state. Tellingly, at this stage she confessed her guilt, but blamed Robert for disclosing the information. She insisted that she'd had 'connection' (as she delicately phrased it) with Robert only three times, and never went to bed with him. Nevertheless, for James Murray this was three times too many. Rachel and her brother left Craigdarroch for England that same day and James was never to see his beloved wife again.[451]

28

Where is the villain,
the basest dastard?

T he Tuckers were a god–fearing, upright family with very strong moral values and a clear belief in what was right and what was wrong. Any person who had spent a lot of time with Sir John Jervis had to share at least some of his uncompromising values, and no family were more attached to the obdurate Jervis than the Tuckers; Benjamin, the father, had worked for him for a significant part of his life, and the definitive biography of Sir John Jervis was written by Jedediah, the eldest son. They had a statue of Jervis in their garden and Benjamin even named his second son 'John Jervis' in his honour. The three older sons of Benjamin, Jedediah, John Jervis and Ben, all went on to significant achievements in their own lives but, without a doubt, the apple of father's eye was Rachel. Benjamin senior had died in December 1829 and on his death Rachel had inherited a substantial fortune. She was the apple of her brothers' eyes too, but her behaviour brought the lofty pedestal upon which she stood crashing down.

The means by which the marriage of Rachel and James broke down was to have a major impact on the highly moral and religious family unit of the Tuckers, and they were almost broken by the shock of such infidelity and its accompanying shame. The gradual evolution of their thoughts and actions in handling this crisis are vividly revealed in a series of splendidly melodramatic letters.[452]

On first hearing the news, eldest brother Jedediah immediately wrote from the family home of Trematon Castle to Captain James. His utter anguish is reflected, not only by the words he used but also by the noticeable deterioration in his writing as his emotions got the better of him whilst writing the letter:

What can I write – is she not deranged – I am sure grief for my father has killed her intellect; has she not shown any other sign of madness lately – How can I face you again, who so tenderly loved her, so affectionately attended her – our disgrace, our shame – well was my father taken – In mercy was his death – If you *will ever* speak to me. I will shortly go to you. I am afraid you will not meet me. Where is the villain, the basest dastard?... I am sure she will die shortly, it were a mercy; and yet to think that I have written that of Rachel. It is a blow that must tell soon and truly. Do not hate us, nor me, for I loved her most – I shall hate her most. We all send our love to you.[453]

The Tucker family throughout their correspondence rarely wavered in their sympathy and sorrow for Captain James' position. Most of the correspondence to Captain James came from Jedediah, the oldest son, but the other brothers also contributed and they shared similar sentiments.

Jervis, who was later to go on to become an Admiral in the Royal Navy, shared the same respect for Captain James that is evident in his brother's letters, but his messages often had a much stronger religious overtone. On 29th August, shortly after the first letter from Jedediah, Jervis Tucker wrote:

Next to the sorrows of a heartbroken husband... My dear Murray that no one feels our horrible situation more than myself, and I most sincerely pray that the Almighty will comfort you in your affliction and lend my sister that repentance which may enable us to think that she may, by the remainder of her life, spent in penitence, receive from him that forgiveness of her sin, and hopes that she is not cut off from life eternal. I look at the letter with a doubt that almost makes me mistrust my eyes. I almost think it fiction, the very thoughts, that her that was, so religious, so charitable, so dear a sister and so good a daughter (who) has brought this heartbreaking disgrace upon the family, is too much for a brother to bear... I thought that (she) was as pure as it is possible for a mortal to be – alas what a change... I trust that the almighty may give you strength.[454]

The youngest brother, Ben, had accompanied Rachel on her journey from Craigdarroch to London. He wrote immediately upon arrival and brought interesting news of Rachel's defence of her actions; allegedly, Robert Mackenzie had threatened to kill himself if she did not comply:

> Temple (postmark Friday 30th August 1831)
> I and my miserable sister arrived this morning – she has borne her unhappy journey far better than I could have expected and is totally composed but truly in a sad and wretched condition... oh that such a poor pitiable rascal as that should have the power to spirit so much happiness and cause such infirmity of woe – But his day must and most certainly will come, and then he will pay the penalty, slight as that penalty will be for his iniquity... She prays you will not believe any... words that you may hear which in the slightest vary the facts that I have related coming from herself – (she) is greatly afraid that people now she is gone and lost will say things of her which are not true. In the infatuation of a moment yielding to and believing a villain's lie that through and by her he was dying... I blame and pity in the extreme but can not make, no not even the slightest excuse for her fall – and that for her brother to say is wretched horrible indeed.[455]

Two days later the initial shock had worn off and the brothers, whilst maintaining full support for James, felt the need to look for explanations and excuses. Jervis found it in the concept of original sin with God unable or unwilling to save Rachel from herself. However, the earthly world could still make a significant contribution and Jervis, along with his brother Ben, was going to demonstrate just that, if together they could only find the errant Robert Mackenzie.

> I have just passed the most bitter day of my life having seen a dear sister, who I thought before this week stood on the very height of human perfection, alas what sinful creatures the very best of us are, and how much at all times we stand in need of God's assistance to withstand temptation... I know my dear brother... even the very best of us sinful and wretched creatures, incapable of ourselves to do anything of ourselves but our sufficiency is of our God...
>
> Sept 3rd. We arrived last night. Therefore send what information you can of the villain ... our hope of finding is but small but it is a long lane that has no turning and if not caught this year may be the next April? If not in this world most definitely will in the world to come.[456]

Ben, who had probably read too many novellas, seemed to be enjoying the whole drama and he relished the role of avenging brother:

> Jervis and myself are off per steam to Edinburgh tonight to try and find that heartless villain – Rachel of course does not know we are going away. Write to me at Edinburgh and make David (James Murray's servant) fish out some arms – direct to Francis Tickle Esq. – Post Office, Edinburgh to wait there till called for. I have changed name for a reason for I have no time to say more.[457]

Just a few days later, on 5th September, the brothers had discovered the 'true reason' for Rachel's behaviour. She had catastrophically been afflicted by madness and was clearly temporarily deranged. That the affair had gone on for some time and Rachel had sent numerous secret letters to Robert did not affect their judgement. Still, she would die soon anyway, and would then answer to her maker:

> ... I am *sure as that I see the sun* which has risen of such sad circumstances that I am *most* certain that when she did fall she was deranged. I knew it the moment I heard it. I believe I wrote it so from Trematon – for believe me – she was not always or naturally bad or vicious – she professed the finest mind and did deserve the character which her father at her marriage gave her, everyone who knew her confirmed it... To exculpate her is god knows the farthest from my most distant thoughts – but compassionately pardon my attempting to look on her deep guilt with those feelings of indignant disapprobation and pitying regret which a brother who was so proud, so fond of her must see so great a fall and sin, committed or rather caused by Insanity having for a moment paralysed such fine feelings, such noble intellect and such devoted affection... I must write that her most solemn oath to God before whom she knows and feels she will very shortly stand to answer for the appeal made, was, that she had been mad and had lost all direction of her thoughts and self.[458]

Rachel clung to the idea that if she could face James and explain, perhaps he might forgive her. Even if the marriage was unable to continue she could ease her own conscience before she passed away. Jedediah's letter to James continued:

> She has I believe submitted to you her only request to see you once more and in your presence acknowledge her shameful sin

and worship your most injured affection... She is... in the highest excitement of fever by which and not by sustenance she is supported – but she will drop soon, indeed so little nourishment does she take that I am astonished she lives.[459]

That Rachel was suffering severely was not in doubt, and five days later Jed reported that her condition had not improved. Her demise seemed imminent:

> ... that I may induce her to take a little other sustenance than dry bread – but hitherto a morsel of that has been her only daily food with a *little* tea; yet her muscular strength flags not, she paces the room, prays in the dust, springs again with returning horror to her feet, *as strongly as I ever saw her in my life* when exhausted drops to sleep and refreshes her dreadful excitement – and such a state as this can't last long, it is physically impossible.[460]

Jed also acknowledged that the search for Robert Mackenzie had been fruitless:

> ... knew their journey to Edinburgh would be useless, such a... hellish coward will not be found there and his Father is besides *far* too cunning. It is not till after a little interval has permitted some rational attempts at quietly detecting him that his accursed fate will be sealed to its just doom ... [461]

Another long letter from Jed, sent on 12th September, also contained a note from Rachel herself, added almost secretly in very small upside down writing on the third page:

> Do *not* disdain my last look... that is my only plea... I must have been mad. Indeed I cannot think it is me – oh that I had been

mad. And do not let them take me out of your reach... I have kissed your feet... sometimes I think I was mad even to ask to see you – but if you could know how my weary aching heart withers for one look of you... [462]

Four days later a discreet and subtle change of tone became evident in the correspondence. Jervis rigorously maintained his support and sympathy for James but it was now the couple's own fault. The reason for their present unhappy predicament was a result of the behaviour of James and his wife and had they attended church regularly this would not have happened!

> I have seen unhappy Rachel. I think her health stays the same and delighted I am to say that she takes some sleep and a little food. She is, my dear Murray as contrite as it is possible for a wretched sinner to be, and it is but justice to her to add, that next to her feelings of the deepest sorrow for having greatly offended the Almighty that her next grief is for the disgrace and ruin that she has brought upon the very best of husbands. I must however say that Rachel is, as well as myself fully imputed that this judgment would not have fallen on your unhappy house if you had not lived so much without God, do not fancy that I am either to palliate her guilt or throw the blame upon you, but I think God has permitted her to follow her evil thoughts and that those thoughts would not so strongly have affected her if she had regularly attended Public worship which I sincerely pray both her and you will think more seriously of... I should not do justice to her, you or myself if I did not point out what I think has been the great cause of this misery and sin.[463]

With the passage of time the Tuckers came to the realisation that maybe Rachel's death was not quite so imminent after all. If she was going to survive, what should others be told?

... she meets the unavoidable with somewhat more calmness; yesterday and today she has eaten a little meat but her only thoughts are what will be your future life, what will ever lighten the gloom or load she has left... but when I do again go into the world the truth appears no longer to be concealed. In one of your letters you desired me to keep all as secret as possible till you saw me – Can you at all conceive how that secrecy is attainable? The legal proceedings of a divorce will announce it with a trumpet's voice and if it does not your separation will, whenever you appear without her... and preserve our reputation as far as possible but as we cannot imagine how... can be stopped and are aware that talk always spreads and magnifies. We... have thought it most prudent that I should quietly inform those who will most wonder and take most interest in order to timely secure their future silence; but we intend if possible to wait till we hear your opinion which I solicit immediately.[464]

By 22nd September the family's anger at Robert Mackenzie still showed no signs of abating and Jed certainly showed a fine command of language in a description of his character:

> As to that basest deformity of hell, that fiend and devilish villain,
> if I knew precisely where he is going the ship registry would
> afford some clue.[465]

Rachel was now beginning to recover, and it appears that James had also indicated that he would follow Jervis' advice, given in an earlier letter, concerning his own devotions, or rather his lack of them:

> Rachel continues to tranquillize (sic), recover her reason and...
> she sings with delight... to every word in your letters which

seem to indicate that you are devoting yourself more to religion than formally.[466]

By the end of September more practical matters began to be considered. James was looking to cash in a marriage bond and was questioning the assets of the marriage. Rachel herself was now very wealthy and the brothers were anxious to ensure that this was not going to fall into James Murray's hands:

> ... as you make no answer to my question to you about your Bond and whether you wish that I pay you £100 on it I conclude I shall shortly again hear from you... her father's disposal of his own property left hers at her sole control – so it was intended and so it continues.[467]

The question of the financial settlement surfaced again in mid-October:

> As... a view of Rachel's property. I do not see that I can say more than I did in my letter of 29th September, her father's dispersal of his own property left... at her sole control, so it was intended also it continues – But you have a copy of his will and can consider it or take advice on it. I shall immediately look about me to raise money to take up your Bond, I shall be obliged if you will in the interim inform me what sum you claim on it and what entries are on its back.[468]

Today, pre-nuptial agreements are not uncommon when considerable wealth is possessed by one of the marriage partners, but an 1827 Murray/Tucker document is an early example of a post-nuptial marriage settlement. The agreement was signed by both Rachel and James and it recognised that in the event of either death the other would inherit, but it was also clarified that the fortune left as a result of Benjamin Tucker's death was to be:

> For the sole and separate use of the said Rachel Lyne Murray and not be subject to the debts, control, disposition or engagements of the said James Murray or any other person with whom she might marry after his decease.

A divorce would not affect Rachel's inheritance but would be financially disastrous for James. He was paid £1,000 by Rachel's father on the event of his marriage to Rachel, but it was clearly intended that he would receive no more.[469]

The search for Robert Mackenzie continued:

> I am so convinced and so we are all that the hound is still in England, that we have again taken steps to discover him, and what is more I don't think he will go or that his accursed coward sire will let him go abroad. They're too much of a kin to separate.[470]

Jedediah, for once, got it very wrong and the Tucker brothers were well off the scent. Robert Mackenzie, clutching £750 given to him by his father, was now well away from Scotland and was shortly to land in Sydney, Australia, to join his brother James. Father was still furious with Robert. Shortly after arriving in Australia, Robert received a letter from his mother telling him to expect strong words from his father but not to reply and to remain cool and calm:

> Father is hot headed and may not mean all he says.[471]

Rachel herself put pen to paper on numerous occasions, and her total shame and degradation shines through, well exemplified not only by her poignant vocabulary but also by the visible signs of despair in her handwriting and presentation. Her first correspondence was left for James at Craigdarroch. At this point in the proceedings Rachel was hopeful that James would forgive and forget:

> The carriage is now at the door but do not cast me off for ever
> – if you would take me to the *outermost parts* of the earth and let
> me be Jane... I would worship you – I cannot believe that *you*
> who are so far above this... (can)... cast me off – for ever.[472]

This initial pleading soon gave way to the reflected concern on the testimony of others. Rachel was particularly worried about what Robert would say, and with some justification. According to his father, George Mackenzie of Coul, Robert was led astray by the older predatory vixen, Rachel. Rachel's only hope was that a meeting with James might allow her to persuade him to forgive her:

> Say you will meet me... say... to a crushed woman... do not care
> for what this world will say it is not like you to care for it – take
> me anywhere – but let me be near you...

James was unmoved by Rachel's pleadings, and in subsequent letters her tone became even more desperate:

> Nothing can be said for me – no excuses are there towards god
> and you... no... sin was ever so great as mine – for no one ever
> had so good a husband – you sent me your forgiveness by Ben
> – oh you think I ever doubted that from you? No and therefore
> was my sin the greater – I never could believe anything said
> against you... I was loved as I loved and lost you and therefore
> is my sin the greater... I write now to entreat you to believe
> nothing of me, vile wretch that I am, for lies have been and

will be said of me... I will tell you truth and nothing but the truth.

How can you care about me if you will cast me off... you know I have friends who would be kind to me and protect me – but they are nothing to me compared to you – go with me – anywhere... do go with me. I will be your slave, anything... [473]

The pleading continued in the same vein for several more letters. By now Rachel was as convinced as her brothers that her time on this earth was coming to an end. James could at least meet with her, so that she could die having had the satisfaction of putting her case and her abject apologies to her husband:

Oh may this make you to pity me, to see me once again... as I am – I am not quite so bad as I appear... oh do be merciful to me, all I ask is to kiss your feet – but... once to see you... I shall go to Elysham (Elysium). [474]

... you are too noble to drive me to despair... to trample on a crushed bosom... there is another world where you will be happy – and after all I have written if it will add to your pain and not alleviate it forgive me then I will not ask it – but it would ease you to hear me – I know it would... I had been your wife ten years a devoted one give me one minute for each year... God will bless you tell me that I may see you... and (I) would die a thousand deaths for you. Just... know that you see me... once more... [475]

It would take a heart of stone not to be moved by Rachel's entreaties but James, a life inured to hardship, was not to be shifted. This realisation would finally come to Rachel and, if she was not going to die after all, she would attempt to ameliorate her own conscience and perhaps do the same for James. Indeed, Rachel was always at pains to emphasise that James had no conscience to ameliorate and she never wavered in her expressions of love for her husband:

In pity see me – you have ever been the best of husbands

(I) will not distract you by more letters. I see you have cast me off – and I fear with justice – May I this once say dearest dearest dearest to you. I have kissed your shoes... but I will not impose any more to... your noble heart.[476]

And you will one day pray that we may again be joined in heaven before God I have loved you more and more – you cannot believe this <u>now</u> you will believe it know it. I cannot account for myself – but I suppose all sinners say that... You have nothing to reproach yourself with towards me.

It will be easy for you to hate me. But no, no, do not, do not, do not hate me.[477]

It goes unrecorded whether James did hate Rachel for her actions, but as a man for whom personal honour was paramount he pursued the divorce with vigour. The action was uncontested, but James' parallel claim for damages against Robert Mackenzie (therefore against George Mackenzie of Coul, as Robert was still under his guardianship) did not go through without a fight. The courts found in favour of James and he was awarded £5,000 in damages plus £8 3s 7d in expenses and £1 3s 7d in fees.[478] Robert was proving to be an expensive son.

On 23rd January 1833 Rachel was formally found guilty of adultery and the divorce was granted.[479] James Murray would never meet Rachel Tucker again.

29

He could not have spoken greater nonsense

Barely a year had passed from the acrimonious breakdown of his marriage when James became embroiled once more in personal turmoil. The dispute between local lairds Hugh Rose Ross and James Stewart Mackenzie, by today's standards, was much ado about very little. The whole incident gradually fizzled out, and has a farcical quality about it which would make the bones of a good comedy drama. For the participants, especially James, the ramifications of the dispute were nothing to laugh about, especially as the backdrop throughout was the fact that James was suffering from a serious health problem.

Nevertheless the whole incident is of considerable interest in that it describes, in graphic detail, the minutiae of the origin and development of a Regency period duel.

The dispute between Hugh Rose Ross and James Stewart Mackenzie was overtly concerned with local politics, but beneath this veneer lay a division concerning issues which in essence aimed to bring about a fundamental change in British society.

Radicalism in the early 19th century was not new. At its core was a belief in the supremacy of Parliament over the monarch. By the early 1800s this ideology was represented by the Whig party. Their manifesto had since widened to include demands for the expansion of the parliamentary franchise, support for free trade, Catholic emancipation and the abolition of slavery. However, such radicalism had been forced to take a back seat in Britain for the previous 25 years or so, as a result of the almost continual state of war which existed between Britain and France. Throughout the period of the Napoleonic Wars the government took very stern measures against any domestic unrest, however trivial.

When Napoleon Bonaparte was finally defeated at the Battle of Waterloo in 1815 the threat of war ended and the Royal Navy reigned supreme, but in the country there was still widespread poverty and high food prices. Leading Whig politicians looked for a return to their reformist agenda and at political meetings speakers such as Henry Hunt complained that only three men in a hundred had the vote. Some of the more hot-headed radicals took the law into their own hands and there was rioting in 1816 and 1817. The Spa Field riots of 1816 led to a vigorous government repression but this didn't stop 40,000 people attending a meeting on Glasgow Green to demand a more representative government and an end to the Corn Laws, which were keeping food prices artificially high. The Peterloo massacre of August 1819 sparked demonstrations across Britain. In Scotland, a rally in Paisley on the 11th September led to a week of rioting and cavalry were used to control around 5,000 'Radicals'. Protest meetings were held, mainly in the weaving areas of Stirling, Airdrie, Renfrewshire, Ayrshire and Fife. There was genuine fear by the establishment and landed gentry that the revolutionary spirit that had been seen in France and Ireland could take place in Britain. To combat such fears there was even a great increase in the recruiting of volunteer regiments throughout the Scottish Lowlands and Scottish Borders.

James Murray's view on these matters appeared unequivocal. He wrote to Aunt Maria Mackenzie on 23rd December 1819, shortly after the news of the Peterloo massacre had reached Ross-shire:

I hope and trust that the vigorous steps the government has

taken will stop the radicals and all the turbulent rascals in their career of wickedness. It makes one's blood boil with indignation to think that a few unprincipled and brazen faced blackguards should have been able to carry things to such a length that they have, that a whole country should have been thrown into a state of ferment by such fellows as Hunt, Cobbet and company.[480]

James, on half pay and living in Ross-shire at the time, reassured Maria, who was living on her estate in East Lothian, that Ross-shire was quiet and free from radicalism:

The country is quiet and only knows (how) such things are by report, and I fancy even little by report.[481]

Later, James was very concerned to learn, in news brought aboard his ship, the Valorous, that less than two years after his confident assertions, major anti-clearance riots had taken place within ten miles of his home at Castle Leod, Strathpeffer. This could be interpreted as an example of James' poor judgement, but in fact it serves to illustrate that the landed gentry were often completely out of touch with the feelings of the bulk of the population, especially in such a period of social turmoil.

Despite the vigorous government repression so welcomed by James, radicalism didn't go away (although full scale revolution did). Two radicals were elected to Parliament during the 1820s and by the end of the decade the Whigs, with their moderate but reforming agenda, had gained power.

The Earl of Seaforth, from a Whig family in Galloway, had already sounded out ministers as to whether he could expect to receive their electoral backing should he decide to stand for Parliament and he had received a positive response. He then promoted a meeting at Dingwall in 1830, where he called for a reform of the 'extremely defective' Scottish representative system.

A committee, chaired by Stewart Mackenzie and including local lairds Roderick Macleod, Kilcoy, Geanies, Coul, Gairloch, Thomas Mackenzie and Charles Ross of Invercharron was set up to promote the cause. A new Scottish representative system was proposed in the Scottish Reform Bill which would introduce wide-ranging changes to the election laws of Scotland and would be a major step, albeit using baby strides, on the road to universal suffrage. The Bill tried to reflect more acutely the population shifts in the country and the rapidly growing urban areas were to be given better representation. Some rural areas would lose out, however and locally Cromartie was one of them, as it was to be united with Ross-shire to form one electoral area, Ross and Cromarty. The total Scottish Parliamentary electorate was about 5,000 adult males, but the Bill would increase this to 60,000 voters (now covering householders of £10 value in the burghs and property owners of £10 or tenants of £50 rental in the country seats). The number of Scottish MPs would also increase from 45 to 53.[482]

Encouraged by local support, Stewart Mackenzie warmly approved the Reform Bills at an Edinburgh public meeting and finally declared his candidature for the 1831 election. Hugh Rose Ross denounced all the candidates as 'unfit', on the grounds that most of the genuine property owners were against reform, and he particularly accused Stewart Mackenzie of seeking to delude the people and being hostile to the interests of Tain and the Black Isle. He particularly objected to the proposed political merger of Cromartie with Ross-shire. Yet despite all, he opted for Stewart Mackenzie even though he thought him 'a bad choice'.

Stewart Mackenzie won his election after a hard fought campaign and in 1831 he became the Member of Parliament for Ross-shire. Giving thanks, he argued that 'timely and effectual reform' was essential, but conceded the validity of some of Rose Ross's objections and, attempting to seize the middle ground, he promised to see if modifications could be made to the Bill without impairing its principles.

The new MP later did little or nothing to attempt any modification of the Bill and conversely proved to be a steady supporter of the details of the reform proposals. For example, when he was presented with a Ross-shire petition against the union with Cromartie, Stewart Mackenzie defended the amalgamation as both logical and harmless, much to Hugh Rose Ross's fury.

Despite the Tory objections the Reform Bill was passed in the House of Commons by the ruling Whig party, but was then rejected by the House of Lords. A further general election took place in the next year when the reformed constituency of Ross and Cromarty had a registered electorate of 516. This time Stewart Mackenzie easily defeated the Conservative, Hugh Andrew Johnstone Munro of Novar, in a poll of 420. Hugh Rose Ross, now firmly against the Reform Act, supported Munro of Novar in the election and there was now little love lost between him and Stewart Mackenzie.[483]

Hugh Rose Ross was a controversial figure. A son of the manse, born in Sutherland in 1767, he went in his teens to the West Indies and there became involved in the supply chain for the British Fleet. He reached the high rank of Deputy Paymaster General in the Government Commissariat Service and, happily for him, managed to build up a considerable personal fortune, although enemies suggested that not all his fortune was earned by morally justifiable means. Concern about the excessive cost of stores in the West Indies led to the establishment of a parliamentary commission and to the accusation and trial of Valentine Jones, the Commissary of Stores, on charges of corruption. It appears that Hugh Rose was a go-between in some dubious transactions between Jones and a merchant named Matthew Higgins. Higgins also used a trading house (involving

Hugh Rose's brother William) to take excessive profits, often under false names. Although Jones was found guilty of corruption, Hugh was not called to trial and was not formally accused of any wrong-doing.[484]

In 1799 Hugh made an astute marriage to Arabella Phipps, the daughter of Isaac Phipps, who, as Paymaster General, was Hugh's boss. Hugh, accompanied by his young wife, returned to Scotland in 1802 rather richer than he had left and almost immediately began the process of buying up sizeable chunks of Easter Ross, ultimately acquiring Calrossie, Glastullich, Arabella,[485] Tarlogie, Morangie and others. It has been suggested that Hugh's new wife was not the only person who accompanied Hugh when he returned to Scotland. Local gossip informed that he also brought back his mistress from the Caribbean and set her up in his home at Bayfield House at Nigg.

Poor Arabella did not live long enough to enjoy their new wealth and status in Cromarty. Her tombstone in the Old St Duthus Church in Tain states simply that Arabella:

... in the act of preparing Medicine for the relief of a sick and indigent Family, suddenly expired on the 9th November 1806, aged 27 years.

Local sources assert that despite the absence of any documentary evidence, her husband's mistress, hiding in an attic at Bayfield House, emerged when the moment was right and murdered the hapless Arabella. No murder case was ever brought but malicious gossip persisted and, allegedly, the tale has been authenticated by descendants of the Ross family.[486]

Local gossip did not help his standing, already low in gentry circles, being a man of 'new money.' He compensated for this by a vigorous approach to local issues. He did much for road works, tree planting, drainage etc. and was a leading light in the formation of Tain Royal Academy. His portrait shows a slight yet proud and dignified figure, a man who would thrive on being considered by his contemporaries to be a pillar of local society.

But there was another side to Hugh Rose. He did not shy away from confrontation and was involved in a celebrated legal action which was to take 40 years and a huge amount of money to reach fruition, and was based on proving that George Ross of Cromarty was illegitimate (thus allowing the inheritance of the estate of Culcairn and Cromarty to fall to himself). Despite its length, he considered the case to be time and money well spent, as he had quite a lot of both. Ultimately his case was accepted and he was successful in his action.[487] From then on he added the name of Ross to his own, styling himself Hugh Rose Ross. A proud and irascible man, he was quick to take offence and was as likely to threaten personal violence as to take matters through the courts.

Hugh Rose Ross was not a person to cross if a quiet campaign, unencumbered by controversy, was sought. The convincing victory of Stewart Mackenzie over Rose Ross's candidate, Munro of Novar, led to bitter recriminations, mainly fought out through the columns of the local newspapers. Two long letters, signed by 'an elector' but clearly the work of Hugh Rose Ross, were the catalysts which ignited a major breech with Stewart Mackenzie. In the first letter of 26th October 1832 Mackenzie was accused in no uncertain terms of failing to honour promises allegedly clearly and unequivocally made, mainly to do with the merger of Ross and Cromarty.[488] Stewart Mackenzie's wisdom was called into question:

> Had Ross (shire) sent its greatest fool to parliament he could not have spoken greater nonsense.[489]

Furthermore his honesty was also deemed to be very suspect.

Here we have got Saint Paul's observation verified. While they promise them liberty they themselves are servants of corruption.[490]

The real objection came in Rose Ross's second letter of 16th November. Whilst continuing to cast scorn on Stewart Mackenzie's actions, he drew particular attention to comments made by him concerning the action of an 88-year-old Sheriff of the county who had changed his mind about an appeal:

> Proclamations made to the world by Seaforth in his letter that the sheriff had been guilty of something approaching perjury... I am also persuaded that Seaforth would never have made such charge against the Sherriff if of equal age.[491]

The accusations of stupidity, corruption and now cowardice proved to be too much for a man who could not cope with the dangerous cocktail of being a proud Highland chief, and the subject of a personal and public attack from a man who held substantially different political beliefs. There was inevitably going to be a reckoning.

30

Measure the earth

On Saturday 17th November 1832 Stewart Mackenzie travelled from Brahan Castle to the home of Captain James Murray at Craigdarroch, and left a letter in which he asked if James would agree to be his 'friend' in a dispute with Hugh Rose Ross:

> ... call on Mr Ross, when I hope, cooler and mature reflection will induce him to retract in writing what he said of me and to give you a written apology, that the public may be informed... If not, you must by post let me know where I shall join you to meet him... I most earnestly entreat you to do this on my behalf.

James had been ill for some time, but rose from his sick bed to meet with Seaforth at Brahan Castle. There he read the relevant letters attacking his friend and, as a result, he formally agreed to act as a 'friend' and to demand a 'meeting' with Mr Ross or an apology.[492] James then sent a letter to Mr Ross, asking Mr Ross to meet him without delay and he, accompanied by Stewart Mackenzie, left for Tarbat House to await a reply. On the road nearing Tarbat in the Black Isle they met Hugh Rose Ross sitting in his carriage. James joined him and a brief discussion ensued, but matters got off to a poor start. James indicated that there was nothing personal as he was simply a cool and dispassionate medium of communication, although nevertheless a bringer of unwelcome messages.

In fact, James struggled to maintain the fiction of him being simply a disinterested messenger. Over recent years his closest friends and acquaintances in Ross-shire had become those who espoused the cause of reform and despite his earlier protestations concerning the action of the reformists, as an elector in the county he would have found it increasingly difficult not to take one side or another. Consequently Ross was not impressed and thought him impertinent in demanding 'a meeting without delay'. Nevertheless he agreed to talk with him and they adjourned to a nearby Inn. There, in a private room, James delivered Stewart Mackenzie's ultimatum:

> I am informed that you avow yourself the author of a letter signed 'an elector'... reflecting on me in language unbefitting a gentleman to use to another. I call upon you to retract, in writing, the whole of that production which accuses me of being guilty of breeches of promise and violation of pledges, which accusations or reflections you must know to be false and unfounded... I require from you a written apology for having thus attacked my character.
>
>   P.S. since writing the above I have seen another letter... I call upon you in a similar manner to retract and apologise.[493]

The strength and vehemence of Rose Ross' response surprised even James Murray. James went on to comment:

> He expressed himself in a loud tone of voice, accompanied by gestures so violent a description as to convince me that any attempt at reasoning was out of the question.[494]

In particular, Ross denied accusing Stewart Mackenzie of cowardice, despite James' protestations that his words, referring to an old man of 88, would bear no other interpretation. Rose

Ross' reply simply confirmed the suspicion that indeed he was not now open to reason.

> I now say Sir that he dared not say that to me which he said of the sheriff.

To make sure that he was not misunderstood he accompanied his statement with a violent blow upon the table. James replied that he had said quite enough; he would have no further conversation with him and, in order to follow correct procedure, Ross should now send his 'friend' to him.[495]

This 'correct procedure' was based upon the well-known course of action to be taken in matters leading up to a duel.[496] The duel, a code of honour, was fought to gain 'satisfaction' and restore honour by demonstrating a willingness to risk life and limb. Killing the opponent was not the primary objective of the duel, but death was not an uncommon result. There were at least 1,000 attested duels in Britain between 1785 and 1845 and the fatality rates were about 15 per cent. It was safer to have a pistol duel than a sword duel and one detailed study showed that six and a half per cent of the 214 participants in the pistol duels were killed and 71 per cent escaped without any injury.[497] Even so, it was clear that a duel was no laughing matter.

Duels continued to take place right into the 19th century, with the largest group of duellists being military officers, followed by the young sons of the gentry. Duelling was also popular for a time amongst doctors and amongst the legal professions. This may account for the fact that, despite the duel being illegal, it was often treated by the courts with extreme liberality. Duelling was strongly frowned upon in official military circles, as it would be possible for an unscrupulous but talented junior officer to challenge and defeat a senior officer and thus gain promotion through the 'dead man's shoes'. Furthermore, it could encourage the disobeying of any order which was unwelcome or disliked, by a junior officer.

Duelling occurred at the very highest levels of society. Four Prime Ministers of the United Kingdom have engaged in duels. William Petty, 2nd Earl of Shelburne fought a duel with Colonel William Fullarton in 1780, followed in 1798 by William Pitt the Younger who fought George Tierney. Famously, George Canning fought a duel with Lord Castlereagh in 1809 and the elderly Duke of Wellington also fought a duel with Lord Winchelsea in 1829.

Duelling was not unknown in the Murray family and James' father Patrick had first-hand experience of a well-known Canadian duel. In March 1795, Patrick Murray's regiment, the 60th Foot, was based near Montréal, Canada. A young ensign named Samuel Holland was in Patrick's company and was the usual high-spirited young officer. Samuel's father, a friend of Patrick's uncle General James Murray, had also served in the 60th and had proudly preserved the pistols he had used in the famous assault on Quebec many years earlier. Samuel's high spirits and his father's obstinate pride were to prove disastrous. The cause of the duel is confusing but Patrick, probably a second for one of the protagonists, has left an account. Captain Shoedde was a serving officer in the 60th. Foot and a close colleague of Patrick. It seems that young Holland may have paid undue attention to his wife and the Captain suspected a rather deeper involvement. Samuel denied any such involvement and consulted his father over whether such an untruth should be further pursued by the satisfaction of honour. His father reputedly replied with the following words:

> Samuel, my boy, here are the weapons which my loved friend
> General Wolfe presented me on the day of his death. Use them,
> to keep the old family name without stain.[498]

Consequently a duel was fought on 24th March, 1795. Shoedde

won the toss of a coin, meaning he could fire first. He shot to kill and the bullet penetrated Samuels's torso just under his ribs. He fell to the ground but managed to recover enough to fire a shot towards Shoedde, which shattered his arm. Samuel was carried from the field to a nearby coffee house, but died shortly afterwards.[499] The incident is still remembered today by the commemorative 'Holland Tree' and its descriptive plaque.

On 23rd August 1826, the last fatal duel on Scottish soil took place, at dawn, just outside the town of Kirkcaldy. After quarrelling over a bank loan, David Landale, a linen merchant, fought George Morgan, a former soldier and at that time his bank manager. By repute, David had no experience of firearms, and he needed to buy pistols and learn how to fire them very quickly. The day before the duel he and his second rushed into Edinburgh and purchased the necessary pistols. The next morning, the two men stood 12 paces apart and, on command, fired simultaneously. Morgan staggered and slumped to the ground, blood pouring from his mouth. Landale, who had never fired a shot in anger before, had fired the more accurate shot of the two men and had killed his bank manager. David immediately fled from Kirkcaldy and headed to the Lake District to avoid arrest. He then adopted an alias and kept a low profile. However, one month after the duel his conscience caught up with him and he turned up for his trial in Perth to face a charge of murder. He was acquitted, and exonerated 'with character unsullied'.[500]

Captain James Murray had agreed to take on the office of 'second' or 'friend' and his task was to conduct the dispute. The 'friend' on each side would attempt to resolve the dispute upon terms acceptable to both parties and, should this fail, they would arrange and oversee the mechanics of the physical encounter. If no agreement had been reached the friends would, between them, determine a suitable 'field of honour'. They would check that the weapons were equal and that the duel was fought in a fair manner.

Even being a second brought its own risks and dangers. In 1712, Charles Mohun and James Douglas, the 4th Duke of Hamilton, had fought a duel. Both were killed but their seconds were arrested, tried and found guilty of manslaughter.

For a pistol duel, the parties would be placed back to back with loaded pistols in hand and, on a given signal, would then walk an agreed number of paces, turn to face the opponent, and shoot. Typically, the graver the insult, the fewer the paces agreed upon. Alternatively, a pre-agreed length of ground would be measured out by the seconds and marked. At a given signal, the duellists would advance to their spot and fire. This system reduced the possibility of cheating, as neither principal had to trust the other not to turn too soon. Another common procedure involved alternate shots being taken, beginning with the challenged firing first.[501]

Before this stage was reached, Captain James continued to search for a solution and now his main task was to reach an agreement with Rose Ross's friend. He was shocked when that friend, accompanied by Rose Ross, entered the room almost immediately after Rose Ross' angry departure. Ross's second was none other than Hugh Munro of Novar, the defeated Tory political opponent of Stewart Mackenzie at the recent election. Murray put Mackenzie's case to Novar who, although expressing sympathy with Rose Ross, did not defend his words used in the recent letters. Murray also strongly argued that it would be inappropriate for Novar to act as a second in this matter as Novar was a recent and high profile political opponent and, should either principal be killed, it would be extremely damaging to him politically. Novar asked for time to consider his position and Captain James gave him until 11am on the next day; the meeting to take place at the Inn at Parkhill by Tarbat House, at which time he said Rose Ross must send a retraction or face a meeting.[502]

Murray explained the current situation to an anxious Seaforth and received a letter in return, by which Mackenzie thanked him:

> ... It will prove, I trust, that cowardice is as little one of my
> characteristics as revenge. Believe me to be most thankful to
> you... for attention to my honour. ... without it I value not life
> itself.[503]

The next morning Novar wrote to Murray and explained that he
would not be able to meet with him until shortly after 11am. He also
pointed out that Rose Ross had written a reply directly to Stewart
Mackenzie. As all negotiations should, according to custom, take
place through the seconds, Captain Murray was displeased and told
Mackenzie so. Stewart Mackenzie assured Captain Murray that he
had not yet received any letter from Rose Ross, but he would not
usurp the role of the second and consequently he would decline to
open any correspondence should it arrive. He reiterated his
determination to satisfy his bruised honour:

> My mind was not made up lightly. I must have complete
> retraction and apology or he or I must measure the earth.[504]

Further hurried notes followed between the two seconds, Murray
and Novar, in which Novar insisted that Rose Ross had written
an answer to Seaforth and put it in the Post Office. Novar finally
turned up to meet with Captain Murray in a field behind Tarbat
House. The time was approaching 6pm and Captain Murray was
by then most annoyed. Although Novar made apologies, Murray,
conscious of his honour as an officer and gentleman, exclaimed
that he:

> could not return to... (... his brother officers) to be taunted with
> having been made a fool of by a parcel of Ross-shire lairds.

Novar appeared to have a letter from Rose Ross with him, but Murray refused to accept it, as he had not seen the earlier letter, allegedly sent via the Post Office. Furthermore, Novar, obviously having considered the advice not to prejudice his own position by acting as a Second, informed Captain James that he was no longer acting for Rose Ross as a friend and Captain Mackenzie would now perform that role. Murray refused to accept this, arguing that Seconds could not be changed at this stage, and he would act with no-one else but Novar. The deadline had now passed, no apology had been received and Novar had not named a time and place for the duel. Consequently James Murray took the decision and insisted that the principals (Stewart Mackenzie and Rose Ross) should meet at 12 pm the next day in the field behind the Novar Inn at Evanton.

At 11pm that night, Murray, staying at Tarbat House, was roused from his bedroom by a visitor, Captain Mackenzie of Kincraig, who was acting as the new 'friend' for Rose Ross. He brought the unpleasant news that he had not come about the forthcoming Mackenzie / Rose Ross duel but instead was to issue a new challenge. Rose Ross was looking for an apology, or a meeting with James Murray, firstly for delivering Seaforth's challenge to him unsealed, and secondly for refusing to accept a sealed letter from him to Seaforth. Should an apology not be forthcoming, and James Murray immediately indicated that he was not going to offer one, then he wished for a meeting at 12am the very next day at Shandwick Gate.

James Murray, a very ill James Murray, now found himself in the ridiculous position of having to appear as a Second for Seaforth at 12am, and also as the Principal, to fight the same man at the same time, but in a location 12 miles apart.

In an attempt to ease the situation James did emphasise to Captain Mackenzie that although he would not apologise, he had not in any way intended to insult Rose Ross by his actions, and

Captain Mackenzie seemed satisfied by his explanation.

The next morning another flurry of letters went backwards and forwards, all failing to improve the situation. As 12am approached, Stewart Mackenzie and James Murray rode to the Novar Inn, but their opponents were, of course, notable by their absence.

As they left the area and neared Alness they met Colonel Munro of Teaninich on the road. Colonel Munro indicated that he wished to speak urgently to James Murray and he asked Seaforth to leave his carriage for a short time and hold Munro's horse whilst he did so. A disgruntled Stewart Mackenzie grudgingly acceded to this request and Teaninich then entered the carriage. On speaking with James Murray he repeatedly explained why Novar had withdrawn from the role of Second to Rose Ross, but Captain Murray, being quite determined not to give way on this point, would not accept any argument. At that point Rose Ross's carriage was spotted and Stewart Mackenzie and Murray proceeded to meet him. They were surprised to see that Rose Ross was accompanied, not by Novar but by Mackenzie of Kincraig. With the whole situation rapidly deteriorating into farce Kincraig then approached Captain Murray and put forward, on Rose Ross's behalf, the extraordinary proposal that Captain Murray should become the Principal and fight Rose Ross whilst Seaforth would then act as Murray's Second. At least some humour was seen in the progression of events:

> Mr Mackenzie (Kincraig) was so struck with the absurdity of this that he could not command his gravity.[505]

In fact, there were some historical precedents for the Seconds also taking part in a conflict. In the early 17th century it was normal practice for the Seconds as well as the Principals to fight each other. Francois de Montmorency-Bouteville, a famous duellist, fought a public duel in January 1627 with a Monsieur Beuvron.

They fought to a bloodless stalemate and agreed to call it a draw, but their Seconds also fought and Bouteville's Second mortally wounded Beuvron's Second. By the 18th century the Seconds' role had become more specific; to make sure the rules were followed and to try to achieve reconciliation; but even as late as 1777 there was still the option of the Seconds exchanging shots in some established duel codes. However, the swapping of the Principal with the Second undermined the whole basic premise of satisfying personal honour, and had never been adopted.[506] Any agreement to Rose Ross's proposal was quite out of the question.

As Murray and Stewart Mackenzie continued their journey in their carriage, they chanced upon Munro of Novar at the edge of the village of Alness, and angry words were exchanged. Munro maintained that he had not 'positively' agreed to James Murray's proposals for Rose Ross to meet with Seaforth this day. Seaforth, rapidly losing his patience, also exchanged angry words with Munro, and it led to Murray leading him away from Munro with the Regency equivalent of that well-worn modern phrase, "Leave him. He's not worth it."

Oh, Seaforth. It is not worth your while to be angry.

The disagreements raged on for the next few days, with letters passing back and forth and allegations and counter allegations being made through the letter pages of the local newspapers. James Murray poured scorn on Rose Ross and his challenge to him:

This gentleman, who sends his challenges at a rate of three per diem refuses to satisfy the man who has called him to account for his misdemeanours.[507]

Seaforth joined the debate too, and also published a statement in the Inverness Journal which gave his interpretation of the affair so far.

In the newspaper Captain Murray's signature is at the bottom of Seaforth's statement, but it is clear that he is affirming that, in his opinion, the statement was a correct and a true statement of the proceedings so far. On reading the statement, Munro of Novar misinterpreted the signature as meaning that Captain Murray was the author of the statement, which incidentally was most unflattering to Munro of Novar. In consequence, Novar then issued a challenge to Captain Murray to withdraw all his allegations and insinuations or give him satisfaction.

Captain James Murray, at that moment very ill and barely able to move, was then in the even more farcical position of being the Second for Seaforth's dispute but simultaneously the subject of two challenges, one from Seaforth's original opponent and one from Seaforth's Second. No doubt, judging by the number and length of letters devoted to this ridiculous disagreement, it was proving to be of great interest and amusement to the readers of the local newspapers.

Murray agreed to meet both his new opponents once he had recovered his health, but fate intervened. On 6th December, Novar, Ross, Seaforth and Murray were bound-over to keep the peace by the Sheriff of Ross-shire. All parties made noises about meetings outside of the county boundary, but this potential path was blocked also almost immediately by a Judiciary Warrant from the Lord Advocate which bound over all the participants to keep the peace in the United Kingdom.

That was effectively the end of the matter. All parties, now safe behind a Judiciary Warrant, continued to argue their case through the offices of the local newspapers. Rose Ross and Novar expressed the view that Seaforth's agent had arranged for the Lord Advocate to intervene in the dispute and both Ross and Novar used very strong and offensive language, particularly against Captain James:

The Captain knows well how to distinguish the difference
between a Principal and a Second – as Second he moved with
the rapidity of lightning – as Principal he reported himself
damaged, laid himself up in dust, where he remained quite snug
from the challenge... which he evaded until the agent of himself
and Seaforth applied by letter to the Lord Advocate... Upon
which the *gallant* officer weighed anchor, came in in full sail, in
all his glory... Where he pronounced YES to the promise to
keep the peace.[508]

Ultimately it was an anti-climactic conclusion to the story, and
today the arguments and counter claims made by all the parties
seem almost childish and trivial in their tone. However, there is
no doubt that all the participants took their duties and the
unfolding events very seriously indeed, and it is just good fortune
that all lived to tell their tales. Seaforth, his initial challenge to Rose
Ross now apparently forgotten, devoted his time to his
parliamentary duties and to forlorn attempts to balance the books
on his vast estate. Novar, never to achieve his ambition of a seat
in Parliament, continued his duties as a significant local landowner
and as a serious art collector, amassing over 2,500 pieces of high
art, including many works by masters such as Turner, Constable,
Watteau and Raphael, by the time of his death in 1864. Hugh Rose
Ross persisted in playing a part in local politics and, it seems, did
not mellow much with age. Five years before his death in 1846,
and at the age of 81, his pride once more got the better of him and
he participated in the last duel to be fought in Ross-shire. The
Inverness Courier reported it in a matter-of- fact manner:

On Wednesday last a duel took place between Duncan
Davidson, Esq. of Tulloch, and Hugh Ross, Esq. of Cromarty
and Glastullich. The quarrel originated in the proceedings of the
county meeting, held lately at Invergordon, on the subject of the

Prison Board. Mr Davidson was Chairman of the meeting and Mr Ross conceived that he interrupted him improperly in the course of the discussion. A duel was the result. The parties met at two o'clock on Wednesday, near the Kincraig Road, by Balnagown Castle... After the usual preliminaries, Mr Davidson fired, as we are informed, 'somewhat in the direction' of his opponent, and Mr Ross discharged his pistol in the air. The Seconds now interfered, and the Principals having shaken hands, left the ground.

Tulloch afterwards said that the meeting took place not because Mr Ross declined to apologise to him, but because he declined to apologise to Mr Ross for having interrupted him, 'as he [Mr Ross] conceived, in an abrupt and uncalled-for manner.'[509]

31

A final legacy

T he last two years had been 'anni horibili' for James
Murray. By 1831 he had become a well-known and
respected member of the Ross-shire gentry. He had
gained the privilege of becoming an elector and secured the
friendship of many of the leading families of the county. He had a
charming and popular wife and together they lived in comfort at
Craigdarroch, well-tended by their servants. Captain James
Murray was a proud man and during his career he had much to
be proud of. The scandals that shook Ross-shire society in 1831
and 1832 took a severe toll on him, and he was never to recover.

There is the suggestion that even before the discovery of his
wife's infidelity he had been suffering from illness. His naval career
had led to him to spend a great deal of his time in the Caribbean
where disease was endemic amongst the British stationed in that
tropical hot-bed of infection. Had James escaped any serious illness
it would have been put down to good fortune. He may also have
been injured following his encounter with Mexican bandits. The
proximity and closeness of his relationship with Doctor Wishart
of Dingwall seemed to be more than just friendship, and the good
doctor was frequently called upon by the Trotter family to use his
professional skills during the period following the breakdown of
James' marriage. Although James was to emerge from the marriage
breakdown with adequate financial recompense, the emotional
compensation was sadly lacking. Even though he maintained his
dignity under the most trying of circumstances there was little

doubt that he was emotionally spent and Doctor Wishart became a constant companion. 1832 saw little improvement. James remained publically very determined and unwavering throughout the divorce procedures, and showed a resolute and indomitable spirit in his pursuit of compensation from Mackenzie of Coul, only recently one of his closest associates.

The events which led to James being 'called out' twice within a week have the hallmarks of a Feydeau comedy farce, but a Regency highland gentleman would not have seen the humour. James gave as good as he got in the dispute which was primarily carried out through the columns of the newspapers, but the imputations on his honour and allegations concerning his personal courage would have been deeply offensive to a proud naval officer. An examination of James' life would have quickly dispelled any notion of cowardice. He had shown courage in the face of the enemy on numerous occasions, and had always come out of conflict with his reputation high and often with a promotion in the offing. However, he showed an unfortunate rigidity in his attitude throughout his role as a Second to Seaforth, especially in refusing to let Munro of Novar stand down as a Second, when all evidence suggests that this was not an unusual occurrence. From this behaviour his own reputation suffered, and led to the challenges he would later receive.

At times James did appear unwilling to meet with Ross and Novar, despite his protestations to the contrary. Almost certainly the reason for this was his ill-health, the recurring fever-based illness such as malaria. In such a situation it would have been almost impossible for him to conduct himself adequately in a duel, and it is to be wondered how he managed to draw upon such a depth of strength to conduct all the frantic activity which took place at that time. A recurring fever-based illness would also account for the periods when James appeared to be in quite normal health, a condition which caused Ross to exclaim, perhaps unfairly:

He then... proceeded to Invergordon (a distance of 20 miles). Mr Ross has shown that Captain Murray was well enough to travel (though not to fight). Captain Murray was capable of writing and signing... a document and be at the same time incapable of drawing a trigger.[510]

It would also explain the apparent sound health that James seemed to enjoy in the December of 1832, when he had the role of Steward at a public dinner in the Royal Hotel, Dingwall in honour of Stewart Mackenzie.[511]

Prolonged illness often has the effect of encouraging the ill-fated recipient to seek comfort wherever and whenever he or she can. James chose to return to the comfort of the village where, as a refugee from war, he was allowed to pursue the normal life of a Scottish child of the late 18th century. He moved back to the Manse in New Abbey in the shadow of the ancient Sweetheart Abbey and was cared for by his sister, Harriet, and her husband, the highly respected Reverend James Hamilton, until he died on Thursday 29th May 1834, aged just 56 years.

In his final will he left all his fortune in equal measure to his three sisters by Eliza, his mother, namely Harriet, Louisa and Theresa.[512] Mary and Isabella, his sisters by his father, Patrick, remained in Canada and were not mentioned in the will at all. There is the suggestion that there had been a family split as a result of their success in gaining land through the military service of their father Patrick, based upon their false evidence as 'sole heirs.' His house at Craigdarroch, still under feu to Mackenzie of Coul, was retained and administered as a rental property for many years by James Hamilton and by David Murray, his long-standing retainer, who continued to live there.

James Murray was the first of his refugee family to pass away, although his mother had died a few years before him. She had returned to New Providence in the Bahamas with her two 'sons', John George King and Podmore Smith, shortly after James had relinquished control of Argenteuil. James did not mention the two boys in his final will and testament and, although Eliza refers to the boys in exactly the same way as she refers to her other children, it is quite possible that they were also adopted whilst she was living in New Providence. A John Podmore, Loyalist, is credited with an estate on the Caicos in 1797 but is not heard from again. It is possible that he died shortly after 1797 and his son was then cared for by Eliza. A John George King appears in Canada with Eliza and then shows up again, this time named John George King Podmore, as a lieutenant in the Royal Navy in 1815. John seems to have adopted the surname Podmore in recognition of his father, probably as he entered adulthood. This same Podmore was also a significant slave owner in the Bahamas, albeit mainly absent, at a time when many of the original loyalist incomers had left the islands. In 1825 Podmore had at least 148 slaves, mainly in New Providence. Eliza had remained a slave owner and is recorded as selling five slaves, namely Roslin, Delia, Amelia, Rebecca and Elizabeth, to Podmore in 1823,[513] although it is likely by this time that most of her slaves had already been passed on to new owners. J.G.K. Podmore became a long standing resident of the Bahamas and enjoyed considerable respect in his position as a magistrate for the islands.[514]

James Murray's sister, Louisa, on the death of her husband Thomas, had inherited the Larbreck estate near Irongray, Dumfriesshire. From 1834 the busy Rev. James Hamilton became her factor until she died in September 1843 in Helensburgh. Like James, she returned to the village of her youth and was interred alongside her half-brother in the burial ground of Sweetheart Abbey.

Just six years later Harriet Hamilton passed away. Unlike James and her sisters she had never left New Abbey after arriving there as a young homeless refugee. Her final resting place, along with her husband the Reverend Hamilton, is in the grave situated immediately next to James and Louisa. The third 'sister', Theresa, outlived them all, enjoying a very prosperous retirement in the affluent city of Bath. She died in 1864, leaving behind a rich portfolio of Georgian property in the area.

James' women all ultimately fared rather better than he did. Matilda Harris, although a wealthy and very eligible lady, remained single for many years and it was not until she was 42 years of age that she finally married, and rather like her relationship with James, it was to a man considerably older than herself.

Even if she was ever allowed out of the sight of her protective brothers, it seemed unlikely that Rachel, after the trauma of her divorce, would re-marry, but she did. The Tucker family's devoutness probably ensured that Rachel, firmly discouraged in contact with other men, could at least make an exception for male ministers and other men of the cloth. When she married farmer George Lee in 1844, it was no great surprise that he was the son of a minister.[515] She seemed to have maintained her liking for younger men and George was six years younger than herself. Nevertheless, she was still a good catch financially, and even in 1851 she (not her husband) was described as being the employer of nine people.[516] Sadly, Rachel remained childless and died in 1871 at Amersham, Bucks, just two years before her former lover, Robert Mackenzie passed away.

Robert Ramsay Mackenzie almost appears as a 'pantomime baddy' in the story of his relationship with Rachel and its tragic aftermath. His later life did little to dispel this image. He proved to be no more reliable and trustworthy in Australia than he had in his home in Ross-shire. In Sydney, after his escape from the clutches of the Tucker boys, he met up with his brother and soon began to speculate in land. A few years later Robert bought Salisbury Station in the New England district and separated from his brother, promising him £3,000, which of course, he was never to pay. By 1839 he was heavily in debt once more and borrowed a further £8,000 from his long-suffering family in Scotland. He used the money unwisely, allegedly living extravagantly in Sydney, and by December 1840 he was £19,000 in debt, but still claimed that he could 'work it out'. It was an empty boast, and by 1844 he had become bankrupt with debts of over £27,000.[517]

It appears that Rachel had enjoyed a lucky escape. It was another woman, Louisa Jones, who finally seemed to sort out the chaotic and erratic Robert. His farming enterprises finally began to make money and in 1859, now financially secure, he entered politics. The Queensland Governor, Sir George Bowen, laughingly described him as 'of high honour and integrity', obviously knowing little of his earlier life. In August 1867, after a period as Treasurer, he was elected as Premier of the State of Queensland. He served for two years before returning to Scotland, where in 1873 he died. He was scathingly summed up as:

> an absentee squatter who could justly be described as a cormorant who left no roots in the land... Physically large, he was limited intellectually and as a leader.[518]

James Murray had not always enjoyed the best of luck. Illegitimacy had cost him an inheritance into the Scottish aristocracy and his early life was torn apart by war and family breakup. His attempt to be colonist and landowner in Canada ended in disappointment and debt and his naval career was cut short before he could gain the flag rank he ultimately aspired to. His personal life seemed destined for upset and failure, and his health in later years was far from perfect.

He left no children but the story of James Murray did not end with his death. His nephew, the son of Harriet and James Hamilton, was christened James Murray Hamilton, and Captain James recognised his pleasure and esteem for the boy in his final

will and testament. Several thousand miles away another James
Murray was also keeping his name alive. Theophilus Yale had been
given his first start in life as a tenant when James Murray was the
Seigneur of Argenteuil, and in gratitude he had named his first
child James Murray Yale in his honour. Theophilus did not survive
long after his son's birth, but the orphan James Murray Yale was
put in the charge of a Thomas Bowren and in early life was
financed by none other than Eliza Smith, James' mother. James
Murray Yale went on to achieve considerable fame and success as
an explorer and trader in North West Canada, even having a fort
named after him. When the fur trade declined he moved into
agriculture, and Murray Yale was credited with developing many
of the largest farms which then existed on the mainland of what
is now British Columbia. Governor Simpson of British Columbia
described Yale as:

> A sharp, active, well conducted, very little man but full of fire
> and with the courage of a Lion. His diminutive size is more
> feared and respected than some of our six feet men.[519]

Apart from the reference to diminutive size it was an obituary that
Captain James Murray would have been proud to have had said of
himself. James Murray was descended from two remarkable
families and was to live through some extraordinary events. In a
more enlightened age James would have inherited the title, wealth
and prestige of the Elibank lordship. Although showing no signs
of resenting his loss of title and his place in the social order, he
was still very aware of the remarkable achievements of his Elibank
relatives, and the people around him were equally aware. He had
to live with this pressure and was not so well known to the general
public, but his own life was just as remarkable as his more
illustrious relatives. He was a man of his time and, like his Elibank
forebears, he lived according to his principles. He courted duty,

always sought to do the right thing and even, occasionally, managed to achieve it. He could wear the epithet, a 'scion of heroes', with pride.

Acknowledgements

esearch for the book presented a great excuse to travel and, consequently, visits to the archives in Dumfries, Edinburgh and London became almost routine. The frequently visited archives and research centres in the UK included the Ewart Library, Dumfries, The National Records of Scotland in Edinburgh, The National Archives in Kew, Dingwall Public Library, the Inverness Archive and Family History Centre, The National Library of Scotland, The Caird Library, Greenwich and the Surrey History Centre. Without exception, tribute should be paid to all the staff, who were most helpful and encouraging. These jaunts also enabled a 'walk in the footsteps' approach, and I thank those who assisted me in my seemingly haphazard itineraries, especially the present owners of Craigdarroch, Coul House, Tulloch Castle and the Novar Inn, all in Ross and Cromarty. In North America the research visits to Florida, Georgia, South Carolina, Montréal, Quebec, and Halifax, were also most fruitful and the friendliness, enthusiasm and help universally received will always remain in my memory. I thoroughly enjoyed the visits to the various Historical Society Headquarters, especially those in St. Augustine, Ormond Beach, Savannah and Charleston; all centres which house fine collections of both primary and secondary information and all freely shared with me. For most of the magnificent research conducted in Canada I have to thank Albert Smith, who has a research nose like a sniffer dog and unearthed some very useful and extremely well hidden data on our subjects. He worked primarily from Montreál, but the author also visited and received kind assistance from staff, in the Chateau Ramezay,

Montreál and the extensive Nova Scotia Archive collection based in Halifax, Nova Scotia.

The eye catching cover was designed and produced by the brilliant Laura Hudson Mackay who combined technical excellence with the imaginative abstract concept of a rope linking and tying James Murray to the sea, to his duty and to the inescapable expectations on his shoulders arising from his illustrious antecedents. Now, why didn't I think of this?

The task of checking, editing and sifting was given to unsuspecting friends and colleagues, who, to a person, gave me positive and helpful advice, encouragement, and, where necessary, (which was all too often, I fear) correction. I owe Alison Burgess, Professor Ted Cowan, Mike Hollis, Sadie Hollis, Ewan and Carol McCulloch, Edith Macdonald, Fraser Sanderson, Elizabeth Weir and Vena Wright a huge debt of gratitude. When I thought that I had finally completed the copy check I passed the work onto Peter Barrett who soon disabused me of that opinion. My grateful thanks to Peter. He did a great job.

Finally, and most importantly, my appreciation must be given to my wife Maureen. She has been part of the project since its inception and has had to live and breathe James Murray ever since, although I trust that James Murray's only surviving image, which shows a most handsome and dashing young officer, played no part at all in her enthusiasm. Research of this nature is often obscure and frustrating. Maureen, by use of unconventional logic, a peek outside of the normal box and a scatter gun approach to library and online resource material has complemented my primitive attempts to follow a more planned, orthodox approach and led us to discover much more than we would otherwise have done.

List of Abbreviations

NAS	National Archives of Scotland.
NA	National Archives (Kew, London).
SHC	Surrey History Centre.
NLS	National Library of Scotland.
SCHGM	South Carolina Historical and Genealogical Magazine.
FHQ	Florida Historical Quarterly.
NYHSM	New York Historical Society Museum and Library.

Bibliography:

The main centres for research were:

Aberdeen University Library.
: *Special collections.*

Archives Nationales du Quebec a Montréal.
: *Legal documentation, wills etc.*

Chateau Ramezay, Montreál.
: *Museum and former home of the Governor of Quebec.*

Dingwall School and Community Library.
: *Local collections.*

Dumfries Archives: including
: *Manse papers (uncatalogued).*
: *Shambellie Papers GGD 37.*
: *William Grierson's diary GGD 23.*

Ewart Library, Dumfries.
: *Local collections.*

Georgia Historical Society, Savannah, GA.
: *Local collections.*

Highland Archive Centre, Inverness.
: *Local collections.*

Lambeth Palace Library.
: *Fulham Papers.*

National Archives, Kew (NA)
: *Manuscript collections including War Office (WO), Admiralty (ADM), Carleton Papers (PRO 30/55) and Wills (PROB).*

National Archives of Scotland (NAS).
: *Mackenzie of Coul Papers.*

Decreets.

New Abbey Kirk Session Records.

Kirkbean Kirk Session Records.

Seaforth Mackenzie Papers.

Cromartie Papers.

National Library of Scotland (NLS)

Extensive collection, mainly secondary sources.

New York Historical Society Museum and Library (NYHSM)

Local and Loyalist collections.

Nova Scotia Archives, University Avenue, Halifax, Nova Scotia.

RN records and military records, especially concerning General James Murray.

Ormond Beach Historical Society.

Local collections.

Royal Naval Museum Library, Greenwich, London.

Naval history collections.

St. Augustine Historical Society, St. Augustine, FLA.

Local collections.

Scotland's People Research Centre, Edinburgh.

BMD, Wills, Census records.

South Carolina Historical Society, Charleston S.C.

Local collections.

Surrey History Centre and Archives (SHC)

Marriage settlements K 95/1/47 and K 95/1/53.

University of Glasgow Library.

Extensive historical collections.

Articles

Constable Archibald, *The Edinburgh Magazine and Literary Miscellany*, vol. 88 (Google eBook), 1821.

Griffiths R.J.H., *Genealogy of James and Lewis Mortlock and Relating to Kirtling, Cambridgeshire.* Update of note in Cambridge Family History Society (May 2003), Havant, 2010.

Kaye, Maggi, '*Some account of the rising of the Levellers in Galloway in the year 1723',* Wood, Maxwell J., (Ed), Gallovidian Annual, Robert Dinwiddie,1923.

Leneman Leah, *Wives and Mistresses in 18th Century Scotland,* Women's History Review, vol. 8, no. 4, 1999.

Lovejoy, Paul, *Olaudah Equiano,* Journal of Slave and Post-Slave Studies, vol. 27, Issue 3, 2006.

Macklin, M., *Memoirs,* St. Augustine Historical Society, El Escribano, vol. 41, 2004.

Osler, Edward, *The Life of Viscount Exmouth,* The London Quarterly Review, Issues 107–110, pp 69–93, 1835.

Parrish, Lydia A., *Records of some Southern Loyalists,* typescript on microfilm, Georgia Historical Society, 1953.

Petrie, Sir Charles, *The Elibank Plot, 1752–3.,* Transactions of the Royal Historical Society (Fourth Series), 14, 1931.

Rose, J., Holland, *British West India Commerce as a Factor in the Napoleonic War,* Cambridge Historical Journal, 3, 1929.

Schafer, D.L., *St. Augustine's British Years, 1763–1784,* El Escribano, St. Augustine Historical Society, vol. 38, 2001.

Schafer D.L., *Governor Grants Diary,* El Escribano, St. Augustine Historical Society, vol. 41, 2004.

Schafer, D.L., *Mount Oswald Plantation,* Florida Anthropologist, vol. 52, nos. 1&2 March–June, 1999.

Shoemaker, Robert B., *The Taming of the Duel: Masculinity, Honour and Ritual Violence in London, 1660–1800,* The Historical Journal, vol. 45, no. 3, Cambridge University Press, 2002.

Smith, Josiah, 1731–1826. *Diary of Josiah Smith, Jr., 1780-ca.,* 1932, South Carolina Historical and Genealogical Magazine, vols. 33 and 34, South Carolina Historical Society, 1932–1933.

Smith, Larry, *Bahamian Heritage in the County of Norfolk,* Bahama Pundit, September 2011.

Stewart, F. J., *Sweetheart Abbey and its Owners over the Centuries*, DGNHAS, 3rd series, Vol. 64, Dumfries, 1989.

Strickland, Alice, *Ashes on the Wind; the Story of the Last Plantations*, Volusia County Historical Commission, Ormond Beach, Florida, 1985.

Tingley, Charles A., *Over the Swash and Out Again*, El Escribano, vol. 45, 2008.

Troxler, Carole W, *Loyalist Refugees and the British Evacuation of East Florida 1783–85,* Florida Historical Quarterly, vol. 60, no. 1, July 1981.

Truckell, A.E., *Some 18th Century Transatlantic Trade Documents*, DGNHAS, series 3, vol. 67, 1992.

Other Printed documents

Commons Papers, *Accounts and Papers, relating to Assessed Taxes, Poor etc.,* 18 volumes, House of Commons, 1831–1832.

Georgia Historical Society Pamphlet, *Savannah in the American Revolution,* Georgia Society Sons of the American Revolution, GA.

Quebec Legislative Assembly Papers, *Titles and documents relative to the seigniorial tenure required by an address of the Legislative Assembly 1851,* Frechette, E.R., Quebec, 1852.

Register of Sasine, Kirkcudbrightshire circa 1791–1795; nos. 1005, 1006, 1017, 1018, 1021, 1022, 1357 and Kirkcudbrightshire circa 1791–1810, nos. 599, 2763, 2764. Also 26th March 1807, no. 2187.

Royal Naval Museum Library, *The Press Gangs and Naval Recruitment, Information Sheet 78,* Greenwich, London, 2001.

Blogs / Websites

Research today inevitably involves the extensive use of online sources and both primary and secondary online material is rapidly increasing in its scope and availability. This study found it particularly useful in two areas. An initial general search often gave very useful background information and also identified sources for more in-depth study. At the other end of the spectrum many local and specialised sources are now going online and are thus available remotely. It is not practical to list all online sources used. Specified authors are listed in the secondary source section but selected online sources that took a more holistic approach are listed below and hopefully give a flavour of the material obtained and consulted.

Admiral Sir William Hope:
www.clanjohnstone.org/pdf/viceadmiral_sir_william_johnstone_hope_gcb.pdf

Battle of San Domingo:
http://www.militaryhistory.about.com/od/NapWarsNaval/p/Napoleon ic-Wars-Battle-Of-SanDomingo.htmwww.militaryhistory.about.com /od/NapWarsNaval/p/Napoleonic-Wars-Battle-Of-SanDomingo. htm

Bahama Pundit: *www.bahamapundit.com*

Duel, Canada:
www.lowensteyn.com/Samuel_Holland/Gedcom/events/ event15.html

Encyclopaedia of Children and Childhood in History and Society:
www.faqs.org/childhood/index.html

Harris Family:
www.mississauga.ca/portal/discover/benareshistorichouse

Historical collections of Georgia:
www.usgenweb.info/georgia/history/hcg-c-g.htm

Highland Clearances:
www.electricscotland.com/ history/ articles/ sheep.htm
Jane Austen: Blogs on social customs etc. in Regency Britain.
http:// janeaustensworld.wordpress.com
Jones, John Paul: *www.jpj.demon.co.uk/ jpjlife.htm*
Legacies of British Slave Ownership: UCL Dept. of History
database. 2013, *http:// www.ucl.ac.uk/ lbs*
Listed Buildings, Dumfries and Galloway. New Abbey:
www.britishlistedbuildings.co.uk
Maxwell, family and genealogy:
www.maxwellsociety.com/ Biography/ 1819century.htm
Nigg and the Black Isle: *www.fearnpeninsula.org.uk/ niggpdf05.pdf*
Parliamentary History: *www.historyofparliamentonline.org.*
Port Royal Battle: *http:// miniawi.blogspot.co.uk/ 2010/ 12/ battle-of-port-Royal-island*
Royal Navy in Napoleonic Times:
www.nelsonsnavy.co.uk/ broadside2.html, and *www.ageofnelson.org*
Schoolteacher, New Abbey: *http:// incrediblefacts.com/ human-endeavours/ the-man-who-wore-scarecrows-clothes*
Slave Registers of former British Colonial Dependencies,
1812-1834: Ancestry.com on-line database, Provo, Utah,
2007.
Strathpeffer:*http:// web.undiscoveredscotland.com/ strathpeffer/ strathpeffer*
Tucker Family: *www.brucehunt.co.uk/ trematoncastle*
Washington, George, Papers. George Washington to Continental
Congress, Cambridge, December 18, 1775:
http:// lcweb2.loc.gov/ cgi-bin

Contemporary Newspapers

Bahamas Gazette.
Dumfries Journal.

Edinburgh Evening Courant.
Galloway Gazette.
Georgia Historical Quarterly.
Inverness Courier.
Inverness Journal.
London Gazette.
Newport Mercury.
New York Gazette.
Pennsylvania Gazette.
Quebec Gazette.
South Carolina Gazette.

Consulted Dissertations and unprinted sources.

Dacam, H. John, *Wanton and Torturing Punishments: Patterns of Discipline and Punishment in the Royal Navy, 1783–1815*, PhD Thesis, University of Hull, 2009.

Livingston, Alistair, *The Galloway Levellers – A Study of the Origins, Events and Consequences of their Actions*, M. Phil. Dissertation, University of Glasgow, 2009.

Peters, Thelma, *American Loyalists and the Plantation Period in the Bahamas,* Unpublished PhD Thesis, University of Florida, 1960.

Prokopow, Michael J., *To the Torrid Zones: The fortunes and misfortunes of American Loyalists in the Anglo-Caribbean basin 1774–1801,* PhD, Harvard University, 1996.

Shirley, Paul Daniel, *Migration, Freedom and Enslavement in the Revolutionary Atlantic: The Bahamas 1783–c.1800,* PhD Thesis, University College, London, 2011.

Smith, Roger C., *The Façade of Unit: British East Florida's War for Dependence*, MA thesis, University of Florida, 2008.

Smith, Roger C., *The Fourteenth Colony: Florida and the American Revolution in the South.* Unpublished Doctoral Dissertation,

Department of History, University of Florida, Gainesville, 2011.

Secondary sources

Aitchison, Peter & Cassell, Andrew, *The Lowland Clearances, 1760–1830*, Tuckwell, East Linton, 2003.

Adkins, Roy and Adkins, Lesley, *The War for all the Oceans*, Abacus, London, 2006.

Adkins Roy, *Trafalgar: The Biography of a Battle*, Abacus, London, 2005.

Allen, Robert S. (ed.), *The Loyal Americans: The Military Role of the Loyalist Provincial Corps and their Settlement in British North America, 1775–1784*, National Museums of Canada, 1983.

Alston, David, *Highlanders*. www.spanglefish.com/slavesand highlanders

Baynham, Henry, *From the Lower Deck: The Navy 1700–1840*, Arrow Books, 1972.

Bell, H.C. & Parker, D. W., *Guide to British West Indian Archive Materials in London and in the islands, National Archives, Kew*, Carnegie Institution, Washington, *D.C.*, Public Domain, 1926.

Bicheno, Hugh, *Rebels and Redcoats: The American Revolutionary War*, Harper Collins, (New edition), 2010.

Blackmore, David S.T., *Warfare on the Mediterranean in the Age of Sail: A History, 1571–1866*. McFarland, 2011.

Blundell, Dom. O.D.O., *Ancient Catholic Homes of Scotland*, Burns and Oates Ltd, London, 1907.

Bouchette, Joseph, *A topographical description of the province of Lower Canada, with remarks upon Upper Canada, and on the relative connexion of both provinces with the United States of America*, Saint-Lambert, Quebec, 1973 (orig. London, 1815).

Brown, Wallace, *The King's Friends*, Brown University Press, Rhode Island, 1965.

Bryant, Joshua, *Account of an Insurrection of the Negro Slaves in the Colony of Demerara, which broke out on the 18th of August, 1823*, Stevenson A., Guiana Chronicle Office, Georgetown, 1824.

Buckner, Phillip, *Hamilton, Sir Charles*, Dictionary of Canadian Biography, vol. 7, University of Toronto, 1988.

Bunnell, Paul, *New Loyalist Index, Vol. 2*, Heritage Books, Maryland, 1996.

Burton, Clarence Monroe, *History of Detroit 1780–1850*, Biblio Bazaar, 2010.

Burton, John D., *The Demographics of Slavery. The Sandy Point Plantation and the Prince Storr Murder case* in Buckner et al, (Eds.), Proceedings of the 10th Symposium of the Natural History of the Bahamas, Gerace Research Centre, San Salvador, Bahamas, 2005.

Butler, Lewis, *The Annals of the Kings Royal Rifle Corps, vol 1. 'The Royal Americans'*, N&M Press, London, 1913.

Campbell, Alexander V, *The Royal American Regiment: An Atlantic Microcosm, 1755–1772*, Univ. of Oklahoma Press, Norman, Okla., 2010.

Campey, Lucille, *Les Ecossais: The Pioneer Scots of Lower Canada, 1763–1855*, Natural Heritage Books Toronto, 2006.

Candlin, Kit, *The Last Caribbean Frontier, 1795–1815 (Cambridge Imperial and Post-Colonial Studies Series)*, Palgrave Macmillan, 2012.

Cashin, Edward J., *The King's Ranger*, Univ. Georgia Press, Athens, 1989.

Chapman, E.J. & McCulloch, Ian, *A Bard of Wolfe's Army; Jas. Thompson, Gentleman 1733–1830*, Montréal, Quebec, Robin Brass Studio, 2010.

Chebroux Alain, *The Seigneury and County of Argenteuil in New Franc.* www.comte-argenteuil.com

Clarke, James Stanier & McArthur, John (eds.), *The Naval Chronicle: Containing a General and Biographical History of the*

Royal Navy of the United Kingdom with a Variety of Original Papers on Nautical Subjects Volume 24 , July–December 1810, Cambridge University Press, 2010, Online Publication, January 2011.

Colley, Linda, *Britons; Forging the Nation 1707–1837,* Yale University Press, London, 1992.

Combe, Andrew M.D., *The Principles of Physiology Applied to the Preservation of Health and to the Improvement of Physical and Mental Education* (Google eBook), Harper & Brothers, 1837.

Craik, William, *Account of,* Farmer's Magazine, vol. XLVI, Edinburgh, 1811, from:
www.kirkcudbright.co/historyarticle.asp?ID=137&p=14&g=4

Craton, Michael, *A History of the Bahamas,* Collins, London, 1962.

Cripps, Derek, *Steel's List of the Royal Navy 1793–1805: Ships Commanders and Stations,* Cripps, Arlington House, 2004.

Cyrus, Thomas, *History of the Counties: Argenteuil Quebec, Prescott Ontario,* (orig. pub. 1896, John Lovell, reprint Mika Publishing, Belleville Ont., 1981.

Davis, Robert, *Christian Slaves, Muslim Masters: White Slavery in the Mediterranean, the Barbary Coast, and Italy, 1500–1800,* Palgrave Macmillan, 2005.

Derriman, James, *Marooned,* Polperro Heritage Press, Cornwall, 2006.

Dictionary of National Biography, vol. 39, Smith, Elder and Co., London, 1885-1900.

Downie, the Rev. Charles, *The New Statistical Account of Scotland, volume 14* (15 volumes), William Blackwood & Sons, Edinburgh, 1845.

Ellis, A.B., *The Defence of Dominica, 1805,* in The History of the First West India Regiment, Chapman and Hall, London, 1885.

Equiano, Olaudah, *The Interesting Narrative of the Life of Olaudah Equiano, the African, written by Himself,* vol. 1, London, 1789.

Fasti, Ecclesiae Scoticanae, Vol. II. *Synods of Merse and Teviotdale,*

Dumfries & Galloway, Edinburgh, Oliver and Boyd, 1915.

Feldman, Lawrence H., *Colonization and Conquest: British Florida in the 18ᵗʰ Century*, Clearfield, Baltimore, 2007.

Foreman, Amanda, *Georgians: A true age of sexual discovery*, 1998. www.amandaforeman.com/express.shtml

Fowler, Simon, *Tracing your Naval Ancestors*, Pen and Word, Barnsley, Yorkshire, 2011.

Fraser, William, *The Earls of Cromartie, vols. 1 & 2*, Constable, Edinburgh, 1876.

Frederick, John, *A Royal American: A New Jersey Officer in the King's Service during the Revolution*, Dog Ear Publishing, 2010 (kindle).

Gauthier, Raymonde, *Les Manoirs du Quebec*, Éditeur Officiel du Québec, 1977.

Gilchrist, M. M., *Patrick Ferguson: 'A Man of Some Genius'*, NMS Enterprises, Edinburgh, 2003.

Glover, Gareth, *Wellington's Voice, The candid letters of Lieutenant Colonel John Fremantle, Coldstream Guards, 1808–1821*, Frontline Books, September 2012.

Goldman, Lawrence (ed.), *Oxford Dictionary of National Biography, 2005-2008*, OUP, Oxford, 2013.

Gordon, Anne, 1997. *Nigg – A Changing Parish*, 1977. Retyped and Reprinted by Whiteford, Liz at http://www.fearnpeninsula.org.uk/niggpdf05.pdf 2000.

Gordon, Arthur, *Life of the Very Reverend Archd. Hamilton Charteris*, Hodder and Stoughton, London, 1912.

Griffiths, R.J.H, *The Genealogy of James and Lewis Mortlock*. Update of note in May 2003 issue of Cambridge Family History Society, Havant 2010. www.mortlock.info/encyclopedia/kirtling.pdf

Groome, Francis H. (ed.), *Ordnance Gazetteer of Scotland: A Survey of Scottish Topography, Statistical, Biographical and Historical*, Thomas C. Jack, Edinburgh, 1882–1885. (online at scottish-places.info/parishes/parhistory1055.html)

Hamilton, Joseph, *The only approved guide through all the stages of a quarrel: containing the Royal code of honour; reflections upon duelling; and the outline of a court for the adjustment of disputes'*, Hatchard & Sons, London, 1829.

Harper, Malcom, *Rambles in Galloway*, Fraser, London, 1896.

Harris, Richard C., *The Seigneurial System in Early Canada*, McGill-Queens University Press, Kingston, 1984.

Harvey, A.D., *Sex in Georgian England*, Duckworth, London, 1994.

Higgs, Liz Curtis, *My Heart's in the Lowlands: Ten Days in Bonny Scotland* (Google eBook), Random House LLC, 2009.

Hill, J. R. *The Oxford Illustrated History of the Royal Navy.* Oxford University Press, Oxford, 2002.

Hume, John, *Dumfries and Galloway*, Rutland Press, Edinburgh, 2000.

Hunter, James, *A Dance called America*, Mainstream, Edinburgh, 1994.

Hyam, Ronald, *Empire and Sexuality: the British Experience*, Manchester University Press, Manchester, 1990.

Irving, L. Homfray, *Officers of the British forces in Canada during the War of 1812-1815*, Welland Tribune Printing, 1908.

Jakobsson, Stiv, *Am I not a Man and a Brother? British Missions and the Abolition of the Slave Trade and Slavery in West Africa and the West Indies 1786–1838*, Gleerup, Uppsala, 1972.

James, William and Chamier, Frederick, *The Naval History of Great Britain, from the Declaration of War by France in 1793 to the Accession of George IV*, (1837), 6 vols., Conway Maritime Press, 2002.

Janzen, Olaf U., *A Reader's Guide to the History of Newfoundland and Labrador to 1869*, Grenfell Campus, Memorial University of Newfoundland. http://www2.swgc.mun.ca/nfld_history/

Jasanoff, Maya, *Liberty's Exiles: American Loyalists in the Revolutionary War*, Vintage, New York, 2012.

Johnson, Joseph, *Traditions and Reminiscences of the American*

Revolution in the South, the Reprint Company, Spartanburg, South Carolina, 1972.

Johnston, F. Claiborne, (ed.) Hollis Hallet C, *Early Colonists of the Bahamas*, Juniperhill, Bermuda, 1996.

Joyce, R. B., *'Mackenzie, Sir Robert Ramsay (1811–1873)'*, Australian Dictionary of Biography, National Centre of Biography, Australian National University, vol. 5, 1974.

Kennedy, Benjamin (ed.), *Muskets, Cannon Balls and Bombs*, Beehive Press, Savannah, Georgia, 1974.

Kiernan, Victor Gordon, *The Duel in European History: Honour and the Reign of Aristocracy*, Oxford University Press, 1988.

Kipps, Andrew, *New Annual Register, or General Repository of History, Politics and Literature for the year 1785*, G.G.J and J. Robinson, 1786. (Google eBook)

Lamb, W. K., *'Yale, James Murray'*, Dictionary of Canadian Biography, vol. X, (1871–80) University of Toronto, 1959 (online).

Landale, James, *Duel: A True Story of Death and Honour*, Canongate Books, Edinburgh, 2005.

Laughton, John Knox, *Inglefield, John Nicholson (1748–1828)*, Oxford Dictionary of National Biography, Oxford University Press, 2004.

Laughton, John Knox, *Hope, Sir William Johnstone (1766–1831)*, Oxford Dictionary of National Biography, Oxford University Press, 2004.

Lavery, Brian, *Nelson's Navy: The Ships, Men and Organisation, 1793–1815*, Conway Maritime Press, London, 1989.

Lawrence-Archer, James Henry, *Monumental Inscriptions of the British West Indies*, Chatto and Windus, London, 1875.

Lawson, Philip, *The Imperial Challenge: Quebec and Britain in the age of the American Revolution*, McGill, 1994.

Lee, Cora, *Illegitimacy during the Regency.*
http://coraleeauthor.wordpress.com/category/british-regency

Leech, Samuel, *Thirty years from home, or a voice from the main deck* (Google eBook), C. Tappan, 1844.

Lewis, James A., *The final campaign of the American Revolution: rise and fall of the Spanish Bahamas*, University of South Carolina Press, Columbia, S.C., 1991.

Lieven, Dominic, *Russia against Napoleon: The Battle for Europe, 1807 to 1814*, Penguin, 2010.

Lyon, George, *Journal of a Residence and tour in Mexico in the year 1826*, vol. 2, Murray, London, 1828.

Macdonald, Donald, *Lewis – A History of the Island*, Gordon Wright Publishing, Edinburgh, 1978.

Mcgowan, Winston R., Granger, David A. J., Rose, James G., *Themes in African Guyanese History*, Hansib Publications Limited, 2009.

Mackenzie, Alexander, *The prophecies of the Brahan Seer*, Eneas Mackay, Stirling, 1899.

Mackenzie, Alexander, *History of the Mackenzies: With Genealogies of the Principal Families of the Name*, A. & W. Mackenzie, Inverness, 1894.

Mackenzie, George Steuart, *General View of the Agriculture of the Counties of Ross and Cromarty* (Orig. pub. 1813), Book on Demand, Miami, 2013.

Mackenzie, John M. and Devine, Thomas M., *Scotland and the British Empire*, Oxford University Press, Oxford, 2011.

Mackey, Frank, *Done with Slavery: The Black Fact in Montréal 1760–1840*, Queen's Press, McGill, 2010.

Macleod, Innes, *Discovering Galloway*, John Donald, Edinburgh, 1986.

McNeill, John Robert, *Mosquito Empires: Ecology and War in the Greater Caribbean, 1620-1914*, Cambridge University Press, 2010.

MacPherson, James Le Moine, *Picturesque Quebec, vols. I and II*, BiblioLife, (reprint), 2009.

Mahan, Captain Alfred Thayer, *The Life of Nelson: the Embodiment of the Sea Power of Great Britain*, 2 vols., Little, Brown, and Company, 1899.

Mahon, Gen. Reginald Henry, *The Life of General the Hon. James Murray: a Builder of Canada*, John Murray, London, 1921.

Mahon, Major-Gen R. H., *The Life of General The Hon. James Murray, with a Biographical Sketch of the Family of Murray of Elibank*. www.electriccanadian.com/makers/murray/chapter15.htm

Marshall, John, *Royal naval biography, or Memoirs of the services of all the flag-officers, superannuated rear-admirals, retired-captains, post-captains, and commanders, whose names appeared on the Admiralty list of sea officers at the commencement of the present year 1823, or who have since been promoted*, 12 vols., Cambridge University Press, Cambridge, 2010.

Morrison, Alfred J. (Translator and editor), *Travels in the Confederation [1783–1784], From the German of Johann David Schoepf*, Franklin, New York, vol. I and II, 1911.

Moultrie, William, *Memoirs of the American Revolution: So Far as it Related to the States of North and South Carolina, and Georgia*, vol. 2, Longworth, Georgia, 1802.

Mowat, Charles L., *East Florida as a British Province*, University of California Press, Los Angeles, 1911.

Murray, Colonel Hon. Arthur C, *The Five Sons of 'Bare Betty'*, John Murray, London, 1936.

Murray, Captain James, *Statement by Captain James Murray as to certain publications in the Inverness Newspapers*, Inverness, 1832.

Murtie, June C., *Loyalists in the Southern Campaign of the Revolutionary War*, Genealogical Publishing, Baltimore, 3 vols., 1981.

Nelson, Larry L., *A man of distinction among them, Alexander McKee and British Indian affairs along the Ohio Country Frontier 1754–1799*, Kent University Press, 2001.

Noble, Rev. John, *Parish of Fodderty, vol. 14, The New Statistical Account of Scotland,* 15 vols., William Blackwood & Sons, Edinburgh, 1845.

O'Brian, Patrick, *Joseph Banks A life,* Collins Harvill, London 1998.

Osler, Edward, *The Life of Admiral Viscount Exmouth,* Bibliolife, London, 2007.

Pappalardo, Bruno, *Tracing your Naval Ancestors,* P.R.O., London, 2003.

Perkins, Roger and Douglas-Morris, Kenneth J., *Gunfire in Barbary: Admiral Lord Exmouth's battle with the Corsairs of Algiers in 1816, the story of the suppression of white Christian slavery,* K. Mason, 1982.

Philippart, John, *The Royal Military Calendar, Or Army Service and Commission Book: Containing the* Services and Progress of Promotion of the Generals, Lieutenant-generals, Major-generals, Colonels, Lieutenant-colonels, and Majors of the Army, According to Seniority: with Details of the Principal Military Events of the Last Century, vol. 5 Valpy, A.J., (Google eBook) 1820.

Porter, Roy, *English Society in the Eighteenth Century,* Penguin, London, 1982.

Ramsay, John, *Scotland and Scotsmen in the Eighteenth Century,* vol. 1, Edinburgh, 1888.

Richards, Eric, The *Highland Clearances,* Birlinn, Edinburgh, 2013.

Richards, Eric & Clough, Monica, *Cromartie Highland Life 1650–1914,* Aberdeen University Press, Aberdeen, 1989.

Riley, Sandra, *Homeward Bound: A History of the Bahama Islands to 1850,* Island Research, Miami, 1983.

Rodger, Nicholas A.M., *The Command of the Ocean,* Penguin, London, 2005.

Rodger Nicholas A.M., *The Wooden World,* Collins, London, 1986.

Rogers, George C., *Evolution of a Federalist: William Loughton Smith,* USC Press, Columbia, 1962.

Rowland, Lawrence S., *History of Beaufort County, South Carolina,* University of South Carolina Press, Columbia, 1996.

Russell, Peter E., *'Hay Jehu' in Dictionary of Canadian Biography,* vol. 4, University of Toronto, Université Laval, 2003.

Salamé, Abraham V. A., *Narrative of the Expedition to Algiers in the Year 1816: Under the Command of the Right Hon. Admiral Lord Viscount Exmouth,* (Google eBook, Digitised 20 Nov 2007), J. Murray, 1819.

Saunders, Gail, *Bahamian Loyalists and their Slaves,* Macmillan, London, 1983.

Saunders, Gail, *Slavery in the Bahamas 1648-1838,* Media Publishing, 1995.

Scott, Walter, *The Miscellaneous Prose Works: Periodical criticism,* vol. 7, Baudry, 1838.

Searcy, Martha C., *Georgia-Florida Contest in the American Revolution 1776–1778,* University of Alabama Press, Alabama, 1985.

Siebert, Wilbur Henry, *Loyalists in East Florida,* 2 vols. Gregg Press, 1972.

Sinclair, Sir John (ed.), *The Statistical Account of Scotland 1791–1799,* vols. 2, 3&15, EP Publishing, Wakefield, 1973–83.

Somerville F., Tawse J, Craigie J, Urquhart A, *Decisions of the Court of Session from 12th November 1832 to 12th July 1833,* Adam and Charles Black, Edinburgh, 1833.

Smith, Paul H., *'Loyalists and Redcoats; a Study in British Revolutionary Policy,* Chapel Hill, N.C., Univ. of N. C. Press, 1964.

Smith, John Jay, *Celebrated trials of all countries, and remarkable cases of criminal jurisprudence,* Godey L. A., 1836.

Spruill Marjorie Julian, Littlefield Valinda W., Johnson Joan Marie (eds.), *South Carolina Women: Their Lives and Times,* 3 vols. University of Georgia Press, GA, 2009.

Stagg, John C. A., *The War of 1812: Conflict for a Continent,* Cambridge Essential Histories, Cambridge University Press, Cambridge, 2012.

Stewart, Francis John, *The Stewarts of Shambellie,* vol. 2, Edinburgh, 2002.

Sutherland, Alexander, *The Brahan Seer: The Making of a Legend,* Lang, Peter, AG, Internationaler Verlag Der Wissenschaften, 2009.

Taylor, Stephen, *Commander: Life and exploits of Britain's Greatest Frigate Captain,* Faber and Faber, London, 2012.

Thomas, Cyrus, *History of the Counties, Argenteuil, Quebec,* John Lovell, Prescott, Ontario, 1896. (Reprint Mika Publishing, Belleville Ont. 1981).

Thomas, Earle, *Sir John Johnson; Loyalist Baronet,* Dundurn Press, Toronto, Ont., 1986.

Thomas, Earle, *'Johnson, Sir John,'* in Dictionary of Canadian Biography, vol. 6, University of Toronto, 2003.

Thomas, Evan, *John Paul Jones: Sailor, Hero, Father of the American Navy,* Thorndike, Waterville, 2003.

Thomas, Hugh, *The Slave Trade, 1440 – 1870,* Picador, London, 1997.

Trotter, Bruce, *Galloway Gossip,* Courier and Herald Press, Dumfries, 1901.

Warren, Mary B., *South Carolina Newspapers, The South-Carolina Gazette 1760,* abstracted by Lowery Robert S. and Warren Mary B., Heritage Papers, 1988.

White, Rev. George, *Historical Collections of Georgia: Containing the Most Interesting Facts, Traditions, Biographical Sketches, Anecdotes, etc., relating to its History and Antiquities, from the First Settlement to the Present,* Pudney & Russell, New York City, 1854.

Wilkins, Frances, *The Dumfries and Galloway Transatlantic Slave Trade,* Wyre Forest Press, Worcs., 2007.

Willcox, William Bradford, *Portrait of a General; Sir Henry Clinton in the War of Independence,* Knopf, Random House, 1964.

Winfield, Rif, *British Warships in the Age of Sail 1793–1817: Design, Construction, Careers and Fates,* Seaforth Publishing, London, 2008.

Wright, J. Leitch Jr., *Florida in the American Revolution,* University of Florida, Gainsville, 1975.

Wyannie Malone Museum, *First Loyalist Settlements in Abaco,* Hope Town, Bahamas, 1979.

Notes

Prologue

[1] No first-hand record survives of the engagement between HMS Northumberland and the French vessel, L'Imperial', during the battle of San Domingo. The descriptions of action below decks that are transferrable and common to all major ship engagements have been based on the first-hand account of Samuel Leech, who was present at the encounter between HMS Macedonian and USS United States in 1812.

Chapter 1: Bare Betty

[2] NAS, CS 46/1833/2/59.
[3] A Curry in Cockney / Glaswegian rhyming slang is called a Ruby, based on Ruby Murray, formerly a very popular Irish singer.
[4] NAS, GD 32/23/9.
[5] Ramsay, 1888.
[6] He met and corresponded with Patrick on numerous occasions, declaring that he never met his lordship without going away a "wiser man". It was during a visit to Patrick at the Elibank family seat of Ballencrieff in 1773 that by repute the famous quote concerning horses and oats was born. In Dr. Johnson's dictionary, oats were defined as "eaten by people in Scotland, but fit only for horses in England." Patrick's retort to this was "That's why England has such good horses, and Scotland has such fine men!"
[7] Petrie, 1931, pp 175–196.
[8] NAS, GD 32/24/61. Letter from George Murray to his brother James.
[9] Gilchrist, 2003, p. 40.
[10] For a full account of the life of this remarkable man see Gilchrist, 2003.

11 Anson's Centurion became the first European warship to visit China.

12 Given the horrific losses to Scurvy, it is surprising that there was not an investigation into its cause and cures, especially as Anson's men were observed to improve when onshore and receiving fresh fruit and vegetables. James Lind read the ship journals and conducted his own investigations and in 1747 proved conclusively that the receipt of fruit such as oranges and lemons would lead to dramatic improvement and resistance from Scurvy. In the way that official cogs often move slowly it was 50 years before Lind's recommendations were implemented.

13 A piece of eight was a Spanish coin comprising approximately one ounce of silver.

14 NAS, GD 32/23/9. George maintains that the return to Britain was against his inclinations but he was overruled by his superior officer.

15 There were a number of disputes over the prize money and it had to be settled in a court of law, causing considerable acrimony between the Captains. Anson was awarded three–eighths of the prize money, estimated at £91,000. This can be compared with the £719 he earned as a Royal Navy Commodore during the three years and nine months voyage. An ordinary seaman would have received about £300, which amounted to about 20 years' wages.

Chapter 2: The suppression of vice and immorality

16 Harvey, A.D., 1994, p. 4.

17 Ibid. p. 156.

18 Foreman A., 1988.

19 Lee C., 2012.

20 Robert Burns graphically described contemporary attitudes to illegitimacy, and especially the terrible crime, in his eyes, of not recognising and supporting an illegitimate child, in his poem 'The Libel Summons' (1786).

21 NAS, GD 32/24/26. Letter to General James Murray 1777.

22 Ibid.

23 NAS, GD 32/24/71/3. Letter: James Murray to Mrs Williams.

24 NAS, GD 32/24/12. Letter from Rev. Gideon Murray to Gen. James

Murray, Nov. 1759. A 'yellow admiral' was the Royal Navy's method of superannuating older officers and was, in effect, equivalent to being retired on half pay.

[25] NAS, GD 32/24/61. Letter Admiral George Murray to General James Murray, Sept. 1761.

[26] Mahon, 1921, p. 49.

[27] Ibid. George went on to ask James to burn the letter and not to 'suffer any part of it to be returned here and used against me.' George's conscience was far from clear.

[28] NAS, GD 32/24/15 Letter: Mrs Maria Mackenzie to Gen. James Murray, Feb. 1763.

[29] National Archives, WO 12/7000: Muster Roll 60th foot.

[30] Fraser, W, 1876, pp. 257–258.

[31] Butler, 1913, pp. 199–200.

[32] A number of Swiss nationals joined the 60th foot and fought with distinction in North America. Perhaps the most famous name was Prevost, two of whom achieved the rank of General in the British Army.

[33] www.Royalprovincial.com/military/courts/ cmfitzpatrick.htm

[34] Frederick, John, 2010.

[35] Searcy, M.C., 1985, p. 87.

[36] National Archives, PROB 11/1111.

Chapter 3: Help me to be pure – but not yet

[37] The War of Jenkins' Ear was a conflict between Great Britain and Spain from 1739 to 1748. Its unusual name refers to an ear severed from Robert Jenkins, the Captain of a British merchant ship by a hostile Spanish boarding party. This ear was exhibited before Parliament and provided the excuse for declaring war against the Spanish Empire.

[38] At least that is what a contemporary viewer, Johann David Schoepf, thought. Morrison (ed.), 1968, pp. 139–140.

[39] Ibid. p. 229.

[40] Joseph Smith's Diary. SCHM 33, p. 90.

[41] Now all contained within the boundaries of Tomoka State Park and the city of Ormond Beach. The protected ruins of his sugar mill still exist in Ormond Beach.

42 Tingley, C.A., 2008.
43 There is no direct evidence that Richard Oswald ever visited his massive plantations in Florida.
44 The 'three chimneys' site is now lovingly cared for by the Ormond Beach Historical Society.
45 Siebert, vol. 2, 1972, p. 330.
46 Schafer, Daniel L., at www.unf.edu/floridahistoryonline//plantations/plantations/Julianton_Plantation.htm
47 Smith, Roger C., 2011.
48 'The Intolerable Acts' was the American nickname for a series of laws passed by the British Parliament in 1774 relating to Massachusetts as a result of the Boston Tea Party. These acts stripped Massachusetts of much of its self-government and caused outrage and resistance in the other American Colonies.
49 Ibid. note 47. Also Siebert, 1972, vol. 1, p. 17, 80, Mowat, 1911, p. 87. Smith regarded it as highly unlikely that Lt. Colonel Fuser was directly involved in any Sons of Liberty campaigns in East Florida, but he did contend that Fuser was constantly and publicly at odds with the Governor.
50 Searcy, Martha C., 1985, p. 106.
51 National Archives, PROB 11/1111/350, Fuser, Will.
52 Smith, Roger C., 2011, p. 189.
53 National Archives, PROB 11/1111/350, Fuser, Will.
54 Butler, L., 1913, Vol. 1, Appendix II. (Memoir of Major Patrick Murray).
55 Archives Nationales du Quebec a Montreál, Microfilm 3795, Agreement & Subrogation by Mrs Smith to Sir J. Johnson, 1806–6–10.

Chapter 4: Come and take it

56 Butler, L., 1913. Appendix II. 'Memoir of Major Patrick Murray', p. 288.
57 Ibid. However, Searcy, 1985, p. 87, argued that Patrick's account was greatly exaggerated.
58 Cashin, E., 1989, p. 211.

59   Although it was several months before he could walk and he suffered from headaches for the rest of his life.

60   Cashin, E., 1989, p. 305. The American colonists who remained loyal to the British monarchy and the soldiers fighting on behalf of the King were often called Tories, Royalists, or King's Men.

61   Letter, Brig.-Gen. Prevost to Sir Henry Clinton, C. in C. July 11th 1778 in Carleton papers, vol. 12.

62   Butler, L., 1913. Appendix II. 'Memoir of Major Patrick Murray', p. 308.

63   www.exploresouthernhistory.com/fortmorris

64   Butler, L., 1913. Appendix II. 'Memoir of Major Patrick Murray', p. 309.

65   http://www.usgenweb.info/georgia/history/hcg-c-g.htm: The Reminiscences of Captain Roderick McIntosh are contained in a letter written by John Couper Esq., at the age of eighty-three, found in the History of Gilmer County, Georgia. He refers to McIntosh as the 'Quixote of Georgia'.

66   Butler, L., 1913. Appendix 11. Memoir of Major Patrick Murray, p. 311.

67   Ibid. p. 313. Patrick had urged its capture but his advice was rejected. He even offered to hold the port against all comers with his company. Patrick was not slow in pointing out his own valour and foresight.

68   Ibid. pp. 311–318, and miniawi.blogspot.co.uk /2010/12/ battle-of-port-royal-island

69   Moultrie, 1802. The American commander, General Moultrie, had no doubt that it was an American victory. Rowland, 1996, also supports this view.

70   Butler L., 1913, p. 313. Also National Archives, WO 12/7033, Muster Rolls 4th Battalion 60th Foot. This shows that Patrick Murray was away on 'General's Leave' until late 1783.

71   Ibid. pp. 308.

Chapter 5: Defeat from the jaws of victory

72   Kennedy, 1974, p. 107.

73   Archives Nationales du Quebec a Montréal, Microfilm 3791. Last

Will & Testament of Mrs Eliza Smith, 1806–6–9.

[74] NAS, Last Will & Testament of Captain James Murray, SC 16/41/9 (Kirkcudbright Sherriff Court) and also Archives Nationales du Quebec a Montreál, Microfilm 3206, Last Will & Testament of James Murray, 1804–3–12.

[75] Taylor, S., 2012.

[76] Patrick Murray had been given leave of absence by General Prevost (Carleton Papers, vol. 12, April 1779 (Letter: Prevost to Clinton) and so was probably not present during the siege.

[77] Georgia Society Pamphlet, Savannah in the American Revolution.

[78] Georgia Historical Quarterly, Vol. 35 (1951), pp. 56–57. Minutes of the Governor and Council of Georgia, Oct– Dec 1779.

[79] Bicheno, 2010.

[80] Siebert, 1972, Vol. I, pp 79–80, p113. Fuser's death was reported as being on February 5, 1780.

[81] It is purely coincidental that the very name chosen by Jane Austen for the girl whose background was unknown but was possibly of 'gentle' birth was Harriet Smith, and Harriet, of course, became the unfortunate protégé of Emma in the book of the same name.

[82] Webber, M, vol. 33 (1932) pp. 90–140 and vol. 34 (1933). Joseph Smith, of no relation to Eliza, kept a fascinating diary in which he recorded everyday events in the town whilst he was a prisoner there.

[83] Ibid. vol. 34.

[84] National Archives. WO 12/7035 and WO 12/7036. Muster of the 4th Battalion, 60th Foot, 1800–1802.

[85] Ibid. WO 12/6935.

Chapter 6: The best small village in Scotland

[86] The bridge, now improved and strengthened is a double-arched span today.

[87] Groome, F. H., 1882–1885.

[88] Stewart F. J., DGNHAS, 1989, pp. 58–70.

[89] Called 'the old house'.

[90] Aitchison, P. and Cassell, A., 2003.

[91] http://www.britishlistedbuildings.co.uk. New Abbey, Dumfries and Galloway

92 Sinclair, 1973–83, Vol. 2, New Abbey.

93 Ibid.

Chapter 7: It's who you know

94 NAS. CS 46/1832/2/144.

95 Register of Sasine, Kirkcudbrightshire circa 1791–1795; nos. 1005, 1006, 1017, 1018, 1021, 1022, 1357.

96 Register of Sasine, Kirkcudbrightshire circa 1791–1810; nos. 599, 2763, 2764.

97 Mary was remembered in a song by Robert Burns (Ode, sacred to the memory of Mrs Oswald of Auchincruive). Burns had no love for either Richard or his wife Mary, and their slaving and armament supply background was well known.

98 Wilkins, F., 2007. On his death Richard Oswald left over £500,000, which Wilkins estimated would be worth over £337 million today.

99 Richard married Louisa or Lucy Johnstone and Robert Burns, obviously forgetting his minor feud with the Oswald family, composed his verses, "O wat ye wha's in yon town" to her.

100 http://www.electriccanadian.com/makers/murray/chapter15.htm; correspondence in which James Murray is wishing to use the not inconsiderable influence of Oswald to assist him in his governance of Canada.

101 The importance of patronage from such a well-connected and influential landowner as Richard Oswald cannot be underestimated, and his influence in North America, especially in Florida and South Carolina, was very considerable.

102 Farmer's Magazine, Vol. XLVI, 1811, pp. 145–165, inc. letters from Helen Craik, daughter.

103 Ibid. p. 152.

104 Ibid. p. 153.

105 Trotter, B., 1901, pp. 440–431.

106 Thomas, E., 2003 and www.jpj.demon.co.uk/jpjlife.htm

107 Military personnel often used the term 'butcher's bill' to describe the level of casualties suffered during a hostile engagement.

108 Blundell, Dom. O.D.O., 1907.

109 www.maxwellsociety.com/Biography/1819century.htm

Chapter 8: Keep your heid doon

[110] Stewart, F.J., 2002, P. 44–45.

[111] This house, no longer lived in by the Stewarts, housed the National Museum of Costume until 2013.

[112] Dumfries Archives, GGD 37/8/1/7, Shambellie Papers; letter from Jas. Murray to William Stewart, 1788.

[113] Dumfries Journal, 8th December 1818.

[114] Stewart, F.J., 2002, vol.2.

[115] This James Murray of Broughton and Cally was not the widely reviled Murray of Broughton, the secretary of Charles Edward Stewart during the 1745 rising.

[116] Catherine came to terms with Ann, her husband's illegitimate daughter, but James Murray of Broughton later eloped with Grace Johnston, with whom he had four children. Catherine wrote to Ann shortly after the event and asked her not to contact him whilst "his frenzy remains".

[117] Lady Catherine took a special interest in Ann and her husband, who initially lived as farm tenants on the Cally Estate before moving into the Stewart family home at Shambellie with their (then) 15 children.

[118] James Alexander through marriage became James Alexander Stewart Mackenzie and married into the Seaforth dynasty.

[119] Stewart F.J., 2002. vol.2, p. 101.

[120] About this time James was desperately looking for finance to purchase promotion and Dorothea was writing to her brother complaining of being almost destitute.

[121] NAS, GD 32/24/55. Letter from William Young to Gen. James Murray.

[122] Dumfries Archives, GD 37.

[123] Stewart F.J., 2002. vol. 2, pp. 99–100.

[124] Ibid. p. 96.

[125] Fasti, 1915.

[126] The discontent was sometimes linked to political demands for more democracy but there is no evidence that the New Abbey protests were connected with this broader political ambition.

[127] National Archives, WO 12/7033. 4th Battalion, 60th foot muster rolls.

[128] In the Dumfries Archives, a letter from John Wright was filed alongside other documents connected to the Reverend William

Wright. It was part of the collection of the renowned antiquarian Dr. Robert Corsane Reid (1882–1963). He served with distinction as Secretary, President and Editor of the Dumfries and Galloway Natural History and Antiquarian Society for many years. Dr. Reid assumed a connection between John Wright and the Rev. William Wright but does not indicate what that connection was.

[129] It was common for different ships to have the same name and several ships of the time were called the 'Betsey'. Spelling was also inconsistent and it should not be assumed that the 'Betsey' was necessarily a different ship from the 'Betsy.'

[130] Dumfries Archives, Bundle GGD 498/2/7.

[131] Dumfries Archives, New Abbey Manse Papers, Box 13 (uncatalogued).

[132] Wilkins, F., 2007 established that there was significant involvement of people from south west Scotland in the slave trade, pp. 19–23, and a number of local Scots were based in Liverpool and associated with the trade at that location, p. 26.

[133] Thomas, H., 1997, p. 526.

[134] The 'George Washington Papers, December 18, 1775,' and Smith, Roger 2008. These papers apparently prompted Washington's request to Congress for direct military action.

[135] National Archives, PROB 11/1111/350.

[136] National Archives, WO 12/7033. 4th Battalion, 60th Foot muster rolls.

[137] Walter Newall, son of William Newall, became a celebrated architect in south west Scotland, being responsible for many prominent buildings, including Moat Brae, the home of J.M. Barrie of Peter Pan fame.

[138] Stewart, F.J., 2002, p. 66. The subscribers, mainly but not exclusively local, were, Rt. Hon. Earl of Selkirk; William H Maxwell, Constable of Nithsdale; James Murray of Broughton; William Craik of Arbigland; Richard Oswald of Auchincruive; William Stewart of Shambelly; George Maxwell of Munches; John Maxwell of Terraughty; Robert Brown of Milnhead; James and Mary Maxwell of Kirkconnell; John McCartney of Halkerleaths; The Rt. Hon. Lord Linton; Ralph Riddell of Cheeseburn Grainge; Mrs. Dorothea Riddell, sister of Mrs Maxwell; William Glendonwyne of Parton; The Revd. James Muirhead, Minister at Urr; Revd. William Wright, Minister at New Abbey; Adam Craik, younger of Arbigland; Thomas

Bushby of Ardwall; Thomas Stothard of Arkland; George Chapman, late Rector of the Grammar School, Dumfries and Robert Riddell, younger, of Glen Riddell.

Chapter 9: *We will die with our swords in our hands*

[139] Siebert, 1972, Vol. I, pp. 79–80 and pp. 132–133.

[140] This was not just idle talk. Loyalist schemes, such as those of the mercurial William Augustus Bowles, were put forward on numerous occasions over the next few years, but none had any real foundation.

[141] Schafer, D.L., 2001.

[142] National Archives, CO 23/25/24. Letter from Lord Germain.

[143] National Archives, CO 5/560. Letter to Captain Bissett in London.

[144] Craton, M., 1962, p. 166.

[145] Shirley P., 2011, p. 101. The majority of his volunteers were probably Bahamian residents sympathetic to British rule, and they far outweighed the Loyalists in terms of numbers.

[146] Jasanoff, M., 2012. P. 220.

[147] Craton, M., 1962, p. 161. Deveaux was awarded 250 acres in New Providence and 1,000 acres on Cat Island, thus becoming a neighbour of Eliza Smith.

[148] Wright, 1975, p. 99.

[149] National Archives, CO 23/25/247. Memo of British American loyalists still in East Florida.

[150] Ibid. ADM 49/9. Also Troxler, C.W. 1981, p. 23.

[151] Shirley, P., 2011, pp. 110–111, quoting the words of Bahamas Governor Maxwell.

[152] National Archives, CO 23/25/137–138.

[153] Shirley, P., 2011 p. 122, quoting a proclamation by Governor Powell of September 1785, that each head of family would receive 40 acres of land plus an additional 20 acres for every other family member.

[154] Wright, 1975, p. 135.

[155] Ibid. pp. 25–26.

[156] Jasanoff, M., 2012, p. 221.

[157] Morrison, 1968, p. 262–64.

[158] National Archives, CO 23/25 f139.

[159] Shirley, P., 2011, p. 28. Prior to 1783 only five of the Bahaman group

of islands had any substantial human population. By 1800 Human settlements had extended for hundreds of miles across the Island Archipelago and at least eight more islands now held substantial populations.

[160] Ibid. p. 95. At most there were only 500 acres of cultivated land in the whole island group.

[161] Shirley, P., 2011, p.108. He estimated that circa 1,200 white and 3,600 black people moved to the Bahamas from East Florida.

[162] Jasanoff, M., 2012, pp. 221– 243.

[163] Saunders, G., 1983. P. 17.

[164] Ibid. Also National Archives, CO 25/25/75.

[165] National Archives, CO 23/28/150. Even Col. Brown got caught up in the protests when he was arrested on Abaco for leading what was termed a 'race riot'.

[166] Jasanoff, M., 2012, p. 243.

[167] Bahamas Gazette, various, circa 1785–88.

[168] Bahamas Gazette, 24th September 1785.

[169] Ibid. October 21st 1786.

[170] Kipps, A., 1786.

[171] http://incrediblefacts.com/human-endeavours/the-man-who-wore-scarecrows-clothes

[172] Stewart, F.J. 2002.

[173] Ibid. also Dumfries Archives, GGD 37/8; Shambellie Papers.

Chapter 10: Go to sea young man

[174] Parliament did not rescind the charter in 1790 and actually extended it, but only for twenty years at a time. The charters granted in 1793, 1813, 1833 and 1853 successively scraped away the Company's commercial rights and trading monopolies. In 1857, the year after the Indian Mutiny, the Company lost all its administrative powers and its Indian possessions and armed forces were taken over by the Crown.

[175] NAS, GD 32/24/55. William Young to General J. Murray, 2nd April 1787.

[176] Ibid.

[177] Ibid.

[178] NAS, CS 46/1833/2/59.
[179] Burton, Clarence M., 2010.
[180] Ibid.
[181] Nelson, Larry L., 2001.
[182] Burton, Clarence M., 2010.
[183] Russell, Peter E., 2003.
[184] Archives Nationales du Quebec a Montréal. Microfilm: Civil Records (births, marriages and deaths).
[185] http://www.comte-argenteuil.com/DOCe.htm
[186] Harris, Richard C., 1966, p. 86.
[187] Bouchette, J., 1973.
[188] Archives Nationales du Quebec a Montréal. Microfilm: Act No. 953, 23 May 1793.
[189] In 1789, Charles Stewart of Shambellie, New Abbey paid £479 7s 9d in total to purchase an ensign rank in the 2nd foot for his son James. A Royal Naval commission would be at least the equal of this.
[190] National Archives, CO 23/30/217. Lists of tracts of land granted, 1788–1789.

Chapter 11: A career begins: The Topaze

[191] National Archives, ADM 9/4/1030.
[192] Lavery, B, 1989, p. 88.
[193] Rose, J. Holland, 1929, pp. 34–46.
[194] Admiral Lord Nelson never did and suffered from sea-sickness throughout his career.
[195] National Archives, ADM 52/3497 Masters Log: Topaze, and ADM 51/1269, Captains Log: Topaze.
[196] The Andromeda was then captained by Prince William Henry, the future King William IV.
[197] National Archives, ADM 51/1269. Master's Log: Topaze.
[198] Ibid.
[199] Ibid.
[200] A temporary mast, using any materials available.
[201] Nova Scotia Archives, Halifax, NS. MG 100 vol. 227#29 (mfm 9744). A list of prize money received by all the crew of HMS Topaze from the action of 22ril 1798. Captain Church of the Topaze received

£176.00, a considerable sum for a relatively small action.

202 National Archives, ADM 51/1269. Master's Log: Topaze.

203 Lavery, B., 1989, pp. 90.

204 National Archives, ADM 52/3498.

205 Ibid.

206 Ibid. The Master's log of the Topaze is quite clear about who captured the ship. However the entry for the action in 'The London Gazette (no. 15295. p. 1082, 20th September 1800) does not mention the involvement of the Topaze.

207 The London Gazette: no. 15241. p. 285. 22nd March 1800.

208 National Archives, ADM 52/3498.

Chapter 12: From the House of Shame to the House of God

209 Cashin, E., 1989, p. 13.

210 Ibid. p. 137. He was a prisoner in his own house, which was brick built and heavily fortified.

211 White, G., 1854. Colonel Thomas Brown of the King's Rangers' reply to David Ramsay's History of the Revolution of South Carolina, pp. 614–620.

212 Cashin, E., 1989, p. 137.

213 Another brother was Robert, a trader, who lived with the Creek Nation and had an Indian Family. Their family resided in Augusta, Georgia.

214 Johnson, J., 1972.

215 National Census, 1851.

216 The impact of Scots has been examined in detail by David Alston.www.spanglefish.com/ slavesandhighlanders

217 Slave register of Former British Colony dependencies, 1812–1834. ancestry.com

218 The status of 'slave' had never existed under English common law or Scottish law. Technically, since slaves did not legally exist, holding a slave was never made specifically illegal until 2010.

219 New York Historical Society Museum and Library: nyhs_sc_b-02_f-13_044.

220 Ibid. nyhs_sc_b-02_f-13_040-001.

221 Ibid. nyhs_sc_b-02_f-13_004.

222 http://slaverebellion.org/index.php?page=the-brig-Royal-charlotte-1763, citing the Newport Mercury 6 June 1763; New York Gazette 13 June 1763; Pennsylvania Gazette 16 June 1763.
223 Religious meetings for the slaves had to take place after the work of the day had finished and so were held in the evenings.
224 Rev. John Smith, letter dated 21 August 1823, quoted in Jakobsson, 1972, p. 323.
225 Ibid. pp. 323–4.
226 National Archives, CO 111/45. Sir Benjamin d'Urban to Earl Bathurst, 30th September 1824.
227 McGowan, 2009.
228 Legacies of British Slave Ownership, University College London, Dept. of History Database, 2013. The former slave-owners were given a total of £20 million in compensation by the British Government.
229 Dumfries Archives, Manse Papers, box 13 (uncatalogued). Letters from Louisa Grierson to James Hamilton.
230 Dumfries Archives. Manse Papers, box 16 (uncatalogued). Record of Ministers in New Abbey.
231 Stewart, F., 2002 p. 46. In 1727 the Kirk Session spent £107 on building a new Manse for the Minister, next to Sweetheart Abbey and the existing Parish Church. This house was extended and completely renovated in 1802 and remains much the same today.
232 Gordon, A., 1912.

Chapter 13: The angel of salvation

233 Craton, M., 1962, p192.
234 National Archives, CO 23/26/204. Eliza would have been delighted to get so much land on this healthy Island. It was reported that over 2,000 people now lived there and sickness was almost unknown. There was no doctor on the island.
235 National Archives, CO 23/30/217–219. List of the tracts of land granted to the inhabitants of the Bahamas from 8th April 1788 to 31 December 1789.
236 They were Lord Dunmore (Governor), Alexander his son, Lady Gambier (wife of former Governor), Lt. Col. Thomas Brown

(Loyalist hero) and the family of John Moultrie (former Governor of Florida).

237 She received 4,000 acres of land on Cat Island.

238 This organisation was set up to represent the interests of the incoming Loyalist people, but inevitably it was primarily concerned with the white slave-owning group of refugees with mercantile, military and professional backgrounds.

239 National Archives, CO 23/30/217–219. Of the recipients of land grants only 41 out of the 605 in total were female. The size of land awards ranged from 4,000 acres to less than 20 acres. Eliza had one of the largest grants awarded to a woman.

240 Riley, S., 1983 pp. 189–190.

241 Jasanoff, M., 2012, p. 243.

242 National Archives, CO 23/41/110 and CO 23/44/182–183.

243 Ibid. 23/44/182–183: Letter from James Moss.

244 National Archives, CO 23/48/144–146.

245 Shirley, P., 2011, p. 191.

246 Occasionally, owners would decide to release some of their slaves. The release was formalised through a 'manumission', i.e. a document granting the slave his or her freedom.

247 Shirley, P., 2011, p. 185. Dunmore was accused by the Loyalists of 'indulging slaves' and 'encouraging manumission'.

248 Ibid. 'Bahamian Manumissions 1782–1800,' pp. 294–308.

249 Ibid. numbers 461 and 465.

250 Ibid. In the Bahamas only two other Rosett(e)(a)s, Rosetta Wilson (in 1797) and Rosette Cox (in 1798), gained their freedom between 1782 and 1800.

251 Smith, L., 2011.

252 Archives Nationales du Quebec, Microfilm 2152, Wills, donations and disposals (1800–1850). Quittance du Hons. James McGill & Pierre L. Panet, Ecuyers, en faveur de Patrick Murray ecuyer et subrogation a Dame Eliza Smith, 28 –8–1802.

253 Or perhaps because of... . Eliza may have been anxious to involve her son in her financial ventures.

254 Archives Nationales du Quebec, Microfilm 2858, Deed of sale of seigneurity of Argenteuil from Patrick to James, 30–4–1803.

255 Archives Nationales du Quebec a Montreál, Notary records of John Gerbrand Beek, Microfilms 2859 (Lukin), 979 and 1502 (Beek).

Transfer of Murray debts from Nicholas Montour to Sir John Johnson.

256 Archives Nationales du Quebec a Montreál, Notary records of P. Lukin, Microfilm 2859. Obligation for two sums of money with interest due by Patrick Murray, James. Murray & Mrs E. Smith to Sir John Johnson, 30–4–1803.

257 Earle, T., 2003.

258 Archives Nationales du Quebec a Montreál, Notary records of P. Lukin, Microfilm 3392, 22–10–1803.

259 Ibid. Microfilm 2861, Letter of Attorney, Mrs E. Smith to John Armstrong, 2–5–1803.

260 Ibid. Microfilm 3207, General Power of Attorney from James Murray to Patrick Murray & Mrs Elizabeth Smith, 12–3–1804.

261 Thomas, C., 1971 p. 8.

262 Ibid. Scotch Settlers of Argenteuil, p64.

263 Mackey, F., 2010, p. 50.

264 http://pages.videotron.com/myfamily/siteanglais/anglais. html#James.

265 Richards, E., and Clough, M., 1989. Letter of the 25th Nov. 1820 from Patrick Murray to Lady Maria Hay Mackenzie. This probably refers to the 1790 land purchase, made whilst Patrick was Chairman of the Hesse Land Board.

266 Thomas, C., 1971, pp. 71–72.

267 Ibid. pp.72–73.

268 Ibid. pp. 72–73.

269 Archives Nationales du Quebec, Microfilm 3791, Last Will & Testament of Mrs Eliza Smith, 9–6–1806.

270 Ibid. Microfilm 3792, Sum of money due by Mrs Eliza Smith to James Reid Esq and Power of Attorney from Mrs Eliza Smith to James Reid, 9–6–1806.

271 Ibid. Microfilm 3795, Agreement & Subrogation by Mrs Smith to Sir J. Johnson, 10–6–1806.

272 See various blogs concerning the world of Jane Austen, e.g. http://janeaustensworld.wordpress.com for discussions concerning the woman's role in Regency society.

273 Quebec Gazette, No 2187, 26th March, 1807.

274 Archives Nationales du Quebec, Microfilm 3995, Deed, Sale & Concession of Land by Patrick Murray to Robert Simpson, 3–4–

1807 and Microfilm 4033, Concession by Patrick, as Attorney to James, to Uriah McNall, a point of land commonly called Calkins Point, 11–7–1807.

275 Archives Nationales du Quebec, Microfilm, 4448, Land Concession by Sir John Johnson to Judah Center, 3–7–1810.

276 Thomas, C., 1896, said Major Murray sold Argenteuil to Sir John Johnson in 1814 but Thomas, E., 1986, p. 155 quoted late 1807 or early 1808 as the sale date. This date is supported by Gauthier, R., 1977, pp. 26–27.

Chapter 14: Hero: San Domingo and Dominica

277 National Archives, ADM 52/3681. He would have been relieved that he did not spend too much time on the Ruby because, judging by the frequency of flogging, it had serious disciplinary issues and was an unhappy ship.

278 Ellis, A.B., 1885, pp. 103–117.

279 He is normally named as Sir Samuel Hood but James Murray used the name James, although clearly referring to the same person.

280 National Archives. GD305/unlist/30. Cromartie Papers, 1816–1819.

281 Ellis, A.B., 1885, pp. 109–115.

282 The Naval Chronicle, Vol. 17, p. 128. This means that materials unfit for purpose had been used in the refit of the Centaur. Corruption and corner-cutting in the shipyards was rife and considered a major scandal of the period.

283 Poor Thomas Matthews died of dehydration only the day before they reached the safety of the Azores.

284 Laughton, J.K., 2004. Also archive.org/details/cihm_91969. Captain Inglefield's narrative of the loss of the Centaur, in 1782, 'being a literal extract of his letter to the Admiralty.' This detailed Captain Inglefield's personal account of the loss of the Centaur and was published shortly after the event. A dramatic painting of the incident was later made into a bestselling print.

285 Rodger, N.A.M., 2004, pp. 528–575.

286 A cousin of the famous Lord Thomas Cochrane, nicknamed the 'sea wolf' for his astonishing successes against French vessels of war.

287 Lavery, B, 1989, pp. 200.

288 Speed of fire was considered more important than accuracy, and the objective of most captains was to engage the enemy at very close range.
289 National Archives, ADM 51/4480, Northumberland, Captain's Log. 290291 http://www.militaryhistory.about.com/od/NapWarsNaval/p/Napoleonic-Wars-Battle-Of-San-Domingo.htm and Rodger, N.A.M., 2004, p. 546.
292 National Archives, ADM 6/100, passing certificates.

Chapter 15: You'll laugh when it's all over

293 James, W., 1837, p. 375.
294 Ibid. Vol. III, p. 376.
295 National Archives, ADM 51/2072. Unique, Captain's Log, 1807–1808.
296 Ibid.
297 National Archives, ADM 37/2959, Unique Muster, 1808.
298 http://www.nelsonsnavy.co.uk/broadside2.html
299 National Archives, ADM 51/2072. Unique, Captain's Log, 1807–1808.
300 www.cariwave.com/regiments_of_the_british_west_indies_and_bermuda.htm
301 National Archives, ADM 51/2072, Unique, Captain's Log, 1807–1808.
302 Ibid.
303 Ibid.
304 Ibid.
305 Articles of War, Number 15, 1757.
306 Hill, J. R., 2002, pp. 135–137.
307 Rodger, N. A. M., 1986.
308 http://www.nelsonsnavy.co.uk/broadside7.html
309 Lavery, B., 1989, p. 122, quoting Naval Records Society, Captain Boteler's recollections.
310 Ibid. p. 123, quoting from Sheehan, J.J., History of Kingston upon Hull, 1864, p. 148.
311 Information Sheet 78, the Press Gangs and Naval Recruitment, Royal Naval Museum Library, 2001.

312 The British asserted this, but Spanish reports deny commencing any hostile action towards the British ship.

313 National Archives, ADM 51/2072, Captain's Log, Unique. 1807–1808.

314 Ibid.

Chapter 16: Martinique and Guadeloupe

315 ADM 51/2072, Captain's Log, Unique. 1807-1808.

316 The mutiny at Spithead (an anchorage near Portsmouth) in 1797 saw sailors on 16 ships protesting against the living conditions aboard Royal Navy vessels and demanding a pay rise. Pay had not increased since 1658, but high inflation during the last decades of the 18th century had eroded the real value of the sailors' pay. Admiral Lord Howe negotiated an agreement leading to a pardon for all crews, a pay rise and abolition of some of the worst abuses prevalent in the Royal Navy at this time.

317 Rodger, N.A.M., 2005, pp. 447–451.

318 Adkins, R., 2005.

319 James, W., 2002.

320 National Archives, ADM 51/1948, Captain's Log, Neptune.

321 Derriman, J., 2006.

322 National Archives, ADM 51/2733, Captain's Log, Recruit.

323 Ibid.

Chapter 17: It wasn't us Sir: Oberon and the North Sea

324 Lieven, D, 2010.

325 Ibid.

326 National Archives, ADM 1/2175, Letter, Murray to Admiralty.

327 National Archives, ADM 51/2633, Captain's Log, Oberon.

328 Lavery, B, 1989, p. 131.

329 National Archives, ADM 1 /2178, Letter to Admiralty.

330 Ibid. ADM 1/ 2175, Letter to Admiralty.

331 Ibid. ADM 53/945, Ship's Log, Oberon, 1813–1815.

332 Ibid.

Chapter 18: Too much Hope

[333] Stagg J. C. A., 2012.

[334] MacPherson, J., 2009. The nickname had added piquancy in view of Patrick's frequent conflicts with lawyers over matters of his debt.

[335] NAS, GD305/unlist/30 (1816–1819). Letter in Cromartie Papers.

[336] Dumfries Journal, 1811, Microfilm 15/1 3D, Ewart Library, Dumfries.

[337] NAS, CS 46/1833/2/59.

[338] Laughton, J.K., 2004, and www.clanjohnstone.org/pdf/viceadmiral_ sir_william_johnstone_ hope_gcb.pdf

[339] National Archives, ADM 9/4/1030.

Chapter 19: The trident vibrates

[340] National Archives, ADM 37/5948.

[341] Davis, R., 2005.

[342] Ibid.

[343] National Archives, FO 113/4, Report of William Shaler, 30 August to 5 November 1815.

[344] National Archives, ADM 53/1256, Satellite Logs.

[345] Ibid. and Taylor, S., 2012 (ebook location 4906).

[346] National Archives, FO 3/18, McDonnell to Bathurst, 20 May 1816.

[347] Taylor, S., 2012, location pp 4933–4938, quoting Exmouth Papers, box 18, Exmouth to Sidmouth.

[348] He later rescinded this order.

[349] Salamé, A. V. A., 1819 and Taylor S., 2012, location 5289.

[350] Taylor, S., 2012, location 5272.

[351] James, W. and Chamier, F., 2002, ebook p. 292 and p. 399.

[352] National Archives, ADM 53/1256, Satellite Logs.

[353] Osler, P., 1835, p.89.

[354] Taylor, S., 2012, Location 5573.

[355] Salamé, A. V., 1819, p.48.

[356] Perkins R. & Douglas-Morris K.J., 1982, p. 107.

Chapter 20: A nest of idle vagabonds

357 National Archives, ADM 37/5949, Satellite Muster.
358 Mackenzie, A., 1894.
359 Letter online at: http://freepages.genealogy.Rootsweb .ancestry.com /~coigach/cromartie.htm
360 Smith, J. J., 1836.
361 Richards, E. and Clough, M., 1989. C.P. Laing to Hay Mackenzie, 20 Sept 1814.
362 Ibid. p. 150.
363 Ibid. pp. 149–151.
364 NAS, GD 305/unlist/30, bundle 30, 1816–1819.
365 Noble, Rev. J., 1845, Parish of Fodderty.
366 http://web.undiscoveredscotland.com/strathpeffer/strathpeffer
367 NAS, GD305/unlist/30, bundle 30, 1816–1819.
368 Ibid.
369 Ibid.

Chapter 21: The perfect girl?

370 NAS, GD305/unlist/30, bundle 30, 1816–1819.
371 Ibid.
372 http://www.bonhams.com/auctions/15265/lot/264
373 National Archives, WO/65/65, Army Lists from 1815–1818, and PROB/11/1823, Will of John Harris. Also Philippart, J., 1820.
374 NAS. GD 305/unlist/30, bundle 30, 1816–1819.
375 Ibid.
376 Ibid.
377 Richards, E. and Clough, M., 1989, letter (now missing), CP Bundle 31, Patrick Murray to Mrs Hay Mackenzie, 25th Nov. 1820.
378 Ibid.
379 NAS, GD 305/unlist/32, 1822-1824.
380 Archives Nationales du Quebec a Montréal, Microfilm C-2550, pp. 72870-72873, Murray, Patrick.
381 This is further evidence to suggest that Patrick Murray was not the father of Harriet and Theresa, but it is not conclusive as James Murray is also not declared as a legitimate heir. This action may have

caused difficulties to develop between James and his half-sisters as they were later excluded from his will.

Chapter 22: Valorous

382 National Archives, ADM 37/6787, Valorous, ship muster.
383 Mahan, Captain A.T., 1899.
384 National Maritime Museum, GB 0064 TUC, Tucker papers.
385 www.brucehunt.co.uk/trematoncastle Saltash and Tamar Valley History website.
386 Constable A., 1821, p. 92.
387 N.A.S., CS 46/1833/2/59. Decree of divorce, Captain Jas Murray v Rachel Lyne Tucker.
388 http://www.mississauga.ca/portal/discover/benareshistoric house. A description by Matilda in a later letter to her brother in Benares House. She ascribed his temper to his Irish origins.
389 National Archives, ADM 37/6787, Valorous, Ship muster.
390 Ibid. ADM 51/3529, Valorous, Captain's Log.
391 N.A.S. CS 46/1832/144, Decreet, Capt. James Murray V Robert Ramsey Mackenzie.
392 Adkins, R., p. 32.
393 O'Brian, P., 1998 pp. 45–56.
394 www.heritage.nf.ca/lawfoundation/articles/royalnavy
395 National Archives, ADM 52/4648, Masters Log, Aug 1821–Feb 1824 and ADM 51/3529, Captain's Log, Feb.1821-Dec. 1824.
396 Ibid. ADM 52/4648, Master's Log, Aug 1821–Feb 1824.

Chapter 23: I was not sober one hour

397 Ibid.
398 The literal translation of the Gaelic surname MacNamara is 'son of the sea'. Whether James McNamara saw any amusement in this ironic definition is unknown.
399 National Archives, ADM 53/1256.
400 Ibid. ADM 52/4648, Master's Log, Aug 1821–Feb 1824, and ADM 51/3529, Captain's Log, Feb.1821–Dec. 1824.

[401] For a detailed discussion of discipline and punishment in the Royal Navy at this time see Lavery, B., 1989 and Rodger, N., 1986.

[402] National Archives, ADM 52/3681, Master's Log, HMS Ruby.

[403] Leech S., 1844.

[404] National Archives, ADM 51/1269 Captain's Log, Topaze.

[405] Baynham, H, 1972, p. 136.

[406] www.cariwave.com/regiments_of_the_british_west_indies_and_bermuda.htm The official line is that they were all incapacitated by illness.

[407] National Archives, ADM 51 and 53, Masters' Logs and Captains' Logs of ships Topaze, Ruby, Centaur, Northumberland, Ballahoo, Unique, Neptune, Recruit, Oberon, Satellite and Valorous.

[408] Ibid.

[409] Rodger, N.A.M., 1986 p 82.

[410] Ibid. pp. 84–85.

[411] Lavery, B., 1989, p. 205.

Chapter 24: The last cruise

[412] NAS, GD 305/unlist/32, 1822-1824.

[413] Buckner, P., 1988.

[414] National Archives. CO 194/65.

[415] Ibid.

[416] Lyon, G., 1828.

[417] Combe, A., 1837, pp. 69-70.

[418] Admiral George Murray and promotion to 'Flag rank' i.e. Admiral. Promotion to flag rank from Captain was from the Navy List, and once a name reached the top of the list (through death, resignation etc.) an Admiral rank was automatically awarded.

Chapter 25: The day will come

[419] Accounts and Papers, 1831–1832, p.12.

[420] Downie, C., 1845, New Statistical Account.

[421] Inverness Courier, July 23 1834. The house and grounds were described with especially high praise for their gardens. The house

was said to 'comprehend every article requisite for a genteel family.'

[422] NAS, CS 46/1833/2/59.

[423] Tomnahurich Hill to the south west of Inverness was several miles from a sea inlet.

[424] It has been calculated that at the end of the 18th century the Scottish highlands accounted for over a third of the total Scottish population. Today it is less than 10 per cent (figure depends upon the definition of the boundaries of the 'Highlands').

[425] Drumossie Moor is the name of the moor above Culloden where the 1746 battle took place.

[426] Mackenzie, A., 1899 and Sutherland, A., 2009.

[427] James Alexander assumed the surname Stewart-Mackenzie after his marriage in 1817 to Mary Mackenzie (the Hooded Lassie).

[428] Macdonald, D., 1978, p. 37.

Chapter 26: They live in the midst of filth and smoke

[429] Kaye, M., 1923, quoting a letter by John Maxwell, Esq. of Munches, to W. M. Herries, Esq. of Spottes, 1811.

[430] Although a tough taskmaster, Craik did have the respect of all his contemporaries. It is perhaps significant that when John Paul Jones, whose father had been a gardener on Craik's estate, attacked the British coast on behalf of the fledgling United States he chose to try to kidnap the Earl of Selkirk and left William Craik's estate alone.

[431] Livingston, A., 2009.

[432] Described on information boards situated by the Steamboat Inn, Carsethorn. The reason given by the families for their decision to emigrate was 'to get more bread'.

[433] Richards, E., 2013. Military service absorbed some of the excess highland population. More than 48,000 men between 1756 and 1815 served in the armed forces, but the population continued to grow.

[434] Ibid. ebook location 1152.

[435] Ibid. ebook location 1035.

[436] For example, Patrick and James Murray had made strenuous efforts to recruit highlanders to their Seigneury in Argenteuil, Canada.

[437] Mackenzie, G.S., 2013.

[438] Ibid.

439 Ibid.
440 The Edinburgh Evening Courant, 9th August 1792.
441 The Edinburgh Evening Courant, 11th August 1792.
442 Richards, E. & Clough, M., 1989, p. 163.
443 Richards, E. & Clough, M., pp. 163–164.
444 NAS, GD 305/unlist/30, Cromartie Papers, Letter 22nd March 1824.
445 Ibid. Blackmoor, letter, 12th July 1825.
446 Scott, Sir Walter, 1838, p138.

Chapter 27: Has he told everything?

447 NAS, CS 46/1832/144, Decree, Capt. James Murray v Robert Ramsey Mackenzie.
448 N.A.S. CS 46/1833/2/59, Decree of divorce, Captain James Murray v Rachel Lyne Tucker.
449 Ibid. Proof in action of Divorce.
450 Ibid.
451 Ibid.
452 NAS, CS 46/1833/2/59. Decree of Divorce.

Chapter 28: Where is the villain? The basest dastard

453 The letters are unsorted and are bundled together, with the witness evidence appearing in the divorce papers.
454 NAS, CS 46/1833/2/59, personal letters (1).
455 Ibid. personal letters (2).
456 Ibid. personal letters (3).
457 Ibid. personal letters (5).
458 Ibid. personal letters (6).
459 Ibid. personal letters (7).
460 Ibid. personal letters (8).
461 Ibid. personal letters (9).
462 Ibid. personal letters (12).
463 Ibid. personal letters (13).
464 Ibid. personal letters (14).
465 Ibid. personal letters (17).

466   Ibid. personal letters (20).
467   Ibid. personal letters (20).
468   Ibid. personal letters (21).
469   Ibid. Personal letters (23).
470   Surrey History Centre Archives, K 95/1/47 and K 95/1/53, marriage settlement.
471   N.A.S. CS 46/1833/2/59. Personal letters (24).
472   NAS, GD 1/1149/46, Mackenzie of Coul papers.
473   NAS, CS 46/1833/2/59, Rachel Tucker letters (unsorted and undated).
474   Ibid (unsorted and undated).
475   Ibid. 25 (unsorted and undated).
476   Ibid. 25 (unsorted and undated).
477   Ibid. 25 (unsorted and undated).
478   Ibid. 25 (unsorted and undated).
479   NAS, CS 46/1832/2/144.
480   NAS, CS 46/1833/2/59.

Chapter 29: He could not have spoken greater nonsense

481   Richards, E. and Clough, M., 1989. Letter from Cromartie Papers, now missing, p. 159.
482   Ibid.
483   http://www.historyofparliamentonline.org/volume/1820-1832/constituencies/ross-shire
484   Ibid.
485   Alston, D, www.spanglefish.com/slavesandhighlanders
486   He named the Arabella estate after his first wife.
487   Gordon, A., 1997.
488   Somerville F. et al, 1833, pp. 338–339.
489   Inverness Journal, 26 October 1832.
490   Ibid.
491   Ibid.
492   Inverness Journal, 17 November 1832.

Chapter 30: He or I must measure the earth

493 The terminology used at the time may cause some confusion today. A 'meeting' in this context refers to a duel and the 'friend' is the duellist's supporting Second.

494 Murray J., 1832. Statement, p. 5.

495 Ibid. pp. 5-7.

496 Ibid.

497 Hamilton, J., 1829. This book, in its 251 pages, detailed the codes of engagement.

498 Shoemaker, R.B., The Historical Journal, 2002, pp. 525–545,

499 MacPherson, J., 2009, p. 416.

500 www.lowensteyn.com/Samuel_Holland/Gedcom/events/ event15

501 Landale, J., 2005. An account of the last Scottish duel written by an ancestor of one of the protagonists.

502 Hamilton, J., 1829.

503 Murray, J., 1832, pp. 7–8.

504 Ibid. p. 9.

505 Ibid. p. 10.

506 Ibid. p. 19.

507 Kiernan, V. G., 1988.

508 Inverness Journal, Friday, Dec 7th 1832.

509 Inverness Journal, Friday 14th December 1832.

510 Inverness Courier, January 27th 1841.

Chapter 31: A final legacy

511 Inverness Journal, December 14th 1832.

512 Ibid. December 31st 1832.

513 Scotland's People. SC 16/41/9, Kirkcudbright Sheriff Court records, will of James Murray.

514 Slave Registers (1812–1834), 2007.

515 He was the investigating magistrate in the celebrated 1833 Sandy Point Plantation murder case, when a black overseer was charged with the murder of a black slave.

516 The Rev. Timothy Tripp Lee, Vicar of Thame, Henley on Thames.

517 1851 National Census. Norwood Farm, Ivor, Bucks.

[518] Joyce, R.B., 1974.

[519] Ibid.

[520] Lamb, K.W., 1959.

Index

Cistercian, 4, 7, 48, 49, 50
Clan Mackenzie, 222, 225
Clare, William, 210
Claus, Major William, 88
Clinton, General, Sir Henry, 31,
    42, 43, 310, 317, 318
Cochrane, Admiral Alexander,
    138, 155, 159, 329
Coigach, 184, 185, 333
Coinneach Odhar, *see* Brahan Seer.
Colvend, 53
Commissary of Stores, 264
Common grazing, 229, 230
Conan House, 241, 242, 245, 246
Conon, river, 241
Constantinople, 174
Contin, 221, 233, 244
Continental system, 162
Copenhagen, 164
Corbett, 187, 188
Corn Laws, 261
Cornwall, 199, 215
Cornwallis, Lord, 74
Corruption, 150, 198, 199, 264,
    267, 329
Cottars, 50, 229
Cotton, 71, 80, 82, 108, 116
Coul, 229, 232, 241, 242, 243,
    244, 245, 257, 259, 263,
    282, 283, 289, 293
Court Martial, 16, 148, 159,
    165, 166, 167
Craigdarroch, 221, 244, 246,
    249, 257, 268, 281, 283, 289
Craik,
    James, 56
    William, 54, 55, 56, 57, 61,
        229, 302, 321, 336

Crawford, passenger on
    Valorous, 217, 218
Criffel Hill, 46, 47
Cromartie, 8, 12, 125, 182, 183,
    185, 186, 188, 189, 221,
    222, 237, 263, 264, 294,
    303, 308, 329, 332, 333,
    337, 338
Cromarty, *see* Cromartie
Culloden, 3, 60, 223, 336
Culrain, 236
Cumberland Island, 33
Cumberland, Duke of, 61
Curacao, 152
Cyrus, 34, 79, 302, 310

Dalbeattie, 46
Danish ships,
    Jorge Henrick,164
    Stafeten, 164
    Wegvusende, 164
Darwin, Charles, 217
Dashwood, Captain, 178
Davidson, Duncan, 224, 243,
    279, 280
Davy, John, 152
Davy, Sir Humphrey, 224
De Courcy, 170
De Romanoff, Count, 163
DeLorimier, William, 119
Demerara, 107, 110, 112, 171, 301
Denmark, 164, 167, 168
Denness, Seaman, 211
Derrick, Richard, 211
Dervorguilla, 48, 51
Desertion, 9, 148, 200
D'Estaing, Vice Admiral
    Comte, 39

Index

Index